The Blind Shepherd

Tomas W. Schafer

SMB
Sunrise Mountain Books
Boise, Idaho

THE BLIND SHEPHERD
©Copyright 2020 Tomas W. Schafer

ISBN 978-1-940728-16-2

Library of Congress Control Number: 2020904642

Published by Sunrise Mountain Books
13347 W. Tapatio Drive
Boise, Idaho 83713

Printed in the United States of America

Foreword

God's Word is rich, vibrant, full of life and direction. In studying His Word, there are moments when a certain passage strikes a particular chord within a person. At that moment the mental wheels begin to turn and questions are posed that often lead to further in-depth study.

Such is the case pertaining to The Blind Shepherd. The Gospel of Matthew states that Christ Jesus restored the vision of two blind beggars outside the city of Jericho. One was named Bartimaeus but the second person is not named. Nor is there any other reference about this person. In addition there are no other details about Bartimaeus, only of his faith in Christ that He would restore his sight.

My research began to explore who these two blind men were. The result is over 400 hours of pouring over Biblical studies, commentaries as well as historical documents to glean answers to the questions surrounding these two individuals. As a result, the basis for this book began to take shape and evolve into the final manuscript.

Along the road of research much interesting and revealing information was uncovered pertaining to those times. The various pieces of the puzzle were sorted through and categorized into a story that encompasses the initial 75 years of the first century.

In many ways that particular period of time shaped and influenced today's world in ways both spiritual and secular. The wealth of material to choose from was organized to focus on those events and people most instrumental in the making of history during those 75 years. There are also those individuals who either have no place in history books or are relegated to footnote status. Yet their personal lives served as a guide for the countless others who lived and endured through those turbulent years.

The two blind men briefly mentioned by Matthew are examples of those caught up in the events that impacted their lives but who are now relegated to footnote status. This book is historical fiction to give insight into what the people of that era thought, lived, and believed.

It should be no surprise that their experiences are very similar to what people encounter today. History has a way of dispelling myths and misconceptions. The historical facts thereby form the foundation for the fictionalized parts of the book.

LIST OF CHARACTERS and Pronunciation Guide

Mattan (Ma/*tahn*)..... the blind shepherd
Terach (Ter/*ack*)..... father of Mattan
Beulah *Byoo*/lah..... mother of Mattan
Amram, Eiton (*I*/ton), Gavriel (*Gav*/real)..... brothers of Mattan
Hadassah Had/*ahs*/ah..... wife of Bartimaeus
Nigrid (*Nye*/grid)..... chief administrator of Herod over Judea
Zaccheaus (Za/*key*/us)..... tax collector
Jesus Barabbas (Jesus Bar/*ah*/bus)..... shepherd/ rebel member of Zealots; also called Barabbas
John of Gischala (Gis/*shaw*/la).... leader of rebel group Zealots
Menachem (Men/*nock*/em).... leader of small group of rebel Zealots
Herod The Great..... ruler over Judea at time of Christ's birth
Quirinius (Qui/*rin*/ius)..... Governor over Judea at time of Christ's birth
Archelaus (Ar/chell/*ay*/us).... son of Herod The Great
Apostle Paul..... good and faithful servant of Christ Jesus
Channah (*Hah*/nah)..... sister to Mattan
Iza (EE/sah)..... 1st wife of Mattan
Nadan (Naw/*dawn*).... Father of Iza
Devorah (Dvo/rah)..... Mattan's wife
Bartimaeus (Bar/tim/*ay*/us)..... blind man healed by Christ Jesus

Chapter 1

The lone figure dismounted from his horse and stood looking up at the dark night sky. There were numerous stars shining brightly and deep in the heavens but a new and unusual star he had never seen before shone brighter than the others. The silhouette observed this strange star for a brief time, then turned his gaze from the heavens to the buildings of the small town that surrounded him.

He detected no candle lights piercing the darkness of the late night hour. The inhabitants of the buildings were fast asleep. The shadowy form breathed a sigh of relief that he could move about undetected to accomplish his mission. Reflexively, he touched the hilt of his short sword with his right hand, receiving assurance it was available should the need arise.

Satisfied no one had noticed his arrival, perhaps due to his dark attire, he peered towards his destination. One small light served as a beacon to guide his way. After surveying the surrounding terrain that bordered the beam of glowing light, he began to move toward his target. He slipped effortlessly and silently among the bushes, stopping periodically to listen for sounds coming from the light source.

His breathing remained calm. There was no panic or fear within him. His eyes riveted on his mission in a manner not unlike the abundant wolves of the region. Once his surveillance was completed, he began slowly to make his ascent up the small incline a few steps at a time. He would take two steps, then stop and listen. Confident the sounds coming from the light source were only expected ones, the black shadow relaxed and resumed his quest.

When he was within twenty paces of the light source, he could make out details. There was a small fire burning in the front entrance of a cave. The fire revealed five human figures kneeling at the cave's entrance peering inside at some object. The five silhouettes periodically turned towards each other, indicating they were conversing, probably about the object of their attention, the same one he pursued.

The man in black hesitantly took two careful steps before pausing again. The voices and the movement from within the cave gave him no cause for alarm, so he stealthily proceeded. When he was merely four paces from the kneeling silhouettes in front of the cave, he could finally see inside.

To the left were several beasts of burden including an ox, a mule, and two donkeys. Looking back to his right, he noted a newborn infant lying in part of a trough used to feed the animals. The infant was wrapped in traditional Jewish swaddling clothes and was fast asleep. Behind where the infant lay was a man of medium height conversing with a woman. They both were looking down and talking in soft voices.

The dark stalker followed their gaze and discovered a young woman lying on her side on fresh straw. Similar to the infant, she, too, was in deep sleep. The man took a blanket from the woman standing next to him and leaned down to drape it gently over the sleeping young woman. When he stood upright he had a few final words with the older woman who then turned to leave the cave.

As the woman began her exit, the sleuth quickly stepped back into the dark night to remain undetected. In front of him the five kneeling figures stood up and opened a path for the older woman's departure. Once she was through the human gate, she wrapped her cloak tightly around her and made her way down the small incline. As she departed, the five figures gathered again into a tight group and stood looking at the man in the cave.

The man inside spoke to the onlookers. They turned to leave, following the path the older woman used down the slight slope. The curious spectator made sure he was completely hidden by the foliage. As the five men moved past him, the shadowy tracker took one long intense look at the scene inside the cave, then silently followed the group.

At the bottom of the slope one of the men looked behind him and recoiled with a cry of alarm. His companions' heads snapped in the direction of his focus and they, too, were startled by the sight of the dark silhouette who was backlit by light from the cave. One held a long stick in his hand and made a menacing defending motion with it towards the black ghost.

The dim figure quickly assured them, "Have no fear, my friends, I intend no harm to you!" He slowly moved closer to

8

allow the frightened men to make out his appearance in the darkness. The defender with the staff stepped forward, staring intently at the approaching murky form.

Suddenly, the man put his stick down with great relief and a little irritation, sighing, "Ah, Terach, it is you. Why did you sneak up on us like a robber of the night?"

"My friends, I apologize for frightening you, but I had a strange experience. Following the encounter, I came here, but I wanted to make sure it was no subterfuge to do me harm."

Someone eagerly asked, "Terach, is it possible we all have had the same strange encounter?"

Before Terach could answer, another blurted out, "I was tending to my sheep in the sheepfold next to my house, when suddenly a very bright light shone all around me. I could detect a form in the middle of the light. It was as if the night had turned to day! It was very bright, yet I could see clearly. I became frightened, and grabbed my rod. At that moment, a voice from above me said not to be frightened but to rejoice for this night the messiah we all have been waiting for is born here in Bethlehem! The voice said to come and see the messiah, here in Bethlehem, and to tell others about his arrival!"

The breathless reporter finally took a breath, quickly glanced at his cohorts, and added, "The light and the singing awoke my family and they came out of the house, wondering what was going on. I quickly told them it was strangers passing through and for them not to be concerned but to go back into our house."

Murmuring voices affirmed the man's depiction of their similar experiences. One chimed in, "It is as our friend has said, Terach. The commanding voice sounded excited as it gave me the same instructions. When it finished speaking, there was singing from a host of unseen voices, proclaiming glory to God and peace toward men! Then as suddenly as the bright light appeared, it was gone! I could hardly move, trying to understand what had just happened. I looked up into the dark sky around me, but there was no sign of anyone."

There was hushed silence. The last man of the group testified, "I made haste from my house here to see what this thing is and met my four friends." All heads nodded confirmation of what the shepherd farmer relayed. Then he asked, "Terach, did you perhaps have the same encounter as the rest of us?"

The five shepherd farmers moved closer to their friend and leaned in eagerly to hear his answer.

"My friends, I, too, had the same encounter and it concerned me, also. I decided to follow the instructions of the voice, and came swiftly on my horse, just as the voice told me to do. I saw you in front of the cave but was wary until I knew for certain what was taking place."

Terach paused and briefly looked up the incline at the lighted cave. His eyes came back to his companions. Taking a deep breath, he softly asked, "Is it possible this event is as the prophets have foretold—the new messiah has been sent to us— just as God has promised?"

Before he could continue, a member of the group interrupted. "Terach, we all know you have the ability to read the Torah, and *you* instruct us with God's sayings." The man extended his arm toward the lighted cave and continued, "How can a newborn infant of man be our messiah? And why is he of lowly human parents and not of royal birth as the Pharisees say? And why be born in a cave intended for animals? This goes against all that we are taught by the Pharisees and rabbis."

Another argued, "Yes, Terach, I for one will not heed the voice's command to go forth telling others of this night to rejoice. This is not how the messiah will come to our aid. When people see this lowly situation, they will ridicule me. I do not feel like rejoicing over this matter, do you?"

A final voice blurted out his frustration, "We shepherd farmers do not wish being even more despised by our fellow Jews. Telling them of this event will only make matters worse for us. The Pharisees and the rabbis will become deeply angered." The spokesman paused, then added with a disgusted tone, "Besides, they won't listen to us, anyway."

Terach tried to calm their confusion with his quiet, steady voice. "You are right. There are many questions to be answered. But for now, return to your homes and prepare for the morrow when we begin the harvest celebration of the Feast of Tabernacles. When it is morning, gather your families and return here to our regular site. I will recite the words from the Torah appropriate to this feast. We must obey God's command of keeping this first day of the feast holy. Afterwards we can discuss this strange occurrence and try to make sense of it. "

Following Terach's leadership, the mystified men dispersed into the late night, pondering their astonishing experience. Their homes were located on the outer edge of Bethlehem and were within a quarter mile of each other. It did not take them long to return to the safety of their houses.

Terach silently scrutinized the scene lighted by the small fire. There was no movement within the cave, just the flickering of the small flames of the warming fire warding off the chill of the mid-autumn night. His mind was racing, analyzing what his five fellow Jews had just told him. He compared their experiences with his own. His thoughts shifted to the Torah passages that foretold the coming of the great messiah. This scene did not align at all with the expectation in the minds of the Jews who were fervently waiting for their Savior. It was unsettling.

After his brief moment of introspection, Terach decided he would return to his family and get a bit of sleep before returning to Bethlehem to begin his role in the celebration of the Feast of the Tabernacles with his fellow countrymen. Thankfully, the distance from this cave to his desert camp was not that far, and his speedy horse could traverse the distance in a short amount of time.

With that, Terach quietly made his way to where his steed awaited. He mounted his horse, urging it quickly back to camp. As the stallion made ease of the terrain, Terach was deep in thought. Could the prophecies actually be coming true? Could this really be the messiah? But, why an infant in such lowly conditions? The potential that indeed the prophecies were being fulfilled made the hair stand up on the back of his neck.

Beulah was waiting for Terach, and she worried about the lines of concern that shaped her husband's face as he stood inside their tent. Her candle only dimly illuminated his countenance, but it was enough for her to know something of great magnitude had impacted Terach. Beulah's first words were, "Are we in danger, my husband?"

Terach eased his way to their sleeping pad and took off his mantle and sandals before quietly answering, "It doesn't appear to be so. Nevertheless, this strange phenomenon requires much attention."

Beulah could see the weariness that possessed her husband. She did not pursue the matter, knowing that Terach would reveal all to her in good time. She lay down next to him and moved her body close to his in an effort to ward off the cold that covered Terach's exhausted body.

In spite of unanswered questions and much to ponder, the comfort of their nearness allowed them both to fall asleep almost immediately.

Chapter 2

The night dew was just beginning to dissipate when Terach, Beulah, and their four young boys reached the outskirts of Bethlehem. The small town was very quiet. Only a couple of barking dogs heralded the family's approach.

Terach slowed his horse to allow Beulah and the three older boys to come closer, riding their donkey. Once they were beside him, Terach leaned towards his wife and said, "Go to our regular meeting place. I must attend to a matter before we begin our observance of the holy feast."

A perplexed Beulah nodded and urged the donkey with the giggling boys onward. Terach immediately swung his horse to the western hills that bordered Bethlehem. He made sure his youngest son, Mattan, was secure in the saddle with him. Mattan let out a shout of delight as the strong stallion burst forward. The youth was happy to share this new adventure with his father. Mattan's happy squealing brought a smile to Terach.

Their destination was not far from Bethlehem. Terach stopped his horse at the base of the incline to the cave he had visited just hours before. On foot, he and Mattan quickly proceeded up to the mouth of the cave. Mattan struggled to keep up with his father and was panting with quick little puffs when they reached their destination.

Upon their arrival, Joseph rose to greet the visitors. "Shalom to you. I am Joseph of Nazareth. May I inquire what your purpose is here?"

Terach answered, "My name is Terach. I am a shepherd and wonder if you are inclined to celebrate the Feast of the Tabernacles during your stay in Bethlehem?

Joseph sensed the shepherd's sincerity and gently replied, "As you can see, my wife has recently given birth to her son. She is tired, weak, and unable to travel. As a Jew, I am unable to fulfill my responsibility to do pilgrimage to Jerusalem for this holy week."

Terach felt comfortable at the man's answer. He offered, "Would it be permissible with you, then, that others and my family come here for the reading from the Torah?"

Joseph looked surprised and answered, "This would be most pleasing. I am greatly honored by your gesture. The midwife will be arriving at any time now and also will join our observance of this holy day."

Terach smiled at Joseph, gathered up his young son atop his shoulders, and headed down the incline. Mattan held tightly and giggled with each bouncing step as they raced down the slope.

When Terach arrived at their usual gathering place, the other shepherd farmers were there with their families talking with Beulah. Terach did not dismount, but summoned all to follow him to the cave that the traveling family was sharing with the animals.

Because of the ritual observance required of the last feast observed by the Jews, Terach wasted no time in producing his Torah from a bag fastened to his horse. Reverently, the nomadic shepherd unrolled the scroll and began to read from its contents. Joseph was taken aback at the passion and eloquence of the shepherd's voice. Rabbis that Joseph knew did not display such reverence when reading from the Torah that contained God's Word.

The reading did not last long. Terach directed the gathered crowd to continue their observance of the holy festival with the traditional feast. Joseph was disappointed he had no contribution for the festival. Terach sensed Joseph's displeasure and assured him, "Do not fret about having no food for the festival. Our wives always produce sufficient food. Your present circumstances do not permit adherence to the law of the Torah."

Joseph relaxed and smiled at Terach. "Terach, there is one observance I can do in obedience with the law. I will present the newborn son to the world."

Terach studied Joseph's face and saw how he hoped approval would be given. "Joseph, we would all be proud to be guests at this presentation."

Terach, the farmer shepherds and their wives, and the children all gathered around the mouth of the cave to listen to Joseph's presentation. Even the animals in the manger stood motionless, as if understanding the significance of the moment.

After the presentation and the festive meal, the shepherds dispersed to their homes located throughout the surrounding terrain to continue the God-ordained ritual. The holy feast required the Jews to build temporary make-shift tents with palm leaves for the covering. Throughout the first day of the holy festival there would be no labor, and all food was eaten cold. This was done in observance of the forty years their ancestors spent wandering in the desert before entering the Promised Land. The next five days' observance would include daily readings from the Torah; but the Jews could resume semi-normal daily activities until the last day of the feast. On that day they would abstain from warm food and would not labor. They would sing praise songs throughout the seven-day festival to Almighty God for His blessings to them.

The Feast of the Tabernacles was also a celebration of the harvest from the year's toils in tilling the soil and for the shepherds' caring for their sheep. It was also a bridge between the waning days of summer and the imminent approach of the winter rainy season. This feast was one of seven observed by the Jews that required a pilgrimage to Jerusalem. Since the farmer shepherds could not leave their animals, they celebrated the feast with the nomadic shepherd Terach.

When the farmer shepherds were gone, Terach remained behind to speak with Joseph. "How is it that you travel to Bethlehem this time of year, and with a wife so close to giving birth?"

Joseph was unapologetic in giving his answer. "We are from Nazareth. But because Caesar Augustus has declared a time for a census we had to return here. Our Jewish leaders require us to return to the home of our ancestors for their own tax purposes. Both Mary and I are of the line of David, and for that reason we must return to Bethlehem, David's city."

Inwardly, Terach bristled at the word taxes. It was a sore subject to the shepherd who hated the concept, especially how the Jewish Sanhedrin had incorporated aspects of this heathen law into the Jewish culture. Terach's mind quickly went to a time when he refused to pay the Jewish tax and at one point informed the rabbi in charge of collecting the tax that when he and the other nomadic shepherds were allowed to freely participate in regular Jewish society, and when they would be welcomed to attend a synagogue, and not be despised, then he would pay. The embarrassed rabbi merely turned and walked away, never again confronting Terach about paying his Jewish taxes. Inwardly, the rabbi felt content that Terach, his family, and all the other small group of nomadic shepherds would burn in hell for their rebel attitudes.

Terach gathered his thoughts back to the present moment and asked Joseph, "What livelihood do you do to honor God?"

Joseph straightened and with joy announced, "I am a carpenter as my father was."

His proud claim was verified by Terach's inspection of Joseph's thick fingers and powerful forearms, his stout shoulders and back. Being a carpenter was a tough job that demanded a great deal of physical strength and endurance. Joseph's muscular body manifested the natural results of years of toil and training to perform the various tasks of his trade.

"I can see by your physical appearance you have spent many years learning your craft. I laud you, Joseph, on your God-given trade."

From that point on, the two men became more relaxed with each other and their conversation continued for quite some time.

As the hour grew late, Terach said, "I must return to my home. Beulah and our boys will wonder what has happened to me. I'm pleased we have had this time together. Tomorrow I shall return to read more of God's blessings from the Torah and I invite you to join us."

Joseph nodded his acceptance and said, "I appreciate your willingness to include me and my family to participate in this holy festival."

Terach gave one final statement. "Joseph, we shall do the reading here. That way you don't have to leave your newborn son, and your wife can participate as well." With that, the nomad shepherd mounted his trusty Arabian stallion and headed west where his family and multitude of sheep awaited his arrival. During his ride back to his tents, Terach was pleased that he and this Joseph were amiable towards each other. In light of the shocking visit and news about the messiah's arrival, Terach wanted to scrutinize this family to determine if this event could actually be the fulfillment of the Torah's prophecies. He chided himself for questioning an event that had been prophesied in God's Word. Yet, it was mind-boggling that it could actually be happening in his own lifetime! If so, it would be very interesting how this messiah would change the world.

On the second day of the Feast of Tabernacles, Terach gave his reading and invocation to a larger crowd than on the first day. Included in this new number were women, children, and the elderly males who were too old and infirm to make the mandatory pilgrimage to Jerusalem. The final feast and holy observance by the Jews required all males to trek to Jerusalem with an animal sacrifice to pay homage to Almighty God for His grace of leading the ancient forefathers out of Egypt and into the Promised Land. The Jewish religious structure left out women, children, and the elderly.

God's direct command had been strictly observed down through the ages, and at this particular moment all the able men were in Jerusalem. They pitched makeshift tents made of thin sticks covered with palm branches and other tree leaves. They ate inside their tent, consuming only the same cold food as their forefathers had.

A smattering of able-bodied males remained in Bethlehem. These were individuals deemed as outcasts of Jewish society and were restrained from participating in the three pilgrimage feasts. The list consisted of nomad shepherds, retail shop owners, butchers, dung collectors, and youths not old enough to attend the synagogue. Some of these people out of curiosity made their way to the cave, where the traveling Nazarene couple was located, to observe the holy festival.

Many wondered, why a cave and this one in particular? It was not the regular meeting place where Terach usually read from the Torah and prayed blessings for the people.

One of the farmer shepherds who had been confronted by the angels about the birth of the messiah went about informing this diverse crowd what the angels had directed to all the shepherds in the area. Without exception everyone who heard the outlandish fantasy of this shepherd disregarded his words. Some verbally rebuked him and a couple of women accused him of false prophecy. The Gentiles present merely shrugged their shoulders, discarding the fulfillment of God's prophecy as if it were a fairy tale.

Several of the outcast men in attendance stared at the farmer shepherd with steely eyes, but refrained from making any accusations against him. They closely observed everything this man did and whom he approached. Similarly, Terach meticulously monitored the actions of his fellow Jew but did not interfere with the man's actions.

After the brief ceremony ended and the crowd dispersed, the outcast men made their way toward Terach. The leader of the group stepped forward and warmly greeted him. "Terach, your words were very powerful today and touched my heart deeply.

This last feast of the year is a good way to prepare for the coming winter and your words give comfort."

Terach acknowledged the kind words from the man who he knew was the leader of a group of outcasts. "It is good to see you again, Jesus Barabbas. I'm glad you were able to attend."

The powerfully-built man smiled and jubilantly proclaimed, "Ah, my friend, what would this holy holiday be without you! My men and I would be left to only partially observe God's command as we tend to our flocks in the coastal regions of our lush valley."

Jesus Barabbas jerked his head towards the town and vehemently said, "These hypocrites who talk about God yet prevent us from participating in His holy feasts treat us with distain, mockery, and contempt!" As he spoke his face reddened with emotion, and he waved his hands widely to include everyone who lived in Bethlehem.

"Barabbas, it does you no good to get so angry. The Jews who follow the man-made teachings of the Sanhedrin will not change. We get along well without them. Their laws cannot keep us from honoring God."

The angry man looked intently at his close friend and silence filled the air. Suddenly, Barabbas threw back his head, and his keffiyeh head covering made a soft sound as it waved in the breeze. The outer cloak, his similah, parted and fluttered like a ship's sail as Barabbas threw his arms up towards the heavens. Everything about Barabbas seemed always to be bold and dramatic. "Terach, you always have the right words for me!" Barabbas tilted his head and squinted with one eye. The corner of his mouth curled upward. "You are a wise man, which is one of the things I like about you. What I like most is that you are honest and do not attempt to appease these religious fools. I respect you and it is why I call you my friend all these years we have known each other."

"Those same characteristics are what I like about you as well, Barabbas. In addition to being the same age, we are like brothers."

Barabbas stuck out his chest and gave his good friend a warm hug. Then he stepped back, as a concerned expression took hold of his face.

"My friend, I must convey to you that the words spoken by our Jewish brother about this new messiah could cause harm to come to him. Because I trust you, tell me what you know of this so-called messiah?"

Terach relayed what the angels had told him and the other shepherds, and how he had come to this cave to inspect the situation for himself. As he spoke, Barabbas' brow furrowed in concentration and he gave his full attention to Terach's incredible story.

When the shepherd completed his narrative, the scar-faced man asked, "What do you plan to do to determine if there is truth in what was spoken to you and the other Jewish outcasts?"

Terach had, indeed, already made a plan. "My friend, I plan on questioning and observing this Nazarene couple throughout the remainder of this holy festival. Afterwards I shall decide if there is more to be done."

Barabbas nodded. "That is a wise approach, Terach. Once the men of Bethlehem return from Jerusalem, it will be more difficult to obtain answers. As a nomad shepherd, the local rabbi and his henchmen will dissuade you from staying here and force you out to the plains with your sheep and goats. I cannot help you at that time." Barabbas laughed and finished, "But my friend, I also can make my own inquiries in ways that will benefit us both."

The muscular shepherd squinted and stated, "My friend, I will meet with this Nazarene, talk with him, and observe this so-called messiah."

Terach placed his right hand on Barabbas' strong shoulder, and smiled. "Barabbas, I know you will be effective in securing information about this new development. Visit with me in the plains at our home later and we shall compare what each has learned."

Barabbas squeezed his lips tightly, nodded, and gave his commitment. "It is as you say, my friend." With that, he turned and with his hirelings made his way up the slight incline to the mouth of the cave.

The shepherd's eyes followed the group as they stood at the entrance to the animal manger. He pondered how much he could learn from this Joseph of Nazareth in the few remaining days of the festival. He had so many questions. Terach wondered how many of them could be answered. He withdrew his gaze from the manger to rejoin his family and led the way back to the grassy plains and their tent home.

Each day of the Feast of Tabernacles, the residents remaining in Bethlehem and the small band of shepherds affiliated with Jesus Barabbas wearing their long, black goathair cloaks, came forth from their make-shift tents and met Terach and his family at the foot of the cave that housed the family from Nazareth. After ceremonial reading and blessing, some of the townspeople lingered behind, scrutinizing this little family with the strange fantastical story. Several of the women huddled together as they slowly walked back to their regular homes, murmuring about the Jewish man's claim the infant was the prophesized messiah that all of Israel longed for.

The women whispered, "How could the promised messiah come from Nazareth—nothing of value has ever come from there?" And, "This infant is of peasant birth; only a royal heritage could be the lineage of the true messiah." The most skeptical among them sneered, "Why would God tell these lowly commoners about the promised messiah and not our valued religious leaders?" There was considerable doubt about the shepherd's words given to them the first day of the feast. Each woman's reactions reflected the erroneous teaching of the ruling Pharisees.

Every day of the designated festival, Terach spent some time conversing with Joseph, interspersing questions. Beulah engaged the young new mothe, but she made sure she stayed out of the way of the midwife who attended to the young woman daily.

Back in their tent home, Terach and Beulah compared their findings and shared their thoughts about this new family. The fact was, to their disappointment, neither learned much about this traveling family and the fulfillment of God's prophecy. They did not speak much about what the angels had heralded earlier.

On the last day of the sacred feast no work was allowed. On that day, Terach's youngest son, four-year-old Mattan, crept close to the trough where the baby named Jesus lay. He was tentative as he approached the infant. Mattan was unsure of himself, but summoned his courage to satisfy his curiosity about the infant. This was the first human newborn baby he had ever seen. At the side of the trough, Mattan's head barely reached over the top of the trough to see the tiny infant.

The curious lad stood motionless, staring at the form wrapped tightly in the traditional swaddling clothes. A flat rock was close to the trough and Mattan was able to carry it to where the child lay. The dark-headed boy stepped up on the rock to get a better view. His little fingers gripped the side of the trough. Terach stood nearby, carefully observing his youngest so, but did not interfere. He wanted to see not only what the youngster would do but also how his son would react to the infant. The shepherd's eyes likewise honed in on what the infant's parents would do.

Terach noticed Joseph had turned away from his young wife and peered at the shy little boy who was staring wide-eyed at the baby Jesus. Joseph looked towards Terach and silently smiled that it was alright for Mattan to view the newborn messiah. Mary was distracted by Beulah and did not notice the little onlooker.

Without any announcement or request for permission, Mattan reached over and gently placed his chubby little hand on the baby's bound chest. To his surprise, the infant cooed in delight and began to squirm as if in an attempt to free himself from the tight cloth. Mattan's eyes widened in shock but he did not move his tiny hand which lightly rested on the baby. He was transfixed.

Stretching with all his might, Mattan grasped the edge of the trough and leaned over the side as far as his little body could reach. With his chest balanced on the trough, the determined boy moved his little head towards the baby. Carefully he leaned down and gave him a kiss on his covered head. As Mattan lifted his head, his eyes locked onto those of the baby Jesus. They stared at each other for some time and then Mattan broke out in a happy smile. The elated youth slowly lowered himself from the trough. He stepped off the rock and turned around to see his father looking intently at him. Mattan smiled gleefully at Terach and moved toward him. At his side, the little shepherd boy looked up at his towering father and softly proclaimed, "I really like this baby Jesus."

Terach reached out and took his young son's small hand and together the two made their way back to where Terach's horse was waiting for them. Beulah followed, and gathered up the other children. They quickly piled into the cart that would carry them back to their home on the grassy plains, jostling for their favorite places. Mattan wanted to ride with his father, so Terach secured his young son to the front of the saddle. Throughout the entire ride back to their tent home, young Mattan spoke excitedly about his experience and how much he wanted to see the baby Jesus again. Terach assured his young son he would.

Chapter 3

After the Feast of Tabernacles concluded, the able-bodied Jewish men returned to Bethlehem to resume their normal activities. The nomadic shepherds had returned to their flocks in the grassy plains that stretched between the outskirts of the small town to the coast of the Mediterranean. It was a broad valley and quite capable of supporting large numbers of animals.

Terach was the largest owner of the dwindling number of nomadic shepherds. His flock of Awassi sheep numbered well over four thousand plus an additional 875 Nubian goats. To adequately care for such a large number of animals, Terach had forty hirelings and thirty dogs to assist in herding his vast sea of woolly mammals. The dogs were excellent at keeping the sheep from straying, and the hirelings were adept at pacing the animals so that the grasslands did not suffer permanent damage from the volume of hungry four-footed feeders.

To not interfere with the farmers who surrounded the perimeter of Bethlehem, Terach moved his flock further west. This was strategic because the grass nearer the coast was taller, lush, and less grazed. Terach had no issues with the farmers of Bethlehem because they only had twenty sheep on average in their flock. They considered themselves farmers first, and animal raisers, second. They did not use the term shepherd due to dictates by the Jewish Sanhedrin.

The purpose for even a small number of Awassi breed sheep was as a source for milk that was made into cheese. The relatively small amount of wool was a revenue source for the farmer. When it came time to butcher one of the animals, the hide provided clothing mainly for the farmer.

Terach also had an agreement with the farmers that every year he would have his hirelings shear the farmers' sheep at no charge. In addition, the Jewish shepherd kingpin would also exchange ewes from time to time to ensure purity of the farmers' flocks. The alliance established by Terach was with the farmers throughout the entire region of Judea that included south of Bethlehem, and all the way north to Jericho and into Galliee.

Terach was widely known for his sharp business mind, honesty, fairness, and even temperament. Even so, the Jewish sheep lord could be demanding and severe with anyone who attempted to take advantage of him. He particularly loathed the rabbis and the religious leaders of the Jews for their dictates that made him and all the other remaining nomadic shepherds' outcasts and unwelcome members of Jewish society.

At an early age, Terach had been taught by his father how to read. This was highly unusual for the time. Only the Pharisees and the Sadducees held the reputation of being able to read. It was part of their control over the Jewish nation.

When Terach turned fourteen, his father had presented him the gift of a Torah. It was essentially the Old Testament, and was greatly valued by the Jews. Terach's father had obtained the sacred book while conducting a business transaction with one of the rabbis. He had exchanged several lambs for the holy book. The Rabbi would have faced severe punishment from the ruling Sanhedrin had word leaked to them about this transgression. Terach had guarded it as a coveted treasure, and immediately immersed himself in reading all the scripture contained in the revered book.

Based on his reading, he became angry and hardened towards the Sanhedrin for turning shepherds from a position of acceptance and esteem into the dregs of society. God's holy word placed great value on shepherds; but the Sanhedrin followed the mind warping of the Egyptians who detested all nomads, especially shepherds because of how the flocks would eat the crops grown by the Egyptian farmers.

For the entire four hundred years of captivity, the Jews had been lectured and duped by the Egyptians to the point that even after the Jews were safely in the Promised Land, they maintained the Egyptian attitude concerning shepherds and nomads.

Terach got a measure of retaliation every year when Passover took place in April. Animal sacrifices were required, and the preferred victim was a lamb of purity and without blemish as dictated by God's law given to the Jews' ancestors. Terach always had a large number of suitable lambs and his breeding methods resulted in obtaining top price for his animals.

The business-minded shepherd also sold large quantities of wool to the Nigrid top overseer in Jericho. The cheese from both his sheep and goats was highly valued by Jewish merchants. There was a long list of mainstream Jews who clamored for the cheese produced by Terach. All these factors resulted in Terach being wealthy and a man of influence to many, except to the Jewish religious community and those they influenced.

Unbeknownst to the religious bigots, Terach had a solid alliance with King Herod who narcissistically referred to himself as The Great. Herod allowed the successful Terach to graze his vast flock throughout all of Judea. He slyly instructed his Nigrid in Jericho to reduce the tax levy on the shepherd. On one occasion, Herod deemed Terach "King of the Shepherds," a moniker based on Terach's flock greatly outnumbering all the other nomadic shepherds'.

But the history of Terach and his position of favor was not known to the Nazarene carpenter, Joseph. The carpenter was more impressed at Terach's knowledge of the Torah and for the power of his delivery of God's word.

Joseph was surprised when Terach introduced him to the main shopkeeper in Bethlehem. "My friend," Terach addressed the shopkeeper, "I have a favor to ask of you. Is there available housing here for this man and his family? They have traveled from the far north of Galilee for the census and need adequate housing."

The shopkeeper looked first at Terach, then at Joseph, and replied, "I know of a house that is available due to the death of the occupant. But first I must know what this man's occupation is."

Joseph took the opening and informed the shopkeeper that he was a carpenter and that he had brought his tools with him. He expected that they would be assessed as required by Herod and the Romans who allowed him to rule.

Satisfied with the stranger's answer and preparedness, the shopkeeper led them to an abandoned house where the traveler and his family could reside while waiting for the census takers. It would provide a safe and weather resistant shelter for the young mother Mary to gather strength after her arduous ordeal of rough travel and subsequent childbirth. Joseph was very thankful for Terach's involvement on his behalf. This served as a bonding between the two men, which Terach appreciated since part of his purpose was to learn if the baby Jesus was indeed the promised messiah.

Four days after the completion of the Feast of Tabernacles, Terach received word that one of the nomadic shepherds who aligned his smaller flock with that of Terach's had been taken to Bethlehem by the chief rabbi's henchmen. The shepherd was accused of the Jewish crime of false pretention to prophecy because of telling several women about the angels that heralded the arrival of the promised messiah.

Five witnesses came forth and accused the shepherd. The crime carried severe penalties. The chief rabbi and two of the main elders convicted the shepherd and sentenced him to be whipped. The shepherd had no defense other than his own word, and the court ordered him to receive twenty lashes. The sentence was carried out immediately, with the usual exception--the shepherd received only 19 lashes in accordance with Jewish corporal law of giving one less, in case of a miscalculation.

One of the older Jews of Bethlehem was assigned to administer the lashing because a man in his prime strength could kill an offender with the punishment. Normally, once the sentence was carried out, the offender would be welcomed back into Jewish society with full membership. However, this was not the case for shepherds and others who were deemed dregs of Jewish society. The disdained shepherd was not given ointment for his wounds. Instead, he was roughly escorted out of Bethlehem where he was spat upon, ridiculed, and humiliated.

Upon hearing about the incident, Terach rode to the shepherd's tent that was located behind and to the east of Terach's main flock. The angered shepherd leader dismounted his Arabian stallion and purposefully strode into the victim's home. Terach looked down to see the shepherd lying on his stomach. His wife was applying ointment to the wounds.

Terach could vividly see that some of the lashings had carried over the shepherd's shoulders. Terach knew there were wounds on the man's chest as well as on his back. Despite the freshness of the wounds, Terach assessed they would begin to heal quickly.

In a calm voice Terach asked; "Massai, tell me how this happened?" The shepherd completed his rendition of the arrest and lashing. Terach inquired, "Who were the rabbi and the judges?" Massai gave Terach the names between winces as his wife applied more ointment to his wounds. "Now, tell me, Massai, was the only reason you were lashed due to your relaying what the angels told us the night of the promised messiah's birth?" Massai could not speak, but weakly nodded yes as his wife assisted in getting his tunic back on his wounded body. The shepherd let out a sigh of pain once the tunic was put on.

Terach looked at the ashen-faced shepherd and soothingly advised, "Rest, my friend, and do not attempt to perform your responsibilities in caring for your flock. My men will do this for you." As Terach turned to leave his fellow shepherd, he hesitated and asked one final question. "Massai, does anyone else know about your trial and conviction?"

The worn-out pained shepherd's brow wrinkled in contemplation. After a moment of thought he replied, "Of course. The citizenry of Bethlehem and I think maybe one of King Herod's men who was in town purchasing items from the main shopkeeper. Other than that, I do not know, Terach."

Satisfied with Massai's answer, Terach nodded his head and left the tent. His cloak flapped around his angry steps and lifted in the breeze as he mounted his stallion.

Back at his tent home, Terach relayed his visit to Beulah, and the two discussed the situation at length. Beulah had the ability to calm her husband and keep him from acting impulsively. "My husband, refrain yourself from attempting to do harm to the rabbi and the judges. They were following the Jewish laws. Besides, at this point in time, we do not know if what the angels told you and the other shepherds is really the truth. This must be determined before we shepherds tell others about the strange event."

Terach's facial expression softened and he leaned over to give Beulah a kiss on her cheek. Tenderly, he took her hand in his and kissed the back of her hand. "You are correct, my lovely wife. I shall heed your wise advice."

Several days after discussing the lashing of Massai with Beulah, Terach was checking on his flock in the uppermost region of the grassy plains which sustained his flocks with winter habitation. The shepherd lifted his head and sniffed the air with his nose. The air had the smell of an impending winter storm. Instinctively he pulled his goat hide cloak tighter around his body.

After talking with his hireling assigned to that region about the approaching storm, he was satisfied the sheep would be well cared for and protected, so Terach turned his stallion northward. The horse proceeded at an easy pace and its master enjoyed the view of the rippling grassland. Terach never tired of viewing the open plains regardless of the season. He felt thankful for God's grace in renewing the rich grasses that supported not only his but the other nomadic shepherds' flocks.

Approximately two miles into his journey, Terach noticed figures on horseback approaching his position. Immediately the shepherd reined in his stallion to better observe the stick figures. The stallion had also noticed the approaching small group and nervously stepped side-to-side and snorted to alert his master. Both man and beast prepared themselves for potential danger. It was not uncommon for Syrian marauders to invade Judea, plundering all that they could.

As the small group grew larger in their path of intervention with Terach, the shepherd tightened his grip on his barbed rod normally used to control and direct the sheep. He also looked down to his side to make sure his short sword was readily available should he need it for defense.

The steady advance of the small group now changed from stick figures to that of recognizable men. The group of five riders came within one hundred yards of Terach, and he recognized one of the advancing horsemen. Terach breathed a sigh of relief. He relaxed his grip on the rod, and raised his hand overhead in a sign of non-hostility towards the riders. Despite this gesture, the stallion remained nervous and continued his shifting stance.

When the small group stopped in front of Terach, the leader let out a boisterous laugh and said, "Terach, what are you doing this far ahead of your flock and your home?" The leader's voice was jovial and teasing. He did not wait for an answer to his question, but adopted a more serious tone, "I have need to speak with you. This can be done here. There is no need to proceed back to your home." The leader's facial expression conveyed the sincerity of his words.

"Barabbas, there is a small cave just west of us that we can use and get out of this cold blast of air ahead of the advancing storm." The shepherd turned his steed and led the way to the cave. Once inside, Barabbas wasted no time getting to the topic of his concern.

"I have information concerning the Nazarene named Joseph. I also made inquiry about the lashing of Massai. No doubt you, too, have information on these matters that we can share with each other." With a nod from Terach, Barabbas went on. "This Joseph personally told me he is a carpenter in Nazareth and an elder in the synagogue there. He is in Bethlehem for the census because this is his origin but none of his family remains alive. He has no relatives or friends in Bethlehem."

Barabbas paused to catch his breath and give Terach time to ask any questions. Terach took the opportunity and held up his hand to keep Barabbas from interrupting. "This is most interesting, my friend. This Joseph told me the same that he informed you."

The still black-clad Barabbas smiled broadly and began to share more details, communicating with his arms and hands as he always did when he wanted to command the conversation and emphasize a particular point. "Joseph and the woman continued to reside in Nazareth until he was commanded to return to Bethlehem for both the Roman and the Jews' census."

Barabbas paused, mainly to rest his arms, and then continued. "Joseph did not offer any information or knowledge about the angels heralding the birth of his infant son or about the child being the promised messiah. But, Terach, you and I saw the angels and heard the message! Even so, Joseph did not deny that the new born baby was the messiah."

Barabbas then inquired of his friend, "In light of this information, how can it be that the promised messiah spoken about in the holy book can come from this type of beginning?" The perplexed nomad added another perplexing thought, "Wouldn't the chief priest, the Sanhedrin, and the rabbis know of this, based on their knowledge of the Torah?"

Terach was momentarily silent before he gave his reply. "When I spoke with Joseph during the Feast of Tabernacles, he did not reveal any of this to me." Terach mused, "Nor did he claim his infant son indeed is the much sought messiah." Terach paused to let this settle in Barabbas' mind before he continued. "I, too, have grave concerns about this story of the baby being the promised messiah, despite what I heard from the angels."

Barabbas jumped in, "What do you plan on doing to get more answers to these perplexing events?"

Terach straightened his posture and replied, "I plan on making frequent trips to Bethlehem throughout the winter months until it is time for me to begin the journey leading my flock north to Jericho. On these visits to Bethlehem I will purposefully engage Joseph and ask him pointed questions, especially about what he can tell me about the baby Jesus being the promised messiah."

To ease the concern of Barabbas, Terach added, "My friend, I believe we should meet periodically until such time it is necessary to make that move north and east with our flocks and share whatever new information we gather about this man and his family."

Barabbas clasped his hands together and his voice erupted, "Excellent, my friend!"

Satisfied the topic of Joseph and the infant Jesus was resolved, Barabbas shifted to Massai. The nomad's voice lowered almost to a growl. His face showed deep anger and hostility. "I have learned about this rabbi and the elders who convicted Massai of false pretention to prophecy. He did not take the time to question Massai in depth. He and the others convicted him simply on the basis of being a shepherd. It's a matter of control for this contemptable pig. He does not want the Jews of Bethlehem to give credence to anything Massai or the rest of us shepherds say."

Terach solemnly nodded. "I, too, have reached that same conclusion, my friend. This is a continuation of what began when our ancestors were in captivity to the Egyptians. The rabbi could have discussed this with me, since Massai on occasion aligns his flock with mine. In addition, he knows that I perform the reading of the sacred Torah scripture and was there when Massai spoke about this messiah. The fool knows full well we shepherds are in close communication with each other. Beulah convinced me not to engage with this rabbi as it will do no good; and alas, I must agree with her."

Barabbas shook his head and made a fist, speaking angrily, "No, my friend! This matter shall be resolved that all who participated in Massai's lashing and humiliation shall know of their despicable deed."

At that point, they could already smell and hear the beginning of the rain that the wind had summoned. Barabbas peered outside the cave and said, "My friend, this storm forces us to rest here until such time we can depart to the warmth of our homes." For the next two hours the men shared goat jerky and talked about the impending winter and when they would proceed northeast to Jericho.

When the storm abated, the men rose to leave. Terach gave his friend one final piece of advice, "Don't attempt to harm the rabbi or the judges. It could have grave consequences for all of us."

With that, the group dispersed and on the cold trip back to his tent home Terach could not stop contemplating Barabbas' words about dealing with those involved in Massai's lashing. Terach knew the power of Barabbas and his passion. He was more concerned for his friend than any of those associated with the incident surrounding Massai. The rain began to resume, and Terach hunched his body, secured his cloth head covering, and made sure his cloak protected him. He did not have to urge his stallion to quicken the pace back to his home.

On the rain-soaked ride, Terach shifted his thoughts to Joseph and the question surrounding the infant Jesus. The shepherd had many thoughts and questions and was eager to confront Joseph for the answers. But his curiosity would have to wait until after the first hard storm of the winter waned.

Two days after the storm ceased, Terach inspected his vast flock, checking with the hirelings to make sure there was no loss of sheep. The Awassi breed was very hardy and could withstand inclement weather conditions. Just the same, Terach exhibited the age-old shepherd creed of caring for his flock. It was more than economic loss that concerned Terach. He and the other nomadic shepherds had a genuine softness in their hearts for the animals they believed God put under their care.

It took Terach an entire day to inspect both the sheep and the goat flocks. He was thankful for God's provision of his Arabian stallion that made the process go quicker. It would have been extremely difficult for Terach to undertake such an endeavor on foot. The four thousand head of sheep stretched several miles wide. The large number of goats was separated from the sheep and Terach had three of his hirelings pasture them along the row of small hills that the goats preferred. This added to the distance the shepherd had to regularly cover to determine the condition of his vast flocks and herds.

When the shepherd finished his duties, he swung his steed around in the direction of his tent home. He was but a short distance from the tent when all four of his boys came racing out excitedly to greet him. In a cacophony of youthful energy, each shouted their reason for priority to climb aboard the steed and be with their father. Little Mattan had a special seat just behind the saddle horn while his older brothers fought for position on the remaining spots. The stallion did not refuse the additional weight. Once the noisy crew was aboard, Terach slowly guided the stallion the final short distance to their tent home.

Mattan always giggled when riding with his father. The swaying of the horse gave the youngster delight. He could hardly wait until such time he was old enough to ride a horse by himself.

Inside the tent, the aroma of hot food filled the air. The warmth from the small fire was an added bonus to the chilled Terach who relished even more the warmth from his sons' hearts. For a short period of time he wrestled with his horde of boys and made sure to include Mattan, who was brave enough to enjoy the activity. Still, Terach made sure the wrestling did not get too rough for his youngest son.

Terach and Beulah had an opportunity to converse privately after the meal. The tired boys were put to bed on their straw mats covered with goat hair skins for protection from the straw and for needed warmth during the cold winter. The shepherd looked lovingly at his sons, then turned his attention to his wife.

"Tomorrow I will go to Bethlehem and engage Joseph. I want to see what he and his wife, Mary, have done to the house the shopkeeper opened to them. This will also provide me opportunity to obtain information concerning the questions we have discussed about him and his family. Is there anything you suggest I say or ask of this man?"

"You are wise enough to be subtle in your questioning, my husband. The only thing I suggest is not to demand too many answers from the man. This might make him suspicious of your intentions. Do you detect he may not be friendly towards you because you are a shepherd and he was an elder in the synagogue back in Nazareth?"

"Thus far he has been receptive to my presence. I believe he was surprised by my reading from the Torah during the Feast of Tabernacles. This gave him some insight as to who I am. I hope this man is not like the other religious leaders in despising shepherds." Terach reached for his wife's hand and firmly clasped her fingers. He drew her close and looked deep into her eyes. A tone of uncertainty crept into his typically confident voice. "Tomorrow will be a big day, hopefully to resolve this confusing issue about the infant being the promised messiah."

Chapter 4

Terach left early in the morning for Bethlehem. He drew in a deep breath of the crisp fall air and felt the coolness penetrate his lungs. Its crispness coupled with the chill and the dew on the grass always mildly excited the shepherd ever since he was a small boy. He looked toward the horizon. The first rays of the sun were announcing God's new day. He lingered in relishing the moment until the Arabian stallion snorted and threw back its head, signaling his eagerness to move faster.

The shepherd made sure his small goatskin bag contained food provided by Beulah. He opted to leave his barbed rod at home, but retained the short sword for protection should the need arise. Terach was fond of the short sword instead of the usual knife utilized by the farmer/semi-shepherd. The short sword was a gift from King Herod who acquired it from a Roman centurion sent to make sure Herod was ruling in accordance with Roman dictates for conquered nations. The sword was better suited than the knife for self-protection when encountering a marauding predator around the sheep. There were times when a weapon such as the short sword was better suited to deal with adversity than the shepherd's rod.

Now that the colder winter season had reached the grassy plains, Terach exchanged his usual short tunic for a longer one that afforded more protection against the blustery wind and rain. His longer tunic coupled with a longer cloak mantle made mounting the stallion more awkward. A few grunts assisted him into the saddle. Once aloft, Terach easily adjusted his clothing so that the short sword and the food pouch would travel well and not drop to the ground and become lost. On this particular day, Terach quickly made his adjustments as his prized stallion quickened the pace to Bethlehem.

From where his sheep were pastured and his tent located, the ride to Bethlehem would take nearly one hour. Terach prepared for a relaxed ride. He knew to maintain an easy pace so as not to tire out his reliable Arabian horse.

At the outskirts of the town Terach engaged one of the farmer shepherds for preliminary business. Terach assured the farmer that he would exchange two of his younger ewes for the farmer's two older ewes so that the forthcoming lambs would be pure and not subject to disease and mental weaknesses that inevitably accompanied inbreeding.

After taking care of this minor bit of business, Terach focused his direction to the house that Joseph and his family now occupied. As he approached the house, Terach could see that Joseph was making some repairs to the roof. The carpenter took notice of his visitor and shouted down to the horseman, "Terach, I am almost finished with this repair and then we can talk."

It did not take the proficient craftsman long to repair the roof. Joseph's efficiency and skill impressed the shepherd. Once on the ground, Joseph invited his visitor inside his newly acquired abode. He guided his visitor to the table where Mary had prepared the morning meal. She had observed the arrival of their guest and prepared sufficient sustenance for them all while Joseph's tools tapped on the roof. The young mother attended to her new-born infant, then placed the enticing meal on the table located in the main portion of the house.

The three sat down and Joseph asked his guest, "Terach, what brings you away from your flock to Bethlehem? It is quite a distance from where your sheep are pastured to town, and the weather is very unsettled for travel."

Terach casually answered, "It is that time of year when I exchange some of my ewes for those of the various farmers located along the outskirts of Bethlehem. I determine how many ewes will be needed and then return for the exchange."

The shepherd could tell Joseph and Mary were satisfied with his truthful answer. Terach shot forth his initial question to the carpenter. "Joseph, have you met with the shopkeeper and the rabbi to determine how much and what kind of carpentry is needed in Bethlehem?"

Joseph looked pleased as he replied, "Both the shopkeeper and the rabbi have guided me to work. The synagogue is in need of some repair and the shopkeeper has engaged me to make some yokes and plows that he can sell to the farmers. He told me there is much work available in Bethlehem, especially now that the prior carpenter has died. I shall have enough work to provide for Mary and the baby Jesus. This is a blessing from God because this census can last a long time." It was not unusual for the combined census dictated by the Romans and by Herod to last up to two years based on the thoroughness of the soldier census takers.

Taking a bite of the fresh-made bread, Terach dipped it in the hummus and sipped some of the flavorful wine before he queried his host. "Do you intend on returning to Nazareth after your obligations when both the Roman and the Jewish census are completed?"

Joseph looked forlornly at the inquisitive shepherd and softly said, "King Herod has all but destroyed Sepphoris where much of my work was located. The city is in ruins. My hope was that Bethlehem would be in need of a carpenter." His face brightened as he noted, "And God has answered my prayer with His grace and blessing."

Terach had heard of the destruction of Sepphoris, but since it was far north, near close proximity to Galilee, it was of minor importance to the nomad. Still, it answered the question about this carpenter and his intentions. The shepherd proceeded with his effort to unearth more information. "Joseph, have you been approached by the rabbi in this district of Bethlehem to participate in the synagogue?"

Joseph did not seem alarmed by the question and replied, "We have talked and I have been accepted into the synagogue, and Mary also with the women there, as well."

While he thought, Terach slowly tore off a piece of the fresh bread and purposefully reached to dip it into the hummus and also take a piece of flavorful falafel. As he did so, he carefully controlled his intonation as he asked, "Did the rabbi share any information with you about the recent lashing of the shepherd Massai?"

Again the carpenter appeared calm and not alarmed. And Terach could tell from a quick glance at Mary that she was relaxed with the question. Joseph took a sip of his wine then remarked straightforwardly, "The rabbi said it was because the shepherd made a false pretention to prophecy."

Terach was glad Joseph knew this and was willing to address it. Terach quickly probed, "What type of false prophecy did the rabbi say the shepherd made?"

Again Joseph simply replied, "That Bethlehem was the site of the arrival of the promised messiah and that angels told him and the other shepherds to announce the messiah's arrival." This time Joseph's tone changed and he was more selective in choosing his words. Mary also shyly looked down at the top of the table.

It was all Terach could do to keep his hand from quivering with excitement over his inquisition of the carpenter and his wife. As casually as he could, Terach took a sip of his wine then looked directly into his host's eyes. "You know, of course, the shepherd Massai was referring to your newborn son Jesus. Do you believe the angels mentioned by Massai were stating that your infant son Jesus is this messiah that has been promised to us Jews?"

The couple stared blankly at their guest then turned and looked at each other, speaking a silent language between them. As Terach waited for a response to his question, he looked first from Mary to Joseph and then back again. As this intermezzo continued, Terach's heartbeat quickened and the palms of his hands became moist. He found himself holding his breath in anticipation of what he was about to hear from his hosts.

Joseph slyly nodded to his wife and Mary turned toward Terach. The young mother took a deep breath, cleared her throat, and began her narrative. "Three months prior to my becoming pregnant I was sleeping, when an angel of Almighty God came to me and said, 'Rejoice highly favored one, the Lord is with you; blessed are you among women.' The angel's words troubled me and I was confused by such a greeting."

Mary paused with a glance at her husband before continuing her chronicle. "The angel told me not to be afraid because I had found favor with God. He went on, saying that I would conceive in my womb and bring forth a son and shall call His name Jesus."

Again Mary hesitated and took another deep breath. She lowered her eyes and in a less tentative voice continued. "The angel's voice became excited as he proclaimed this Jesus will be great and will be called the Son of the Highest and the Lord God will give Him the throne of His father David." Mary cleared her throat once more. "The angel sounded emphatic in saying that Jesus will reign over the house of Jacob forever, and of His kingdom there will be no end."

Mary raised her head and looked directly at Terach to gauge his reaction to what she knew was an astounding tale the shepherd probably would have great difficulty believing. Her expression was calm but she was waiting for Terach's reaction. The shepherd sat with a calm composure and deep interest in the woman's account. Sensing her hesitation, Terach nodded his head toward Mary and softly urged her to continue.

The young Nazarene woman relaxed and picked up where she left off. "I asked the angel, 'How can this be? I do not know a man, not even my betrothed husband!' Quickly the angel said, 'The Holy Spirit will come upon you, and the power of the Highest will overshadow you.' He went on to say, 'The Holy One who is to be born will be called the Son of God.' I was stunned by these words and at first I remained silent. Then I told the angel 'Behold the maidservant of the Lord! Let it be to me according to your word.' I had nothing else to say at such an astonishing thing. When I finished giving my reply, the angel disappeared. I sat on my bed, my heart was racing, and I tried to make sure I wasn't merely dreaming. Three months later it became evident I was pregnant."

Anticipating Terach's thinking, Joseph leaned towards the shepherd and said, "Terach, you have heard Mary's account of her experience with Almighty God, but it doesn't end there. I have my own description that will answer some of your questions." Terach felt his body tense as he wondered what else was involved with this incredible story.

Joseph took a sip of wine, drew in a deep breath, and continued the amazing story. "As Mary has stated, we were betrothed in Nazareth and the official ceremony was scheduled to take place on the anniversary of our betrothal. The evidence of Mary's pregnancy changed everything. Continuance of our Jewish betrothal tradition would not be possible. As an elder in my synagogue I knew the ramifications. Our story would not be believed. It would destroy Mary to seemingly be bearing a child out of wedlock. Her apparent infidelity would not allow us to continue our marriage covenant. There was only one provision. With two witnesses I could privately divorce Mary and not subject her to public ridicule."

Joseph stopped his report, remembering those painful decisions. He looked at Terach to gauge his reaction. Joseph knew his guest was fully aware of Jewish law pertaining to the seriousness of infidelity. Satisfied the shepherd was not exhibiting signs of a spirit of condemnation, Joseph opted to continue relaying his version of the implausible story.

"Before I could act on divorcing Mary, an angel of the Lord also appeared before me saying that I should not be afraid to take Mary as my wife, because, he said, that which was conceived in her was of the Holy Spirit and that she would bring forth a son and he was to be called Jesus, for He will save His people from their sins."

Joseph placed his hand on top of Mary's and smiled warmly at her placid face. Gently he squeezed her hand, then turned to face Terach. "Similar to Mary's encounter with what could be the same angel, I became aroused from a very deep sleep, deeper than what I've ever experienced. I knew in my heart the encounter with the angel was real because a great peace engulfed my body."

The powerfully built carpenter sighed and quietly finished, "I went to Mary and took her as my wife. Shortly after that, the proclamation was made in Nazareth about the census by the Roman Caesar Augustus and we made plans for our journey here to Bethlehem. It took us much longer because I had to devise a route that would not be as difficult for her condition. Long distances can cause difficulties with pregnancies." Again the carpenter looked affectionately at his young wife and he gave another gentle squeeze to her hand.

Joseph decided to make one important final admission. "Since I decided not to divorce Mary, we still have not known each other as husband and wife."

Joseph's candid words seemed to hang in the air, and silence filled the room. Terach was flabbergasted by both narratives. It was nothing as he had expected. The shepherd's mind raced for words and also for a plan of action to respond to this improbable tale that easily could be construed as fantasy. After a prolonged period, the shepherd finally composed himself and saw both his hosts were looking at him, highly anxious to hear what he would say.

The stalwart leader of the nomadic shepherds of Judea placed his hands on top of the table and sympathetically shared his thoughts. "I do not doubt your renditions concerning the birth of your son Jesus. For quite some time I've immersed myself in the study of the Scriptures in the Torah. As you spoke, several of God's prophecies came to my mind that foretold of this day. I believe God's Holy Word, and have personally wondered when Almighty God would fulfill His promise to His chosen people."

Terach momentarily paused before continuing, "Still, this news comes as a great shock, especially when we have been taught by the Jewish religious leaders the messiah would be of regal birth, with power and influence to establish a formidable army capable of dispatching the Romans who now control our existence."

The shepherd leader's thoughts suddenly went to a troubling question he had. "When you heard how Massai heralded to the Jews what the angels told us nomadic shepherds, myself included, about this Jesus being the promised messiah, why did you keep silent?" Terach emphasized, "Especially when the rabbi and the court convicted Massai of false pretention to prophecy. You have dealings with the rabbi and could have verified what Massai told to the people during the Feast of The Tabernacles."

There was sadness, but no hesitation from Joseph as he answered the shepherd's query. "Neither Mary nor I were released by God to confirm the fulfillment of His prophecy. His Holy Spirit tethered our mouths shut. In addition, I know how the Jews feel towards shepherds. My confirmation of Massai's claim would have made no difference in the minds of the rabbi and the elders of the synagogue."

Terach leaned back as he listened to Joseph's reasoning. He saw the carpenter's serious expression of sincerity, and stoically uttered, "You are correct, Joseph, about the reaction of the Jewish leaders of Bethlehem. I also believe these same leaders would have taken measure to discredit you and not allow you to either work or attend the synagogue here. It is unfortunate how the power of the religious leaders can negatively impact people's lives."

Joseph and Mary listened closely. When Terach finished, he saw a relaxation in his hosts. Their faces showed a sense of relief. Their demeanor changed as frozen rigidity thawed and tension evaporated.

Terach took note of this and decided the atmosphere was conducive to continue his questioning. "What do you propose to do concerning the rabbi and the elders from here on out, concerning this fulfillment of prophecy?"

Joseph raised one eyebrow and semi-shrugged his shoulders. "Obviously, we must continue to follow God's direction. His timing is always right. It appears right now that He does not want us to introduce Jesus as the promised messiah because nobody in proper Jewish society would believe our assertion." The carpenter briefly looked at Mary, then back at Terach as he continued, "We are mere servants of Almighty God. We will do His bidding as He directs us to do in His perfect timing."

Joseph shot a question of his own to Terach. "How do you foresee yourself and the other shepherds handling this revelation?"

Terach did not have to ponder the question very long. He answered, "As for us shepherds, based on what you have just told me, coupled with what the angel spoke to us, we will spread this news to those who will hear our words. Some already have. All those deemed outcasts of Jewish society shall hear of this magnificent event, but it will be their choice to believe and receive this news, or not. It is obvious the Jews steeped in Jewish tradition will rebel against such news."

The conversation ended. Terach left Bethlehem to meet with the various farmers about their small sheep flocks. Joseph resumed his repair to the house God provided for the Holy Family. Mary realized it was time to nurse her newborn son. For the time being, life returned to everyday normal tasks.

Once his mission with the area farmers was completed, Terach began the journey back to his tent home, approximately four miles southwest of Bethlehem. Despite the lateness of the day, the shepherd felt no urgency to hurry home. Rather, Terach utilized the time to ponder the earlier conversation he had with the Nazarene family. There were several nagging questions in his mind. As was his custom, he would discuss with Beulah the revealing conversation he had just had with this newly arrived couple to the town. Her insight and wisdom would be of great help in comprehending the shocking story.

Terach gathered his goat hair cloak tighter around his body as a sudden chill coursed through every fiber of his being. The shepherd was unsure if it was due to the wind suddenly rushing a cold blast in his direction, or if it was from his speculation concerning this unusual family's secret.

The chill remained with the shepherd as he completed his journey home. His arrival coincided with the last rays of the day's sun fading into the twilight.

When the four young boys had finally depleted their youthful energy and fell asleep, Terach and Beulah moved to a corner of the tent where their bed was located. From that quiet place they could discuss the day's events. Beulah was particularly anxious to hear what her husband's interrogation of the newcomers from Nazareth revealed.

Beulah sat transfixed throughout Terach's entire report. At times her eyes widened in astonishment and disbelief. When he finished, she was silent for a short period of time, mentally sorting through the strange explanation given by the Nazarene couple. Terach paid close attention to his wife's eyes. When she was deep in thought and contemplating her words, her eye movements reflected careful evaluation. They did that now.

Finally Beulah sighed. She reached for her husband's hand and stroked it. Softly, she cleared the catch in her voice. "My husband, I agree with you about these strange encounters both Joseph and Mary had with an angel. Had one of God's angels not spoken to you and to the other shepherds about the birth of this promised messiah, I would totally discount what this couple told you." Beulah squeezed Terach's hand to emphasize her sincere feelings. "You must search the scriptures to verify what God's Word has to say about His promise to His chosen people. It is important to learn of any timing God might have said in His holy word about His promised messiah. As you do this, I believe God will speak to you, and will give you His discernment and wisdom so that you can take action accordingly. If you find anything that does not align with God's prophecy, then you will know this couple are imposters out for some gain for themselves or are agents of the devil."

Terach was relieved by her advice. "Your words are the same as my thoughts, dear wife. This is the proper course of action I must take."

Beulah nodded her head, smiled, and gave Terach a gentle kiss on his cheek. When she leaned back she looked deeply into his serious eyes. "Should the Tanakh, the Torah, vindicate this couple's story, you will have a much greater decision to make concerning them and what you should do about this revelation. This could be very important."

Terach bowed his head slightly and quietly confirmed his wife's statement. "Again you are correct in your assessment, Beulah." The stymied shepherd finished, "Only Almighty God can direct my words and my actions concerning this development." At that, Terach looked up into his wife's soft face. He would not take his task lightly. They embraced and lay back on the bed, silently clinging to each other for some time, each deep in their own thoughts.

The last words spoken were from Beulah whispering into her husband's ear, "If this infant is indeed the messiah, the world will change in ways we cannot envision."

Finally, they fell asleep, wondering, but without answers.

Chapter 5

For the next several days Terach was busy directing his hirelings on the care of his massive flocks of sheep and goat herds. When the day's work was complete, each night after his children were sound asleep, the shepherd undertook the task of researching the Tanakh/Torah scriptures for insight into God's promise of sending a messiah to His chosen people. Several candles were burned as Terach's research continued. Beulah was of great help by keeping the four boys very active after their evening meal, until they were all so exhausted all they wanted to do was lie down and sleep. This gave Terach more time in the evening to pursue his quest.

The Tanakh given to Terach contained the five books written by Moses, which the Jews referred to as the Torah. Other books were divided into two separate sections. The middle section contained the writings of all the major prophets. Terach took his time researching each book for clues to what the angels announced about the arrival of the promised messiah.

It was a slow process and at times frustrating for the shepherd. Finally after three weeks of study, Terach found the answer he was searching for. He sat transfixed, staring at the words he had just read. Suddenly he realized he had been holding his breath, and he released it with an audible huff. Beulah was finishing some sewing repair to one of the boys' tunics. Startled, she put down the garment and anxiously looked in the direction of her husband. Her suspicions rose, and she excitedly asked, "What makes you gasp, my husband?"

Terach blurted out, "Beulah, the answer! I've finally found the answer to our quest!" Beulah quickly held a single finger to her lips, signaling her excited husband to lower his voice. The elated shepherd stammered as he pointed his finger at the portion of the scroll that lay open before him, "It's... it's very clear... and there can be no mistake. What I've found can change the lives of all Jews forever!"

Beulah moved closer to her husband and placed her hand gently on his shoulder. "Terach, do not raise your voice so much, you will wake the boys. Speak softly to me." The wide-eyed shepherd was motionless with awe.

Terach gathered his composure and took a deep breath. He read to his wife the words contained in his Tanakh. "*But you, Bethlehem Ephrathah, though you are little among the thousands of Judah, yet out of you shall come forth to Me the One to be Ruler of Israel, whose goings forth are from of old, from everlasting.*"

Beulah's eyes widened and she squeezed her husband's shoulder as she fought to remain calm. She inhaled deeply and wanted to know exactly where such prophecy came from. "Where did you find these profound words?"

Terach smiled in wonder and replied, "They are in the book of prophecy written by Micah. These were God's words given to the prophet that we, now in this time, could read them and know He has kept His promise to all of Judea."

The shepherd took Beulah's hand and smiled at her astonished expression. "My wife, the messiah is as the angels spoke to myself and the other shepherds. There is no reason to doubt."

Beulah relished the joy and confidence that she saw on her husband's face. Suddenly though, her countenance changed to grave concern, "Do you intend on confronting Joseph and Mary with this or go to the rabbi with this news?"

Terach assured her he would not approach the rabbi or any of the elders with this earth-shaking news. "They would not listen to me, or believe anything I may tell them. They will either label me a heretic or totally disregard God's prophecy to protect their religious mantra." The shepherd theologian let his words sink in before adding, "And no, I will not confront Joseph and Mary. During my earlier conversation they indicated they would not tell the rabbi or the elders about their experience with God's angels."

The shepherd slowly stroked his beard and emphatically assured Beulah, "I shall stand back and monitor how Joseph and Mary proceed. They claim God will direct them. I certainly will not interfere in any way." Terach tenderly took hold of Beulah by her shoulders and drew her closer to him. She was trembling. He wrapped his arms around her and quietly said, "This is unknown territory we face. Our main approach is to wait and see how this promised messiah grows up and makes himself known to his people. It will be important to learn what kind of a leader he will become."

Beulah wrapped her arms around Terach and they each pondered not only what God's Word spoken through His prophet Micah said, but also Terach's speculation that was beginning to dispel some lingering doubts.

Five days later the shepherd rode into town, intent on conversing with Joseph and also doing some business with the retail shop owner. Terach opted to get the business dealing out of the way first.

When he stepped inside the shopkeeper's place of business, the owner immediately informed him the census taker had arrived in Bethlehem. The census taker was also the assigned tax collector for King Herod's appointed Nigrid, or overseer, for Judea. The Nigrid recruited tax collectors and acted as Herod's general business administrator throughout Judea.

In addition to the census taker, the Jewish high priest Ananus ben Seth sent one of his scribes to assist the local rabbi in monitoring the census and the tax collecting. To make sure everything was accomplished to King Herod's satisfaction and mainly to Rome's, a contingent of no less than twelve Roman soldiers accompanied the tax collector. They were posted around the synagogue to prevent any riots from erupting—always a perceived threat due to the Jews' hatred of Roman taxation.

Terach thanked the shopkeeper for the information. They conducted their business dealing and the shepherd left. He hesitated in proceeding to meet with Joseph. The shepherd's indecision did not last long. He pulled on the reins and turned his stallion away from the direction where Joseph, Mary, and their infant messiah lived and headed back to his tent home.

Shepherds avoided all towns during the census taking and yearly tax collection. The Romans were aware of their nomadic lifestyle and as such did not tax them at the same rate or frequency they did the dwellers within the towns. Rome's representatives were content with taxing the shepherds when they sold their wool, cheese, hides, and the lambs. Rome did not view nomadic shepherds as sources of wealth. The Roman rulers were more concerned that the shepherds might ignite or foster an uprising against the Roman authority.

For this reason, Roman soldiers periodically inspected the nomadic shepherds while they were in the fields with their flocks. Should an uprising occur, this was the logical starting point where the Romans decided to look first. The Jews hated the Roman system of taxation because it was oppressive and disproportionate to the income of the people. The original tax was severe enough, but the graft of the tax collectors who added more money for their own pockets made the taxation extremely burdensome.

Adding insult to the overzealous tax system was how certain Jews would align with the Romans to become their tax collectors. The Romans recruited such Jews because the local synagogues were the locations where tax monies were secured. Only Jews were allowed in the synagogue and the Romans honored this rule in an attempt to avoid igniting an uprising among the conquered Jewish people. The Jews who became tax collectors for the Romans were viewed as traitors and were ostracized from the Jewish society. This put tax collectors in the same category as nomadic shepherds—at the lowest level.

Terach avoided all towns during this period of time and especially at the beginning of the Jewish New Year, which occurred in March. It was during the Jewish New Year celebration that the Jewish religious leaders imposed their tax on all of the Jews. The customary tax levied was one half shekel per male per household. Males ranging from age twenty to sixty were assessed the yearly charge.

The tax money had a dual purpose. First it was as a census count that replaced the counting of each individual. Each half shekel represented one adult male. The second purpose was to send the funds to Jerusalem to provide for the public sacrifices and the upkeep of the Temple. All the nomadic shepherds refused to pay this tax because of the low status accorded them within Jewish society.

Once when confronted by the rabbi assigned to secure the tax, Terach and several of the nomadic shepherds said, "You despise us, refuse to allow us into the synagogue, and hold us back from participating in the holy feasts at the Temple, yet you want us to pay a tax to you. We never will pay any tax to you until such time we are elevated back to how God viewed shepherds during the time of Abraham, Jethro, and Moses!"

When word of this refusal reached the ears of the high priest and the Sanhedrin, it was quietly decided not to pursue the matter of taxing the shepherds. Naturally, their resistance further sealed the Sanhedrin's decision to keep the nomadic shepherds out of mainstream society.

Once the Roman census and tax collection was finished, Terach returned to Bethlehem. His main goal was to talk with Joseph and finalize one last piece of business with the local shopkeeper. For this trip, little Mattan pleaded with his father to take him along. Mattan wanted to see the baby Jesus once again. Terach cheerfully agreed. He always enjoyed the extra time with his youngest son.

This time, Joseph was busy working on fabricating some yokes for the shopkeeper. The carpenter was able to work from his home, as most craftsmen did. This made it quite convenient for Terach to converse with Joseph. It also easily allowed Mattan to be with Mary and the infant Jesus. It was all Terach could do to control Mattan who wiggled in his eagerness to leave the stallion and see Mary and her newborn son. When his father finally placed him on the ground, Mattan ran as fast as his little feet would carry him into the house to be with Jesus.

Terach purposefully approached Joseph who put down his tools and invited his guest to sit beside him. The carpenter had worked up a sweat through toiling with the yoke fabrication. He wiped his brow and heaved a sigh of relief, glad to take a break from his work. "Terach, your arrival allows me to momentarily stop my efforts." Joseph joked as he added, "Should I continue my efforts I would dry up from thirst." The congenial host invited his guest, "Terach, would you accompany me to get some water?"

The shepherd said yes and the two stalwart men sat down on a bench.

"Tell me, Terach, what brings you to Bethlehem?"

The shepherd casually replied, "I have some business to finalize with the shopkeeper before I take my flock west to the seacoast where the grass is rich for the sheep and the goats. This begins our winter pasturing as we slowly move northeast to the upper Jordan Valley to Jericho."

Joseph showed interest and inquired, "How long will you be at the seacoast pastures?"

Wiping some errant water from the side of his mouth, Terach answered, "Until the cold winds from the northeast begin to cease. That will be our signal to begin moving the flock northward. In January the pregnant ewes will lamb. After that, we will proceed to Jericho to arrive in time for the spring shearing and the sale of the best lambs to the Nigrid there. The lambs will be sold as Passover sacrifices. It is an important business period for myself and the other nomadic shepherds."

Terach then smoothly changed the subject. "Joseph, due to my migration with the flock, I am curious to know if you now propose to inform the Jewish religious leaders about Jesus being the promised messiah? This intrigues me very much."

Joseph looked intently at Terach. He thought how good it was to know someone who understood the precarious position he and his family were in. He replied, "Very soon after the Romans completed the census and the tax collecting, I was present in the synagogue with the rabbi and the elders. They were complaining about the abusive tax levied by Rome plus the additional tax King Herod placed on the people to restore his treasury from the expense of his many building projects."

Joseph stopped to take a long gulp of water before he continued. "Of main interest to me were the comments of great hope for the promised messiah to arrive soon and free the Jews from Roman suppression. All of Judea wants a warrior messiah to destroy the Romans! There is much discontent throughout Judea, including Samaria, over this issue."

Terach confirmed it, informing Joseph, "Yes, word from Jerusalem is that the promised messiah will come from the elites of the religious leaders. He will be of noble birth and raise a powerful army before he reaches the age of twenty." Terach wondered what Joseph would say to this.

Joseph verified Terach's statement, "The same talk reached north to Nazareth and often the people would act in a frenzy about this desire. Alas, the rabbis and the Sanhedrin have done nothing to dispel such rumors."

Terach did not have to quiz his host about the warrior messiah, because Joseph quickly echoed his thoughts. "Obviously, Jesus is God's promised messiah, but he is not of noble birth." Joseph swept his arm in the air, to indicate his simple dwelling and workshop. "I certainly am not of nobility and more importantly, I am not the father of Jesus. Besides, the religious leaders would never accept that their desired messiah would come from Nazareth. To announce Jesus as the promised one to the religious leaders, as well as the Jewish people would result in Mary and I being ridiculed, possibly even being removed from Jewish society for false prophecy." Joseph lowered his head and emphasized, "It is probable they would even stone all of us to death."

Silence filled the air and the only sound was from some chatting birds outside Joseph's abode. The two men looked at each other in silent understanding. Finally Terach admitted, "Unfortunately, you are correct, Joseph. The Jewish leaders, as well as the people, are locked in on their perception of the promised one." Disgust entered into his voice, "And anything outside their perception is dismissed."

Joseph spoke quietly but confidently, "I know you won't speak about this to any of the Jewish leaders. But I certainly won't ask that you not talk about this with the other shepherds. I am certain that in God's timing, He will loosen both Mary's and my lips about Jesus. Until such time, we must remain silent."

Terach felt genuine concern and wanted to know, "I assume you, Mary, and Jesus will remain here in Bethlehem, or do you intend on returning to Nazareth?"

Joseph wiped his brow with his forearm as he disclosed, "Sepphoris was the business hub of the region. Since King Herod destroyed it, carpentry as well as other jobs are very limited. I can adequately support my family with the work that is available here in Bethlehem. It is my intent to remain here and become more active in the community."

Terach smiled at this news. "I'm glad you intend to remain here, Joseph. Every season I return here with my flock, I shall look forward to renewing our friendship." The shepherd looked towards the house and chuckled, "Besides, my youngest son Mattan wants all the time he can get with the little one, Jesus. He regards him as his younger brother and enjoys being around him very much."

Joseph was already chuckling before Terach finished speaking. "Mattan certainly does enjoy his time with Jesus, and Mary is quite delighted to have your son visit and assist her in caring for her son."

Terach slapped his knee with his hand and concluded, "I must finish my business here and return to my flock. Do you mind if Mattan remains here while I go about my business?"

Joseph waved his thick hand indicating there was no problem. With good humor, he said, "Mary will make sure Mattan and Jesus do not wander off. He will be here when you decide to return to your home."

Terach did not take long dealing with the shopkeeper. When he returned to Joseph's house, he found Mattan sitting in the shade holding the infant Jesus and talking to him. The baby's eyes were focused on Mattan's. Mattan's sweet voice and gently bobbing head made the infant coo and form a slight smile. Terach was surprised how much Mattan was devoted to this infant.

He was not at all happy to relinquish Jesus back to Mary. The youngster wanted to stay awhile longer with his new friend. He resisted to the point that Terach finally had to become stern and plop him decisively on the saddle for their return home. As Terach headed back home, Mattan strained to peer around his father for one last look at Jesus and Mary who stood watching their guests' departure.

Within days after the last visit to Bethlehem, Terach began leading his flock further west to the rich grassland near the seacoast. The size of the flocks and herds made for slow going, but at least the weather did not add problems with cold or rain. During their westward journey, Mattan often asked how soon they would return that he could be with his new friend.

That winter was cold and rainy, causing Terach and the other few nomadic shepherds to be extra vigilant in caring for their flocks. It was a season that the shepherds longed for the ending of, so that they could begin the journey north to their destination of Jericho. Terach enjoyed knowing their paths often paralleled the routes of the three great patriarchs of the Jewish people, Abraham, Isaac, and Jacob.

By the end of January the nomadic shepherds' trek came to a halt when they reached the area that was a comprised of the Jordan Valley and the Rift Valley's numerous hills with caves. To the east lay Jericho, a hub of commerce between the port city of Caesarea and Jerusalem which lay to the south.

The nomadic shepherds were relieved to reach this fertile grassland. The hills provided thankful relief from the harsh winds that funneled through the Jordan Valley. Shortly after arriving at his traditional pastures, Terach was visited by his friend and fellow nomadic shepherd, Jesus Barabbas. "I'm glad you survived the harsh journey north, my friend," said Barabbas from atop his horse. Terach motioned for his weary looking visitor to dismount. The shepherd stretched and grunted in an attempt to relieve his stiffness from long hours in the saddle.

When Jesus Barabbas completed his effortful task, Terach stated, "I also praise God for your safe journey here as well, Barabbas. Come and join me for some hot liquid. I hope you have brought me some interesting news."

The two friends went inside the warm tent and Barabbas extended his greetings to Beulah and teased the four young boys who always looked forward to a visit from Barabbas. Mattan sprang forward, grabbing Barabbas by the leg, twisting him in an attempt to get the man down to the ground. Barabbas always complied in the familiar game.

Once Barabbas finished his usual teasing of the boys, he sat down next to Terach. He wrapped his big hands around the hot mug and lowered his head to smell the aroma of the spice tea. "Beulah, should this dog I call my friend ever decide to divorce you, I shall immediately take you as my wife after I separate his head from his body for being so stupid. You make the best tea that I've ever tasted."

Beulah tilted back her head in musical laughter and joked, "Alas, Barabbas, I would be too much woman for you; and besides, you would have great difficulty providing for me and my sons in addition to your other wife and children." Terach joined their laughter. He especially enjoyed how easily his wife handled bantering with his close friend.

Barabbas laughed loudly, until a serious expression took hold of his face. "Since I arrived here ahead of you, Terach, I've had opportunity to go to Jericho and learn of the latest news. It appears that King Herod is in fear of not having sufficient money to continue his extravagant lifestyle. As such, he is planning on adding greater taxes to all the people of Judea. This means when we take our wool, hides, cheese, and lambs to market at Jericho this spring, we will be forced to pay a greater tax. This is very upsetting to me, the other shepherds, and the many merchants who travel to Jericho to do business."

The aroma of the spice tea enticed Barabbas to pause and take a sip. It warmed his body as it slid down to his stomach. Barabbas watched Terach as he drank. He was eager for his friend's reaction to the taxation news.

Terach sat with a thoughtful expression on his face. The shepherd leader seemed to be in no hurry to answer. He took a slow sip of his own spice tea, relishing its warmth, before revealing his thoughts to Barabbas. "My friend, have you forgotten that we have a special arrangement with the Nigrid of Jericho? In exchange for lower taxation, we supply the Nigrid with extra lambs that he sells for the Passover Feast."

Barabbas' troubled look did not change. He replied, "I have not forgotten, my friend. Nor have I lost my memory that you are the one responsible for this special arrangement."

Barabbas placed his mug down and drummed his fingers on the table as he continued in a stern voice, "I do not trust the Nigrid. He is one of those Jews who have sold out to the Romans, becoming their idiot puppet. He does the bidding of King Herod as well as the Roman emperor, and obviously at the expense of us, his own people."

The nomad felt growing anger at the thought of how the Jewish Nigrid had become a traitor to his own people. He took a deep breath and slowly exhaled, all the while remaining locked on Terach's eyes. When he had sufficiently controlled himself, he admitted, "You are better equipped to deal with this traitor than I am, praise God. It would be difficult for me not to cut him with my knife to satisfy my anger towards him. When you are settled in your pastures, maybe you can talk with this traitor about the new tax."

Terach gently touched his friend's shoulder and gave him solace, "Barabbas, certainly I will do this. I'm glad you informed me of this development before I ventured to Jericho. It will be a few days before I'm available to meet with the Nigrid. Would you like to accompany me to Jericho for the meeting?"

Barabbas smiled broadly at the invitation extended to him by his friend. He slightly lowered his head and cocked one eyebrow as he replied, "I was hoping you would ask me to accompany you." The burly shepherd laughed loudly and clapped his hands together. He leaned toward his friend with one eye slightly closed and continued, "Rest assured, my friend, I shall also contain my anger and not cut the throat of this despicable traitor we have to deal with."

The two shepherds spent the remainder of their time together catching up on the travails they each encountered on their journeys to the northern pasturelands. As the sun slipped lower on the horizon, Barabbas ended his visit with his best friend and mounted his horse for the ride northeast to his home and family.

The next day, Terach rode into Jericho and immediately sought out the Nigrid of Judea. The two men had established a mutual respect aside from the fact they both were considered outcasts of Jewish society. The Nigrid respected Terach for his business sense, his strong character, and his strength in standing up against the Jewish leaders. Terach respected the Nigrid for his honesty in their business dealings as well as his being helpful when issues arose for which Terach needed extra assistance in resolving.

One of the Nigrid's house servants directed Terach to the main living part of the mansion that at one time had been utilized by King Herod. Since the king was often building himself new mansions, this particular one was given to the Nigrid so long as he remained favorable to the king. Terach remained standing in the opulent room until the Nigrid made his appearance. The men greeted each other warmly and sat down to conduct their business.

Both men liked to address whatever issue that brought them together without fanfare or undue delay. Terach opened their discussion by relaying what Barabbas had told him the day before. The Nigrid confirmed Terach's story. "Your friend Barabbas is correct in what he has told you, my friend. King Herod is in need of more money and with the consent of Rome; he will inflict additional taxes on all of Judea."

The Nigrid saw Terach's anxious frown. He quickly spoke to ease his friend's concern. "Do not fear, my friend. You and the other shepherds I have the special agreement with will not incur additional taxes." Waving his hand as if powered by the sea, he added, "The king has given me certain latitudes in this matter. Besides, the number of the trade caravans frequenting Judea has grown that taxes imposed on them will diffuse any perceived shortage of tax from you shepherds." The Nigrid chuckled at the thought of his deviousness.

Terach relaxed at these words of assurance and thanked his friend for his generosity. "My friend, I shall relay your words to Barabbas and the rest of the shepherds. They will be greatly relieved."

Then the Nigrid leaned toward Terach and spoke confidentially, "I want to be the first to inform you to prepare for changes. Herod's health continues to deteriorate and there are times he does not operate lucidly. He makes irrational decisions that his assistants totally disregard. It is a time of uncertainty for all."

Terach was listening intently to what his business friend was telling him. The Nigrid continued, "Rome is paying close attention to Hero. And monitors his actions that they do not result in an uprising in Judea. It is no secret how the Jews despise the Romans, but they are prepared to handle this. What is of major concern to Rome is that Herod will undermine his relationship with the Jewish leaders and that it results in rebellion. The Jewish leaders remain thankful to Herod for his building and improving the Temple. But this will cease should overtaxation change their minds and lead to rebellion."

The leader of the nomadic shepherds sat comfortably in the luxurious couch. He studied the Nigrid and he determined the body language of the overseer of all Judea was tense as he carefully posed his question. "What do you believe Rome would do should Herod cause an uprising by the Jews?"

The Nigrid closed his eyes, tightened his lips, and briefly tilted his head back. He pursed his lips, and answered, "The emperor will act quickly. Herod will be removed. Rome will take direct control over all of Judea, including Samaria." The Nigrid momentarily paused, shrugging his shoulders. "I suspect they will appoint a governor to replace Herod. Beyond that, I do not know the extent of Rome's plans."

The two men knew this topic was at an end and changed course to discuss their specific business dealings. They agreed the Nigrid would buy all the wool, hides, cheese, and the newborn lambs as well as those born during the regular lambing season. The agreed-upon price was very fair to Terach, so he also negotiated the same agreement for the other nomadic shepherds.

Once business affairs were taken care of, the Nigrid had an exemplary savory meal brought in for them. As the two dined, Terach felt the timing was right to discuss one final item with his business friend. It was the same unrelenting topic in his mind. "My friend, have you heard word coming out of Bethlehem about the supposed birth of the promised messiah the Jews have been hoping for since the ancient of times?"

The Nigrid put down a piece of bread he had dipped in the garum sauce and looked steadily at his guest. "Oh yes, I have heard. And also that the shepherd who initiated such rumor was beaten for his pretention of prophecy." The Nigrid let out a short laugh and added, "Terach, you should realize after all these years of our dealings together there is very little I do not know about what happens in Judea." Then the governor of Judea turned serious and emphasized, "It is my business to know what takes place not only for my benefit, but also to apprise Herod in such a manner it does not harm me."

Terach smiled weakly and let his host continue. "Terach, you and the other shepherds winter your flocks in that area and probably have the same information I have gleaned." The Nigrid waved his hand in a dismissive manner and resumed, "My informants stated a couple from Nazareth are the parents of this so-called messiah but to date there is no indication this infant is the promised one." It was the Nigrid's turn to query his guest. "Terach, does my rendition of this event coincide with yours?"

Terach quickly answered in the affirmative and asked, "Do you intend on continuing monitoring these parents?"

The Nigrid very quickly stated, "Of course. It is my duty to inform Herod of anything that has potential to impact his reign. Personally, I am interested if this infant is indeed the one the prophets of old spoke about. It goes without saying that should this Jesus raise up a mighty army against the Romans, I want to position myself in a favorable position to him should he overthrow Rome's dominance here in Judea. I have grave doubts he will be able to accomplish such a task, but in any event I will be prepared to switch my allegiance."

Terach chuckled noticeably. "Excuse me, but I do not mean that as any disrespect. I would not expect you to do otherwise. In fact, should I be in your position, I would do the same thing." The Nigrid laughed heartily and held his hands to his stomach in amusement. Both men raised their wine mugs in a toast to each other and finished their meal. Terach thanked his business friend for the business deals, and the shared information, as well as the exquisite meal.

The shepherd leader left the mansion and looked to the sky as he was so accustomed to do. The clouds indicated a storm was moving in. Terach could not help but think that another ominous human storm was approaching, as well. This man-made storm could be more devastating than what nature normally hurled. He turned his horse's head in the direction of his camp and the horse set its own pace in returning to familiar territory. Along the way, Terach's thoughts were wondering what the Nigrid did *not* tell him about what he knew of the Nazarene family or what was on the minds of those in power.

Terach startled his stallion as he laughed aloud over his thoughts. The shepherd leader thought it very ironic that the common Jew knew nothing of the supposed arrival of the promised messiah; yet those in leadership capacity and the secular government were all paying close attention to this development, and formulating plans how to stop this newly announced savior.

As for himself, the shepherd was hoping this Jesus was indeed God's promised savior to the Jews. But doubts remained in his heart about what the eventual outcome would be and if he would even be alive to witness God's plan in action.

Chapter 6

The following months were uneventful for Terach and his fellow nomadic shepherds. Their business with the Nigrid was lucrative, and after the Passover Feast the shepherds began their springtime return journey to the southern part of the Jordan Valley. The routine of the nomadic shepherd's life resumed as it had for many past generations. Terach always insisted that the other nomad shepherds who had much smaller flocks lead the way. The majority of the smaller flocks proceeded down the west side of the Jordan River. Terach's vast flock stayed to the east of the Jordan River, thereby allowing all the shepherds ample fresh grass for their animals.

From the southern tip of the Sea of Galilee down to the northern edge of the Dead Sea, both sides of the Jordan River were fertile and lush with tall nourishing grasses. The entire coastal plain that comprised the Jordan Valley was 150 miles long with a width of 25 miles at one point towards the southern boundary. This fertile abundance accommodated not only the needs of the nomadic shepherds but also the farmers who lived in the region who were able to grow a variety of crops. In the minds of both the nomad shepherds and the farmers was ever-thankfulness to God for His blessing of such rich land.

The plush soil of the Jordan Valley was also a magnet for trade caravans. One originated north of Antioch, Syria, and went through Damascus southeast of Jerusalem and parallel to the Dead Sea. This was called the King's Highway. The other main trade route stemmed from Antioch along the Great Sea (the Mediterranean) and included the cities of Sidon, Tyre, Caesarea, Ashkelon and Gaza. This route was referred to as the Via Maris.

There was a connecting route the Jews called "The Sacred Bridge" that joined the two routes using Jerusalem as the mid-point. The sacred aspects were due to the geographical location of the city of Shechem. It held economic, cultural, and deep religious significance to the Jews.

The Romans noted military strategic aspects of the two main trade routes and the Sacred Bridge as well as the Jordan Valley. They sent engineers to improve these land arteries, thereby making travel easier and quicker. Because Rome was constantly in need of food, the military assigned a two-pronged involvement to Judea. Part of this assignment was to foster development of abundant crops. Included in this first part was the lessening, to a certain degree, of taxes imposed on the farmers. The part relished most by the military was to protect this valley at all costs. The main source for invaders was via the Great Sea and the plethora of harbor cities along the coastline. Roman encounters with various invaders were frequent and with the same result; the Romans always won and mostly with very limited loss of life.

Consequently, the Roman soldiers maintained an equitable relationship with the nomadic shepherds who roamed the entire Jordan Valley. It was not unusual for the nomadic shepherds to encounter at least two cohorts of Roman soldiers during their trek either north or south. Terach convinced the smaller nomad shepherds to gift the soldiers with cheese, goat milk, and either a female goat or sheep. It was not for charitable reasons. The shepherds received favor and were given added protection by the soldiers.

In mid-summer of the year following the birth of Jesus, Terach came into contact with one of the Roman cavalry units. He knew the centurion in charge and therefore was not alarmed by their presence. The centurion took Terach aside and asked, "Terach, I know you spend part of your winter nearby Bethlehem. Do you have information about this rumor of a new Jewish leader being born in Bethlehem last fall?"

The question caught him off guard, but he did not flinch. Casually, he answered, "Yes, I know of this birth. I was present shortly after the infant came into this world. His parents are from Nazareth and were in Bethlehem to properly register for the census ordered by Rome."

The centurion leaned forward and rested his elbow on the saddle horn for his second question. "Do you believe this infant to be this promised leader the Jews often talk about? The one who supposedly will raise up a mighty army against Rome."

Terach maintained a matter-of-fact demeanor as he answered the centurion. Waving his hand in a dismissive gesture he said, "At this point in time, I do not believe Rome has anything to fear from the birth of this infant. He does not satisfy the criteria established by the Jewish religious leaders."

However, the centurion persisted in his questioning, "I have knowledge of the expectations of your Jewish principals. Let me ask you, Terach, do you believe these Jewish bosses will announce this leader's arrival?"

This time, Terach shrugged his shoulders nonchalantly and shook his head. "I do not believe the high priest, the Sanhedrin, or the scribes really think the messiah indeed has arrived in Judea."

The centurion seemed satisfied with Terach's answers and rose up to an erect posture. He changed the subject to less important matters. The two men talked at length, and then Terach made good on his gift-giving and presented the centurion with ample amounts of fresh cheese, milk, and one female goat. The centurion made one last statement before leaving the area, "Terach, I know how the Jews despise nomad shepherds, but that you are highly regarded by many people, both Jews and others. For this reason I trust what you say. You know, of course, it is my duty to keep abreast of anything that Rome considers potentially harmful. Thank you for your input." The Roman military unit left to patrol their assigned portion of the Jordan Valley.

Later, Terach discussed with Beulah the meeting with the centurion and his line of questioning. "My husband, this development is such that when we arrive back at Bethlehem, we must find out directly from Joseph and Mary if they have been contacted either by the Romans or any of the Jewish authorities." Beulah feared they had. She paused before finishing her thought, "Assuming that both Joseph and Mary will be forthright with us."

It was early fall when Terach and the other shepherds arrived at their winter pasturelands. There was much to do with getting the flocks settled in the new environment. Both Terach and Beulah were anxious to finish their respective tasks so that they could hurry on to Bethlehem. Once the resettlement was completed, Terach, Beulah, and their children, including enthusiastic little Mattan, made a visit to Joseph, Mary and the nearly one-year-old Jesus.

Immediately Mattan separated himself from his family and bolted to the home of the baby. His quest was to find Jesus and resume their friendship. Mary met Mattan at the door and greeted him with a hug. Beulah was close behind her rambunctious youngest son and was pleased at how well Mary looked. The three older boys entertained themselves with childhood games and Beulah went inside to chat with her younger friend.

Once inside the home, Beulah saw how much the infant Jesus had grown. "Mary, you are doing well in the care of your firstborn son! He appears strong, healthy, and certainly is growing."

The young mother smiled broadly and accepted her older friend's compliments with a blush. "The midwife assisted me the first six months after Jesus was born, making sure I knew how to feed, clothe, and generally care for Jesus. She indicated Jesus was quite healthy and that should I encounter anything I wasn't sure of handling to summon her."

Beulah bobbed her head in understanding. "Jewish midwives are very good at what they do and I believe know more than the doctors who seem befuddled at the care of an infant. I personally know the midwife who assisted you. Her character and reputation are very good."

At that point both women were startled by a shriek and turned their heads toward the sound. They saw Mattan on his hands and knees with the little Jesus on Mattan's back. They were playing and the shriek came from an excited Jesus full of joy. The women giggled and turned back towards each other, satisfied that all was well.

The two friends chatted for a while about motherhood, and Beulah gave Mary some suggestions regarding her developing child. "Beulah, I'm ever so grateful for your kindness towards me. You are really the only confidante I have since Joseph and I arrived here in Bethlehem."

Mary was comforted by Beulah's smiling response. The young mother did not want to embarrass Beulah, but she wanted to share her feelings with her newfound friend. "I do talk with several of the women I've met at the synagogue, but I purposefully refrain from sharing much with them."

Beulah's heart began to race. This was the perfect opening for her to find out if Mary or Joseph had been open with members of the synagogue about Jesus being the promised messiah. "In essence then, Mary, you have not shared with any of these women about Jesus being the promised one the prophets have foretold?"

The young mother of Jesus shook her head no, and briefly looked down at her hands that were cupped together in her lap. She said, "It is quite clear that no one will truly accept that Jesus is the promised one to the Jews. They are adamant that the messiah will be of royal birth by a member of the Pharisee class and be from Jerusalem. I fear that should I, or Joseph, speak about Jesus being the promised one, we would be ridiculed and severely punished." Mary cleared her throat and finished, "But really, Almighty God has not yet released us to make such announcements."

Beulah nodded her head slowly as she listened. Mary's statement served to confirm that nothing had changed in the year they were away from Bethlehem concerning the heralding of Jesus as the promised messiah. "I understand, Mary, and I believe you are wise not to say anything about this to anyone, especially the rabbi or his wife or any of the elders."

With grave concern, the shepherd's wife asked, "Have you been visited by any Roman authorities with inquiries about Jesus being the leader who will free the Jews from Roman domination?"

Mary was startled by the question, and her eyebrows rose in surprise. "There have been no soldiers or government authorities here to question either Joseph or myself about this matter." Mary's expression became worried and she leaned toward her older friend. In a serious tone she asked, "Should I be concerned about this possibility?"

Beulah gently grabbed Mary's hand and softly said, "There is no reason to be alarmed, Mary. It was merely a question of curiosity on my part."

Their conversation was interrupted by sounds coming from outside the house. The two women went to determine the source of the ruckus and witnessed the boys were in a heated disagreement about something associated with one of their games. Beulah quickly separated the warring youths and forced each one to sit in different spots along the outside of the house. Beulah turned her attention to Mary and apologized, "I'm sorry for the behavior of my older sons. It is time that I return them to our home and have them do their jobs before they get in anymore trouble. We will talk again soon, my friend." The disgruntled mother gathered up a sullen Mattan and she and the other boys boarded the horse-drawn cart and headed west toward their tent-home in the pasturelands.

Soon after her arrival back at her home, Terach came riding in on his stallion. Beulah was glad he did not need to stay longer in Bethlehem because she was anxious to share with him what she had learned from Mary. While the boys went about their daily chores, the two adults sat with warming tea and exchanged what information each had gathered while in Bethlehem.

"My dear wife, what Mary told you is the same as what Joseph shared with me. It is clear this couple does not trust anyone, Roman or Jew. This is odd, considering at some point they will have to announce Jesus being the promised one to form alliances to build his army."

Terach abruptly changed the subject. "I have made arrangements with the shopkeeper here to use his home as the site for the reading of the Torah during the upcoming Feast of the Tabernacles. As usual, the local rabbi won't allow us to use the synagogue while he and the other able-bodied men go to Jerusalem and the temple to celebrate the holy observance."

Beulah sighed, "Nothing will change our plight. But still these religious hypocrites cannot keep us from honoring God and observing His holy feast." The two discussed how different this year's observance would be than last year's. "We won't be celebrating at the cave where Mary gave birth to Jesus. This year we will have more room and comfort at the shopkeeper's home."

During the feast that year there was no nomad shepherd making any statement the Jewish authorities construed a violation of their religious laws. Massai welcomed this the most and was in a relaxed mode throughout the entire observance. After the feast was concluded, the shepherds returned to their flocks in the southern Jordan Valley and waited out the early winter. The trade route caravans made fewer stops at Bethlehem because the crops that were harvested had already been sold to the traders.

In December Terach's herd slowly moved north parallel to the Via Maris trade route. The other nomad shepherds also ventured north, but well ahead of Terach's sheep and goats.

Towards the end of December both groups' respective herds began the twice annual birthing of sheep and goats. Terach and his hirelings separated the pregnant ewes from the rest of the flock. They created a sheepfold out of brush, branches, and rocks that prevented the ewes from escaping. Over the next few weeks, many hours were spent observing the ewes. When a pregnant sheep exhibited signs of labor, either Terach or a hireling was on hand to make sure there were no problems associated with the birth of the lamb. It was a long tiring time for man and also the dogs that served as sentries around the sheepfold. It was also a time of training for Terach's sons. Even Mattan got involved, much to his delight. He felt manly, being able to participate in this process.

When the last ewe gave birth, it was a time of relief as well as celebration. It was common for a ewe to give birth to twins. In fact Terach's methods of breeding and caring for his flock resulted in the highest twin birth rates among the shepherds and even the farmers who had small flocks.

Fifteen miles separated Terach from his friend Jesus Barabbas, and when he had finished with the lambing and getting sufficient rest from his efforts, Terach rode northeast to meet with Barabbas and learn how his lambing season went.

As usual, the burly Barabbas greeted his friend with a boisterous laugh, a kiss on each cheek, and a hearty slap on the shoulders. "It is good to see that you are surviving the winter thus far, my friend. How was your lambing this season?"

Terach smiled broadly at his friend and returned the hearty shoulder slap. "God has blessed us with an abundance of lambs. We will have sufficient number to expand the flock and many more to sell for the forthcoming Passover celebration. We did not have a single deformed lamb or lose a single ewe to the birthing."

Terach searched his friend's face to get an advance on how Barabbas' lambing went. "I, too, was blessed by Almighty God. We did not have that many twin births as you do, but every lamb is strong, healthy, and can be presented as suitable for the Passover. My ewes are recovering nicely from the birthing and we should not encounter any problems as we proceed to Jericho and the auction to the Nigrid."

Barabbas had his friend stay for the traditional midday meal and they talked about the lushness of the winter grasslands and about the increased number of spring and summer trade caravans along both major trade routes. Terach was vigilant to learn if Barabbas had obtained any information about the young family in Bethlehem. But his extroverted friend did not reveal any knowledge about the baby Jesus being the promised messiah.

Barabbas did share a rumor that caused Terach to take notice. "A member of one of the trade caravans from Damascus informed me that King Herod's health continues to worsen. There are times the king becomes delusional and he has several days in great pain. I believe it is God punishing him for his wicked ways."

Terach looked thoughtful at this news. "My friend, this development about Herod's health can be such that Rome will replace him as their client-King. Herod has done some good for the Jews but still he is ruthless, unpredictable, and prone to exploit the Jews unnecessarily. He claims to be a Jew and provided the funds to build the temple in Jerusalem, yet the money came from heavy taxation the Jewish leaders overlook." Barabbas nodded his head in agreement as he chewed a piece of falafel wrapped in bread with hummus.

The guest shepherd finished taking a bite of the fresh bread baked by Barabbas' wife. As Terach ate, Barabbas finished Terach's thought. "We must stay alert to other developments with Herod's health that we may plan how to deal with whoever replaces him should he die. It is important we quickly share what information we obtain that we all can remain unified."

For the remainder of the late winter months, Terach's thoughts concerning Herod's health were relegated to the back of his mind. The nomad shepherd leader's focus was on making sure the lambs he designated for the Passover celebration remained unblemished. He instructed his hirelings to maintain good feeding and nutrition habits for the ewes, to ensure that their milk and cheese would be of the highest quality for the Jericho market. Terach included all four of his sons in the process. The patriarch was pleased how quickly his boys were learning the proper care of the animals. Terach was especially impressed by Mattan's attention to detail despite being only five years old.

As winter gave way to spring, the nomadic shepherds converged on Jericho. The smaller flocks arrived usually one week ahead of Terach's. Herod's Nigrid negotiated fairly with these shepherds, but anxiously waited to see what Terach would have to offer. The Nigrid always awarded top prices to Terach, not because of their friendship, but because of the high quality of the shepherd leader's goods.

Shortly after all the shepherds arrived in Jericho, the annual shearing began. It took approximately two and a half weeks to complete. That particular spring there was a copious amount of wool. Each sheep gave nearly ten pounds of wool much to the delight of both the shepherds and the Nigrid. As usual, Terach was the last to sell his wool, cheese, milk, and hides. While some of the shepherds negotiated with other buyers, Terach sold exclusively to Herod's Nigrid.

Per their usual arrangement, the Nigrid invited Terach to his home to finalize their business and to engage in much desired conversation. When the food the Nigrid provided his top supplier arrived, the congenial host immediately launched into a topic of interest to both.

"Terach, I know that you have difficulty obtaining news of interest while you are in the grasslands. I have a development you need to hear immediately." The Nigrid quickly continued, "Herod recently received esteemed visitors from the east. These men of affluence inquired about a new king of the Jews being born in Judea and asked Herod if he could tell them where to find this new king." The Nigrid stopped to let Terach absorb this news. Terach held his breath, anxious to hear the rest.

The Nigrid excitedly went on, "Herod had these affluent men stay at his palace while he summoned the priests and scribes in search of knowledge about the new king." Again the Nigrid paused, this time to take a bite of the meal that was before him and to sip the fresh wine. Terach was intently studying the face of his host, and was mildly annoyed to have to wait to hear what else the administrator of all Judea had to say. He felt his stomach begin to churn over the implications of this event.

"I know the rest of this news will greatly interest you, my friend. The scribes and priests stated the promised messiah would be born in Bethlehem."

Terach sat back and said to his host, "This is in line with what the prophets have foretold."

Pleased with Terach's reaction, the Nigrid continued enthusiastically, "Herod relayed what the scribes and priests said to these three rich men who then set out for Bethlehem. Herod pleaded with them to return and tell him about this new so-called king that Herod could also honor his presence."

Terach took a big swallow of his wine and spoke before the Nigrid could interject his thoughts. "Of course, Nigrid, you and I know that Herod would never honor another king. His intentions are to have this new king killed so as not to lose his power." The Nigrid tilted his head and nodded solemnly. Terach added, "Tell me, my friend, how long ago did these proceedings take place? Have these three men from the east returned with the news Herod's seeks?"

A cool breeze filtered through the room, causing the men's head coverings to flutter. The Nigrid looked unconcerned as he figured the time span and distances. "It has been four weeks now. Their journey was such... they should have arrived at Bethlehem, honored this new king, and returned by now. I suspect these men have journeyed to other destinations, wherever those may be. I think it remote they will return to Herod's palace."

Terach pointed a piece of fresh bread at his host and spoke with emphasis, "I agree with you, my friend. Perhaps they did go another way. If they are wise they will see through Herod's ruse. And I anticipate Herod's fury at the news of a rival king plus displeasure with these foreign men from the east will cause him to take impulsive action before long."

The Nigrid put down his wine goblet and leaned on his elbow towards his friend. "It is already as you say, my friend. While you and the other shepherds were involved with the shearing, Herod dispatched troops to Bethlehem with instructions to kill all male boys two years or younger. This is his way of making sure the new king will not remain alive to threaten his rule."

A flash of horror coursed through Terach's body. He thought of Joseph, Mary, and the young Jesus who was the age Herod had placed a death sentence upon. He realized there was no way he could warn the family or all of Bethlehem of the impending death force about to invade their community.

The Nigrid saw Terach's reaction and asked, "Why does this news cause such concern to you, my friend? Do you have family in Bethlehem that could come under Herod's death order?"

Terach stared without blinking and almost under his breath revealed, "I know of one family in particular this would have a disastrous impact. They have a son Herod's troops will murder. In addition, there are maybe another fifteen such youths on that death list."

Silence filled the room, magnifying the sense of the spring breeze that made its way throughout the house. It did not take long for a somber mood to envelope the room. The Nigrid looked at his anguished friend. He smiled and optimistically offered, "Herod has made several rash proclamations that haven't been carried out because of their absurdity. While this one is different, I have very good sources who tell me the soldiers will not abide by this death sentence. It will have to be the Romans who do

Herod's bidding, and the garrison commander will not engage in such an activity that could cause an uprising among the Jews."

Terach took a moment to ponder the Nigrid's words and hoped he was right. He took another bite of his well-prepared meat. It now seemed flavorless and unappetizing. He slowly chewed the morsel and stared at his host. When he had swallowed, he earnestly inquired, "My friend, I know you speak the truth. If anyone would know the mindset of the Roman commander, it would be you. What do you think will happen next?"

The Nigrid shrugged his shoulders and revealed, "Herod comes closer to death with each passing day. His depression and paranoia consume him. This, coupled with his kidney problems, make his death more impending. The Romans are quite aware of Herod's health problems and have made plans who will replace him. Whoever is chosen, the result will be great change for everyone living in Judea."

Terach eagerly asked, "Do you foresee these changes being for the better or worse for Jews, Samaritans, and all the traders who frequent Judea?"

Again the Nigrid shrugged his shoulders as he weighed the possibilities. "The changes will be such the Jews and Samaritans will have to adjust or suffer the wrath of the Romans. As for the traders, little of importance will impact them. The Romans value good business and the tax money they get, so I do not see any negative impact on business matters. The big question remains how the Jews and the Samaritans handle these new demands. I do not foresee these factions uniting against the Romans. The hatred they have for each other runs too deep for this to take place."

"I believe you are wise in your words, my friend. It will be interesting and possibly shocking what takes place," said Terach. The two men finished their mea, and talk switched to matters of business and the Nigrid's involvement in the various businesses he owned throughout Judea. The Nigrid was one of a few Jewish men who dealt favorably with the Samaritans, and Terach was always interested in the mindset of fellow Jews who were at war with their own kinsmen over religious issues.

After the Passover feast concluded, the shepherds gathered their flocks for the return journey to the southern part of the Jordan Valley. Terach made sure he visited Barabbas and relayed the news and developments shared by the Nigrid. Terach was taken aback by his fellow shepherd's response. "Terach, these changes that are soon to arrive concern me greatly. I believe they may even change my life and possibly yours in ways neither of us really wants or is prepared for."

Terach thought about Barabbas' words but especially his melancholy attitude and resignation to things that had not happened yet. There was no way of knowing what would indeed happen.

When Terach returned to his tent he shared his thoughts about Barabbas with Beulah. Her only reply was, "Whatever happens, Terach, we must never lose sight that God is with us. He really is in control and we are His children."

Throughout the spring and summer journey back to Bethlehem and the southern part of the Jordan Valley, the shepherds encountered more trade caravans than the previous year. The ample fruit and crops grown by the farmers in all the towns located within the lush valley's borders was increasing because of the bumper crop. Terach and the other shepherds increased their treasuries selling mainly cheese and a few ewes to these traders.

Once again Terach encountered the same centurion as in the previous year. This time the centurion brought news to the nomad shepherd that delighted him. "My sources tell me that Rome put a stop to Herold's soldiers in carrying out his directive to kill all the youths two years old and younger in Bethlehem. The majority of Herold's assassins have fled the land and now are part of the Roman army." Terach could not contain his emotions and raised both hands high, giving thanks to God. The centurion watched this display and smiled tolerantly at the reaction of the nomad. After the presentation had been completed, Terach eagerly told Beulah of this important news. She too was ecstatic and they hugged each other tightly.

The tiring and demanding trek came to a close in the early fall of the year. The nomad shepherds once again settled in their winter pastures and prepared for the first wave of rainy weather so typical of the seasonal change. Once his flock was settled and the hirelings properly instructed in their duties, Terach and his family ventured into Bethlehem for their usual fall business. They were anxious to also resume their relationship with Joseph, Mary, and little Mattan's favorite playmate—the now two- year-old Jesus.

Terach and his family's first stop was at the house where their friends from Nazareth lived. To their dismay and shock, the house was empty, and signs indicated it had been for some time. Concerned, Terach sought out the shopkeeper for knowledge of what had happened to the Nazarenes. "It was very unusual," said the shopkeeper. "Three very rich men from the east and their sizable caravan arrived here and sought the carpenter and his family. Their interest in this family was of great surprise to all here in Bethlehem."

The shopkeeper scratched the top of his head and continued, "I found it very odd how these rich men presented gifts to the son of the carpenter and bowed in honor of him. After two days these men and the entire caravan left." The shopkeeper pointed in the direction they chose, explaining, "They went southwest toward Herodium. But this has been quite some time ago, Terach."

The agitated shepherd pressed the shopkeeper, "Have there been any Roman soldiers come this way after the men from the east left?"

The befuddled shopkeeper shook his head, "None at all. Only you nomads have come."

Terach pushed for more information. "Did the Nazarene family say anything to anyone before they left? Maybe telling you or the rabbi where they were going and why?"

Again the shopkeeper shook his head decisively. Terach realized it was no good to question the shopkeeper or anyone else in Bethlehem concerning the mysterious vanishing of the Nazarene family. He thanked the shopkeeper for the information and promised he would return later to discuss business with him.

That evening when Terach and Beulah were alone, they discussed the strange departure of their new friends. "I can't help but believe their disappearance is related to what the Nigrid told me back in Jericho," said Terach. "Somehow, Joseph must have learned of Herod's plans to kill all the young boys here in Bethlehem. This is very strange because the Nigrid indicated nobody knew about Herod's death order except the Nigrid and the soldiers Herod told to carry out his sentence."

The perplexed shepherd's wife voiced her worry in a somber voice, "The uncertainty I have is where did they go and if we will ever see them again?" Beulah's words hung heavily in the air and the couple became hushed. When they curled up together on their mat, each mulled over their separate thoughts about their friends' disappearance until they fell into an unsettled sleep.

Chapter 7

The monster brutality of raging winter eventually lost its battle against the relentless resistance of youthful springtime. It was worth celebrating. Spring season in Jericho began a festive period of the year.

The milder temperatures, usually in the low to mid 70's, brought with it a light-heartedness to the region's people. Flowers bloomed, and numerous palm trees sang the soft song of spring through their branches. There was renewed interest in the land, and people looked forward to the forthcoming growth of grapes for production of wine. Perfumes would be made from the array of flowers abundant to the city and the upper Jordan Valley. The land would gush out a wide assortment of herbs and spices thanks to the rich alluvial soil and quenching of mineral spring water.

Normally, the overseeing Nigrid had a bounce to his step during this time of year. He enjoyed traveling throughout the Jordan Valley inspecting his and King Herod's agricultural holdings to gain an idea of how bountiful the fall harvest would be. The Nigrid often lingered during the journey to savor each location and its diverse array of sensory delights.

However, this particular spring, the Nigrid was sullen, listless, and in emotional turmoil. He had no appetite for food or drink, his sleep was but a few hours each night, and his brow seemed permanently creased. It was all caused by King Herod.

Herod's diminishing health had resulted in ever greater depression and paranoia that he successfully passed along to his underlings. Painful kidney disease coupled with genital gangrene fueled his mental difficulties. The king was prone to rash decisions that resulted in great cruelty and it was mainly directed towards the Jews who despised him.

Most recently, when Herod had returned to his palace in Jericho from one of his four mansions, he had 42 people burned alive because young men led by two teachers of the Law, Judah ben Sarifai and Mattatias ben Margalot, had torn down the Roman eagle symbol Herod attached to the Temple gate. This was done on the rumor that Herod had died from his ailments.

This act by a small contingent of Jews caused a ripple effect through Herod's inner circle. No one felt safe or immune from the king's irrational behavior that too often caused needless death. Of particular concern not only to Herod's inner circle but to all of Judea were the secret police employed by the king to ferret out those who opposed the king's actions. The secret police would monitor and report back to Herod any indications of potential protests by the Jews.

The identity of the secret police was not known, even by the inner circle, thus creating perpetual alarm and dread in the minds of those close to Herod. Added to their angst was the development of Herod imprisoning his oldest son from his first wife Doris. It was no secret that this son, Antipater, hated his biological father and sought any means to kill him. Upon learning this, Herod enticed both Antipater and Doris to Jericho from the safety of their Roman house and immediately arrested Antipater.

Herod petitioned Emperor Augustus for permission to try and execute both his son and former wife. During the interval of waiting for Augustus' decision, Herod spent time in the healing baths of Callirrhoe. Upon his son's return, Herod gave orders to imprison the most distinguished members of Judea for execution at the time of Herod's death. By this means, Herod hoped to cause a great lamentation of his passing. Initially, the Nigrid was deeply concerned for his own life; but because he was an agent of Rome, the governor of the region escaped Herod's wrath. Nonetheless, it was an intensely emotional and uncertain time for the Nigrid and the other Roman agents located throughout the region.

In his prison confinement, Antipater heard the cries of those chosen for execution and took them to mean Herod had died. Gleefully, Antipater endeavored to bribe his jailer to release him so that he could ascend to the vacant throne. The jailer instead reported the bribe to Herod, who immediately ordered Antipater's death. Herod then sent word via carrier pigeon to Augustus informing him of Antipater's treason and subsequent execution. Herod's reputation was widely known. After receiving the message, Augustus said to his secretary, "It were better to be such a man's swine rather than his son."

After the execution and imprisonment of the distinguished men of Judea, the Nigrid met secretly with the only member of Herod's inner circle he felt could be trusted, Nicolas the king's finance minister. "Nicolas, my heart is sick over these events and I'm distressed at what Herod might do next. He could vent his delirium on any one of us."

Physically, Nicolas could be described in words that also fit the Nigrid. Both men had short stature, slim builds, and dark hair. Differentiating the two was the finance minister's response to Herod's paranoia. He developed a twitching of one eye and the nervous habit of biting his fingernails.

The older man understood the Nigrid's reaction. Looking furtively around, he whispered, "I feel the same as you do, Nigrid. The rest of Herod's household and those close to him hope he will die soon, for us all to be rid of this monster." The two men exchanged what knowledge each had secured about Herod's potential actions. Most of it was deemed rumor, but nonetheless cause for further worry and anxiety. "Nigrid, I do not know how much longer any of us can sustain this existence. Each day Herod grows worse and the depression and paranoia increase. Nobody wants to be in his presence. We all hope Rome takes action soon to resolve this terrible problem."

Five days after their melancholy conversation, Herod died. The intense pain from his ailments had caused the king to thrash about, scream, and plead God for mercy. But no one entered Herod's chambers to minister to him. Their callous attitude was, "He pleads to God, let God handle him."

In line with the custom of the time, Herod's body was encased in funeral cloth, and the same day transported with great pomp by his personal bodyguards, totaling 2,000 fierce mercenary soldiers, from Jericho south to Herodium. There his body was enshrined in a mausoleum prepared years before Herod first took ill.

The day of Herod's death was marked on the Jewish calendar as a festival. The secret police disbanded, and their identity was never known. But much speculation was this force was made up of Jews who sought favor of Herod.

Herod's inner circle traveled with the body to Herodium, and once the mausoleum door was sealed shut, a collective sigh of relief was heard. When the entourage returned to Jericho, the usual custom was for a seven-day period of mourning. This meant a time of reverence with no celebrations.

Contrary to this common Jewish custom, the Nigrid invited Nicolas to his mansion for a celebration dinner. No other members of the inner circle attended—although, unbeknownst to the two administrators, Herod's own son Archelaus also had a celebratory party attended by his friends and those seeking his favor.

Nicolas lifted his wine goblet towards his host. With a beaming smile he exclaimed, "At long last, Herod is dead! May our troubles now turn to better days."

The Nigrid also smiled broadly and touched the goblet of Nicolas with his own, confessing, "There is great relief in my heart this day. Now hopefully we can return to calmer, more restful days without fear of our own demise."

The two men went into the dining room of the mansion formerly used by Herod. Nicolas was greatly impressed by the bounty that lay before them. On small individual tables positioned in front of the customary reclining couch reserved for eating, were bowls of goat cheese, fresh bread, and the fish sauce garum so favored throughout Judea and the other nations of the Roman Empire. Wine was plentiful and satisfying, as were dates, olives and pomegranates.

As the meal progressed, eggs, wild onion, and garlic were served along with a lentil soup garnished with sweet smelling herbs. Finally, a roasted lamb was presented along with a small bowl of honey that each diner dipped small pieces of the meat into. The atmosphere was jovial, and the food was sumptuous and more than satisfying.

Once the final bite was consumed, Nicolas bowed to his host and said, "Nigrid, your hospitality is greatly appreciated, as is our shared relief of not having to endure Herod any longer! It has indeed been a great trial for us, especially once Herod's diseases took hold of his body and his mind. This opulent feast is just the right cure for our bodies and minds!"

The Nigrid laughed aloud for the first time in many months at his guest's declaration. "Herod was always ruthless and prone to cruelty. Yet, he was also more predictable, which made it easier to stay within his graces. I tell you, Nicolas, thoughts kept returning to my mind during Herod's last days to meet with him and run my dagger deep into his heart. Alas, this was impossible due to the constant presence of his bodyguards."

Nicolas tilted his head to one side, pondering the Nigrid's confession and searched his host's eyes. "I, too, harbored such thoughts, Nigrid. I'm sure there were others within his family and the inner circle who felt the same as we did. It will be interesting what develops now that Herod's throne is vacant."

The Nigrid raised one eyebrow and speculated, "Indeed, it will be interesting, and the successor to the throne will be announced soon. As for you and me, I sincerely hope we will retain our current positions. Your experience and knowledge of Herod's finances and mine of his business holdings make us of value to whoever the successor will be," said the Nigrid. Nicolas raised his glass toward his host.

Herod had left a will that originally stated that Antipas, brother to Archelaus, was to be Herod's heir to the throne. Just before his demise, Herod had changed his will and named Archelaus as his heir. Many within Herod's inner circle believed Archelaus somehow manipulated his father into making the change. It would be in keeping with his sly character.

Following the official reading of Herod's will, couriers were sent to Rome with news of the new heir. The Emperor of Rome was either to acknowledge and approve of the new heir, or reject the king's choice and appoint someone else. It was felt that Emperor Augustus would not reject Archelaus, mainly because Herod's son foretold the emperor that in the event of Herod's death, things would not change in governing Judea. This was to the emperor's liking because it meant stability would prevail in the region. Rome did not like rebellions and this assurance by Archelaus swayed both the emperor and the Roman Senate.

Before the arrival of the couriers to Rome, Archelaus ascended to the throne just before the Passover observance. The arrogant eighteen-year-old created an elaborate ceremony and demanded the presence of Judea's top business leaders and the Jewish religious Sanhedrin. Both Nicolas and the Nigrid were ordered to attend. The two men felt this was a positive omen for their respective continuation of duties and personal profit.

As he approached the new golden throne, Archelaus was dressed in white and adorned with expensive jewels. Nicolas later commented to the Nigrid that the smile on the new king's face more closely resembled a smirk. The ceremony proceeded as planned and Archelaus was officially recognized by all of Judea as its new king.

Within days following the ceremony, the Jewish leaders approached the new king, seeking the punishment of those responsible for the deaths of 40 young men and two teachers who earlier removed the edifice of an eagle placed at one of the Temple gates. This act was grievously offensive to the Jews and taken as a symbol of Herod's disregard for the Jews' religious customs. The 42 Jewish men had been burned alive and now the Sanhedrin wanted revenge.

In addition to the punishment of the slayers of the Jewish young men, the Sanhedrin also wanted Archelaus to replace the high priest appointed by Herod. They wanted someone of greater piety and purity. The members of the Sanhedrin who petitioned Archelaus felt confident the new king would grant their wishes.

Indeed, the teenage king acceded to the demand of a new high priest, but balked at punishing those responsible for the burning of the 42 Jewish men. "Please, I ask you to be tolerant and wait until Caesar confirms my place on the throne. After I'm confirmed, I will address your concerns in these matters, plus the lowering of taxes you so desire."

Standing in the background while the teenage monarch made his statement, Nicolas felt the new king was getting angry with the populace. The youthful dictator did not like being treated as, in his words, "a mere servant to the masses." Nicolas had a very uneasy feeling when the meeting was over as the new king went to dine with his friends.

When news of the teen king's avoidance to honor earlier assurances filtered down to the people, there was great consternation among the Jews. Many took their wailing and mourning for the 42 dead Jews to the Temple. Their loud pronouncements made their way to Archelaus who immediately became concerned about the escalating threatening behavior. The new monarch was deeply concerned how Rome might react to this news.

Members of Herod's army were sent to the Temple to qualm the crowd, but were stoned to death by the angry Jews. At just after midnight, the new teen king ordered the entire army to the Temple. The result was 3,000 Jews were killed, another 800 maimed, and the angry new king ordered the Passover observance cancelled.

Thus began the teenage monarch's reign. The Sanhedrin immediately dispatched a sizable party to Rome to protest the confirmation of the new despot. To their dismay, Augustus ruled that Archelaus was worthy to succeed his father. Further, Rome declared the new monarch could appoint to the position of high priest anyone he desired. The hearts of the Sanhedrin's representatives sank. They had hoped the government would turn over traditional religious matters back to the Jews.

Judea's new youthful tsar took his confirmation from Rome as a sign of carte blanche and set out to put his opponents in their place. Taxes were not lowered, but actually raised. It was the duty of both Nicolas and the Nigrid to make sure the new impositions were carried out. Their transition was not a joyous occasion for either administrator.

Over breakfast one morning, the Nigrid grumbled to Nicholas on the progress of the new enforcements. "I tell you freely, Nicolas, these new taxes are making the people angrier than they ever have been. Archelaus' enforcers don't hesitate to beat anyone who voices opposition. There is great discontent among the Jews."

Nicolas responded, "I am aware of what you tell me, Nigrid. Archelaus hides much of the additional money from Caesar, whom I fear is aware of such actions. I can tell you that this added wealth is not being dispensed for the good of Judea or any of the towns that need assistance."

Archelaus' kingdom was comprised of Judea, Samaria, and Idumea. The changes taking place were made known to the various bands of nomadic shepherds. During their annual trek from the south of the Jordan Valley northward toward Jericho, Jesus Barabbas went to his friend Terach to discuss the situation and hear what Terach would say. Exasperated and angry, he exploded upon the scene.

Terach as usual was calm, and realistic. "Barabbas, I do not see any real change between Herod and his successor. The family blood remains the same; and I fear matters will only worsen as the Jews oppose their young king."

"Terach, I am of the same mindset as you. When the last Passover was cancelled, that was a big indicator of Archelaus' mindset. He cares nothing for the Jews or our sacred feasts!"

Terach warned, "The new king's wrath is focused mainly on those who dwell within the cities and villages. Thus far, he has left us nomad shepherds alone. But this could change at any moment. As we travel to Jericho, we must be alert and wary of such change. My hope is that he will retain the same policy as his father invoked throughout his reign."

Jesus Barabbas suggested, "When we arrive at Jericho we both must gain the ear of the Nigrid and inquire what he knows, since he is one of the new king's administrators. Surely he will be able to give us advice." There was an uncertain pause before Barabbas finished, "Hopefully, we will not be subject to what is happening throughout Archelaus' swath of vengeance and greed."

With grave concern, the two friends ended their conference and returned to their respective flocks and herds.

Many miles away in the bustling city of Heliopolis, news of Archelaus reached the ear of a workman. The carpenter paid close attention to the stories conveyed by the trade caravan members who brought news along with an assortment of goods for sale and exchange. The woodworker asked many questions of the caravan crew, making sure he was apprised of everything taking place throughout Judea.

When his workday was completed, the carpenter hurried to his home in the small nearby town of Metariyeh where he lived with his growing family. His young wife had recently given birth to her second child, a half-brother to her first son whom she had named Jesus.

Mary saw the consternation on Joseph's face when he came into the house. Joseph relayed what the trade caravan merchants had spoken about Herod and now Archelaus. "I fear, dear Mary, this latest news means we must remain here in Egypt much longer than we envisioned. Archelaus appears to be much like his father and I dreadfully fear this youthful king will want to follow his father's order to kill Jesus. Should we return to Bethlehem and this young despot learn that Jesus was the reason behind Herod's order to kill all the young children, Archelaus will attempt to complete his father's order," Joseph lamented.

Mary took his hand and said, "God gave us a vision and a message to flee Herod and now we must pray for His divine guidance in this development as well. We must continue to trust in our Lord."

A short time later, God's divine intervention took place, giving Joseph and Mary a dream to return to Judea. In the dream, the couple was instructed to avoid Bethlehem and go to Galilee instead. Joseph and Mary knew they must obey His command without any reservations or doubt. They knew they could not return to Bethlehem. God provided the means by which they finalized their decision to return to Judea.

The trade caravan merchants informed Joseph that Caesar Augustus had given Archelaus the majority of Judea, but it did not include the region of Galilee and other northern areas.

When the carpenter told his wife about this division, it sealed the decision to go to Galilee. "God has confirmed to us that the words of these trade merchants coincide with the vision He gave us in our dream. We must not tarry. Let us prepare to leave immediately."

God's special family sold their household items, gathered their personal belongings and Joseph's vital carpenter tools, and secured passage with the trade caravan that was embarking on its return journey to Antioch. The family retraced their steps from when they had fled Bethlehem for Egypt. The trade caravan slowly made its way northward first to the city of Gaza, then to Ashkelon, and after many days it reached Caesarea.

At Herod's city built to honor Rome's Caesar, the family left the trade caravan and proceeded northeast with a smaller traveling group to Nazareth. They had come full-circle. God gave them additional assurance of their obedience to Him when they learned that all of Galilee was under the command of Herod's son Antipas, who thankfully was not cut from the same cloth as his father or his much younger brother, Archelaus.

Antipas was given the region as part of both Herod's will and Caesar Augustus' executive order. Antipas knew he must exhibit loyalty to Rome and he personally wanted to create a more positive image than that of either his father or brother. One of the first acts by Antipas was to command a rebuilding of Sepphoris, the once thriving commercial hub of southern Galilee.

Work on reconstructing the city began in earnest with Rome's explicit approval. The timing was such that Joseph immediately found carpentry work. He located a suitable house for his family outside of Nazareth. The distance from his home to Sepphoris was less than three miles. In addition, the building resurgence and the influx of new people to the area eliminated previous gossip concerning the purity of Mary and her being with child prior to a marriage finalization with Joseph.

"God is blessing us greatly, Joseph! My heart praises Him daily for His guidance and protection over us."

Joseph was quick to agree with his young wife. "Indeed, Mary, you are correct. I have peace in my heart that all will go well for us here."

The nearly 81-mile distance separating Nazareth from Jerusalem, and the 70-mile distance from Jericho became buffers between two vastly different worlds. Galilee was thriving, peaceful, and growing. Jerusalem was wailing under the oppression of Archelaus, and Jericho was ruptured from dealing with the cruelty of the new teenage puppet king and the deeply concerned trade merchants that frequented the area.

Jericho functioned well in commerce due to the combined efforts of Nicolas and his friend the Nigrid, but the inner circle associated with the young puppet king was split in their allegiance to the new master of cruelty.

Wary of the fluctuating temperament of the people, Nicolas privately sought out Archelaus. The minister of finance knew that the best way to sway the new master of cruelty was not to get into conflict with his decisions. Rather he would lead him through suggestion and innuendo to the desired decision. Before his meeting with Archelaus, Nicolas first sent in one of the military officers with a report on the ever-growing discontent of the people about the heavy burden of taxation levied upon them. Next, Nicolas adroitly submitted a report on how much money was being lost by the reduction of the trade caravans not only to Jericho, but to Jerusalem as well.

When Nicolas met with Archelaus, the new ruler initiated the topic of the two reports he received. "Nicolas, I need your advice concerning two reports I've received." Nicolas breathed a sigh of relief as he listened to the information he already knew.

When Archelaus finished, the confused young ruler said, "Can you advise me what I should do in these matters?"

Striving to contain his pleasure over his successful strategy, Nicolas proceeded to give the sound tactical plan. Inwardly, he realized that Archelaus would either reject the plan entirely or modify aspects of it to meet his own mindset. But he was surprised at the despot's decision. "After listening to your suggestions, Nicholas, I've come to the conclusion that I shall refrain from new taxes on the Jews. Instead, I shall focus on the region of Samaria. Henceforth, their taxes shall increase twofold. Further, you are to only submit one quarter of that amount to Rome."

The finance minister stood dumbfounded at Archelaus' decree. Nicolas knew he could not object to the lunacy of this decision. Nor could he point out the impact this decree would have on the Samaritans, much less the ruling Romans. He could only feign loyalty and obedience in spite of his terrible misgivings. "It shall be as you say, Archelaus." The disappointed finance minister slowly turned and made his way out of the despot's office. He had misjudged the king. Nicolas quickened the pace as much as his short legs would allow and went to the despot's minister of business, the Nigrid, to apprise him of what was about to take place.

The Nigrid stood up from behind his desk after being informed of the despot's lunatic decision. He placed his hands behind his back, paced back and forth, and scowled. "Archelaus is doing a very bad thing with this new decree. He does not realize how angry and bitter both the Jews and the Samaritans are over his cruelty and his taxation. I fear for the tax collectors who frequent these regions to perform their duty. I will request a heavier guard for them, otherwise they will be killed. When Rome hears of my request it will be interesting what action the emperor takes."

Nicolas agreed with the Nigrid's assessment and added, "I believe there will be more to come from our new potentate. He is unpredictable and anything can happen."

The finance minister's prediction came to pass within a short period of time. Archelaus found a new way to further anger the Jews and insult them religiously, as well. The callous potentate violated Mosaic Law when he married the widow of his brother Alexander despite the fact Archelaus' own wife was still alive. This, coupled with the hatred the Jews still harbored over Archelaus' murdering of 3,000 Jews during the sacred Passover celebration, created a smoldering volcano.

In addition to the monarch's violation of Mosaic Law of marriage, the young despot began instructing the high priest how to religiously govern the Jews. He demanded changes to the Temple money changing, and wanted more money from the yearly Jewish tax of one shekel per adult male. These actions solidified the opinion of the Sanhedrin that in spite of his pretense and lip service, Archelaus really wasn't Jew intent on honoring either the Torah or the Talmud.

In the end, Archelaus paid for his aloof, arrogant attitude of sovereignty. The Jewish and the Samaritan leaders petitioned Caesar with a long list of grievances against Archelaus. This, after a mere five and a half years of rule by the young king. Caesar Augustus listened attentively to the complaints from the religious leaders of their two sizable regions.

After the angry leaders finished their litany of grievances, Augustus said, "I hereby decree that henceforth from this day, Archelaus shall no longer be the ethnarch of Judah. He will immediately be recalled to Rome at which time I shall punish him. Further, I do decree that Rome will appoint a procurator as governor over all of Judah. He shall be under the direct supervisor of the legate of Syria. In addition, I shall add 60 cohorts, for 680 soldiers to Judah. They shall be garrisoned at both Caesarea and at Jerusalem." The religious contingent did not know that the Roman emperor had inside knowledge of the situation and used this grievance as an excuse to take the action he wanted.

With that, the short reign of Archelaus ended. He was exiled to Gall where he died at the age of thirty-five. But troubles for both the Jews and the Samaritans did not end with the removal of Archelaus. Little did the diverse religious leaders of Judea realize what would happen to them over the next 63 years.

Chapter 8

The Jewish and the Samaritan religious leaders had barely returned to their respective headquarters when an announcement was sent forth that a new Roman delegate had arrived in the port city of Caesarea. The delegate was officially called a procurator and he would be the governor over all of Judea, including Samaria. The procurator's name was Coponius, a member of the equestrian order of elite heritage.

Coponius was in his mid-thirties at the time of his appointment by Caesar Augustus. His previous governing experience was low level, and he saw this promotion as a way to impress Rome and perhaps be able to advance his career.

His appointment was an unexpected test to himself in the process of attempting a positive demonstration to Augustus. Prior to the reign of Herod, the Roman Senate was set to appoint a local governor to Judea. They opted instead on allowing Herod to rule based on his convincing them he would rule with an iron hand and would improve the region. In Rome's eyes, Herod did what he promised. The problem arose when Archelaus proved to be inferior. His actions were actually fueling sparks of Jewish rebellion. What Rome especially frowned upon were the repeated mini-revolts by both the Jews and the Samaritans during the youthful despot's tenure.

Rome again decided to take complete control over the region and made it an official province of the Roman Empire. This meant both the Jews' and the Samaritans' authority would now be severely limited. The Jews would no longer have jurisdiction over crimes or could institute capital punishment. The Romans would assume the role of chief taxation. There would be limits on religious observances. The final straw in this haystack of change was the great influx of Roman soldiers to the region.

Herod had his own small army, and his personal bodyguard contingent was 2,000 strong, fierce, and ruthless. However, they were nothing compared to the Roman military, the most feared and well-trained force of its time.

Caesar declared that the Roman capitol of the region would be in the thriving port city of Caesarea. The procurator would hold court there. Three times a year he would make official appearances in Jerusalem, planned to coincide with the three major religious feasts observed by the Jews. At each of these feasts the number of Roman soldiers would triple, much to the dismay of the Jews. There was already a sizable Roman garrison established in Jerusalem. The unavoidable military presence was seen and felt each day of life in the Jewish community.

Coponius wasted little time in proving his sovereign rule over Judea. One of his first acts was to order the minting of a special coin of his own design. The design reflected his personal idea of what he esteemed of special value. It would be the legal tender throughout the region and recognized through all of the Roman Empire.

When the new coin was dispensed throughout Judea, it was an unmistakable signal to the Jews and the Samaritans that their desired freedom was not to be. The Jewish high priest Ananus ben Seth was beside himself, and had the daunting task of addressing the Sanhedrin concerning this devastating development.

"Members of the Sanhedrin, it is with great sorrow and consternation that I must inform you of the results of what my scribes have learned concerning what the Romans are imposing upon us." Ananus ben Seth paused and looked about the meeting room that contained the elites among the Pharisees, the Sadducees, and their scribes. All eyes of the august ruling body were directed at the high priest. Satisfied he had their complete attention, he continued, "The quarrels and riots that took place between us and Archelaus during his despicable reign have now led the Romans to impose a heavy hand over us." Ananus ben Seth's voice dropped. He could not contain his emotions and mournfully wailed the inevitable result, "We have no recourse but to abide by these new impositions. To do otherwise will result in all of Jerusalem being destroyed." At his declaration, the

Jewish ruling body groaned and many joined in the high priest's wailing as if mourning the death of a loved one.

Regaining his composure, Ananus ben Seth raised his hand for silence. When the great room quieted he said, "We have no power to combat these oppressors. We must remain on the good side of this new Procurator Coponius, as he is the voice of Rome. He has literal power of life or death over us." Again there was much moaning and murmuring throughout the assembly. The air within the great room was heavy with despair.

The high priest once more held his arm high for silence in order to continue his presentation. "Thank you for your cooperation. We must instruct all the rabbis throughout Judea to inform the men of the synagogues to use restraint when dealing with our oppressors. I fear that should a riot or battle ensue in any one of our towns, it will have disastrous consequences for all of Judea." At that point the assembly fell eerily quiet. Dozens of eyes were trained on Ananus, searching for some sign of hope; but there was none. Some closest to the high priest witnessed him quickly wiping tears from his eyes.

After a moment, one of the Pharisees asked the high priest, "Do you believe that should the Samaritans cause the ire of this Coponius, he will in turn carry out his wrath against us?"

Ananus put his hand to his bearded chin and reflected briefly. "I really don't know the answer to that question. These Romans often are brutal, but at other times reasonable. I hope we will be spared should the Samaritans do anything to incite the Romans' ire. It depends whether or not this procurator knows the difference between us of the true faith and the accursed Samaritans."

With deflated hearts and burdened emotions, members of the Jewish ruling committee hung or shook their heads. The Sanhedrin dissolved the special meeting. The leaders set about to carry out the high priest's orders to instruct the numerous rabbis how to carry out Ananus' plan of action. Many realized the plan's goal was basically appeasement.

Three days following the special meeting of the Sanhedrin, the high priest Ananus was summoned to meet with Coponius at his headquarters in Caesarea. The message was very simple and straightforward, "Come immediately that I may instruct you on the new order of things in Judea." Ananus' stomach tightened at the terseness of the procurator's order. It was clear Coponius had total contempt for him as the primary representative of the Jewish people he would govern.

The high priest was led into the room which served the Roman court of justice at times and as a meeting room for the procurator when needed. There was a platform upon which an ornate chair was placed—the judgment chair of Coponius. The atmosphere in the room was not inviting. Ananus truly felt a foreboding as he gloomily waited for Coponius to make his appearance.

The procurator strode into the room wearing the customary toga with the colored stripe indicating his official rank. Coponius moved smoothly with smug confidence. His tall stature enhanced his demeanor. Casually, he ascended the five steps to the top of the platform and took his place in his judgment seat. The procurator's entrance was highly orchestrated and meant to intimidate.

The high priest of the Jews was forced to remain standing, a clear indication of his stature with the Roman authoritarian—just another man about to receive Roman judgment and sentence. The role of the high priest being the final authority was deliberately minimized by this arrangement. He did not enjoy this realization, and anger simmered within him.

Coponius wasted no time getting to the point of why he summoned the Jews' highest leader. In a staccato shrill-like tone, he launched his attack, "You received my initial announcement from my assistant and now I want to add details to that order. Rome will establish a full garrison of soldiers in Jerusalem to be housed in a facility we have selected and will shortly renovate to our specifications. Our normal military force in your capitol will total 480 well-trained battle-tested infantry. We also shall bring forth sixty mounted archers should the need arise to restore order to the city and to the region."

Coponius stopped to allow Ananus time to visualize the thrust of the military power available at his disposal. He noticed a cringe in the high priest's guarded expression. Coponius slightly smirked at the effect his description had had on the Jew.

The procurator slowly ran his right hand through his curled short hair and continued emphatically, "From this point on, Rome will have final authority and supervision over your temple. Further it will be I..." He exaggerated the word, I, "who appoints and disposes of your high priest. This has been agreed upon by Caesar. It is long overdue, based on the numerous insurrections committed by you people," he sneered.

Hearing the procurator's words was like having a double-edged sword run through his body. Ananus could not keep from stepping backward in shock. Quickly, he straightened his shoulders, but not before Coponius took notice of the impact his decree had on the high-ranking Jew. Coponius again smiled an ugly smirk. Ananus' reaction inspired ugly pride, and a tone of jubilance entered Coponius' voice. "Rome has evaluated the Jews' actions to this point, and believes this action is necessary to quell all future uprisings from you people. You Jews have tested Rome's patience to the point it no longer can trust that you will obey our rules over you."

Ananus was still in shock from Coponius' words. He was marginally able to relax only when he heard the procurator say, "As for now, I have no desire to replace you as high priest over your people. Periodically, we shall communicate with each other. You must immediately inform me as to any developments within your religion and your people that might impact how I deal with you. I, alone..." and again he emphasized his personal reference, "...I reserve the power to adjudicate all capital offenses, as well as civil and religious. There will be no exceptions! Any violations of these commands will result in severe punishment for you, for members of your ruling body, and for the populace who violate our laws."

A pronounced silence filled the room. The only sound Ananus heard was his own heavy breathing. He was stunned and unable to move. But there was more to come from the elated Roman who spitefully spat, "Oh yes. One other thing. Because you people say your God owns the land, and your people do not, Rome has decided that in accordance with its well-known policies, Rome shall own all land throughout Judea. As such, all Jews who have farms, own businesses, and reside in houses shall pay a lease to Rome for use of Rome's property."

Ananus could not believe what he had just heard. In one fell swoop, all venerated Jewish tradition concerning land had vanished. God's covenant with His people and their land—His land—had just been swept away by meaningless human decree.

The Roman procurator was not finished. He looked down at the shrinking high priest, then leaned forward to make his next decree. "Furthermore, all food that is bought or sold in all of Judea shall henceforth be taxed by Rome. All inheritances shall also be taxed. And those traveling the major roadways throughout Judea shall pay a toll for use of these routes."

Coponius finally stopped to let his decrees resonate with the Jewish leader whose usual pomposity was now completely deflated. Ananus ben Seth had nothing to say and it was evident that Coponius was in no mood to entertain any delay or negotiation on his new ruling. The high priest of the Jews realized the sentencing of the Jews was over. As such, Ananus reluctantly bowed to the procurator, turned, and slowly left the judgment hall with stooped posture and a heavy spirit.

The newly appointed Roman administrator watched from his perch as the broken figure of a man shuffled out of the courtroom. Coponius gripped the arms of his judgment seat. He squinted scornfully as the Jew exited the room. When the doors shut and he was alone in his judgment chamber, he slowly stood up, smiling broadly, meticulously adjusted his finely made toga, and exited through the same side door he had entered. His cadence and demeanor portrayed the winner of a great battle victory.

It was time for his next appointment. He hoped it also would lead to a more profitable and enjoyable stay in this despicable land occupied by arrogant, insurgent-minded people.

When the high priest returned to Jerusalem, he presented his disheartening news to the members of the Sanhedrin. After relaying the decrees of Coponius, he dismally placed both hands atop his ornate headdress. He began to move his head side to side, remembering the ancient promise written in Genesis 49:10 *"The scepter shall not depart from Judah, nor a lawgiver from between his feet, until Shiloh (Messiah) comes; and to Him shall be the obedience of the people."*

Ananus forlornly lamented aloud, "Woe unto us! For the scepter, our symbol of power, has departed from Judah and the Messiah has not come! God's promise has not been fulfilled. We do not have His favor."

The various members of the Sanhedrin began to sway side-to-side with arms locked around each other. Extensive moaning and groaning echoed in the great assembly hall.

What the august Jewish leaders did not know, nor would they have accepted, was the truth that a small Jewish boy was growing up in Nazareth, Galilee, waiting for the precise timing to make Himself known as God's Promised One. Indeed, prophecy had been fulfilled. Shiloh was among His people, but the people would have deaf ears and blind eyes to His arrival.

While the Jews were bemoaning their worsened fate, Nicolas and the Nigrid sat together over breakfast and discussed their individual meetings with the new procurator. The Nigrid was the first to give his evaluation. "Nicolas, based on what we each experienced with Coponius, I believe our respective meetings were tests to determine our loyalty to Rome. Caesar is concerned whether we will perform our duties to benefit Rome or if we will be obstinate like the Jews."

Nicolas sat back in his chair and looked anxiously at his colleague. "I believe there was more to our individual interrogations than mere loyalty, my friend. Coponius was searching to determine if we have been carrying out the taxation duties as directed by Rome; and if Herod was taking too much for himself. Rome lives by heavy taxation. I detected the new procurator has plans for additional taxes he did not disclose to us."

The Nigrid's eyes widened in surprise. "Do you suppose, Nicolas, that Coponius will unveil more taxes soon?"

Nicolas nodded his head without hesitation. "This man is devious, Nigrid. He has his own plan, and it will be implemented shortly. Coponius' fact finding will determine the date of his plan's revelation."

"Do you think the two of us will be instrumental in carrying out this plan for Coponius, or is it possible the procurator will replace us?" Nicolas put down his piece of bread. He pursed his lips together and continued, not waiting for the Nigrid to answer. "I believe that Coponius will use us to implement this plan. Why not? We have experience, plus knowledge of these people that is valuable to him. Part of my concern is our personal safety in doing so. The Jews have a history of rebellion against those who rule over them. I fear, my friend, it will be only a matter of time before the simmering volcano erupts. We must prepare ourselves for such an explosion."

The Nigrid slowly chewed his breakfast morsel as he thought about what Nicolas had just said. When he finished, the Nigrid extended an open hand toward his colleague. "Nicolas, indeed it shall be the two of us caught in the middle of this impending eruption. We must remain united and devise our own plan of survival." Nicolas picked up his wine goblet and thrust it toward the Nigrid, saluting the formation of their private pact.

The two administrators shifted their topic to the upcoming major festival that was most sacred to the Jews, the observance of Passover that took place each spring. It would be a time when all of Judea descended on Jerusalem. There was much money to be made from this sacred festival and the duo wanted to make sure they secured their portion of the bounty. Since neither man was Jewish, they did not care about the religious aspects of the observance. Their focus was on the money and profit easily attainable from the religious event.

Sizeable profits could be made for the Nigrid from the sale of lambs found unblemished and suitable for the Temple sacrifice. He would purchase these animals less than five months old from his trusted friend, the nomadic shepherd Terach. In addition, Terach would supply the Nigrid ample amounts of goat cheese, and sheep and goat hides.

Nicolas would be in charge of dealing with the Jewish Temple moneychangers. The influx of people to Jerusalem for the sacred festival meant different currencies would be presented to purchase the sacrificial animals. Jewish moneychangers would exchange these different currencies for the Jewish shekel. It was Nicolas' duty to intervene with the moneychangers and swap the currencies for the preferred Roman coins. Of course, Rome expected this switch to be profitable for the Roman treasury. Their greed and deceit all added to the frustration of the Jewish Sanhedrin.

In the past, Herod had been somewhat lenient during this sacred festival to show pretended compassion for the Jews. His motivation was mainly to hold back revolt against his otherwise ruthless domination. Nicolas and the Nigrid secretly wondered if the new regime would adhere to these patterns of Herod.

When the sacred festival officially began, Coponius traveled from Caesarea to Jerusalem along with extra Roman soldiers to maintain order. The newly appointed procurator remained in the background as an observer of the event he had only heard about. The procurator was seeking information about how the Jews observed this religious festival—with a keen eye to strategize for his new taxation plan.

Both the Nigrid and Nicolas knew about the directive Coponius had given Ananus in their first meeting. The two administrators were curious as to what Coponius would do following his first exposure to Jewish customs and sacred rituals. To their surprise, the Roman authoritarian was generally satisfied with his initial list of changes and new taxes. The one area that was differed from King Herod's policy was that nomadic shepherds would now be taxed on the various goods they sold. This tax included the sale of lambs for the pilgrimage feasts, all hides, cheese, and items they used in the common bartering system that permeated the region.

The Nigrid was assigned to inform the nomad shepherds of the new change. He knew it would not go well and he worried about the reaction that he would face. He needed to sway Terach first because the other shepherds looked to him as their leader. The Nigrid hoped there would be no major hurdles involved. Nevertheless he prepared himself emotionally for just such a development.

The Nigrid sent a message to Terach that he had a matter of utmost importance to discuss with him. This was an unusual occurrence. He knew he would not be required to meet unless something of significance was pending. Terach was a non-official leader of the minority group; he suspected the topic to be directly related to the arrival of the new Roman procurator. He had to travel a full day back to Jericho to meet with the Nigrid, but he responded right away.

The special session between the two men took place immediately upon Terach's arrival in Jericho.

There were the customary snacks and drink served during the meeting and the Nigrid got straight to the point of the summit. In a simple, straight-forward manner, the Nigrid explained the new tax decreed by Coponius. Terach showed no emotional reaction. After the Nigrid finished his announcement, Terach chose his words carefully before he gave his reply.

"Nigrid, this development is something I have sensed would take place when Rome made Judea a province of their empire. Of course, I had hoped we would be spared involvement because of our lowly status within the Jewish community. Obviously, this is not to be, so tell me when and how often we shall be subject to these new taxes?"

A barely audible sigh of relief left the messenger's lips. "I shall not collect any taxes until next year's Passover, Terach. But be prepared that the rest of your journey can be such that when you engage anyone for business at those towns—the ones where you do business with the trade caravans—the tax will be collected. The tax collectors at these business centers will be informed of Coponius' decree."

Terach tightened his lips and slightly shook his head. "No doubt, these minions will be quite eager to pad their pockets as well. Do you have any advice how myself and the other nomad shepherds can lessen this new tax?"

"There is none, my friend. Be assured, if there was any way I could help you and the other shepherds, I would. Do not be surprised if this new Roman has other ideas in mind to benefit himself at the expense of yourself and the Jews at a later time."

"There is nothing else, then, to be discussed, Nigrid, so I will take my leave now and ponder your words as I return to my flock. I shall arrange a meeting with the other nomad shepherds who travel the same route I do and relay this development to them. Be aware, Nigrid, that some will not receive it well." Terach was anxious to conclude the interruption to his rounds.

The Nigrid realized that his business associate was beginning his routine trek back to the southern part of the Jordan Valley and didn't want delays. It was vital for Terach to accompany his animals because undue delays could cause negative results for the shepherd leader. Naturally, this would also detract from the Nigrid's benefits, too. Before Terach could leave, he offered him one more piece of advice. "It is possible that along your journey some of the Roman soldiers will be lenient, especially should you give them extra gifts. These soldiers do not receive much pay, so anything that benefits them will be greatly appreciated."

Terach rose up from the reclining couch, gave his business associate the customary exit hug, and mounted his stallion for the trip back to his flocks and waiting family. The shepherd leader pondered the Nigrid's advice concerning this new decree and made a mental note to share it with his fellow nomad shepherds. However, Terach wondered which of the other shepherds would be most irate and obstinate against the new tax. The one name that stood out among the other shepherds was Jesus Barabbas. His temper often resulted in violent action, much to the discomfort of anyone Barabbas had issue with.

True to Terach's prediction, Barabbas was the most demonstrative and loudly vocal of the shepherds. He screamed, "Terach, this procurator is a puppet of the devil! He creates much hardship for all Judeans. He must somehow be taught a lesson about his wicked ways! I believe his actions will cause new hostilities between the Jews and the Romans!" With each explosive phrase, the volatile nomad pounded his fist into the palm of his opposite hand.

Terach was prepared for Barabbas' fit of temper. He firmly interjected, "Barabbas, it is with great sadness that I must agree with your words. But I must also strongly implore you and the other shepherds. We must remain united in this matter and not lose our heads. Our actions must not cause distress for the others." The assembled group of nomads murmured at length, but a pact was established to follow Terach's directive before the shepherds dispersed to their respective flocks. Only Barabbas remained behind.

Terach was glad his friend opted to stay. Barabbas flailed his arms and paced about, causing his cloak to flutter and unfurl behind him. He vented his frustration while Terach merely stood by and watched the dramatic demonstration. Barabbas finally stopped his harangue. He turned to Terach, pointed his finger, and said, "My friend, assuredly I tell you that this imbecile from Rome will rue the day he imposed such wickedness!"

The hard-hitting changes imposed by Coponius swept throughout Judea, Samaria, and even north to Galilee. The Jews' reaction was even more hostility toward their conquerors, mixed with many more prayers that God would send their hoped-for messiah to eliminate the Romans from their daily life.

One Jew decided it was time to stand up to the oppressors. The Jew became known to the Romans as Judas the Galilean. He amassed a band of guerilla warriors that inflicted physical as well as mental pain to the oppressors.

After Quirinius, Roman Legate to Syria, ordered a census, Judas of Galilee and a Pharisee named Zadok found they were in total agreement about the Roman' newly imposed taxes. They vowed to resist the buildup of Roman soldiers and the establishment of a large garrison in the region of Galilee.

The two Jews founded what became known as the "fourth sect" or the Zealots. The first three sects were the Pharisees, the Sadducees, and the Essenes. Many Jews of the time were furious over how the Sanhedrin, comprised of these three religious orders, kowtowed in submission to the Romans. The newly formed Zealots espoused a return to the fundamentals of Jewish traditions and rituals and preached that God alone was the ruler of Israel. This was in stark contrast to the numerous rules and rituals established by the Sanhedrin.

The Zealots went about urging all Jews not to pay any taxes to Rome. There were many friendly ears to the Zealots' pontifications. Within a short period of time, the preaching of the Zealots captured the attention of Coponius, as well as Ananus and the other 70 members of the Sanhedrin. Both leaders had deep concerns, but for different reasons.

Converts to the Zealots became very vocal in their denunciation of Judea's two ruling authorities. They began a campaign of disruption throughout Judea. Bands of Zealots attacked Roman squads while they engaged in their routine scouting missions. The Zealot bands also attacked various trade caravans, taking all money and valuable spices that originated in Egypt and items grown in Judea. The most highly prized commodity was salt, one of the most desired and expensive items sought not only in Judea but also in Rome. Salt was important as a preservative for many foods.

As Zealot strikes and guerilla missions increased, Coponius became greatly agitated. He convened a private meeting with his two administrators, the Nigrid and Nicolas, in Jericho to seek a solution to the problem that was becoming known not only to Quirinius in Antioch, Syria, but also to Caesar in Rome. It was a position the procurator of Judea did not like. Coponius actually feared for his life from the rebels. An even greater personal threat to him was from Rome.

Coponius paced about the business meeting room in the Nigrid's mansion. The Nigrid and Nicolas looked on from their seats. Normally, the procurator strutted about in arrogance over his autocratic rule, but now he looked worried. When the Roman official became irritated or anxious, he would run his fingers throughout his hair. His hair showed these signs of distraction as he thought about his growing problems.

Between paces, Coponius stopped and peered at his two administrators. "I have read both of your reports about the diminishing treasury and the decision of the trade caravans to demand heavier protection during their trek through Judea. At the current rate of disruption, one quarter of the treasury will be lost within six months should these rebel Zealots continue to operate."

Coponius looked to see if his administrators would add further information to their previous reports. When neither man spoke, the Procurator to Judea forged ahead. "Based on your reports, I have spoken with the garrison commander in Caesarea to increase his patrols south to Adasa. I travel to Jerusalem to instruct the garrison commander there to do likewise all the way south to the border with Egypt and to the coastal towns along the Great Sea, the Mediterranean. Both commanders have a free hand to do whatever is necessary to capture these despicable Zealots. All sympathizers of these rebels will also face severe punishment should they be caught aiding the Zealots in any way."

The Nigrid and Nicolas sat still, listening to the frantic procurator. Both men knew the decree by Coponius would be difficult to carry out due to the mindset of the Jews and their growing hatred towards both Coponius and Rome. They knew better than Coponius the current number of soldiers was not enough to carry out his band-aid plan. They waited until their supervisor finished before they voiced any thoughts.

Finally, Coponius placed his left hand on his toga with his official colored stripe. He took a deep breath and slowly exhaled, a sign of personal satisfaction at hearing his own words. His look of satisfaction indicated he would now listen to any thoughts of the two administrators. Nicolas was the first to speak.

"Judea is a large area for this limited number of soldiers to patrol, Coponius. Because the treasury is the main cause of concern, I foresee the increased patrols being utilized to protect the trade caravans on their journey either to Egypt or their return to Rome. There simply aren't enough soldiers to both protect the caravans and to ferret out the rebels and those who aid them."

Coponius' eyes narrowed. He did not like hearing the truth spoken by his unemotional administrator of finance. He turned his piercing eyes on his administrator of business affairs, the Nigrid, for his opinion. The small man was not intimidated by his taller superior. He sat relaxed in his chair. Calmly, he looked at the harried Roman and stated, "In addition to what Nicolas has spoken, you must realize there are many caves, hills, and canyons surrounding Jericho where these Zealot rebels can establish bases. It will be extremely difficult to search these areas. The Zealots and their growing followers know this region far better than the Roman soldiers." The Nigrid hoped this last comment would strike a warning chord with Coponius' ignorance of the land's topography.

Coponius fumed. He wasn't accustomed to being instructed by underlings. He stared at the administrators and was incensed over their calm demeanors. He seethed, "I believe there is a way to protect the trade caravans and expose these Zealot rebels."

Having reminded himself of this, he relaxed, and undisguised arrogant haughtiness formed on his face. "I have already recruited many spies who reside in the main towns where these Zealots and their followers will frequent. These ears of Rome will be subtle and clandestine in obtaining the necessary information needed to capture the agitators. I have no doubt this problem will rectify itself in a short period of time."

Satisfied with himself, Coponius gave each man some final instructions, then left for Jerusalem to meet with the garrison commander. After his departure, the administrators remained in the room for their private discussion.

"Our esteemed leader is quite pompous in his assessment of the situation, and his solution is ludicrous," the Nigrid observed.

Nicolas tipped his head to one side and chuckled with a wry smile. "Tell me, do you foresee any lessening of anger on the part of the Jews or other people with the Romans?"

"No, and Coponius and Caesar fail to understand the mindset of the Jews. They will never accept worshipping false gods as the Romans expect." The Nigrid emphasized his final statement, "It is not the increase of taxes that infuriate the Jews. It is their religious belief that only God can tax, only He can own the land, and only He will lead His people."

"I am Greek and have not lived here long enough to have the insight you do, Nigrid. I thank you for enlightening me the way you have on so many occasions in my dealings with these people. But tell me, my friend, knowing how the Jews feel about these issues, why do you cooperate with the Romans in your business deals, including the collection of the many taxes— knowing they will despise you?"

The Nigrid did not hesitate to answer. "I was ridiculed by the Jews when I was younger due to my small stature and my father's occupation of being a butcher. King Herod found out about my plight and took pity on me. He made me his chief business administrator, knowing I would relish getting a form of revenge on those who castigated me and my family. I admit it. I do enjoy inflicting emotional and economic pain on these fools."

Nicolas sensed the anger and pain in the Nigrid's brief narrative. Not deterred by his friend's demeanor, Nicolas continued, "It is safe for me to assume then, my friend, that you will comply with Coponius' orders?"

The Nigrid answered enthusiastically, "Oh yes! I will do all that I can to bring about the end of these Zealot dissenters! I will enjoy using everything at my disposal to learn of their identities and those who aid their cause." The Nigrid suddenly halted before giving his final statement. "Besides Nicolas, what these bandits are doing is very bad for business. Both you and I have our personal wealth at stake in this matter. It behooves us to protect our valuable interests."

The discussion was complete. The Nigrid summoned his servant to serve the evening meal for the two comrades. The remainder of their conversation explored how to cooperate in their efforts to expose and eliminate the Zealots.

Coponius' efforts proved unsuccessful. After one year of frustration, Quirinius and Caesar had had enough. The Legate to Syria dispatched a huge force of well-trained soldiers, including cavalry archers to Galilee, the headquarters of Judas the Zealot and his fellow conspirator Zadok. In a bloody series of battles the two founders were captured and crucified.

A bloodless victim of Quirinius' campaign was Coponius. The Legate of Syria and supreme governor over all of Judea finally had enough of the arrogant first procurator to Judea. With Caesar's approval, Coponius was ordered back to Rome to answer for his ineptitude and failure to handle the Jewish insurrection. Quirinius instructed his assigned squad of soldiers to make Coponius' journey back to Rome as uncomfortable as possible.

Despite the deaths of the Zealot leaders, the group of insurrectionists remained committed to their cause. They were scattered throughout all of Judea as a result of Roman force. Every region had at least one band of Zealot operatives. Coponius' spies were uncovered and put to death by the Sanhedrin because they were Jews' deemed traitors. The spies formed by both Nicolas and the Nigrid were reluctant to perform their assigned tasks for fear of receiving the same fate, so the network of sleuths dissolved. The climate of revolt remained strong and served as an enticement for many others of a certain mindset to carry on what the Zealot founders initiated. One of the recruits to the fourth sect was Jesus Barabbas.

Chapter 9

Terach watched from atop his trusted stallion, proudly surveying the movement of his sizable herd of goats and sheep. He and the other nomad shepherds had completed a profitable sale of their animal products in Jericho. It also was a good year for unblemished lambs that brought a handsome price as sacrifices for the annual spring Passover festival.

The shepherd was pleased that his flocks were growing and remained healthy. The grasslands were providing plenty of nourishing food for them. He knew the other nomad shepherds would be experiencing a similar blessing from Almighty God. Terach often gave thanks to God for how well his four sons were developing skills necessary to be successful shepherds.

As the shepherd continued his assessment, he heard the sound of an approaching horseman behind him. Terach turned his stallion and immediately recognized the waving arm of the rider who was traveling quickly to meet with him. It was his friend Jesus Barabbas.

Barabbas stopped his horse beside Terach. Perplexed, Terach inquired, "Barabbas, what brings you here away from your flock? Is anything wrong?"

His fellow nomad waved with his hand in a negative gesture and shook his covered head. "No, my friend, there is nothing wrong. But I've come to speak with you about a serious matter."

Barabbas did not wait for his friend to inquire about the nature of the issue. He adjusted himself on his saddle and boldly announced to Terach, "I want to sell you my herd of sheep and goats, and include my hirelings."

Terach was completely taken aback by Barabbas' announcement. He pulled tightly on the reins and his horse moved jerkily backward. Terach's face showed signs of shock and amazement. "My friend, why do you make this request of me? Are you ill and need to make a change for your family?"

The nomad shook his head and his head covering fluttered in concert. "No; my health is good. The reason I make this request of you is I have decided to join the Zealots in their growing mission against the Romans." Seeing Terach's concern, Barabbas quickly explained his reasoning. "My anger with the Romans for leavening a harsh tax on us shepherds continues to grow stronger within me." Barabbas clutched his chest with his right hand to add emphasis to his words. "This last sale in Jericho was the final straw for me, Terach!" Jesus Barabbas momentarily paused and forcefully exclaimed, "I believe it is my duty to combat these Roman pigs and get them to rescind their taxing on us."

A sudden breeze coursed between the two shepherds that made Terach involuntarily shudder. He looked at the hard, tense features in his friend's face and plainly saw bitter resentment. Terach spoke calmly to Barabbas. "My friend, I cannot in all good conscience buy your herd and take over your hirelings for you. How will you and your family survive?"

Barabbas leaned on his saddle toward Terach and replied, "The Zealots plan on raiding the trade caravans, stripping them of valuable goods destined for Rome. In addition, we will continue to sell these goods at a significant reduction to those in need of those items." Barabbas finished, "We trust our Lord for His providing for us in our quest."

Terach had a dozen questions in his mind. He searched his friend's face for signs of anything that did not ring true. His mind quickly analyzed Barabbas' plan and saw what he must do. "Barabbas we have been friends a long time and shared many moments together. I do not feel it is right for me to purchase your flocks. As such, what I will do is take over managing your flocks for you. When it comes time for our bi-annual sale of products, I will get the best price possible. All this money shall be yours. It will be a way you can provide for yourself and your family should your Zealot campaigns go wrong."

Terach saw the magnitude of surprise in Barabbas' face and held up his hand for silence while he continued his proposition. "We can arrange a meeting place and time whereby I can present your earnings to you. At any time, my friend, you have the authority to change our agreement."

Shock came over Barabbas. He stammered, "My friend, your proposition is something I did not conceive taking place."

Barabbas quickly wiped away an escaping tear and took a deep breath. "I-I-I'm both surprised and grateful for your proposal. I do see the wisdom in your offer. We can meet here on the plains outside Jericho two days after the Passover festival. I will be close to the hills and the caves around Jericho where we will base our operations. In the fall, we can meet again at Bethlehem during the Feast of the Tabernacles. I do enjoy your reading from God's word. It will give hope to my soul."

At that, the two shepherds moved their horses closer together and they locked each other's forearms for their agreement. It was sealed with trust and love for each other. There was no need for any type of contract. There was nothing stronger than a man's word. Before Barabbas left, he made a final statement, "I shall bring my droves and my hirelings to you within the next two days. I must meet up with the other Zealots soon."

Terach acknowledged this part of the plan and said, "The grass is plentiful here and I can delay my journey back south past Tekoa. We will have plenty of time to combine our droves." Jesus Barabbas smiled gratefully at Terach, then turned his horse and quickly disappeared over the horizon.

Terach kept his horse steady as he watched Barabbas disappear from view. During the time it took for Barabbas to fade from sight, Terach contemplated what had taken just place, and moreover what the future held. Terach had an uneasy feeling in his stomach about Barabbas' decision. The nomad was prone to impulsive behavior and a short temper, both of which could factor into trouble for the newly recruited Zealot.

That evening after their boys were asleep, Terach and a very pregnant Beulah discussed the development with Barabbas. The uncomfortable mother-to-be said to her husband, "You made the right decision in your agreement with Barabbas, Terach. No one will do a better job than you. I am proud of you. I share your deep concern about our friend joining this band of rebel Jews. They will be hunted by the Romans and I'm not sure how the other Jews will treat them and their efforts to eliminate the Romans from all of Judea."

The couple changed the subject to happier things—the impending birth of their fifth child. Beulah patted her bulging tummy and indicated she felt their baby would come into the world very soon. "Our little Mattan asks me every day when his little brother will arrive that he can care for him. He tells me he wants to do for his brother what he could not do with his friend, the baby Jesus of Mary and Joseph. Mattan misses that time he had with their child," sighed Beulah.

"I know how Mattan feels about a new brother. He has asked me several times about Joseph and his family and wants to know when he can once again play with baby Jesus," said Terach. "Maybe, someday, we will meet up with that family again. I have much respect for Joseph."

Beulah had fond memories of those days, too. "Despite being a young mother, Mary exhibited to me and to the midwife she will adequately care for her first son. I have no doubt, she and Joseph will have more children, and each will be well cared for."

When Terach next met with Barabbas, he informed the converted Zealot of a change in plans. "Barabbas, I have given much thought to our agreement and believe we must make changes." Barabbas was startled, but before he could ask the obvious question, Terach explained, "It will not be good for either your flocks or mine to combine them into one. Your flock needs to continue the route you have established over the years. In this way, both flocks will continue to get the necessary nourishment they need to thrive."

Barabbas squinted and asked his friend, "How do you propose to monitor my flocks should bandits or my hirelings decide to steal them?"

Terach quickly assured him, "One of my most trusted men will take your place. In addition, I intend on exchanging a few of my hirelings with yours. That way, there should be no conspiracy to steal your flocks. More importantly, my friend, my two oldest sons are quite capable of managing your flock."

The converted Zealot put his hand to his dark beard and stroked it gently. He looked down in contemplation, then back up into Terach's face. "I will agree to these changes only because of my trust in you, my friend. Because of you, your sons are trustworthy and wise. It is settled."

Terach's men completed the exchange that same day and both droves began their journey to the southern part of the Jordan Valley. One week into their trek, Beulah gave birth to her fifth child. At first, she was concerned how her family would accept having a daughter and a sister instead of another male. She needn't have worried. Terach and the boys each immediately began to love and care for Channah, the youngest member of their family. Little Mattan stood beside his mother as she nursed the newborn infant. In as deep and boisterous a voice as his little throat could muster, he said, "I shall help you take care of my sister and when all my chores have been completed, I will care for her."

Beulah smiled lovingly. She placed her left hand on her young son's head and gently stroked his tousled hair. She gazed into the youth's eager sparkling eyes and replied, "Thank you, Mattan. I know you will do a good job in caring for your sister."

Because Mattan was considered still too young to be with his father and the sheep and the goats for a prolonged period, he was instructed to assist his mother as much as possible. Thus, he took on the role of caring for his young sister. As a result of their daily involvement with each other, the siblings formed a special bond, despite Mattan's being six years older than Channah. He became very protective of her to the point of fighting his brothers when he deemed their involvement with their sister to be too rough or hurtful to her. This greatly amused the older brothers.

Terach and Beulah often intervened in these skirmishes, yet both parents were proud of Mattan's willingness to protect Channah. In many instances when young Channah would find herself in trouble or get bruised, it was Mattan who usually was the first to come to her aid. This practice was not lost on Terach who felt this quality in his youngest son would serve him well as he grew older and became more involved with the business of the sheep and the goats.

Part of Jewish family life was the responsibility of parents to educate the young. As the youngest member of the family grew, Beulah instructed Channah on the duties of a good Jewish woman, and Terach taught their four boys about the manly duties instructed by God in His teachings. Terach taught all the children and Beulah about God's Word. He read daily out of the Tanach or Torah. Mattan usually raised the most questions and he was quick to memorize scripture passages. As he grew older, he took pride in being able to recite many different passages from God's teachings. This pleased Terach very much.

When Mattan reached age ten, he was overjoyed with the announcement that he would begin his apprenticeship with the flocks. The youth believed his repeated questioning of his father as to when he could join his older brothers in caring for the flocks had finally paid off. He overlooked the fact that time and age were the main factors in Terach's decision to advance the youth beyond camp duties. In addition, Channah was now old enough she did not require the care that was needed when she was an infant and a toddler.

Mattan was eager to learn every aspect of being a shepherd. Initially he had difficulty handling the weight of both the shepherd's rod and the staff. Both tools were too big and clumsy for him to use. He would not be coddled, and he steadfastly refused to carry only one tool at a time. He emphatically insisted that Terach let him handle both tools "because that's what shepherds must do." Terach became very proud of Mattan's persistence. Along with teaching the use of the rod and the staff, Terach taught his youngest son how to use the sling to hurl stones.

Many days it seemed Terach would stumble over Mattan who hovered close by, as the youth wanted involvement in every aspect of becoming a good shepherd. Mattan became sullen if Terach did not spend much time instructing him on the use of the sling. He saw it was used to ward off predators and also to bring straying sheep or goats back to the main body of the flock. It was an essential tool.

Whenever he had a spare moment, Mattan practiced using the sling. He wanted to become as proficient with the shepherd's tool as young David did. Mattan envisioned himself as David slaying Goliath or a predator such as a bear, a lion, or a wolf. The youth would pick out a rock, a bush, or a mound and pretend it was some sort of predator. Quickly he would unleash a smooth stone at the makeshift intruder. As he practiced with the sling, he became more proficient at hitting the most vulnerable and lethal spots of a predator.

On one occasion, Mattan wanted to exhibit his proficiency to show Terach how much he had improved in using the sling. The opportunity presented itself when Mattan and Terach were inspecting a portion of the flock of pregnant sheep. An adult hare sat some thirty-five yards away from the pregnant ewes.

Easily, Mattan placed one of his smooth stones in the sling, and in a flash hurled the stone toward the unsuspecting hare. Terach carefully watched his youngest son. The shepherd leader saw the quickness of Mattan's movements and his strength in hurling the stone. Terach was pleased how much of Mattan's technique was similar to his own.

He also noticed the intensity of Mattan's concentration as his son released the stone. The senior shepherd followed the trajectory of the stone, as it perfectly hit its target, the chest of the hare. Immediately upon impact, the unsuspecting hare fell over. Mattan was the first to bolt towards the slain animal, with Terach catching up to inspect the results. As the two ran to the hare, the startled ewes scattered a short distance away, turning to observe the unusual activity of the humans.

Mattan stood over the dead hare and touched it with his staff, making sure the animal was dead. The youth then took out his knife and proceeded to cut its throat and let the blood drain from its body. When this was done, Mattan looked up at his father, and with a hopeful smile, asked, "Did I use the sling as well as David would have?"

Terach returned the smile and kindly answered, "You did very well, Mattan. But remember, it's one thing to hit a hare but quite another to kill a raging predator who is attacking the flocks or even you. A raging predator can cause you to hurry your throw because you are distracted by its charge. I am sure David knew this and adjusted to the charging animal."

Mattan looked at his father, not with disappointment, but with the knowledge that Terach had been in a similar situation as David to recount such an experience. "Will I someday meet up with a raging animal like you and David did?"

Terach looked down at his growing son and replied, "Sooner or later, a shepherd will encounter such an animal and it will be his duty to protect his flock. Pray, my son, that Almighty God will protect you in such a time and give you courage to do your duty."

Those words resonated in Mattan's heart, and very often he conjured them up in his memory to strengthen his responsibility as a good shepherd. Mattan also compared his technique with the sling and other shepherd duties with those of his older brothers. Despite his youth, Mattan felt in his heart he was becoming as good as his older brothers. His secret goal was to become better.

Many nights Mattan put himself asleep thinking of the time he would become a shepherd. Some days, when he returned to their tent home, Mattan would pull Channah aside and tell her about his day's activities. Usually, his young sister was mesmerized at her favorite brother's endeavors. But when he excitedly depicted the scene with the hare, little Channah put her hands to her ears and yelled at Mattan to stop his story. This surprised Mattan, and he never again told Channah a story that would upset her.

When Mattan reached age twelve, there were significant changes within his family structure. His oldest brother Gavriel got married and took over as head shepherd of Barabbas' herds. Eitu, the next oldest, was assigned to Terach's goat herd, and Amram became Terach's assistant with the main flock of sheep. Mattan was in apprenticeship with each of his older brothers and Terach, moving from one section to another, and learning about the care of pregnant ewes, both sheep and goats.

It was a time of increased responsibility and a somewhat hectic lifestyle. When not out with the flocks and herds, Mattan and Channah continued their education through Terach and Beulah. Mattan's interest in the Tanach and Torah grew. He found himself studying God's word more intently. Like his father, Mattan thought about how the ancient shepherds were treated compared to the current situation within the Jewish society.

On one occasion, Mattan admitted to Terach, "Father, I understand now why you do not like the Jewish leaders who have made us outcasts with our own people. It is sad how their man-made rules and religious mantras really disobey God's teaching and instruction in the Tanach and the Torah. I find myself hating these religious leaders."

Terach was mildly surprised by the strong words of his youngest son. "Mattan, I'm glad you have discerned how religion works throughout all of Judea and is against God's teaching. You must always be wary of these religious purveyors of filth. Someday they will go too far in their rules making. I fear it will be bad for the entire Jewish nation."

When Mattan turned twenty, more changes began to unfold that affected him. Judea was now under its fourth procurator, a Roman named Valerius Gratus. Rome appointed its fourth Legate of Syria, Lucius Aelius Lamia. Each appointment had negative impacts on the Jews of Judea as well as on the Samaritans.

Gratus' main focus was to create wealth for himself at the cost of both the Jews and the Samaritans. Significantly impacting the Jews was the Roman procurator's continuing practice of appointing the high priest, thereby eliminating the Sanhedrin from its traditional role. This fueled the infuriation of the Jews' religious body. The main populace was equally concerned because they had no voice in the selection of the high priest. Adding to that, another source of great irritation and hardship was the increased taxation that Gratus instituted.

With every procurator's focus on increasing their wealth at the expense of the Jews, the Zealots' influence grew and their numbers increased throughout the entire Judea province. The number of dissenters was also growing throughout Samaria, although the two factions did not align with each other.

On one occasion, Barabbas met with Terach divulging, "My friend, more Jews are seeking to join our force because of the deplorable actions of the Roman procurators and the governor in Syria! We are establishing factions in more towns throughout Judea." The shepherd-turned-rebel guerilla fighter smiled at his friend and said, "It is most ironic that many in our ranks are Pharisees, rabbis, and men of good standing within the Jewish community. They even align with us shepherds whom they previously deemed outcasts."

Barabbas chuckled aloud over his last statement. "Imagine such elites fighting side by side with such despised shepherds!" He shook his head, adding, "Despite our shared fight against the Romans, we outcasts do not trust these other members of the Zealots. We remain wary of them and believe they would quickly betray our force should they be captured and tortured by the Romans."

Terach listened attentively as Barabbas relayed the developments that the nomad shepherds and others in remote regions of Judea did not know were taking place. When Barabbas sat down to eat the savory meal provided by Beulah, Terach finally had an opportunity to speak. "Barabbas I'm glad you are taking measures to protect yourself and the other outcasts of your group. Tell me, what is there I can do to assist your efforts?"

Barabbas wiped his hand over his mouth and his eyes darkened as he answered his friends query. "My friend, it is important you do not acknowledge having contact with me or other members of our band. Always be wary of the rabbis you encounter during your trek throughout Judea." Barabbas emphasized, "When in Jericho, you must be most attentive of spies—they can be anybody."

Slightly alarmed, Terach asked, "What about the Nigrid and Nicolas? Do you foresee them as being agents of the Romans against you?"

Barabbas quickly reassured him, "No, I really do not. I believe they will continue their official duties as ordained by the procurator. The Nigrid is one of the outcasts of the Jews and Nicolas is Greek; but both men are intent on making money. As you know, money knows no allegiance to anybody. Both these administrators are acquiring large sums for themselves and they will put politics and religion aside to amass their fortunes. They have no interest in helping Rome or anyone except themselves!"

This meeting marked the first time that Terach's sons, including the younger Mattan, were allowed to join the discussion with Barabbas. All of Terach's sons were very interested in the changes taking place and what impact they would have on their personal lifestyle. Mattan was the first to speak. "Barabbas, what are your plans now that the Zealots are gaining more influence throughout Judea?"

Barabbas smiled at the young man he considered to be a nephew. The rebel looked at his small audience, pleased with their interest, then directly at Mattan. "We are increasing our tactics against the trade caravans and the Roman outposts where the number of soldiers is small enough we can harass them. At the present time, the majority of rabbis throughout the towns of Judea approve of our methods." He winked and said, "They give us their support, and of course are very appreciative of the money we give them from the pillaging of the trade caravans and selling these goods."

Terach gave Barabbas the money obtained from the sale of his sheep and the by-products, and bid his friend farewell. He made sure Barabbas knew that he looked forward to their next meeting outside Bethlehem later in the year during the Feast of the Tabernacles.

Once Barabbas exited, Terach turned to his four sons. "We must be vigilant in not betraying Barabbas in any way. Control your lips at all times. Remember, the Romans will also punish us should they find out we have any dealings with these Zealots."

The shepherd father emphasized, "Before any of you decide to join these rebels, remember we have a great responsibility to God to care for the creatures He has entrusted to our care." He turned his attention to his youngest son and added, "Mattan, you are betrothed to Iza and soon will be a husband to a wife. You will be the last of my sons to take a wife. Your duty is to her. There will always be hostility between the Jews and the Romans. We cannot change that. They are too powerful for us, and I fear these Zealots will not overpower them. The Zealots are destined for failure—at what expense remains to be seen."

The sober reality of the times as taught by both Terach and Jesus Barabbas had a great impact on the thinking of

Terach's sons and the teen-aged Channah. Though there was much wondering in their minds, they felt no sense of doom.

Terach's offspring assured their father they had no intention of joining forces with the growing Zealots. They had no desire to further antagonize Rome with their presence and added labels of "outlaws" and "enemies to the empire."

The shepherd leader felt as if a great load of worry had been lifted off his shoulders as he heard their firm statements of intent. "Good. Now let us focus our efforts on our return trip to the south of Judea. We have a considerable distance to travel before the summer sun dries out the grass for our animals."

Before the family separated to go, Eitou spoke, "And remember, we must not be late for our youngest brother's wedding ceremony at Bethlehem! His father-in-law would be very angry and possibly whip all of us for embarrassing his fair daughter!"

Eitou's brothers as well as Terach laughed heartily. The fact of the matter was that each of the male family members were gratified that Mattan had been paired with a fine Jewish woman of character.

When Mattan had reached age twenty, Terach had begun the custom of selecting a suitable bride for his youngest son. After much research, he and Beulah reached the conclusion that the daughter of one of Bethlehem's established merchants would make Mattan a good wife. Her family did not despise shepherds and Terach had good business dealings with the father of Mattan's soon-to-be bride.

Per the custom of the time, Terach had approached Nadan to begin the shidduch, the matchmaking process. Because both men liked each other and had mutual respect for the other, the process was eased. In matchmaking, Jews relied on the character and intelligence of the parents of the proposed mate, believing that the offspring would inherit their qualities, as well as be ingrained and trained by their parents.

Nadan had been pleased that Terach approached him about matching Iza with Mattan. Several other fathers had also approached Nadan, but he had refused their offerings of marriage to his daughter. To the Jews of the time, marriage was about social, religious, and economic standing. Single young adults were not allowed to select their own marriage partner. The marriage agreement was not between two individuals, but between the two families.

The custom was for the fathers to agree on the matchmaking and establish the price of the dowry (mohar) to be paid to the father. The sum given to Nadan was fifty shekels. In addition, Mattan would give Iza the sum of fifty Roman denarii. The gift to Iza was a representation of Mattan's respect for her. The fifty shekels to Nadan was considered compensation, in that Nadan was losing a valuable member of his family who assisted his wife in all the household tasks.

Nadan often was ridiculed by the area's other prominent Jews for allowing his daughter to be betrothed to a nomad shepherd. The social and religious implications caused these prominent Jews to believe Nadan was crazy. They unkindly concluded such reckless behavior was motivated by Terach's wealth.

Regardless, once the agreement between Terach and Nadan was reached, the two young people were brought together in a bashow. It took place in the home of Nadan with all the family members. The purpose was to determine if Iza and Mattan would be compatible. After some socializing, the young couple went into a separate room to speak just between themselves.

For Mattan and Iza it was not an awkward moment. They had first met when Mattan was fourteen and Iza was eleven. Whenever Terach had business dealings with Nadan, Mattan usually tagged along. With his usual curiosity in full force, he wanted to learn how to conduct business matters. But he also wanted to see the pretty Iza. It was clear that Iza shared as much interest in Mattan that he had in her. However, now, even in their youthfulness, each knew that more than longtime friendliness would be required for a marriage arranged by their parents.

Despite their familiarity with each other, the young couple spent time asking pertinent questions dealing with spending the rest of their lives together. Mattan was both surprised and gratified to learn how serious and intelligent Iza was. He had known her sense of humor and it was much to his liking. But this conversation revealed much more about her.

Iza was impressed at Mattan's gentleness and respect towards her. This wasn't always the case in pre-arranged marriages. In fact, it was, sadly, not uncommon for a newly married couple to discover a dislike for each other that often intensified as the years wore on.

The time was well spent. Iza and Mattan were each confident their marriage would be similar to that of their parents. It would be one of mutual respect, love, and compassion, as well as passion.

Once the bashow was finished, it was customary for the parents to announce the betrothal within four days, which at this time would make it the day before the weekly Sabbath celebration. It was a time to share this happy milestone with family and friends. The betrothal ceremony was very short. Mattan approached Nadan while everyone else stood to the side, looking on. Mattan bowed in respect to his elder and said, "I come to your house, Nadan, for you to give me your daughter Iza as my wife. Let me find favor in your eyes."

Nadan looked with approval for Mattan and answered simply, "Mattan, you have favor with me and my wife."

In the customary manner, Mattan completed the ceremony by saying, "Iza is my wife and I am her husband from this day and forever."

Iza was now legally married to Mattan. But according to the custom of the day, she would remain living in her father's house until sufficient time had elapsed for her to move in with her new husband. That time would be when the nomad shepherd had returned to Bethlehem just before the Feast of the Tabernacles.

Mattan was anxious to begin the journey and to end the year's long delay before he could return to his new wife. Terach enjoyed seeing Mattan's reaction whenever Iza's name was mentioned. He grinned when Mattan's face flushed with embarrassment overt being teased about being a husband. Channah, however, had mixed emotions. She was both happy and irritated with the marriage of her older brother. Her childhood adoration of her favorite brother remained intact as the two grew older, and she felt possessive of his attention. Channah did not joke about Mattan being a husband. She knew her relationship with her favorite brother was changing, and it made her sad.

With the memory of the betrothal ceremony fresh in his mind, Terach stood outside his tent early in the morning and breathed deeply of the crisp fall air. He smiled at Beulah and Channah who stood at the entrance of their tent. Terach turned his attention to his assembled sons and instructed them, "Go to your flocks and tell the hirelings it is time we begin our journey to Jericho and beyond."

Each of the sons eagerly rode off in the direction of their respective flocks. Terach watched them and turned to Beulah with a sigh. "My dear, sweet wife, suddenly I feel old. Soon it will be Channah who becomes betrothed."

A bemused Beulah chuckled and gently rubbed the strong back of her husband. She said softly, "My beloved, we both are growing old, but the Lord gives us favor as well as our family."

After the long arduous journey, the combined sheep caravans arrived at the hills outside of Jericho. The normal business haggling began. This time, Terach allowed his sons to be part of the negotiations. To his surprise and fatherly pride, his youngest son proved to be a savvy negotiator with the Nigrid. The elder Terach was completely satisfied at how well things went, and he made preparations for the next phase of their journey.

Terach informed Beulah before the departure, "I must make one more trip to Jericho and meet with the Nigrid. I will meet you and Channah on the road after you take down our home." Terach swung up on the saddle and turned the reins toward the economic hub of northern Judea.

Business matters with the Nigrid did not take long, and Terach easily caught up with the caravan of his family. There were twenty tent homes that comprised the encampment of the nomad shepherd's family and hirelings. It was the duty of the women to take down the tents and fold them, and place them on the two-wheel carts used specifically for transporting their mobile homes during wanderings.

Each cart was pulled by a single mule and was easy to direct. Older women and young children rode in the front of the cart while those in the prime of life usually walked beside. Terach, always looking for better ways to do things, had constructed his carts in such a manner that everyone could ride, increasing the distance that could be traveled in a day.

The innovative shepherd went to the lead cart and greeted Beulah and Channah. "My, you two are the loveliest women I've seen all day." Beulah smiled but did not turn her head towards her admirer. She lifted her chin and calmly replied, "You have great eyesight for a lowly shepherd. What is the purpose of your flattery?"

Terach smiled. He always enjoyed these little games with his wife. "Obviously, to win your heart. If you have a husband, I will approach him and purchase you and make you the queen of my house." Beulah tried, but couldn't suppress another smile, and it was all Channah could do to keep from giggling.

"I'm afraid it will be too costly for you, a mere shepherd, to buy me. My husband considers me to be of great value. It would probably take ten years of your shepherd earnings before he would even consider such an offer," said the animated Beulah.

"Ah, oh lovely vision; you underestimate my wealth! I could easily pay whatever price your husband demands!"

Beulah turned to Terach with sparkling eyes and said, "Then approach my husband and be prepared for a wondrous gift from God."

Terach shouted out his laughter as he leaned over his horse toward his fair maiden. Beulah leaned towards Terach and the two kissed with obvious affection. It was a difficult maneuver but the two lovers had accomplished it many times. Terach reverted to matters at hand and let Beulah know the plan. "We shall make camp three miles ahead. I will inform our sons and the hirelings to secure their flocks when they get past the hills they are going through. Tonight our sons and the hirelings must remain with the herd. I am concerned about bandits and predators in this region."

Beulah understood, and Channah admired her father as he turned back towards his flocks. The young girl, who now had reached puberty, hoped that one day when Terach would be approached by fathers of eligible bachelors, the man selected for her would be just like her father.

Mattan was the last shepherd Terach instructed about securing his flock for the night. "Mattan, I want you to make sure the pregnant ewes are away from these hills. In the open area, you and the dogs will be better suited to see any predators and will deal with them easier."

The young shepherd replied, "I have a section in mind. It is far enough away from the hills, yet the grass is fresh and the ewes will eat well for their babies."

Terach's had deliberately left Mattan until last. He desired to converse with his youngest son, now a young man, a shepherd, and a husband. "My son, I have decided to change our route back to the south. You can have your wedding ceremony sooner."

To the surprise of the elder shepherd, Mattan shook his head. "No, Father, we must stay our normal course. We know the grass on our regular route will be fresh, green, and full of nutrients. The pregnant ewes need it to give birth to healthy lambs. My wedding ceremony can wait. Both Nadan and Iza know the life of a shepherd. They have accepted its terms."

The elder shepherd leader placed his burly left hand on Mattan's strong young shoulder and looked affectionately at his young son. "Mattan, you indeed are a shepherd and your heart is to care for the flock before yourself. I am proud of you."

Terach carefully reached into a pouch behind the saddle, withdrew a smaller pouch, and handed it to his son. "This is some food for your enjoyment through this night." Terach noticed the sun was dipping towards the horizon. He sniffed the air and looked up at the clouds. "There should be no rain this night, but it will be colder. Find sufficient shelter for yourself. I shall be back tomorrow."

The elder shepherd leader climbed aboard his stallion and gestured farewell to his youngest son, urging the horse towards the encampment that was being set up.

The band of nearly six hundred pregnant ewes was easily herded to the area designated for the night's rest. Mattan's fifteen Canaan breed dogs were quick to get the drove of temperamental sheep and goats settled down for the evening. The ewes shifted their unease from the impending storm and happily indulged in the sweet fresh grass.

The dogs wove their way throughout the flock, trained as they were to inspect the animals for signs of early birth, possible injury, or illness, anything that would signal a need for their master to remedy. Mattan also made his way through part of the flock doing what his trained canines did. After nearly forty-five minutes of inspection, Mattan turned and made his way to the base of a small knoll that would protect him from wind.

Mattan's aba, his outer garment, was made of camel's hair. It was beginning to be too small for him now that he had attained his full manly height and weight. Nonetheless he was thankful for it being waterproof and warm enough to serve as a blanket. He pulled out the pouch his father had given him, and inspected its contents. There was ample bread, cheese, dried fruit, olives, and a surprise honey cake. He smiled at the thoughtfulness of his mother who had prepared the meal.

The young shepherd ate half the meal and saved the rest for his early morning breakfast. He curled up against the base of the knoll and let his mind drift to thoughts of his upcoming wedding ceremony. In his heart he knew Iza would make a good wife and he was immensely pleased that his father and Nadan were of the same mind and had so readily agreed.

Mattan's final thoughts of the night were that he would become the best shepherd of all of Terach's sons and would pass along the family tradition to his sons. He prayed to God for His grace to allow this to happen, then floated away into a deep, peaceful sleep.

Hours later, he was awakened by the barking of one of his Canaan dogs. Groggy, the young shepherd shook his head to clear his thoughts. He stood up and stretched his arms as he headed toward the sound of his sheepdog.

The sun had barely risen above the horizon and shadows still enveloped the landscape. He moved quickly in response to the barking pleas of the sheepdog. As he came closer to the commotion, he immediately recognized the protective stance of the pregnant ewes. They had gathered together in a tight circle facing outward in the direction from which the barking was heard. The other sheepdogs positioned themselves at intervals on the outside of the circle, protecting the animals and keeping them in check. The dogs were persistent, snarling at some unseen intruder.

Mattan quickened his pace, realizing the sheepdog was reacting to a predator had either downed one of the pregnant ewes or was about to attack one. As he hurried towards the threatened sheep, he withdrew his sling from his leather scrip that housed the smooth stones for such an occasion.

His heart was pounding, and Mattan suddenly stopped and peered straight ahead. His sheepdog was fearlessly facing the predator. Its front legs were at shoulder width apart. The protector's hind legs were slightly bent. Its tail was curled in anticipation of battle with the marauder. Mattan's sharp eyes saw a black silhouette in a threatening pose in the dim light. Despite the shroud of grayness, Mattan quickly identified the threat. It was a wolf. It was approximately twenty-five yards ahead of him.

Mattan could see it was a very large wolf. Larger than most he had seen in his young life. Wolves were common to the region, especially now that increased activity of Roman soldier patrols had driven away the once-dreaded lions. In addition to the dispersal of the lions, even bears had left the region for less populated areas and more hidden spaces far away from the Roman soldiers.

The fact this now dominant predator was alone meant one of two things. Either it was an advance scout or a rogue not allowed to be part of the main pack. No matter. In either case, it was on the prowl seeking food.

The predator took note of the human defender interfering with its targeted prey. It slowly backed a short distance away to better assess the situation. While it carefully retreated, its yellow eyes were riveted on the movement of the shepherd-now-turned-hunter. As the animal turned to escape, it took two strides before it felt a searing pain in its right hind leg. It lurched to the ground with a loud groan, much to the delight of the camp dogs.

The 200-pound Syrian wolf regained its upright stance and took another painful step, but once again felt the sharp impact of a stone. This time the stone from Mattan's sling penetrated deeply through the wolf's outer layer of long hair and proceeded through the second shorter insulating layer. It ended its trajectory in the wolf's pelvis near the top of its hind leg. Mattan's powerful throw had resulted in the stone breaking part of the pelvis bone, and it remained lodged in a combination of bone and muscle tissue.

This time the wolf's cry was louder, and was answered with victorious howling from the dogs. In its struggle to escape the shepherd, the wolf dropped low to the ground and began to creep away from its attacker. It managed to reach a large rock without being hit again by another missile from the sling. In less than one minute, Mattan had reloaded his sling three times and shot the smooth stones successfully towards his target. Mattan's years of practice and highly developed skill had paid off.

Safely behind the rock, the wolf painfully turned and looked back towards the victor. Its keen eyesight scanned the form of the missile launcher. It lifted its nose. Two hundred million olfactory cells inside its nose gave the wolf a reference point for its defense. From previous experience, he knew the scent was human.

Its deep yellow piercing eyes honed in on Mattan. The wolf's ears twitched from side to side, determining that the alerted Canaan dog was not pursuing its distant cousin. The wolf was intently observing the actions of the human and his dog. In defense, it perpetually snarled, exposing its fangs. The injured wolf had made up its mind to seek revenge on its attacker and finish its earlier mission of obtaining food. Somehow it mustered strength and disappeared temporarily into the long shadows.

When the wolf disappeared, Mattan thanked his sheepdog for its alertness. Together man and dog went about inspecting the area where the wolf was first spotted. There was no carcass of a sheep and no signs of blood. No sign that the wolf had dragged a dead or injured ewe away. Apparently no loss.

Satisfied there was no harm to any of his ewes, the young shepherd went about calming the rattled band. His efforts were reinforced by the protective actions of his sheepdogs. Soon the ewes calmed down, but they remained in their tight circle. They remained wary of an impending attack.

Mattan noted the reaction of the ewes and knew he wasn't done with the wolf. The sheep evidently smelled the presence of the wolf. He took a sip of water and ate a morsel of his breakfast while his eyes shifted back and forth to the area where he had last seen the wolf. The shepherd knew he had severely injured the marauder, but also knew an injured predator remained a viable threat.

Cautiously, the shepherd stepped forward to be at the front of where the tight band of ewes had made their circle. His hand retained a firm grip on his myrtle wood rod. The three-inch diameter piece of wood was very strong. A length of nearly five feet and a twelve-inch wooden globe atop the shaft made the rod an effective weapon with sharp nails impregnated in the globe.

In addition to the rod, Mattan had a Roman short sword sheathed at his left side. It was a gift from his father who insisted each of his sons and hirelings carry it rather than the traditional small knife most shepherds wore. Terach learned of the versatility of these short swords from Roman soldiers in Jericho. He was impressed with its potential use. The sword's double-sided sharpness provided sixteen inches of death to any would-be attacker.

In his heart, Mattan believed it was just a matter of time before the wolf would return, but he felt ready for such an event. His body remained tense and alert to any unexpected sound or movement that wasn't normal.

The shepherd's mind flashed to his role model, David, and the stories of how as a shepherd boy he had slain several predators prior to killing the giant Goliath. These thoughts helped Mattan remain calm and poised for the imminent battle that he expected would take place.

Twenty minutes later, a shuffling of the tight circle of ewes announced the arrival of the wolf. The sheepdogs began to grumble, and their tails curled in expectation of an approaching battle. They dug their paws into the soft grassy soil for a base to spring forward at any given moment. Mattan's eyes began searching the morning landscape that the rising sun had sufficiently illuminated, transforming the early morning shadows into highlighted details.

The shepherd detected slight movement to his right and he turned for a better view. Slinking close to the ground and attempting to stay hidden by the rocks and flora was the large injured wolf. Mattan's eyes followed every movement of the deadly predator. He faced the assailant straight on and saw intimidating yellow eyes fixed on him. He heard the snarl and saw the long fangs, signaling a battle was imminent.

Slowly, he unsheathed his Roman short sword, gripping it firmly in his right hand. He held the stout wooden rod in his left hand and began taking slow deep breaths.

The wolf was observing his opponent and assessing how it could defeat its nemesis in spite of its severe injuries. The animal's ears repeatedly moved in an effort to detect any approaching interference from the dogs. The rogue wolf's unblinking eyes searched for an opening to eliminate the human who had inflicted injury and thwarted its mission. The wolf peered at Mattan and slowly shifted its position more to the left.

After advancing approximately five yards, the wolf stopped, hidden behind some dense bushes. From there, the would-be assassin waited to see what its enemy would do. The angered animal snarled, again uncovering its lethal fangs. The yellow eyes glared at its target.

Mattan was fully aware of the wolf's movement, but he did not change his position to alert the wolf. With the wolf secured among the bushes, the shepherd carefully eased back towards the rock outcropping behind him that could protect him and provide a fortress to stand on. There were numerous smaller rocks around the bigger ones, and Mattan was confident they would not pose a problem in his defense. In one swift motion, Mattan jumped atop the fortress and prepared himself for the ensuing charge from the wolf.

The young shepherd believed the four-foot height of the rock fortress was high enough that the injured wolf would not have power to jump there and knock him down. This would potentially give him the deciding edge against his adversary. As an enticement, Mattan stood erect in a confident pose, facing the bushes where the wolf was hidden. The death dance was now well-staged.

Without warning, the black monster shot out from among the bushes directly towards its target, the shepherd. The charging wolf bared its fangs, snarling viciously at its intended prey. The jaws, with 200 pounds of pressure per square inch, were on full horrifying display. It halted a short distance from the outcropping, in full view.

Mattan could easily see that despite its injury, his furious combatant was successfully relying on its three healthy legs for speed and power. Their eyes locked on each other, and the wolf's yellowish eyes blazed with ferocity and anger. The animal's head remained steady and pointed directly at the human's throat.

With a noticeable groan the snarling attacker leaped forward, with saliva shooting out its mouth and forepaws stretched, seeking to push its prey down. The wolf had no way of completely knowing the weakness in its right hindquarters. When it made its leap of death, it was with less power than it normally relied on to incapacitate its prey.

Weakness and excruciating pain caused the front legs of the wolf to spread wider than normal. It pawed at the air with its toes and claws as it desperately sought to regain its balance. Its prey had now turned its body and the human's left shoulder was pointed at the wolf's chest. In so doing, Mattan slightly crouched, bending his knees and placing his left foot forward.

The attacker still managed to leap up the four feet where Mattan stood poised for the onslaught. As the snarling wolf came within a foot of Mattan, the shepherd thrust the spiked top of his rod at the open mouth of the attacker. The wolf immediately bit down hard on the myrtle wood shaft and the back four canines used for crushing bone into tiny pieces sunk into the wood so deep, they prevented any release. The immense power of the animal's jaws broke part of the spiked globe away from the shaft. Mattan lost his grip on the rod, and briefly lost his balance. But he had been waiting for this moment when the chest of the animal was fully exposed.

As the wolf lunged upward, the shepherd thrust the blade of his short sword until the hilt fully compressed the long outer layer of fur with the shorter inner layer. There was a muffled gasp from the throat of the attacker and its yellow eyes widened, but the piercing intimidating glare was no more. The blade of the Roman short sword cut through the animal's heart, severing it into two pieces.

The wolf was dead.

But the momentum of the charge against Mattan had caused the shepherd to lose his balance atop his rock fortress. Man and animal went tumbling backward down the rock outcropping and the shepherd struck the back of his head on one of the rocks at the base of the fortress. As both he and the dead wolf continued their awkward tumble, the young shepherd's head turned and struck another sharp rock.

In less than three minutes the battle was over. The wolf lay on its back with the handle of the short sword sticking triumphantly skyward in the early morning crisp spring air. The wolf's coarse tongue hung lifeless out the side of its mouth. Parts of the myrtle wood globe top of the rod were stuck in the roof of the wolf's mouth. Its yellow eyes were now dulled with death. The once regal dominant predator was nothing more than a heap of dead flesh that vultures and scavengers would eagerly visit.

Mattan lay motionless within one foot of the dead combatant to his right. After an uncertain time following the death bout, he was able to place his right hand on the ground to steady himself. With an involuntary groan, he slowly drew up his left leg, and grunted as he attempted to raise his body up, struggling to fight off pain from the brief combat.

Once upright, the shepherd held his arms out wide to steady his balance. He wobbled two steps and fell down to his knees. Slowly, the shepherd teetered at half mast, and then slumped to the ground with a loud thud. Before Mattan felt the grassy plain beneath him, he was unconscious.

His shepherd's aba and tunic were stained with blood— his own and the wolf's. The tight circle of ewes did not disband. They and the dogs remained eerily silent, wondering at the carnage of the battlefield. All of the well-trained sheepdogs hovered protectively close to the flock, sticking out at intervals like cream-colored barbs waiting to impact any new intruder. One lone dog cautiously made his way to the motionless combatants, sniffing the air. The dog was a favorite of Mattan who had raised it from a pup.

He detected both life and death, but when he placed his nose close to Mattan, the dog realized life emanated from his master. He gently licked away some of the blood on Mattan's face and howled his announcement to the other dogs and the flock. Then he settled down next to his limp master and waited for the hoped-for return of life. His protective and loyal instinct prepared to offer its own life for his master.

At the time Mattan first encountered the lone wolf two miles from his brothers, Gavriel and one of his hirelings also battled two wolves that were part of the same pack, working another hunting ground. The slings of the brothers had successfully launched stone missiles and rendered the wolves helpless. The men had disposed of the threat and quickly cut the throats of the two would-be attackers.

Gavriel knew that his younger brother could be in trouble if more wolves patrolled the region, which was usually the case. He ran to his stallion and swung up on the saddle to hurry his Arabian mount in Mattan's direction. Gavriel dug his heels deep into the flanks of his stallion and the horse ran with all its might toward the grazing area of the pregnant ewes.

The distance between the two bands was approximately two and three quarters miles and the swift, sure-footed stallion covered the firm ground in less than four minutes.

When he arrived at Mattan's flock, Gavriel witnessed the huddled sheep and goats along with the Canaan sentry dogs peering in his direction. The older shepherd suddenly saw with horror two silent forms lying on the ground.

Gavriel audibly gasped. In a second he was off his horse, through the grasses, and over the rocks to where the two bodies lay. Mattan's short sword handle pointing skyward spoke of his brother's battlefield bravery and success. As Gavriel looked down at his cataleptic brother he could see dried blood that had oozed out of a wound on the right side of his head. With trembling hands, the older brother called, "Mattan, Mattan, are you all right?" Without waiting for a reply, Gavriel demanded urgently, "Speak to me, brother!" Mattan remained silent.

The older brother tenderly lifted Mattan by the shoulders and discovered more dried blood from behind his head. Gavriel took note there were no bite or claw marks on his younger brother's face or body. The older brother breathed a sigh of relief, and gave God thanks for His grace. He lifted the upper portion of Mattan's body up and rested it against a large boulder.

Mattan's head hung downward and Gavriel deftly inspected his brother for broken bones and was glad to find none. He quickly retrieved a small leather water pouch from his horse and used some water to wash away the dried blood on Mattan's face. Softly, he spoke to Mattan, but still received no response.

Gavriel put a small portion of water to his brother's lips. Once again, he attempted to get Mattan's attention, but to no avail. After several more verbal urgings, Mattan slowly raised his head, which Gavriel gently placed against the rock where Mattan was propped.

The older brother was greatly relieved as the younger shepherd began to regain consciousness. After considerable time,

Gavriel determined Mattan was capable of being moved, so he put Mattan's left arm around his neck. Gavriel shuffled the short distance from the rock to where Gavriel's stallion waited.

Tearfully, he was able to lift Mattan up and drape him across the saddle. The Arabian stallion dutifully accepted the burden without flinching or resisting. Once Mattan was secured across the saddle, Gavriel climbed aboard and headed for the base camp where there would be help.

The distance was approximately four miles and the nervous, shaken Gavriel, his brother, and the Canaan dog arrived safely late in the afternoon.

Channah was outside, pounding the tent ropes securely into the ground when she heard the sound of the approaching horseman. She stood still, placed her hand to her forehead as a visor, and studied the incoming rider. She recognized her older brother and smiled and waved to him. But then, as he quickly approached, her smile turned to mortification. She saw the limp body of Mattan across the horse and feared the worst.

Shaking, she assisted Gavriel in carrying the unconscious body of her brother into the family tent. Beulah's expression of horror and deep concern mirrored Channah's. The three family members placed the limp body of Mattan on a sleeping pad.

Beulah trembled as she attempted to contain her emotions and surveyed the situation. Without hesitation, the distraught mother instructed Channah, "Tell one of the hirelings to return to Jericho and have a doctor come quickly." She turned to Gavriel who naturally detected his mother's anguish. "Go to Terach. He is ahead of our base camp about four miles, inspecting the grasslands."

Both siblings departed the tent on their urgent errands. The hireling rode the four miles to Jericho atop one of the mules used for pulling the cart with the family tents. Gavriel grabbed another mule and rode towards his father. A hireling tended to the exhausted Arabian stallion.

In a daze, Beulah got some water and proceeded to wash the dried blood from her youngest son's face and from the back of his head. She took off the aba and replaced the blood-stained tunic with a fresh, clean one. Her tender actions were what any mother would do, though every mother hoped it would never actually have to take place. Now she sat next to Mattan, looking down at his ashen face, and did what she hated most to do.

She waited.

Chapter 10

A nearly equal distance from the base encampment to Jericho and from the tent to where Terach was inspecting grasslands resulted in Terach arriving at the same time as the doctor from Jericho to attend to the injured Mattan.

Terach nervously stood by while the doctor examined his new patient. His stomach was in turmoil and his breathing shallow as he looked at his youngest son. This was a moment he wished could be reversed, and the realization that it could not, made his angst worse. Terach and Beulah held hands and did not speak as they intently watched the doctor inspect Mattan's wounds.

Within a few minutes the doctor stood up and spoke to the anguishing parents, and to Channah and Gavriel. "Your son will live. He has two puncture wounds to his head, no doubt from the rocks you said he hit during his battle with the wolf. I have bandaged both wounds and you must inspect them daily. He should regain consciousness later this day. When he does, make sure he drinks plenty of water. He will likely feel dizzy and may have headaches. Do not allow him to return to his duties until he no longer experiences dizziness."

As the doctor spoke, Terach put his right arm around Beulah, and Channah pressed into his left side for comfort. Gavriel stood next to Beulah and the foursome listened carefully to the doctor's instructions. They were the usual for that time in dealing with a head injury. "We will do as you say," Beulah promised in a resolute voice.

The doctor made one final statement, "I do not foresee your son not living a normal life. He is strong, young, and with God's help should return to a normal shepherd's life." The doctor moved past the concerned family and left the tent for his return to Jericho. What the doctor did not state was how little the medical community really knew about head injuries at the time, especially internal head injuries. It was fairly common for people who sustained medium to severe head trauma to die within a short time after their event. Those who survived often became disabled and led a life of begging in the major cities.

But within three days, Mattan was back to his normal self. He relayed his deadly encounter with the wolf and learned how Gavriel and his hirelings also slew two other members of the same pack. Gavriel said to his younger brother, "When we removed the hides from the predators, we also slit open their bellies and inspected the contents. There were no signs of sheep or goat but some remains of wild hare. I believe the wolf you killed, Mattan, was old and an outcast from the pack."

As Gavriel spoke, Mattan and Terach listened attentively. "Sheep and goats are much easier to kill than wild animals, and I believe these three wolves were looking for a quick meal as substitute for their failures in killing anything other than a wild hare."

Terach agreed with Gavriel's suspicion. "We are still close enough to the many hills surrounding Jericho that these wild pillagers likely came from dens they established there. This time of year there is plenty of sheep and goats due to our pilgrimage to Jericho for Passover. In addition to us, there are other nomad shepherds these wild raiders can attack."

Mattan said nothing, but his mind flashed to the face of the wolf, the blazing yellow eyes of fury, its intense stare, the exposed fangs, the drooling, and the snarling emitted by his advisary. He inwardly shuddered at the thought that the rest of his life there would be times when he would once again see that same face of evil. The young shepherd wondered if his role model David ever felt the same dread.

During Mattan's recovery, the flocks caught up with the base camp and moved ahead. Once Mattan was capable of returning to his flock of pregnant ewes, he did so with renewed purpose. The women moved the tent city forward. From their original site near Jaba, the caravan of wool, milk, cheese, and meat turned southeast and meandered throughout the rich spring grasslands, following close to the west bank of the upper Dead Sea as they headed toward Jerusalem. Normally, the caravan would stay close to the Dead Sea, which they did, with a dual purpose—determining if Mattan could handle the daily rigors of shepherd life.

By the time the flocks and herds arrived in Bethlehem, Mattan had fully recovered from his nearly fatal encounter with the rogue predator. Nothing about the frightening event was mentioned to either Nadan or to Iza. They focused on happier events—the wedding ceremony.

Nadan had everything arranged by the time the newly acquired family announced their arrival. Per the custom of the time there was a colorful procession of both families through the main section of Bethlehem. The sound of tambourines and rams' horns joyfully heralded the union of wedlock. The procession included friends of both Terach and Nadan and proceeded out of Bethlehem to where the tent city was located. Notably, there were those who did not partake in the celebration—the rabbis, scribes, Pharisee trainees, and others who sought their favor and held tightly to their disdain of shepherds.

The parents and the bride and the groom traveled the celebratory mile in an elaborate cart festooned with flowers. The oxen pulling the cart also wore glorious garlands around their necks. Their horns were painted elaborately for the occasion. The other family members and friends rode either in carts or on mules. The religious leaders of Bethlehem were beside themselves, grumbling that Terach was trampling on Jewish tradition, using rituals they should not be allowed to do because of their outcast status within the proper Jewish community. Terach didn't think twice about his supposed violation. He had decided long ago to disregard religious criticism over man-made rules.

Arriving at the tent city, Mattan was surprised when Terach directed him to a new tent made especially for the newlyweds. "My son, your mother and I gift this tent to you and your bride. My father did the same for Beulah and myself."

Mattan smiled at Terach and placed both hands on his father's shoulders and said, "Thank you, Father, for your gift. I shall honor you with my actions by making this home a place for God. We will welcome you and our entire family members with open arms." His father pulled Mattan close and tightly hugged his youngest son in whom he was well pleased.

Terach returned to the smiling procession while Mattan stood inside his father's provision, waiting for his bride. Nadan escorted Iza to her new home. Terach and Beulah walked behind Nadan and Iza's mother. At the entrance to the tent, Nadan called out the traditional summons to the groom. Mattan replied by inviting them in. Once inside, Nadan took Iza's hand and offered it to Mattan who bowed slightly and took it tenderly in his. Nadan beamed proudly and said, "Your wife is ready to make your home comfortable."

Next came the customary signing of the marriage agreement to give Iza equal rights with Mattan. Iza could have her own property, and retain possession of the wedding gifts from Mattan. They were hers to manage. She could dispose of her property and these gifts as she pleased. The marriage agreement contained a newly implemented provision that Iza could also divorce Mattan. Before the Jews settled in Judea, only the male could file divorce action against the wife. Despite some new leniency, women still were prohibited from attending some of the sacred feasts, could not vote or hold public office, and were restricted to certain parts of the temple.

After the marriage agreement was signed, a boisterous and sumptuous feast began that lasted throughout the day and well into the evening. Throughout the festivities, a separate and private reason for celebration was being lavishly enjoyed by Terach and his immediate family. They were rejoicing and praising God for His grace that had revived Mattan from his head injury and that he could now lead a normal life again.

After the shift in season, the shepherds again headed east past Marsaba to Ein Fashkah, then south down the coastline of the Dead Sea. The journey was slow and deliberate. It was weeks later that the flocks and the tent city finally arrived at the outskirts of Masada.

The rich spring grasses added much needed weight to the sheep and the goats. For Mattan, he was pleased to see the pregnant ewes were getting bags that would soon be filled with white gold—milk for the lambs when they arrived.

Mattan and Iza settled into life with each other, and each day was one of sharing and learning. Many times it was difficult for Iza to adapt to the ways and the life of a shepherd. Having grown up in Bethlehem's town environment, life on the plains was foreign to her. But all concerns of Terach, Beulah, and other family members dissipated as Iza appeared eager and willing to assume her new demanding duties.

Channah took every opportunity to assist her new sister-in-law in learning how to be a shepherd's wife. The teenager liked Iza and enjoyed the times she and Iza could talk and share their views about many things. The surrogate mother to Mattan had adopted a happier attitude toward her brother's marriage, now that she was enjoying Iza's friendship. She enjoyed showing

Iza things that assisted her, and she was relieved that Iza's addition to the family was a positive one.

From Masada west to the Mediterranean Sea city of Gaza, the fertile valley widened. Terach alternated the route of his droves of sheep and goats. The path became a zigzagging journey which took up most of the hotter summer days. The mobile city of animals and people had entered Idumea, which was still under the jurisdiction of the procurator, way north in Caesarea.

To the people who inhabited this vast lush region, Roman politics wasn't an issue. Life went on as it had for centuries prior to the Roman iron fist of control. However, their religious differences had far greater impact on inhabitants of the towns and cities, and travelers to the region.

On one occasion when the shepherds arrived outside the southern part of Beer-Sheba, Iza was personally confronted with religious bias against shepherds. She, Channah, and Beulah went to the city to the local markets for fresh food and other supplies that had been depleted by the long journey from Jericho.

One market vendor refused to sell to the women because they were shepherds' wives. A shocked Iza commented to Channah, "I do not believe we are refused service and treated like inferiors simply because we are shepherds."

Channah merely shrugged her shoulders and replied, "It has been this way ever since our ancestors exited Egypt. The Egyptians taught our people to hate those who God favored. When the Pharisees and the Sadducees gained religious control over our people, they continued the Egyptian hatred for nomads of any kind. We can do nothing about it. But we find ways around such prejudice," she concluded cheerily.

"These people make me feel unclean despite the fact I know in my heart I'm not who they say I am. I had no idea it was this way," Iza murmured.

Channah gave her new sister-in-law a hard look but softly stated, "Iza, it is the same way in Bethlehem and throughout Judea wherever the Sanhedrin have great influence."

Iza was dumbfounded. "I never encountered such open hostility. My family was accepted in society, so I assumed no such unfairness existed."

Channah understood Iza. "Of course you did, Iza. You witnessed it many times; it only became an issue when you and Mattan were matched by our fathers. Once that took place, proper Jewish society then put the same mark on you that it has on us. When you return to Bethlehem, don't be surprised should

127

your family have less social standing." Iza looked at the ground, contemplating this possibility.

The flocks resumed their trek by proceeding north of Beer-Sheba for three days. They headed west along the border of Idumea and onward, north to their destination of Gaza. Throughout the land, God's grace was felt in the lushness of the grass, the fair weather, and no hindrance from robbers or predators.

Earlier when the horde of sheep, goats, and men were encamped at Masada, Mattan began to experience changes within himself that worried him, but he kept them private. He had recurring headaches and pain so intense it caused him to gasp when he moved his eyes. There was also unusual sensitivity to changes in light. Inwardly, Mattan suspected these changes resulted from his death battle with the wolf. He told no one, not even his new wife.

At times, Mattan felt throbbing pressure around his eyes, and only found relief when he lay down on his bed mat. He remained able to tend to his flock of ewes, but was concerned about the upcoming lambing season that would occur around the time they reached Beer-Sheba. More and more frequently, when his headaches occurred, he had to dismount his horse and sit motionless until the pain subsided. His concern grew as the headaches increased, as did the amount of time required to recover from them.

For non-nomadic shepherds, normal lambing season took place in December or January. Terach developed a system that produced two lambing seasons. The shepherd leader passed his methodology on to other nomad shepherds. The results were two lambing seasons, mainly due to the adherence of their routes that provided better grass and other feed for the Awassi breed of sheep.

When ewes ate good nutrient feed, it produced an abundant fat supply that transferred to their milk. Portions of the fat also deposited in their fat tail, and that reserve gave them needed energy when drier conditions developed.

For all of his life, Mattan had witnessed the two lambing seasons and almost took it for granted. Now that he was older and becoming established as a shepherd, he did not take the succulent grass for granted. He was grateful Terach had taught both him and his brothers about determining where the better grasses were located.

At Beer-Sheba the lambing took place as it normally did, and Mattan was the lead shepherd in making sure the pregnant ewes, both sheep and goats, delivered their offspring safely. Out of over six hundred pregnant ewes, eighty percent had twins that were robust and healthy. Only three percent of the pregnant ewes delivered stillborn lambs. This was a major accomplishment for the time. Terach was sure that it was God's grace and blessing to them, and openly praised God for his success. He was greatly pleased how well his youngest son had developed skills in handling the ewes. It was a great responsibility to care for the ewes, and Mattan's reputation rose steadily above others through his consistent management.

During the deliveries of the lambs, Mattan's reoccurring headaches were not improving, and he experienced additional problems along with those he had earlier. His side vision became very restricted; he had a loss of night vision and diminished ability to see in dimly lit environments. The shepherd also noticed that his color vision was becoming eroded. He grew more alarmed, yet he dared not share his fear or these developments with anyone.

In addition to the physical symptoms he was experiencing, Mattan also had a recurring dream that was both disturbing and perplexing. The dream was dramatic, consisting only of two different sets of eyes. One pair of eyes belonged to the demonic wolf. The yellow blazing eyes seemed to penetrate deep into his mind. The other pair of eyes was entirely different. It was those of the baby Jesus when he gazed at them for the first time in the manger.

The two sets of eyes in his dream alternated, coming into focus, and then fading backward away from Mattan's eyes. The yellow blazing eyes were large, glaring, evil, and glowed hideously. Their presence made Mattan feel cold, anxious, and insecure. Producing a dramatic difference were the eyes of the infant Jesus from so long ago, surrounded by warm, penetrating light that made Mattan feel comfortable, safe, secure, and loved.

During this recurring dream, it seemed to Mattan the two vastly different set of eyes were battling each other for control over him. The two sets of eyes revolved around him, shifting their dominating positions rapidly as they whirled. The intensity of the dream always awakened Mattan suddenly. He would sit up abruptly, breathing heavily, sometimes sweating. He would look over to where Iza lay, but invariably saw that she was sound asleep, sometimes snoring.

He was grateful his dreams did not awaken her. He would sit for a few minutes with his knees drawn up and his head couched between his forearms that rested on his knees. Mattan would take a few deep breaths and wait for his heart to stop racing before he would lie back down. The majority of the time he returned to sleep. But when sleep did not mercifully return, he would lie on his back, staring up at the ceiling of hides, and wrestle with the meaning of his frustrating dream. It was a deeply unsettling time for the young shepherd.

During the day while tending to the flock, he attempted to decipher his recurring dream. Always he was stymied, which only fueled his irritation. The disturbing dream dance and his efforts to find its meaning were a private torment.

A week after the lambing, the small itinerant tent town broke camp. Mattan and Terach inspected the ewes and their new offspring and determined the lambs were robust enough for their journey to Jericho. "Mattan, you have done an excellent job in caring for the pregnant ewes. I could not have done better had I been involved. My trust in your ability grows with each day. You are becoming a good shepherd."

Terach's words of praise lifted Mattan's spirits, but only somewhat comforted his concern over his eyesight issues. "Thank you, Father, for your kind words. I know you would not say them unless I did abide by what you have taught me. I vow to continue to learn and hopefully someday will be as good as you."

Terach gently put his right hand on Mattan's shoulder and smiled broadly. "There is no doubt, my son, that one day soon, you will be every bit the shepherd you want to become." Terach relished the idea that when he grew old, became infirm, and died, that Mattan would perfectly continue the legacy Terach's forefathers had established.

When the mass of nearly four thousand sheep, and eight hundred goats, plus seventy humans arrived just south of Gaza, the sense of achievement was clouded by Mattan's worsened condition. He no longer could conceal his eyesight issues. First Iza, then Terach, noticed apparent deterioration in Mattan's perception. He stumbled, not being able to accurately gauge changing levels; he experienced tunnel vision; and constant throbbing pain etched his face with wincing lines.

Iza was the first to approach Mattan. "My dear husband, what causes you such great pain? There have been times you have cried out in your sleep, enough to awaken me. I am concerned about you." At first Mattan brushed off his wife's comments with an off-hand explanation, saying it was only a dream he had. This satisfied Iza, knowing his ugly experience with the wolf. It seemed very plausible and convincing.

However, when Terach spoke with his son about his other manifestations, Mattan could not convince him that his condition was only minor. "Mattan, now that we are in Gaza, I will summon the doctor to examine you. Things that you do gravely concern not only myself, but our whole family. Our hirelings have also made mention to me of your increasing difficulties."

Mattan realized it was fruitless to try to hide his condition any longer. In his heart, he was ready to get relief from the physical pain, as well as the recurring dream. With resignation, the young shepherd sadly admitted, "It is as you wish, my father. I agree to see the doctor."

Terach went into Gaza, but soon learned the doctor was sick and could not attend to Mattan right away. A midwife was available and because they often were sought out in place of a doctor, the shepherd leader persuaded her to come with him to examine Mattan. Many midwives of that time performed duties beyond assisting at childbirth. Indeed, quite a few midwives knew more than the doctors, and as such garnered great respect.

Immediately upon arriving at their base camp, the midwife took Mattan into his tent home. Iza, Terach, Beulah, and Channah were in attendance, looking on anxiously. The midwife did not waste any time. Silently she inspected the two healed but scarred puncture wounds of Mattan's head. She reached into her medicine pouch and pulled out a short metal rod that had a sharp point at one end. Adroitly, she pushed the sharp point into the scar on the side of Mattan's head.

A stream of greenish pus shot out and Mattan emitted a cry of pain. The midwife used the index fingers of each hand and squeezed the area around the wound, forcing more greenish material to escape. This time, Mattan did not flinch or utter any sound. His carefully controlled reaction was quick breathing and a tightening stomach. To his surprise, for the first time since striking the rocks in the heat of his battle, the shepherd felt relief. He uttered a sigh and the midwife grunted. She nodded her head approvingly.

Next, the medical assistant applied the same procedure to the wound on the back of Mattan's head with an identical result. Mattan exhibited no sign of pain, nor did he make any sounds.

131

He merely sat stoically while the midwife performed her medical procedure while the stunned family members looked on.

When she had finished, Mattan slumped down on his mat to the surprise of his fearful and loving audience. The midwife stood and looked down at the now sleeping male. She turned and addressed the attendees in the tent. "He has had much infection that began much earlier. I do not know how much infection remains in his body. I cannot say if what I did here today will eliminate the poison that invades his body. Only time and God will answer this question."

Terach thanked the midwife for her services and gratefully paid her a sum above what she normally would receive. The shepherd leader had one of his hirelings escort the woman back to Gaza. After her departure, Terach gathered the family members who had witnessed the procedure and began the inevitable conversation.

The shepherd spoke calmly and softly, "We all heard what the midwife said. Now each of us must keenly observe Mattan and look for signs that he is recovering or getting worse. Should anyone detect a worsening, inform me at once."

The other family members agreed to do what Terach directed, and the meeting was adjourned. They left Mattan peacefully asleep in his tent. Of this inner circle group, Iza shared their thoughts and concerns. But she had some additional ones of her own.

From Gaza, the rootless nomads slowly made their way north along the Mediterranean Sea, letting the hungry animals eat their fill. It was a pleasure for Mattan to witness the growth of the many lambs. It was also an important time when the new mothers who once again went into heat were united with the rams. For just under sixty hours, the shepherds allowed the rams to mate with the adult ewes. Terach and Mattan calculated that by the time the flocks reached Joppa, the pregnant ewes would give birth just in time for the annual Passover observance. This was not by chance. It was carefully timed to coincide with the Jews' requirement for lambs under seven months of age for a desirable Passover sacrifice.

Daily, Terach observed Mattan's physical mannerisms, dissecting every movement to determine if more infection impacted his vision. Naturally, Iza was especially attentive to the possibility. Unfortunately, none of the family members could monitor Mattan while he tended to the ewes which were pregnant again. Terach's herd of goats and sheep was so large it was divided into sections.

At the front of the steady procession were the pregnant ewes. Their productivity and health requirements dictated that they get the first of the nutritious grass.

The second tier was the main branch of the mixed herd. It consisted of the adult sheep and goats, both ewes and rams. This portion was spread out into a long, wide ribbon that had access to plenty of savory feed. Gavriel was in charge of the main body of animals that usually numbered over three thousand.

Eitou headed up the last tier of the assembly that consisted of the older sheep and goats. These were animals past their prime that were destined for the food market along the way to Jericho. Those that weren't sold during the long trek were auctioned at the Jericho market.

Terach supervised all four sections and scouted the pastureland to make sure the entire band got the richest of the pastureland. Gavriel and Eitou remained tied to their sections, thereby leaving Mattan to tend to his segment alone. It was only when Terach came to inspect Mattan's subdivision that the shepherd leader had a chance to observe his youngest son's physical condition. When the young shepherd was able to return to the base camp, Iza also had her opportunity to scrutinize her husband's physical appearance.

There were times Mattan found himself stumbling when he walked among his ewes, unable to distinguish changes in the terrain. Other times his vision became blurred as he rode his horse in front of the wooly subdivision. Always there was sensitivity to the light that bombarded him throughout the days.

The young shepherd became more anxious about what was happening to his body. He began to wonder if he should inform his family about what was happening to him. Jews at that time weren't known for praying to God, but the shaken Mattan cried out to His Lord for healing and relief. As his condition deteriorated, his cries increased. The decision whether to inform his family was taken out of his hands when an incident occurred between Gaza and the next scheduled stop at Jamnia.

Terach approached the ensemble of wool one day on his return from surveying the pastureland ahead. As he came closer to Mattan's grouping, he caught sight of his son sitting on the ground next to his horse, tightly holding the reins. The young shepherd stood, but appeared disoriented, shaking his head side to side. He fumbled for the saddle horn to grasp as he swung atop his Arabian stallion.

But now seated in the saddle, Mattan appeared confused over what to do next. Finally, he directed the horse to proceed toward the right portion of the spread-out gang of young pregnant ewes. Terach viewed all this silently. He was aghast at the sight of his skilled son's troubles. He nudged his stallion nearer to assist his disoriented son.

At first, Mattan did not recognize the rider approaching him from a distance. He sat astride his mount, leaned his head forward, and squinted intently to identify the rapidly approaching horseman. Terach took note of Mattan's difficulties and called out to his befuddled son, "Mattan, it is I, your father. Do not be alarmed." Terach was surprised his voice did not crack as he fought to keep his voice sounding normal in spite of his screaming emotions.

Mattan relaxed, and waited as Terach closed the distance between the two. The young shepherd waited for his father to speak. "My son, I watched you struggle just now. You are having trouble with your eyesight, am I not right?" The resigned young shepherd admitted such was the case. Terach's heart sank, his posture wilted, and he struggled to softly command, "You will come back with me to our campsite. I will instruct one of the hirelings to take your place. It is becoming too dangerous for you here alone." When he finished speaking, Terach's jaws clenched, creating physical pain that only faintly approached the pain in his heart.

Mattan felt Terach's words sting like thorns. He was crushed by his father's decree but knew it would be futile to argue. "It is as you say, Father." With an audible sigh the young shepherd lamented, "I shall accompany you home." His father took control of the reins of Mattan's horse. Mattan's depression deepened as the duo silently rode the four-mile distance back to their home. Each was overpowered by his own thoughts of dismay, apprehension, and as an intensifying fear of the unknown.

Iza nearly panicked as she listened to Terach's depiction of the events surrounding his decision to not allow his youngest son to continue being a shepherd. The sixteen-year-old was terrified. She wondered what was to become of her new husband. Her earlier unvoiced thoughts and concerns now exploded beyond her imagination.

Beulah took her aside and attempted to soothe the obviously distraught young woman. "Iza, do not be too frightened at Mattan's condition. It is quite possible this is temporary. When we arrive at Jamnia, Terach will summon a doctor to examine Mattan. It could be a return of the infection discovered by the midwife in Gaza. Keep your wits about you and make sure you care for your husband."

The young wife had no response for her mother-in-law. Her thoughts were too jumbled for her to speak coherently. As a show of understanding and obedience, Iza weakly acknowledged Beulah's comfort, and went back to her home and to Mattan.

Inside the tent, Iza saw Mattan slumped with his head in his hands. Cautiously, she approached the sullen figure and gently touched his right shoulder. With a trembling voice she uttered, "My husband, my heart aches for you." She put both arms around his shoulders and rested her head next to his, fighting back her own tears.

Mattan remained silent for some time, but finally said, "Iza, I am deeply troubled. My time as a shepherd may be coming to an end. There were times I realized I could not care for my flock and this troubled me greatly. Now it has come to pass." The young shepherd paused to gather his words. Then in a voice full of distress, he choked out, "When a shepherd no longer can care for his flock, he no longer is a man."

Iza tightly clung to her disturbed husband and would not let him escape her grip. Together the two sat, huddled, worried, and tearful about the days to come.

Chapter 11

Terach and Beulah sat facing each other with forlorn faces. Chilling thoughts about Mattan's vision difficulties dominated their private thoughts and their conversation. In ironic contrast, dancing flames shot skyward from the small fire that warmed the center of their mobile tent home. Beulah bemoaned, "Is it possible for you to take Mattan to Jamnia tomorrow and find the doctor to examine Mattan?"

Terach turned his face away from watching the fire. Prominent lines in his brow and dark circles under his eyes were accentuated by shadows from the dwindling fire. The dark lines accurately portrayed his deep concern over his youngest son's health. Quietly he answered Beulah. "I have thought about that very thing, my good wife. For the sake of everyone, we must learn the extent of Mattan's problem. This awful uncertainty will have a bad impact and cause even more difficulties."

Terach straightened his back and pronounced, "We shall leave at first light. By the time you and the flocks arrive within the next few days, we should have the answer we seek." The elder shepherd slowly rose. He looked down at his dejected wife and said, "I shall go and inform Mattan and Iza of our decision." He turned and shuffled out of the tent, looking and feeling like a man much older than his actual years.

Mattan and Iza were still huddled together when Terach announced his presence. He quickly explained the reason for his visit. "Mattan, you and I shall leave at first light for Jamnia to see the doctor there. Your mother and I are in agreement that it is best for you to see the doctor as soon as possible." Staring at their vulnerable young faces, he offered a bit of consolation, "If there is more infection and it can be removed, then you can

137

resume your position with the flock." It was a feeble attempt to bolster the young couple's spirits as well as his own.

The newly married couple peered respectfully at the imposing figure standing inside their home. Briefly the two exchanged looks. Then Mattan spoke out, "I shall be ready for the journey, Father."

Terach paused, looking down at the despondent couple. His heart ached as he voiced, "Good." The emotional father turned and quickly exited their home.

The ten-mile journey north to Jamnia was uneventful. It provided time for Terach and Mattan to discuss the young shepherd's vision difficulties. The devoted father and son shared their emotions and their thoughts about the situation. This kind of frankness wasn't common among Jewish men at the time, but their hearts and circumstances altered tradition. New respect and a deeper love developed along the route. The journey took only one day as their Arabian stallions easily covered the distance.

Jamnia was a good-sized village and was considered a learning center for that part of Judea. It was required by the Sanhedrin to have both a doctor and a surgeon. Despite being four miles inland from the Mediterranean Sea, the refreshing smell of the sea was present.

Terach received directions to the doctor's home and the pair went directly. His office was situated in the front of his home, a common arrangement. The doctor listened attentively to Mattan as he relayed his experiences after the death battle with the rogue wolf. The young shepherd left nothing out about what he experienced. Terach finished the presentation with his observances of Mattan's problems in the field with the sheep, explaining that he had to take him away from the potential dangers of the pastureland.

After the narrative, the doctor proceeded to examine the healed wounds. The two small scars were testimony of the event. The doctor looked closely and felt around both scars. He applied pressure to each scarred wound, causing Mattan to wince at the examination. When his fingers finished probing Mattan's skull, he sat back on his stool and gave his medical opinion.

"Your wounds have healed and I find no pressure at all. The midwife did a good job of releasing the pus. I do not see hidden signs of infection." The doctor stood up and stroked his bearded chin as he looked down at the two men. "There is no reason to seek the services of our surgeon. There is nothing he can do. It is in God's hands for the restoring of your vision."

With that final statement, Terach and Mattan realized their meeting with the doctor was over. So quickly! The extended uncertainty and angst that preceded the meeting remained. After a prolonged silence they stood up and solemnly followed the doctor out of his office.

The Jews of that time did not distinguish medicine from religion. They attributed health and disease to a divine source. As dictated by the Jewish leaders, healing was God's role and doctors were relegated to being His helpers. As much as shepherds were deemed social and religious outcasts by the Jewish leaders, doctors did not discriminate against them. Terach and Mattan knew the doctor had been honest with them, so they politely thanked him and left.

A winter rain storm rose up and sent dense, chilling drops of water to cover the entire area of Jamnia and the surrounding countryside. Terach and Mattan stood in the doorway of the doctor's office and surveyed the thick stream of water and the small pools in the street around the doctor's home office.

"The nature of this storm shows us it will last quite a while, my son. Let us find lodging here. We can return to our loved ones and flocks tomorrow." Mattan was agreeable to the suggestion and despite having to sit in wet saddles, the disheartened duo made their way to a café that had rooms above the eatery.

Mattan was the first to broach the disheartening topic of his vision difficulties. "Father, with your permission I would like to continue guiding and caring for the pregnant ewes you have entrusted me with." His voice was disconsolate, pleading, and he continued his plea, "I still can see and do what is expected of me. Maybe God will take mercy on me while I'm with my flock and fully restore my sight."

Terach was impressed with his son's request and answered him honestly, "I see no reason at this time for you not to continue your duties with the pregnant ewes. Just the same, I will have one of the hirelings accompany you and remain at your side when you are with the sheep and the goats." Mattan let out a sigh of relief as his father finished his reply, "I, too, pray that God will have mercy on you, Mattan." Inwardly, Terach felt he could no longer petition Almighty God. To do so required hope, and it was a commodity he was empty of.

By mid-morning of the next day the rain had subsided. The two shepherds pointed their trusted steeds southward to meet the approaching mass of herd and caretakers. When they met up with the first wave of animals, they were met by the hireling Terach had instructed to take Mattan's place.

Mattan took the initiative and officially addressed the hireling, "I have returned. I will resume my duties with the ewes. You shall remain with me and assist in whatever way is necessary."

The hireling's eyes shifted to Terach for affirmation of this plan. The distraught father nodded his approval. The hireling smiled broadly at Mattan and said, "It is good that you can return to your flock. I am most honored to assist you, Mattan."

Terach hugged his troubled son, and proceeded south toward the next wave of animal flesh given to him by God to care for. There he spoke with Gavriel. "The doctor had no answer why Mattan is experiencing his vision problems. Mattan and I have agreed that for the time being he shall continue his duties with the pregnant ewes. The hireling will remain with him in case of any difficulties."

Gavriel looked upward and momentarily closed his eyes. He looked at Terach and saw worry and fatigue in his face. With confidence, he assured him, "Whenever possible, Father, I shall go to Mattan and make sure all is well with both him and the hireling. They are not that far ahead of my flocks. I can get to them in a short period of time. My hirelings will be able to keep the flocks together in my absence."

The father and his eldest son forced themselves to converse about other things, mainly about the condition of the grasslands, the change in the weather patterns, and anything else that took their anxious minds off the main topic of Mattan and his health.

The women moving the carts of the rolled up tents were quite vexed the entire time Terach and Mattan left the group. Uncertainty is always more difficult than a concrete problem to solve. When Channah viewed the approaching horseman, she immediately recognized it was her father. The teenager pointed towards the advancing rider and exclaimed to Beulah, "It is Father coming from the north! Everything must be alright because he is alone!"

Beulah inched her neck forward to better see the advancing equestrian. "You are correct, Channah, it appears to be Terach! Don't be too eager in your assessment. Mattan may be back in Jamnia with the doctor. We won't know until Terach speaks with us."

Within minutes of their brief conversation, Terach reached the lead cart containing his wife and daughter. A slight smile was given to them and the shepherd turned his stallion parallel to the cart as it continued to move forward. Channah could not contain herself and she blurted out, "Yes? Is Mattan well and is he with his flocks? Was there any difficulty with the doctor?" Terach held up his hand to silence his eager daughter.

"Please, Channah, I will tell all to you." The two women were all ears as they strained to hear Terach's depiction of the trip to Jamnia. They did not want to miss anything that took place.

After Terach informed them of the developments, Beulah spoke up. "This evening we will have all the women at our house and you can tell them what is taking place. It will be better to say it once to all than to speak with each individually."

Beulah stopped the advancement of the parade of carts earlier than normal. She wanted plenty of time to get the small city of goat hide tents set up for Terach's report to the family about Mattan. She sent Channah to the other women, requesting them to come for dinner at Terach's home where he would relay what had taken place in Jamnia with the doctor.

Beulah made sure that Iza was seated next to her to hear Terach's words. The mother-in-law wanted to be able to comfort Iza in her reaction to the still uncertain news. When Terach finished his presentation, Iza let out a sigh of relief. Beulah and Channah both took one of Iza's hands and gripped them gently. Terach looked directly at Iza searching her features and body language for her true reaction.

"I am pleased that Mattan can remain with his flocks. When we get to Jamnia, I will welcome him home with love." Beulah was particularly pleased hearing the young wife's words. Yet, for some reason the older woman felt something was amiss in Iza's tone.

Later that evening when she and Terach were alone, she mentioned her concern to her husband. "I fear we must closely watch Iza. I believe she is more troubled than what she lets on."

Terach pondered his astute wife's words and admitted haltingly, "I have the same feeling about Mattan."

One week later, Mattan, Gavriel, and Eitou had their respective flocks and herds sequestered along the northeast portion of the village. The day after they settled in, the carts driven by the women arrived. The hirelings and the women had the tent city set up in no time. The three brothers made their way to their respective homes and welcoming wives. They were grateful for the warmth and comforts they had been without for several weeks. Such was the life of the nomad shepherd.

The hirelings took control overseeing the flocks while the leaders took a much-needed break from the animals and the elements. The family gathered for their customary dinner together in Terach and Beulah's tent. Everyone was eager to broach the subject of Mattan because their field duties had not allowed them access to the information at the time it became known. Noticeably, Mattan and Iza did not share their eagerness.

To end all speculation, Mattan took control of the conversation while the others continued to eat the reunion meal. "The doctor said he found no infection and that my wounds have healed with little scarring. His main advice is to petition God for mercy. I will do this, all while pursuing my duties as shepherd to the pregnant ewes." To short circuit the questions and expressions of concern, Mattan abruptly finished, "There is nothing more to be said about my condition."

It was evident to the distressed family that their loved one was reluctant to engage the topic any longer. Each resolved to attempt to carry on in normal fashion to respect Mattan's emotions. However, their façade was a flimsy covering over the depth of their worries for the beloved young shepherd.

From Jamnia, the multitude of sheep and goats continued their customary route north to Joppa, before they turned east to travel along the edge of Samaria. This was the most dangerous portion of the annual loop that Terach and some of the other nomad shepherds made.

Tensions were always high when Terach and his throng of animals and humans entered this territory. The bitter feelings between the Samaritans and their Jewish neighbors sometimes resulted in conflicts between the nomad shepherds and the Samaritans. The shepherd leader warned, "We must be vigilant of Samaritan bandits who are intent on stealing from our flocks. They probably will strike at night."

Terach specifically addressed Mattan and his hirelings. "Mattan, you especially are vulnerable because the pregnant ewes will fetch a high price in Shechem when the Passover feast comes. I will add three more hirelings from Eitou's group to assist while we are in this dangerous region."

Unbeknownst to Mattan, Terach had conferred earlier with his older sons about the situation involving Mattan. The issue of his eyesight worried Terach more than he wanted to let on. He wanted added protection not only for the pregnant ewes, but for his youngest son as well. "Mattan's eyesight still has not returned to normal. He has great difficulty seeing at night and early in the morning when the shadows linger and do not give detail. The hirelings must be Mattan's eyes while we are so close to the Samaritans."

In addition to the threat of the Samaritans, the hill country that dominated the landscape north of Ephraim and continued southeast to Jericho was inundated with many gulches that were perfect for predators, mainly wolves. In the springtime a segment of the Jordan River between Ephraim and Jericho often ran high which made it difficult to get the sheep and the goats across the swollen water.

It was a time of added worry for Terach and his sons. The shepherd leader felt he had instituted the proper precautionary measures to ensure the safety of the flocks as well as his family and servants. Nonetheless, he always relished the time when everyone had successfully made it safely across the Jordan River and could begin the short trek south to Jericho.

The final onslaught of winter caused the living blanket of wool to proceed more slowly than normal. Terach spent longer days traveling ahead of Mattan's mass of soon-to-be-mothers. It was a blessed time in which he could spend time with his youngest son and monitor his leadership skills. Despite his eyesight difficulties, Mattan was able to make appropriate decisions involving his fraction of the flock. Terach was very pleased with his son's compensating efforts and earnestly hoped his son's future as a shepherd could be sustained.

One night after returning home from his inspection duties, Terach commented to Beulah, "Rest assured, my good wife, that Mattan is doing well over this rough part of our journey. At times he falters due to his diminished sight, but he overcomes obstacles well. Have no fear, and relay my confidence in Mattan to Iza and to our mothering daughter Channah." Terach wondered if his exaggerated report would be believed by the woman who knew him better than anyone else.

Terach's body wanted to linger in the comfort of his traveling home, but the shepherd leader knew he must continue guiding the large mass of man and beast safely through the potentially dangerous region. On the morning of his scheduled departure back to the flock he informed Beulah, "Alas, good wife, my body is no longer young and vibrant as it once was. My bones ache and creak. They are begging for more comfort. I always tell them to be patient—less hectic times are coming."

Beulah was concerned for her husband's safety as well as her sons who encountered many hazards as shepherds. The situation involving Mattan certainly intensified her concerns. She watched Terach twist, turn, and stretch until he felt flexible enough to eat his morning meal, then climb aboard his stallion to head back to the main flock. She was glad her husband remained healthy to continue living the shepherd's life that he loved so dearly.

With a happy smile, she stopped Terach before he climbed into the saddle of his horse. She embraced him tightly and would not release him. Lovingly, she whispered in his ear, "Travel with God, my husband. Remember that my love for you is deep in my heart." When she released the shepherd leader, Beulah held out a leather pouch and gave it to him. "This is for you and Mattan tonight when you rest."

Terach adoringly kissed Beulah on her forehead and tenderly stroked the side of her face. "You are a good woman and a better wife." The two chuckled at the comment and Terach rode off to join his sons. As Beulah watched Terach disappear, tears won the battle over control, and her body shook for both her husband and her youngest son.

Due to weather complications it took Terach and the slow-moving entourage one week longer to safely cross the Jordan River and begin the downward trek to Jericho. The winter storms were more like catapulted boulders aimed to cause havoc and disruption.

He purposely held up advancing the flocks so that he, his sons, and the hirelings could rest before continuing to the Jericho marketplace. It was also a time when he manufactured reasons to take Mattan back to the base camp to assure the women of the family that Mattan was doing well and they should not be alarmed at his being away from home.

After the short respite, the travelers eagerly proceeded south to the hub of commerce that was located just north of the Dead Sea. Jericho was a renowned oasis in the Wadi Qelt part of the Jordan Valley. It was 846 feet below sea level with rich alluvial soil and fresh spring water. The nearby spring of Ein es-Sultan, also known as Elisha's Spring, produced an average of 1,000 gallons of water per minute, easily irrigating the 2,500 acres of farmland that produced a variety of crops.

Terach and his family and hirelings always welcomed the sight of the flourishing business-oriented city's entrance Vast groves of palm trees beckoned travelers to the oasis. It was said that the beauty of the palm trees and their abundance relaxed the minds of the many traders who frequented the site on business. Heightened emotions of traders resulted in higher prices for items put up for sale.

Terach and the Nigrid recognized this myth as actual fact and each enjoyed the clamor for the sheepherder's goods. "Once again, God has smiled down on us, Terach. Not only did you have more lambs for sale, but the quality was exceptional! The Pharisees and those pilgrims going to Jerusalem for Passover got their money's worth this year!" exclaimed an elated Nigrid.

After concluding his business with the pillar of business in Jericho, Terach was contacted by Barabbas. Terach's encampment on the northeast side of Jericho was secured and private enough for the Zealot bandit to contact his long-time friend and colleague safely.

Jesus Barabbas was thankful for how well Terach cared for the bandit's sheep and small number of goats. "Terach, my friend, you have done well for me. Better than I expected!" declared a joyful Barabbas. The bandit held the money pouch above his head and exclaimed, "This will greatly aid the coffers of our group and allow us to survive better."

The comrades of the grasslands filled in each other on all kinds of happenings, small and great, that took place over the twelve months of their separation. Barabbas was pleased that his flocks had been supplied plenty of nourishing grass throughout each phase of their nomadic journey. The Zealot bandit was shocked and gravely concerned when Terach informed him of Mattan's vision issues.

"Mattan is a true shepherd, my friend. His bravery with the rogue wolf is unsurpassed. I could not have done better had I been in your son's place. You have reason to be proud of him, Terach." Barabbas then commented on Mattan's future as a shepherd, "I'm not a praying man, but I will approach Almighty God that He will have mercy on you, Mattan, and your family. I also will ask God to restore Mattan's vision back to normal." Barabbas leaned back with a chuckle, "I just hope God remembers who I am and that He won't be surprised by my requests to Him!"

The bandit's eyes welled up as he commented to his best friend, "I am both humbled and honored, my friend, that despite your troubles and worries you were able to make sure my flock flourished. I know this was most difficult for you. I value our friendship even more."

Terach was a little embarrassed by such effusiveness. He hung his head for a moment, then looked at Jesus Barabbas with a smile and simply replied, "Thank you, my friend."

When the somewhat depleted number of sheep and goats once again began their movement south, Terach felt more sorrow over leaving Barabbas and the Nigrid than normal. He always enjoyed time spent with his two colleagues and he missed their insights, their jokes, and most of all their friendship. Recent events that had taken place, especially concerning Mattan, added to his sense of loss.

The animals had to climb out of the oasis valley, and once on the rim of the basin, Terach directed the group east toward the Nabatean border. Despite the more desert landscape, there was sufficient lush spring grassland for the entire animal group.

When they reached the outskirts of Machaerus, Mattan had new difficulties with his eyes. He did not want to alarm his family so he kept this truth to himself. It was his belief that his vision issues weren't that bad and that over time they would lessen and return to normal. But after reaching the southern tip of the Dead Sea and making a turn back up north, Mattan's vision significantly blurred. Frequent headaches assaulted him, and tunnel vision was closing in on his ability to peruse the landscape for potential threats.

At Masaba, the direction of the caravan turned west and traveled along the southern part of Idumea as they headed toward their usual target of Beer-Sheba. Mattan was glad his debilitating vision did not hinder him when it came time for the pregnant ewes to give birth. It was demanding work to make sure the ewes did not lose their lambs during labor and delivery. Terach, the hirelings, and Mattan were able to assist the ewes and protect them and the numerous lambs from marauding predators.

It was a great time of stress for Mattan who worked extra hard to disguise his vision problems. After the lambing season was completed, he felt relieved his father and the hirelings apparently had not noticed his progressing issues. Reluctantly, the young shepherd made his way to his traveling home to spend a short time with Iza and the rest of the family. He kept his distance from his loved ones. It wasn't because he did not want their companionship; he was fearful of drawing their attention to his growing vision problems.

Mattan's condition stabilized for a while, but a series of increased deterioration began at Gaza. He found himself shaking his head in an attempt to clear the blurriness. The tunnel vision shrank and he had trouble in maneuvering around the diverse landscape. Beyond the physical challenges, most of all, Mattan grew upset with the same recurring dream of the two contrasting pairs of eyes. The angry, blazing yellow eyes of the wolf that depicted pure hatred and evil haunted him. But the comfort of bathing in the warmth of the baby Jesus' eyes was enough to keep the young shepherd from crying out as he slept.

At Lydda, Mattan was confronted by Terach. "My son, hirelings and myself have repeatedly witnessed you staggering in the pastureland and have watched as you had to turn your head to see things to the side of you. Tell me, how bad is your vision?"

He was found out. A deflated Mattan admitted his vision problems were escalating. With much effort he sadly confessed, "It grows worse some days, but there are days when it isn't that bad." Then with resolve, he fiercely declared, "I am still able to do my duties as you desire, Father!"

Terach gently placed his hand on his young son's shoulder. "I feel when we get to Joppa, we should visit a surgeon there instead of the doctor we saw last year."

Mattan made no objection to his father's plan. He would follow his father's desires. Terach told only Beulah of his plans, and when the procession reached their regular campgrounds east of Joppa, Terach escorted Mattan to the office in the seacoast city known for its dangerous harbor and Jewish scholars.

The surgeon's office was in his home, the same as the city's doctor. In back of the house was a small building that was lined with marble. This was an operating room common to Jewish surgeons of the time. The surgeon motioned for Mattan to sit in a chair. It was all too familiar. The surgeon probed the side and the back of Mattan's head where his scarred wounds were located. The surgeon looked deeply into Mattan's eyes and stood to one side, asking the young shepherd if he saw him.

The examination was interrupted by the appearance of one of the main rabbis of Joppa. The Talmud required having a rabbi present whenever possible at medical examinations. Part of the rabbi's duties was to ascertain the religious aspect of the patient's case. Having the rabbi present during the examination of his son made Terach exceedingly uncomfortable as he was keenly aware of the religious and social stigma rabbis attached to shepherds.

Following the eye examination, the surgeon quietly gave the bad report. "Your condition is such, Mattan, that I expect you will lose all sight in both eyes. How soon, I cannot say. There are no ointments that can help you and there is no surgery that will prevent the loss of your eyesight. I can only tell you to pray to Almighty God for His mercy."

The room fell silent as the surgeon's words reverberated in the minds of both Terach and Mattan. They were frozen by the news until the rabbi interrupted their thoughts. In an acidly sarcastic voice, the religious priest said, "Shepherds, there is no need for you to pray to God. He will not hear your pleas. You are blemished because of your sin that God knows of full well. Part of this is because you are unclean shepherds. God does not favor your kind."

Terach took a deep breath and slowly rose up to his full height. He faced the rabbi squarely, his eyes ablaze with fury, his jaw firmly set. He locked onto the eyes of the rabbi. The unexpected impact of this made the religious Jewish priest take a step backward. Undeterred, the shepherd leader growled at the priest in disgust. In a stern and deliberate tone, he commanded the rabbi, "You religious fool, you do not have the voice or the mind of God! You do not know who God favors and who He does not. You only know what the Pharisees tell you! Take your leave from us, else I will cut your tongue out and give it to the swine! For it is not to the liking of the buzzards that feed on dead things or to the dogs of the streets."

The angry shepherd began to unsheathe the Roman short sword he worn on his left side. The now terrified wide-eyed rabbi scurried quickly out of the surgeon's office and ran down the street as fast as he could. Terach shoved his short sword back in its sheath and stared at the surgeon who was quick to speak, "Do not believe, Terach, that I share the mindset of that fool. My heart is with both of you at this time."

During the ruckus between Terach and the rabbi, Mattan was nearly oblivious, still stunned by the doctor's analysis. The doctor's words had cut ruinously through Mattan's false hope that his vision would get better.

Neither Terach nor Mattan said anything to the surgeon as they left his office. They remained silent until they were on their way back to their encampment. Finally, Mattan broke the silence with a slow, tentative question, "Do you want me to refrain from being with the ewes, Father?"

Emphatically, Terach bellowed, "No, I do not my son! So long as you have sight, you shall continue being the shepherd God has meant for you to be. We will wait and see what develops and make changes only when it is necessary." Terach swallowed hard, then concluded, "Do not think about what the rabbi said. When we reach home I will inform our family about the visit with the surgeon. I do not intend on telling them what the pig rabbi said, and neither should you. This shall be between only the two of us." Mattan agreed with his father, and the duo rode the short distance awash in their own thoughts.

Mattan continued doing what he loved, making sure the pregnant ewes and their lambs were safe and adequately fed. Terach made more stops to monitor his youngest son than he had in the past. Privately, he instructed his hirelings to watch for any signs of struggles in caring for the sheep and the goats. The shepherd leader noticed that the intuitive Canaan dogs seemed to understand the situation and were also eager to do their part as well.

From Joppa the caravan made its way along the Samaritan border. Along the journey, Beulah relayed to Terach that Iza was grappling with being a shepherd's wife and particularly with the uncertainty of Mattan's vision difficulties. "My husband, our daughter-in-law is broody and gloomy and at times becomes ill-tempered towards Channah, myself, and the other wives. She reluctantly performs her tasks. I sometimes wonder if she even is glad to receive Mattan when he comes in from his flock."

Terach frowned in thought before responding to his wife's assessment, "Have you or Channah or perhaps any of the wives talked with Iza about this?"

Beulah anticipated Terach's question and quickly answered, almost irritably, "We all have on different occasions, but Iza refuses to tell us what troubles her."

Terach scratched his beard, shrugged and concluded, "There is nothing else anyone can do. If Iza does not talk, she does not talk and we cannot help."

The eastward journey from Joppa to Ephraim usually took place early in the spring and was a hectic time for the nomads. Particular care had to be taken for all the sheep and the goats, especially the new lambs. Most were only four months old and were subject to injury over the treacherous terrain.

Terach was grateful that the hirelings and the thirty Canaan dogs were available to guide the lambs and the once again pregnant young ewes. The shepherd leader was particularly concerned about Mattan's ability to navigate the uneven landscape. In addition, Terach was most fretful over Mattan's safety and how he would react should any wolves come from the hills of the region to attack the vulnerable flock.

At the point where the flocks began their journey through the hill region, Terach was scouting ahead when one of the hirelings approached him from the west. "You must come immediately back to the flock! Mattan is in grave condition!" Terach's hidden fears and worries became reality. He swallowed hard and his stomach churned. He turned his Arabian stallion around and spurred the horse with his feet. The stallion shot forward, leaving the hireling to hurry behind on his mule.

When Terach was close to the front of the flock, he saw Mattan sitting on the ground holding his horse's reins in one hand. The shepherd's pet Canaan dog was beside him, licking his face. When the dog saw Terach, he raised his head high and gave out a mournful signal. At the sound of the dog's wail, Mattan turned his head in the direction of the approaching rider. The young shepherd did not move and made no effort to inquire who had come close to him.

Terach jumped from the saddle of his horse and strode to his son, searching frantically to determine if Mattan was injured. The worried shepherd father knelt beside his son and saw there were no wounds or traces of blood anywhere on the young shepherd's body. He looked around for signs of battle or involvement with a wolf. There were none. "Mattan," was all he could say.

Mattan looked in the direction of his father and morosely uttered, "I cannot see." Terach's head went down and his bearded chin touched his chest. "The doctor's prophecy has come true, Father."

The stunned father stared at the forlorn expression shrouding Mattan's face. Tears emerged and ran down the shepherd leader's wrinkled cheeks. Terach reached out and took his son into his arms and held him close. The only sound was that of a chilling wind indicating an approaching rainstorm. No matter how hard the incoming storm would be, it was nothing compared to the emotional hurricane howling in both father and son's hearts and minds.

After some time, the hireling returned. He saw the two sitting silently together. The hireling said nothing, understanding the gravity of the moment. Instead he quietly left to tend to his duties with the flock. The Canaan pet dog of Mattan lay with its head on its paws and gave the hireling no attention. It shared the same misery as its human master's.

Terach's mind slowly turned over the reality of the situation. Holding Mattan tightly, the despondent father softly informed his son, "Let us rise. I must take you back to the encampment. We have six miles to ride. I will take your horse's reins and help guide you." Mattan exhibited no emotion at his father's announcement and followed him slowly, stepping cautiously with his hand on his father's shoulder.

Mattan was able to climb aboard his stallion on his own. When he heard his father doing the same thing, he stammered, "Father, what is to become of me?" Terach placed his hand on the bent shoulder of his son and in a barely audible voice pronounced, "I shall take care of you."

The family was nearly panic-stricken when Terach woefully announced Mattan's blindness. Iza left the family gathering and ran into the tent she shared with Mattan. No one attempted to follow and bring her back. Beulah and Channah's eyes filled with tears that quickly overflowed and slipped down their cheeks. Terach also became choked-up and tears descended down his chiseled face. Mattan was silent, but keenly aware of the distressed sounds that surrounded him. He had no words, and soon he wept along with his family.

Chapter 12

A hireling notified both Gavriel and Eitou they were needed at the base camp. Both shepherds knew it was something serious for them to be called away from their responsibilities. They made haste in returning to the bivouac. Upon hearing the declaration of Mattan's blindness, the older brothers nearly collapsed, their eyes wide with the news. Both unashamedly expressed their angst. Gavriel put his hands to his head and sobbed. Eitou at first stared in disbelief before he also began to convulse.

Later that evening, with great effort, Terach summoned them to his tent. It was necessary to enact a dreaded plan the shepherd leader had devised when Mattan first exhibited his vision difficulties. Terach's hope that the strategy never would take place was now gone.

Eitou was to take Mattan's place at the front of the sheep and goat caravan. Gavriel was to maintain his position with the main flock that numbered over four thousand. One of the senior hirelings was chosen to replace Eitou with the older ewes and rams, thirty percent of which would be sold when they reached the Jericho market.

Terach would continue with his scouting and surveying obligations, and both Beulah and Channah would share the responsibility of assisting Iza in caring for Mattan.

At this family conference, neither Iza nor Mattan were present. They remained in the solitude of their personal tent home. Very little was said by either husband or wife. They were deep in their own thoughts and still in a state of shock from the latest development that was forever changing their lives.

Back at the shepherd's headquarters, when Terach finished giving his directives, Beulah made her own announcement. "We all have been aware Mattan could become blind, and now it is important to control our emotions and do what is necessary for Mattan as well as for ourselves."

The family members listened closely to the matriarch's plea. With confident firmness, Beulah proclaimed, "We must avoid spending time on negative thoughts. They will do no one any good and even make the situation worse. It will be very difficult at the beginning, but we must help Mattan adjust to what has changed for him."

The crestfallen mother's eyes searched each of her assembled family member's eyes as she issued her petition. "Channah and I will help Iza as she assists Mattan in his adjustment to his sightless world. When you men return home, you must speak with us first before approaching Mattan." The emotionally struggling matriarch looked down because her voice was now quivering. "Nobody really knows what lies ahead or what God has in store for any of us." The family quieted as they contemplated their mother's words.

The next six weeks of the final leg of the spring trek to Jericho were very eventful for Terach, Mattan, and all the family. At mid-point of traveling through the hill country, Terach took his blind son with him on periodic scouting surveys.

Both men were cautious and somewhat dubious of Mattan's ability to function without his dominant sense. The blind shepherd sometimes became frustrated and vented his anger at not being able to do what once came so easily and naturally and was expected of a bona fide shepherd.

During those bouts Terach would remain calm and redirect his unsure son. "Mattan, take a moment to smell the air, and feel the breeze on your face. Dismount and touch some of the grass, even taste it. Let your senses become your new eyes. They can guide you, as well as protect you, when you are in need."

Sometimes Mattan listened to his father's words of advice. But at other moments he shook his head negatively and felt a sense of defeat. This was such a time. His emotions anguish erupted, "Of what use is this, Father? I cannot see a ewe or a lamb in distress. Even if one of our dogs tells me something is wrong, I cannot see the location of the animal or what distresses the sheep or the goat and could end up killing it, or even myself!"

Terach did not attempt to argue with his emotional son during such times of anger. He would tell Mattan to stay where he was, saying that the terrain ahead was difficult. The senior shepherd would then ride ahead mainly to let his son cool down. One time during this phase Terach rode ahead, then stopped and turned to watch what Mattan would do when left alone.

Mattan's pet Canaan dog made a short bark. The blind shepherd looked down, and then dismounted from his stallion. Carefully holding the reins with one hand, he stooped down, reaching out to determine if anything was in his path. His intuitive Canaan dog ran into the flock and returned, guiding a ewe and her two lambs to where Mattan knelt.

The dog's tail curled in anticipation and it barked sharply one time. The ewe and the lambs stepped closer to the blind shepherd. Mattan smelled their presence and cautiously reached in the direction he believed the animals to be. His hand touched one of the young lambs and carefully he grasped the confused and trembling sheep.

Tenderly, Mattan drew the lamb to him, all the while speaking soothing words to the lamb and its suspicious mother. The blind man's hands felt the softness of the lamb's wool and its rapid heartbeat. Gently he ran his hand over the young sheep's body, mentally noting it was approximately three months old. As he did this, he felt a huge lump in his throat. He struggled to contain his ragged emotions.

When Mattan's personal inspection was complete, the blind shepherd released the lamb. Immediately it bounded back to the comfort of its sibling and mother. Mattan's pet dog came close to his master. The blind shepherd rubbed the dog's head with one hand and grabbed the back of his neck with the other. He slightly smiled as he leaned close to his pet and softly said, "You did well, my friend. I needed that change to sway my soul." Mattan scratched behind its left ear in a manner he often did to let the dog know it was loved. He whispered, "You know how to give me hope." Inwardly, the blind shepherd wished he could believe his own words.

The blind shepherd released his dog and sat on the grass, breaking off a few blades, sniffing them, and tasting them. Terach quietly watched his son and got choked up. He tightened his grip on the reins, and deftly moved his stallion. He looked over his shoulder, delighted he did not alarm his blind son.

On the days when Mattan remained in the base camp with the women, he appeared to be disquieted and on edge. Beulah and Channah did their best to console their loved one, but Iza remained distant, both physically and emotionally. On one occasion Channah commented to her mother, "I truly believe that if Iza would become more compassionate towards her husband he would respond and not be so irritable."

Beulah concurred with her daughter's assessment. "I agree with you, Channah. I've spoken with Iza about this, but she does not speak to me, merely turns her back and goes off to some task."

What the family did not know was that Iza and Mattan's relationship had deteriorated badly with each new progression toward advanced blindness. The couple ceased all sexual intimacy, rarely spoke with each other, and never shared their emotions or thoughts about what was developing with Mattan. In essence, they were roommates, sharing the same quarters, but not life. Their negative emotions and feelings were turning them into strangers.

When the direction turned south from the border with Peraea, it was an easy journey without major obstacles. The spring grassland was succulent for the sheep and the goats. Terach directed the flocks to follow the border of Decapolis. When it intersected with that of Nabatea, he turned the wooly caravan back west to Jericho for the waiting market.

The situation concerning Mattan had worsened as the crew drew closer to the marketplace. The blind shepherd had more surly days and fewer placid moments. The family was constantly on edge. Throughout this time, Iza became more remote, going through the motions of performing her shepherd wife's duties, but without heart. On the final day of the emotional trek, the traveling city established the camp they would utilize for the next two weeks.

On the first night outside the commerce hub, Terach drew Iza aside from the rest of the family and pleaded with her, "Iza, please tell me what lies in your heart. I will do whatever I can to help you, but I need to know your thoughts to do so."

Iza initially reacted guardedly, as her eyes darted back and forth searching her father-in-law's face. Seeing his concern, she realized his sincerity. She looked deeply into her father-in-law's eyes and confessed in a mournful tone of voice, "Terach, I cannot continue being Mattan's wife. It is too difficult for me. I... I've tried but my heart does not give me what I need to be his wife or your daughter-in-law." The teenaged woman fell silent, attempting to gather confidence to continue. When Terach waited for her to complete her thoughts, Iza took a deep breath and summoned the last of her resolve. The deflated shepherd's wife rapidly blurted out, "When we return to Bethlehem, I shall petition for a divorce."

The force of Iza's words did not shock or dismay the father-in-law. He had expected this would happen and had even discussed it briefly with Beulah. They never spoke of it to any other family member and Terach did not broach the subject with Mattan.

With gentleness, the disheartened shepherd clutched Iza's nervous shaking hands. He gazed into her watery eyes and calmed her emotions. With deep sadness he said, "I shall not interfere with your decision. When my business in Jericho is complete and the Passover feast has concluded, I shall take you to Bethlehem where your father and I can dissolve your marriage."

Iza slightly recoiled hearing Terach's announcement. The emotionally spent young woman did not anticipate such an offer from her husband's father. Her worried face relaxed as she cocked her head and looked at Terach. In a loving tone, the young woman whole-heartedly stated, "You ease my soul, Terach. I am gratified and humbled by your kindness to me."

Terach sadly smiled at Iza and said, "Do not tell anyone of our conversation or our plan." Firmly he added, "No one must know. When we are done here I will announce to the family you and I must return to Bethlehem on urgent matters. Only Beulah will know the full reason for our departure from the group."

Early the next morning, Terach met with the Nigrid to conduct their normal business transactions. The business administrator was very pleased with the increased number of lambs available to him this year. Exuberantly he squealed, "You have had an excellent lambing seasoning, my friend! Only a few were not suitable for the Passover sacrifice. When the Jews view the quality, they will not complain about your price." The Nigrid beamed in anticipation of the increased profit from the sale of the animals.

The Nigrid would be able to sell over 900 lambs to the Passover observers. Five hundred of that number would come from Terach. In addition to the lambs, Terach had an abundance of hides from disposing of the older ewes and rams from both the sheep and goat herds. Again, the Nigrid was ecstatic about the quality of the leather. "The leather will fetch a premium price for the cobblers here and also in Jerusalem. The cobblers' desire for this quality of leather will enable us to greatly increase our price next year."

Jews were very fond of goat cheese, and demand was always high. Of the three products supplied by Terach, cheese was the least abundant because of the lack of an adequate production facility. Nonetheless, what Terach supplied based on the efforts of Beulah, Channah, the other shepherd wives and Iza was excellent quality. The Nigrid winked at his friend as he teased, "Unfortunately, for my personal treasury, this cheese will never make it to the marketplace. I will confiscate it for my own use. Of course, Terach, you will receive the market price."

The Nigrid observed that Terach was not his normal jovial self. Usually the two would jostle each other in mock haggling, but they both knew the astute business administrator would always pay the nomad shepherd the top price. Terach's items were superior in quality to what others offered the Nigrid. The mock haggling was just for the enjoyment of both men.

"Terach, why are you so somber? This is not like you, at all." The business magnate for the Roman procurator watched closely and waited for his friend to reveal the source of his woes. After a brief interlude, Terach confided in his friend and business colleague. "My heart is heavy, my friend, and I desperately need your services." The Nigrid was taken aback at the solemn and desperate tone of his friend's voice.

For the next twenty minutes, Terach told the Nigrid everything about Mattan's blindness and that Iza was going to divorce the blind shepherd. "I know you will keep what I tell you in confidence, my friend, especially about Iza. I told her only Beulah would know of her plans. My main concern is Mattan. Obviously, he no longer can continue being a shepherd."

At that point, Terach relayed to his business colleague and friend stories about Mattan's struggles out in the field and the difficulties Mattan had with even the simplest duties of a nomad shepherd.

Terach paused to consider how to make the hardest part of his request from his friend. In a decisive tone, he began, "My friend, I do not want my son relegated to being a beggar sitting at the Temple in Jerusalem!" Then, with a snort, he added, "Of course, this would never happen! Because as a shepherd, he would not even be allowed next to the other beggars!"

The frustrated and worried shepherd clenched his teeth before going on. "Nor do I want my son sitting here in Jericho begging for alms from strangers!" Terach looked desperately at his friend with pleading. "Nigrid, I seek your advice. What can you do, if anything, for Mattan?"

As Terach's words reverberated in the enclosed patio, the Nigrid swallowed hard before replying to the morose shepherd.

The business icon offered his friend his consolation. "My friend, I am deeply saddened for your family as well as for Mattan. I, too, do not want to have your son, my adopted nephew, relegated to beggar status!" He paused, in order to compose himself. "I must ponder this situation before I settle on a solution. It may take some time, but rest assured, Terach, I will not fail you. I will confer with some people I know who may be able to assist us."

Terach exhaled. His shoulders and expression relaxed. He leaned back in his chair and queried his chosen problem solver, "How long will this take? Iza and I will leave on the morrow for Bethlehem. Two days from now the bands of sheep will begin their journey south. After I finalize the divorce with Nadan, I will return north to Qumran, then east around the top of the Dead Sea. From there I must proceed south to catch up with the flocks. Gavriel will do my scouting, but the main band of sheep and goats requires his supervision. I cannot return here."

The Nigrid's brow furrowed and his lips compressed as he listened to his friend's quandary. He remained quiet and thoughtful for a short time. He rubbed his smallish hands together, and a slight smile formed. "Let Mattan be my guest here in my home. You won't have to waste valuable time returning here to Jericho. This will give me much needed time to examine Mattan's mindset and determine what is best for him."

Terach held his right index finger to his bearded cheek as he listened to the proposal. When the Nigrid had finished his summation, the nomad shepherd interjected, "I believe your solution will work for everyone, my friend. It is quite possible that Mattan's attitude and emotions will ease while being your house guest. Of course, you realize I won't be able to return here once we reach Machaerus. There is no turning back from there. We cross into Nabatean territory until we reach the southern tip of the Dead Sea and can go west from there through Idumea to Gaza."

The Nigrid bobbed his head in understanding the dilemma confronting the nomad shepherd. "My friend, in this case I believe the extended time is a valuable asset for our cause. This will give me sufficient time to get Mattan established and for him to adjust to a new life. He will need this time to build his confidence without aid of the family. Trust my ability to convince Mattan that he indeed has a new life of opportunity."

Terach gratefully nodded his agreement with the Nigrid's proposal. In a choking voice, Terach uttered, "This is a very difficult situation, my friend. Beulah's, Channah's and my emotions are at a fever level. It will be hard for all of us to do as you say. I trust you to make sure that Mattan will be adequately comforted physically and emotionally during his adjustment period."

The Nigrid leaned forward from his reclining position on his fainting couch. "Terach, convey to your family how much Mattan is family to me. I will not harm him in any way."

The matter was sealed. Terach hugged his short friend who held him tightly for an extended period of time without additional words. When the two separated, each quickly wiped tears away from their swollen eyes.

Terach left the mansion and returned to his own home on the outskirts of Jericho. The shepherd leader notified the family members that he wanted to discuss an important matter with them and that they should join him and Beulah for dinner.

Alone in his tent with Beulah, Terach said, "Nigrid and I have reached a solution for our issue with Mattan. You will be pleased when I tell you tonight." His tone lightened as he announced, "Now I will select several lambs from our band for tonight's meal. We must have a feast."

Beulah peered at her husband with a perplexed look. She would have to subjugate her eager curiosity and be patient. She shrugged her shoulders and said, "It is as you command, my husband."

When the savory meal was finished, the curious family group all looked to Terach to reveal what was the important matter. Looking around at his loved ones, the nomad shepherd leader sat next to Mattan and gently, lovingly, placed his hand on his blind son's shoulder. Calmly, the shepherd leader began, "The Nigrid and I concluded our annual business dealings today. He informed me of his desire to have you, Mattan, be his house guest for a period of time. I believe this is an excellent idea, but we want to know how you feel about it."

All eyes suddenly shifted to Mattan. To the surprise of everyone in attendance, the young blind shepherd remained serene and in an even-tempered voice spoke to his family. With his head tilted slightly upward and his vacant eyes moving from side to side, he announced, "I realize how difficult it will be for me to continue with you on our route to Gaza. It is not safe for me, any of you, nor our flocks for me to attempt to continue being a shepherd. This time with the Nigrid could prove valuable to me, as well." With a sigh, he ended, "I will stay here in Jericho."

Terach was dubious about his son's answer. The shepherd felt his son was too quickly willing to make such a drastic change. In addition, Mattan did not inquire about Iza and if she would be included as the Nigrid's house guest. The astute nomad shepherd decided to pursue his instincts further.

"Mattan, you realize should you remain here in Jericho, none of the family will be able to have contact with you until we return to Jericho next spring. It will be a long time, my son."

The expression on Mattan's face did not change. He remained composed, but he acknowledged, "I am aware of this fact, Father. It will pain me to be so far away from all of you and from my duties with the flocks." His voice hinted of a doleful tone, but he quickly regained a sense of determination and decreed in a firm voice, "There is no other choice."

Channah could not contain herself. She jumped up and bolted to her blind brother's side, sat beside him and threw her arms around his neck. Choking back tears, she blurted, "I miss you already, my brother. No one can tease me the way that you do, or make me laugh so hard that I cry." That being said, the blind shepherd's sister bravely forced a giggle in order to disguise her weeping. However, her wet cheek, pressed against Mattan's, betrayed her tears and deep sorrow at the thought of their separation.

Beulah rose up and went to her two youngest children. The mother sat next to Mattan, took his hand and placed it in her own, then moved them together to her cheek. Her actions spoke volumes. The assemblage of distressed family members heard her silent lamentation in their own hearts.

Gavriel and Eitou briefly looked at each other and exchanged stunned expressions. Eitou turned to Mattan and croaked, "You will be in my thoughts every day, my brother. At night I shall ask God to be with you."

Gavriel's head drooped at Eitou's emotional statement. The oldest brother ran his fingers through his beard, inhaled deeply, and haltingly uttered, "In addition to being my brother, Mattan, you are my best friend. I love you and will join Eitou in asking God to take care of you."

The tension hung heavy in the air and Mattan's brothers and sister had to leave. The thoughts of not having their brother around were too strong for them to remain in the tent home. Each left hunched over, stifling sobs and soft moans. Iza remained in the tent but said nothing. She fleetingly glanced at Terach, then looked back at her blind husband.

Terach had to clench his fingers and bit his lip to contain himself. The words of love exchanged by his children to Mattan penetrated to the deepest part of his soul. Never had he witnessed such signs of deep compassion. Watching Beulah sit silently holding her youngest son's hand to her cheek tore into his heart like the screech of a dying hare. The family's heartfelt reactions and words rang true, in stark contrast to Iza's woeful restraint.

When Terach's eyes met those of Iza, he could imagine how she was feeling through this event. The nomad leader moved to the other side of his blind son and put his arm around Mattan's shoulder. The trio of father, mother, and son sat tightly together, while Iza remained detached, alone, looking down at the dirt inside the tent. She made no effort to become part of the supportive group.

The next morning, Terach took Mattan to the Nigrid's home where the ebullient business icon welcomed him joyfully into his mansion. "Mattan, I'm so grateful you will honor me with your presence here in my home! Please make it your home, as well. My servants and I will do whatever is necessary to see that you are comfortable during your stay with me." Mattan and Terach detected complete sincerity in the business governor's voice.

Much to Terach's amazement, Mattan replied, "Thank you, Nigrid, for your generous hospitality. I know I will enjoy my stay with you until such time that I must leave." The blind shepherd turned, moving his head side to side searching for his father and gently said, "It is time for you to return to our camp to direct everyone on the southward part of the journey. Rest assured, Father, I will be fine. I look forward to this time together with Nigrid." Mattan smiled to indicate his willingness to enter the unknown territory that awaited him.

There was nothing for Terach to say, but he scrutinized Mattan's voice and mannerisms. He found it odd that Mattan did not inquire about Iza and decided he would not bring up the subject with his son. The nomad shepherd guessed the couple had discussed the situation last night together and wondered if Iza informed Mattan of her divorce plans. He felt she had not; otherwise, Mattan would not have been so easy going. The nomad leader was wrong in his assumption. The young married couple had discussed it. Mattan's acceptance of the divorce was based on months of recognition that it was inevitable. In essence, they had emotionally divorced months earlier and neither of them needed the formality of a decree to feel the sting of it.

Terach gave his youngest son a tight hug and whispered in his ear, "You remain in my heart, Mattan. I shall think fondly of you every day. I love you."

The nomad shepherd then broke away from his son, nodded to the Nigrid, and turned to make his way out of the mansion. As he rode the short distance to his base camp, Terach let the tears freely flow down his cheeks. He was grateful that he had no need to hide them. This was one of the more difficult times in his life. He felt tired and very, very old.

Chapter 13

The first thirty days of separation from his family and the only life the young blind shepherd ever knew was a wild combination of placid lakes and stormy seas for Mattan and the Nigrid.

The two quickly established a strong friendship. Nigrid was startled how much interest Mattan expressed in the business world that was the heartbeat of Jericho. His young student asked about many facets of business the common man would not be interested in. Of course, Mattan's foundation was based upon familiar matters involving sheep, goats, and the byproducts they offered.

Mattan's business interest caused the business administrator to pause in his search for a solution to his adopted nephew's need for a new lifestyle. The Nigrid spent several days in deep deliberation. Ultimately, the chief business administrator for all of Judea opted to stay with his original idea, and initiated contact with two people integral to his plan.

The first person involved in the scheme was another blind man who several years earlier had come to Jericho in much the same manner as Mattan. The father of the blind youth, Timaeous, was a Jew who owned a shipping company that operated out of Gaza. His son had been born blind, and by the time he reached young manhood, pressure from the rabbi and the Jewish elders of the synagogue forced Timaeous to take his son out of the community.

Timaeous had regular business dealings with the Judean business magnate. He sought his advice because of the Nigrid's vast contacts and inside knowledge of the goings-on throughout all of Judea.

With the help of a caravan captain, the Nigrid stumbled upon a solution that was quite unique. Happily, it also proved profitable to the business icon. The business magnate helped

Bartimaeus, the blind young man, begin the process of becoming a tentmaker despite the huge setbacks of blindness. The caravan captain had mentioned how he witnessed a blind tentmaker on one of his trips to Persia and was taken aback by how someone blind could skillfully engage in such a craft. Not only was this blind man adept in constructing tents, he was highly proficient in the making of shoes and sandals, complementing work that was common to all tent makers of that time.

With the combined efforts of a skilled tentmaker and his own willingness to learn, Bartimaeus had adapted well to the process and had become so competent that the master tentmaker switched Bartimaeus to constructing only shoes. It was a simple matter of economics. There was more demand for footwear, and this afforded more opportunity for profit. The shrewd Judean business magnate was always interested in ways of acquiring more profit.

At the shoe factory owned by the Nigrid, Bartimaeus was taken to the office of the factory manager for Bartimaeus to be interrogated regarding his ability to meet the requirements of producing a quality product. Once approved and hired, Bartimaeus had quickly risen in the ranks to become one of the top craftsmen.

On a warm, sunny day when the cobblers were taking a break, the Nigrid saw Bartimaeus sitting alone. "Bartimaeus, it is I, Nigrid, and I must speak with you about a matter that deeply concerns me. What you say will greatly sway a decision that I must make very soon."

The blind Bartimaeus heard the gravity of his benefactor's tone, and warmly replied, "I will help in whatever way you desire, Nigrid." Immediately, the benefactor launched into detail about Mattan and spared nothing, knowing that every detail would add to Bartimaeus' understanding of the circumstances.

The blind shoemaker took his time considering the facts of the situation confronting his boss. He repeatedly ran his fingers through his coarse beard while deep in thought. "So, it is not tent making or shoemaking that you want me to help with, eh?" The Nigrid watched the blind man's mannerisms closely. He was greatly pleased to see how the blind shoemaker was giving careful thought to the matter.

After a while Bartimaeus turned his head toward his benefactor and commented, "Nigrid, I believe you should pursue your plan for this blind shepherd. He will experience difficulty in the beginning just as I did; but with repeated effort, patience, and teaching, I believe he will be productive. I caution you, this man's attitude will be his biggest enemy. Be prepared to give the matter adequate time. I will help him "see" that not seeing is not the end of life." They both chuckled at the irony of his words.

Pleased that Bartimaeus' response coincided with his own verdict, the profit seeker thanked his blind shoemaker and let him return to his duties. He knew Bartimaeus would be most valuable to his friend, Mattan. The Nigrid ordered the factory supervisor to increase Bartimaeus' compensation.

Bartimaeus would be an excellent counselor and encourager for Mattan. But the Nigrid had a different skill he hoped to give Mattan for a new business. It wouldn't be shoemaking or tent-making, but something he imagined Mattan would find great pleasure in. And he knew just the person who could teach Mattan the new skills he had in mind. As quickly as his short legs would allow, the jubilant business creator made his way to the second contact on his list.

When the Nigrid arrived at his next stop, it was close to the end of the workday. "Very good," he thought. "This will allow us time to discuss my proposal."

The Nigrid carefully laid out his plan for Mattan with the capable woman who sat non-committed throughout his presentation. Finally, the Nigrid could think of no more details to persuade her. "Now that you have heard of this fine young man and have heard my plan, Devorah, will you participate in assisting this blind young man to build a new life?"

Jadedly, the woman sought out by the Nigrid raised her arm. "Nigrid, what you ask will be most difficult and there are no guarantees this man will learn the necessary skills for this new life. I am very reluctant to take on such a project." It was obvious the woman had more on her mind than what she had spoken. "Frankly, what's in it for me? The time I take to teach and mentor this blind former shepherd will cost me valuable time and money."

The woman was one of the Nigrid's better supervisors. She oversaw several of the Nigrid's businesses. She was known for her patience and skill in teaching those chosen for the Nigrid's profitable businesses. She had been widowed at a young age and forced to work because her deceased husband had no brothers to support her as Jewish tradition usually provided. She had been hired by the Nigrid and soon became his best producer. She had the mindset for business economics and for survival.

"Devorah, let me say that you will have complete control in this matter. Yes, I consider this blind man to be part of my family, but I do not let my affections interfere with sound business decisions. Should this man not be able to learn the techniques and skills needed, you have permission to end his involvement in my business."

This statement gave Devorah the assurance she needed. Her skeptical demeanor eased and she reluctantly agreed to her supervisor's proposal. "I will teach this man what he needs to learn the business. Bring him by when you are ready for him to begin the process."

Excited that his plan was doable, the elated conniver raced to his mansion to inform Mattan that he would begin learning how to become a potter. He was very pleased that his plan could be implemented and he believed that Mattan would welcome the opportunity to learn this new life skill.

Part way back to his office, the Nigrid was intercepted by one of the personnel who assisted Nicolas. "Nigrid, I'm glad to have found you. Nicolas wishes your presence immediately in his office. It is a matter of great importance." Baffled by the hired man's statement, the short-legged administrator followed the messenger hurriedly and soon stepped into his fellow administrator's opulent office.

"Ah, Nigrid. I'm glad you could get here so quickly. I was concerned my messenger would have difficulty in locating you. Please, sit," he said as he gestured toward a nearby couch. "I believe you will want such luxury after I tell you the news." The Nigrid took a seat in one of the ornately carved and cushioned chairs. Nicolas produced two gold chalices, poured an ample amount of wine into each one, and handed one to his colleague.

The Nigrid watched curiously at the co-administrator's actions but did not perceive anything ominous. Nicolas sat on the edge of his desk, and smiled as he looked at his colleague. "I have received word that I am to immediately report back to Rome. Caesar has special need of me there. I will begin the process of packing and arranging transportation of my possessions. I should be able to leave for Caesarea within two days."

So it was not an emergency. "I'm stunned to hear of your good fortune, my friend. Let us have a toast to your advancement," said the flustered Nigrid. "Do you know what duties Caesar has in store for you when you arrive in Rome?"

Nicolas frowned. "I do not." With a shrug he added, "It does not matter. I look forward to going to Rome and making myself known there. I'm sure there will be other opportunities to take advantage of, especially the way in which Rome is expanding."

The befuddled Nigrid took a sip from his gold chalice and asked tentatively, "Who will be replacing you here in Jericho?"

Nicolas smiled broadly and his eyes twinkled. He deliberately took his time in answering his friend's question. With drama he responded, "You are, my friend!"

The Nigrid nearly dropped his wine-filled chalice. Disconcerted, the short man stammered, "How can this be?"

Nicolas jovially leaned towards the Nigrid and explained, "Legate Gnaeus Saturninus believes one man can fulfill both duties in this province. You, my friend, will be the sole administrator for all of Judea, beginning immediately." A gleeful Nicolas laughed aloud at the surprise of his friend.

The Nigrid pondered this new development in his life. He took a slow sip and looked up at Nicolas. "Does the procurator in Caesarea have any objections to my taking on your responsibilities in addition to my own?"

Nicolas shook his head no. "The procurator doesn't care how many administrators there are in Judea. His only concern is that everything functions smoothly and that the taxes are collected on time. You have done well in this area. My duties won't hinder your ability to maintain collection of the taxes."

The departing official took a swig from his gold chalice, chuckled, and winked at his friend with a wry smile saying, "Nigrid, this means that you will now have more opportunity to add to your own treasury. As long as the procurator gets his share of the taxes, he won't interfere with you adding to your coffers." He leaned back and summarized, "You, my friend, will become the richest man in all of Judea."

The two collaborators finished their wine and discussion of the turn of events. With new possibilities whirling in his mind, the Nigrid proceeded to his mansion. A considerable time later, after processing Nicolas' words, he met with Mattan concerning his new career as a potter.

Mattan and the Nigrid sat out on the patio as the sun was lowering on the horizon. The Nigrid made sure it was a fitting meal to herald the new changes for himself and for Mattan. As the two sat munching on honey cakes, the benefactor broke the news to Mattan.

"I have splendid news for you, Mattan. Arrangements have been made for you to begin the process of learning a new skill that will provide you the means to live comfortably and not be relegated to that of a mere beggar." The enthusiasm in the surrogate uncle's voice piqued Mattan's curiosity.

"This is surprising news, Uncle. I did not believe anything could happen so quickly. What is it you have arranged for me to learn?"

The surrogate family member put down his wine goblet and slapped his knees as he excitedly announced, "Becoming a potter! A supervisor at one of our best pottery factories is intrigued at the prospect of teaching you the craft. You are to begin right after the Sabbath."

Mattan was almost shocked beyond words. He could not comprehend a blind man becoming a potter. He expressed his doubt with his benefactor. "Are you sure about this? Making pots and other vessels is not an easy undertaking for one who has sight. How can I, a blind shepherd, ever succeed at such an endeavor?"

Avidly, his benefactor explained, "This supervisor is very accomplished and has taught many others this skill. Most of her pupils did not believe they could master the craft, but they have, and now make excellent works. You can do the same, Mattan, I know in my heart it is within you." He spoke emphatically, but then he lied, "This person has taught other blind people who now are accomplished potters."

"Despite what you say, I do not believe a blind shepherd has the capabilities of undertaking such a challenge. I have grave misgivings about this."

His benefactor encouraged his adopted nephew to think more about it, and excused himself. His attention was divided between Mattan's new undertaking and his own. He needed to address an important issue associated with his new combined duties as finance administrator and business administrator.

Mattan lingered on the patio and felt the first coolness of the twilight wash over his body. The blind shepherd lifted his head towards the heavens and imagined the first stars that would be appearing with the beginning of the night. Dazzling stars he had seen so often while in the field with his flock and took for granted.

The image of those times remained vivid and served to pacify his agitated emotions after hearing the outlandish new career proposal. The blind shepherd was confused and didn't know what to really think about such an abrupt change. He felt his surrogate uncle had lost his senses! It seemed more logical that his experience in selling sheep and goat products would possibly be a better avenue for him to pursue. Being a potter had never entered the realm of possibility in his mind. Nonetheless, the young man knew he had to honor his adopted uncle's efforts and good will on his behalf.

As the air cooled, one of the Nigrid's servants came and escorted Mattan to his bedchamber. The disgruntled, displaced young man was surprised how much time had elapsed while he was thinking about these strange developments.

After the blind shepherd fell asleep, the recurring dream of haunting eyes flooded his mind once again, as it had every night since his lethal encounter with the rogue wolf.

The two-day wait to begin his initial experience in the pottery factory compounded Mattan's doubt and concern. The Nigrid spent the majority of his time adjusting his own added responsibilities of being the Judean finance minister. Nicolas prepped his colleague well in the area of finance, and the Nigrid quickly saw how to combine the two areas into one—cohesively and well-organized. When he was around Mattan, he encouraged him at every given moment.

Early that Monday morning, the encourager and the novice made their way to the pottery factory and Mattan's date with destiny. On the short journey, Mattan's hands began to sweat and his breathing was somewhat labored. Upon reaching their destination, Mattan was brought out of his cloud of deep thought by his adopted uncle's words.

"Mattan, this is the supervisor I told you about, who will personally tutor you in becoming a potter. I must hurry to a finance meeting. I'm sure the two of you will get along fine. I leave you in good hands." With those words, the Nigrid scurried off to his office. Mattan stood uncomfortably waiting for the supervisor to direct him. His blindness had produced a new habit of twisting his head side to side in an attempt to locate what confronted him. He was listening for movement and anticipating some instructions.

"I am Devorah. Nigrid told me you were a nomad shepherd blinded by a battle with a wolf. Is that correct?" Mattan's twisting head stopped and honed in on the source of the words. He was taken aback at hearing a woman's voice. As a shepherd, he had no previous experience with a woman being in a position of authority. He wasn't sure how this would go. In a cautious voice he answered, "What the Nigrid has spoken about me is true. I have been blind nearly one year and am resigned to never being a shepherd again."

Devorah detected deep sorrow in Mattan's voice. Before she could speak, the blind shepherd added, "Do you truly believe that a blind man, a shepherd, can learn the skills needed to be a potter?" Mattan's tone revealed deep doubts, mixed with a touch of disdain.

Devorah opted not to give him false hope. It was not her manner to do so and it wouldn't be fair to her new student. "I have trained many different people, both male and female, who have become excellent potters. Your hands and fingers will become your eyes while you learn. All I can tell you is that I will teach you everything that I have learned. It is up to you to gain knowledge and become skilled in your new craft. As in all things, perseverance and patience will be your friends."

The woman potter reached out and took Mattan's arm saying, "Come with me. I will take you to a private area where we can begin the process of learning." A flash of fear, almost a chill, took hold of the blind shepherd as he was guided by his instructor into this strange new realm of life.

By the end of the second week of their new association, both Devorah and Mattan came to an impasse, each refusing to work with the other. Tension between the two, fueled by frustration, created a situation of near combat. The Nigrid was informed of the situation and summoned the two warriors to his office.

His agitated voice thundered in the meeting room. "You both know the reason why I summoned you here. I am well aware that your hostility towards each other is now having an impact on the other potters. It's affecting their productivity." The Nigrid paused, expecting that his no-nonsense attitude and authoritative tone would correct the ruffled feathers and stubborn attitudes of these two dominant personalities.

The Nigrid observed the crossed arms, hunched shoulders, pouty expressions, and stubborn brows of the two opponents. The battle lines were clear, but inwardly he chuckled. The situation was volatile, yet he knew he was in complete control, so he pressed on.

Maintaining a harsh tone, the arbitrator continued, "There is nothing that can't be fixed. The solution to your shared dislike toward each other will be this. First, you will leave here, go to my mansion, sit on the patio, and talk with each other. You both shall tell the other about your background and how you got to this current chapter in your life."

The Nigrid surveyed his subjects and was not surprised at the expressions of resistance and wonderment on each face. He smiled and persisted. "Second, each of you will tell the other your feelings about who you were prior to who you now are. What were both the good as well as the bad moments in your life? Third, I want you to state to each other the passion you had for what you did in your former life."

Again the Nigrid stopped to survey his audience. Now their expressions merely puzzled. They kept their arms crossed and tight to their bodies. Devorah arched a skeptical eyebrow at her judge. Undeterred, the Nigrid went on, "You will not return to the pottery factory during this time of revelation. You shall do this at my mansion. Spend however long each day it takes to accomplish what I've ordered you to do. I shall not interfere because I must travel to Caesarea and meet with the procurator on official business."

For the third time, the Nigrid momentarily ceased instruction to let his students absorb his orders. "I shall be gone for five days. This is how long you have to reconcile your differences. On the sixth day, each of you shall meet with me at my mansion. At that time, I want each of you to give me your findings about the other person. On that day, I shall render my decision as to what will become of the two of you, based on what you tell me." Slowly and with great emphasis he warned, "Your respective futures will be determined by the amount of cooperation you each give to this assignment."

Both adversaries were stunned. One looked at the Nigrid with disbelief in her eyes. The blind shepherd looked in the direction of the Nigrid with blank eyes, but his face was contorted with anguish and doubt.

The Nigrid suppressed a slight smile and used a hand to hide it from Devorah, but inwardly he was chuckling again. He assessed the dispute as that of two youngsters who needed to have parental intervention in the difficulty... and he had become the mediator. The surrogate parent finished, "That is my order. Do either of you have any questions concerning this assignment?"

There was a brief silence in the office. Devorah cleared her throat and asked, "What happens if we fail at this obligation?"

The Nigrid forced a stern expression on his face and manufactured a harsh tone, "Both of you will be removed from the pottery factory and I will cease being your benefactor. Devorah, you shall have to find other employment. It won't be in Judea. Mattan, you shall either be relegated to beggar status here in Jericho or somewhere else your father and I agree upon. There shall be no other alternative. I have responsibilities to the procurator and as business administrator of all Judea. As such, I do not have time to put up with two obstinate children."

The reality of the impasse flooded each of the combatant's minds. Without looking in the direction of the other, each realized the severity of the dispute. There could be a heavy price to pay for stubbornness. Seizing the moment, Mattan was the first to reply to the directive. He choked out, "I fully understand what you have told us and also how our actions have caused harm to you and to the pottery factory. I will do my best to comply with your order."

Devorah looked over at the blind shepherd and sensed his sincerity. She decided if this pigheaded former shepherd was willing to do what the Nigrid had ordered, so could she. Devorah resolved to be better at resolving the impasse than this blind shepherd who so far had proven to be inflexible in learning a new trade. She asserted her intention. "Rest assured, Nigrid, it won't be I who violates your directive."

Both participants in the plan wondered how much the other was truly willing to comply with the ultimatum. Only time would tell. The Nigrid stood up from his chair and decisively finished the scolding, "Good. Now I must go and attend to business."

To his surprise, Devorah reached out and took Mattan by the arm and gently turned him towards the door of the office. Stiffly she suggested, "Let us immediately get started on what the Nigrid wants us to do." The blind shepherd held his tongue and relented.

The two adversaries walked contritely to the Nigrid's mansion and began the first session.

Chapter 14

It was uncomfortable for the two combatants, in spite of the comfortable chairs supplied to them. The silent tension was obvious. One of the servants gingerly placed a tray of food and wine before them, and quickly departed. The only sound for quite some time was that of chirping birds, a peculiar contrast to the icy atmosphere. However, the warm springtime sun began to have its effect, and the two opponents began to relax in spite of the daunting task they had been charged with.

The minds of both Devorah and Mattan were wondering who would initiate and how brutal the battle would be. Each was braced for an opening salvo. The Jewish custom at the time was male dominance in every aspect of daily living. As such, Mattan was within his right to demand that Devorah begin. Instead, the young blind shepherd opted to come from a different angle.

"I shall begin," he said with authority. "This is most uncomfortable but, nonetheless, I shall tell you about being a nomad shepherd."

For the next twenty minutes, Devorah listened to an honest depiction of the blind shepherd's earlier life. At times she pictured herself on the open plain at night watching the stars and the moon and the occasion shooting star. She began to understand Mattan's great love for his former life, for the landscapes and textures and smells. She shuddered as Mattan relayed his death battle against the rogue wolf and ferocious killing. She winced, envisioning confronting the cold, steely, evil yellow eyes of the assailant.

When Mattan finished that portion of his story, Devorah candidly responded, "I greatly admire you passion and your love for your sheep and the goats. It took courage to face that wolf, Mattan. I sincerely commend you." Mattan had spoken impassively during his recital, wondering what her face was expressing. He was both startled and pleased to hear Devorah's words of honest understanding and appreciation. He had purposely omitted details about his failed marriage. He did not feel right about disclosing this painful personal fact. He indicated it was now her turn to provide insight into her background.

As her narrative unfolded, the blind shepherd aligned with her depiction. He was well aware of arranged marriages and how too often these marriages turned into gender wars. He discovered genuine sadness over the death of her husband and having no relatives to take care of her. During that period, women frequently became harlots or were relegated to cleaning the Temple or one of the numerous synagogues throughout Judea.

It was only when Devorah finished telling how the Nigrid saved her from a most unpleasant life that Mattan awkwardly said, "I did not tell you that I am married, but my wife is traveling with my family back to Bethlehem. I fear she will remain there and divorce me because I cannot provide for her. In my heart I believe she simply cannot bear having to take care of me the rest of her life."

Layers of misconceptions had been pulled back, like layers of an onion. A new kind of quietness settled like a spring cloud over the pair. Both were quite surprised how once started, they openly revealed inner thoughts to each other despite their earlier adversarial attitude. They were learning about each other in ways that would impact them beyond the Nigrid's edict.

Devorah informed Mattan that the sun was setting over the horizon and the blind shepherd smiled, "One of the adjustments I've made since becoming blind is sensing the temperature changes that take place when the sun goes beyond the horizon or when a cloud passes over." This revelation slightly startled Devorah. She made a mental note to explore more aspects of Mattan's blindness when the next session resumed tomorrow. This day had been good progress. As if to celebrate the beginning of a truce, a servant appeared with the day's ending meal.

When the Nigrid left the two combatants in his office, he immediately went to his chosen back-up in the dispute. He felt should difficulties continue between Devorah and Mattan, this deputy had the capability of resolving the issue in a manner that would benefit everyone. The Nigrid truly liked both Devorah and Mattan and was dedicated to resolve their disputes, for he certainly did not want to act on his statement of disposing of them. He quickly went to meet with his proxy.

His meeting with the stand-in was brief and efficient. Satisfied this uncomfortable issue was well taken care of, the Nigrid returned to his office and gathered up all the documents he needed for his meeting with the Roman procurator, Valerius Gratus in Caesarea. The upcoming meeting had the Nigrid unsettled about what was to take place. He remained alone in his mansion preparing for the uncertainty that was before him. Very early the next morning, the apprehensive business administrator settled in his comfortable coach for the journey to Rome's designated capital of Judea. A troop of six very accomplished Roman cavalry archers accompanied the Judean administrator to Caesarea.

That second day, Devorah and Mattan were more comfortable discussing themselves. Gone was the initial hesitancy in sharing personal inner facts with someone they did not really know. Early in the new day's session Devorah unexpectedly took the lead role. "The Nigrid is like an older brother to me. He really does care about my well-being. When he took me on as the pottery supervisor, I did not believe I had the capability of becoming a potter. It was as if he saw something special within me that I didn't know. His insight brought out some hidden talents. I don't know how he knew, but I thank God that he did."

Mattan stroked his soft-haired beard while he listened. When Devorah finished, he interjected, "The Nigrid has been like an uncle to me and my brothers and sister. He has always shown us love and kindness. It goes beyond the fact he and my father are business partners. We all truly believe he is part of our family."

The blind shepherd decided to share more of himself with his counterpart. "This whole experience is very distressing. I'm having a difficult time adjusting to so many new things." He stopped for a moment, before admitting, "Sometimes I believe that I'm going crazy." Despite his blindness, Mattan turned his head in the direction of Devorah and confessed, "One day I dress the way I have all my life in shepherd's clothing, and then without warning I now dress in the manner of a city dweller. The clothes are entirely different and feel strange next to my body." Mattan put his hands to his clothing, slightly tugging at the material. "This strangeness goes to my mind and my thoughts."

Mattan paused to gauge the effect his words had on Devorah. When it became evident to the blind man she would make no disparaging remarks, he continued. "I have to adjust to a strange new house environment, a different way of living the day, different food, and constant questions of what will become of me."

At that point Mattan dropped his guard and spoke candidly about his fears. "Too many times it becomes overwhelming. On top of all this, now I have to learn something that is totally foreign to me. I don't know if my mind is ready for all these changes. I am feeling very troubled."

Mattan felt relief that he was finally able to express his inner thoughts. It was as if a great burden had been taken off his back. He was pleased at his ability to share his emotions and did not believe that the Jewish widow would castigate him. His assessment proved correct.

"I had no idea what you have been experiencing, Mattan. It is beyond me simply because I am not blind. Rest assured, when we return to the pottery factory, I shall not treat you the same as I first did."

Mattan reached out, groping uncertainly for Devorah's hand. She took it in hers and immediately the blind shepherd asserted, "I am now ready to receive your instruction."

In Caesarea the Nigrid had an enlightening experience with Valerius Gratus. The Roman was also a former cavalry officer as was his predecessor Annius Rufus. However, this was the only similarity between the two procurators. Rufus was mild-mannered and content with the money he obtained by over-charging the Jews and the Samaritans in their taxes. Rufus had ruled Judea for only three years before being replaced by Valerius Gratus.

Gratus was vastly different. He was harsh and demanding, with an agenda to maintain absolute control over the Jews, whom he despised for their adherence to their one God who dominated their lives in so many ways.

As the Nigrid braced himself for a different experience with the procurator Gratus, a soldier announced the procurator would meet with him in the elaborate office of the mansion used by all the procurators. Gratus remained seated. Before his visitor was seated, the autocrat brusquely got to the point of the meeting.

"Now that Nicolas has been transferred to Rome, you have added responsibilities as both business administrator and now finance administrator. You realize that in your role of finance manager, collection of taxes is to be your main focus. Do you have a problem being able to carry out both appointments?"

"I foresee no difficulties whatsoever, Gratus. Nicolas and I worked well together and sometimes would take the other's duties should the need arise. I am quite familiar with the schedule and methods utilized by Nicolas. I intend to follow his system. You need not worry, Gratus. There will be no interruption or change in collecting Rome's taxes."

Gratus appeared satisfied with the Nigrid's answers, but his eyes remained unyielding and he grilled the new appointee about certain aspects of the tax procedure. "It has come to my attention that a faction of Jews has arisen. They call themselves Zealots. I am told their purpose is to interfere with Rome's tax procedures. What have you learned about this faction?"

"They are small and do not have much influence with the people, Procurator. Actions by them have not required special attention. Thus far, they have not caused disruption in the tax collection."

"It is necessary, Nigrid, that you keep informed about this group. Do not worry. I believe I have sufficient spies who can keep us apprised of their goings on," said the procurator. "When new information comes to me I will notify you via carrier pigeon so that you can adjust to any new directives I impose."

Gratus waited until the meeting was nearly finished when he sprang his last bit of news to the Judean administrator. "I have decided, Nigrid, that to keep these Jews in line, I will continue the policy established by Archelaus and will appoint their high priest. Of course I will select someone who is most favorable to Rome and one who is easy to control. This will reduce any potential threat these Jewish leaders pose to Rome. Do you agree with this continuation of policy?"

A shocked Nigrid was taken aback by this decision. "This is most unusual, Gratus. The Jews are highly protective of the Sanhedrin and do not accept foreigners interfering with their religious rituals and practices. Especially as it applies to the appointment of the high priest. I fear there will be much resistance to your proposal." The appointee shifted in his seat and continued, "Religion is very important to these people. Rome's interference in their rituals only serves to incite these Zealots. This practice could draw more Jews into their ranks."

"I thank you for your honesty, Nigrid. I've anticipated such resistance and believe there is a way to handle any defiance to my order. You simply have to show them who has the real power and they will acquiesce." Gratus slyly smiled, "When I am through with these religious leaders, they will become like obedient dogs following the slightest directive applied to them."

Nigrid knew it would be futile to disagree with Gratus any further. Instead, the Judean administrator said, "I do not doubt your ability to accomplish such a feat, Gratus. I shall do all that is in my power to assist you and make sure this change takes place without challenge."

Gratus smiled approvingly and offered the Nigrid some wine and cheese. "Together we shall not fail Rome. Now, let us take a break from these tiresome business matters. We have new chariot races planned, and I've been told the drivers are most talented and competitive. Let us go and enjoy ourselves."

Back in Jericho, Devorah and Mattan had exchanged their impasse for common ground to complete their assignment from the Nigrid. As they learned more about each other, each felt confident they would succeed. In fact, they were beginning to actually like the other. Nonetheless, the chosen proxy appeared, per the prearrangement of the Nigrid and to the surprise of the now reconciled opponents. The proxy was Bartimaeus, the blind cobbler.

Bartimaeus was congenial and soft-spoken. He informed both Devorah and Mattan he was directed to meet with them on that day to determine what progress had been made in their reconciliation. He was pleased when Devorah informed him of their newly formed pact.

"This is wonderful news, which I'm sure our patron will be quite pleased to learn. However, I am also requested by the Nigrid to speak with each of you individually. I'm to take as much time as needed to accomplish whatever is necessary to achieve the goal."

Devorah looked into the blind cobbler's face and detected no ulterior motive. If she did, it wouldn't make any difference. She knew that both she and Mattan had to comply with the Nigrid's order. It was a simple matter of life or death. Devorah jumped in, "I shall be the first one to speak with you, Bartimaeus. Are we to speak with you privately?"

The blind cobbler-turned-mediator smiled warmly and turned his head in the direction of Devorah's voice. "Yes, that is what has been directed."

Devorah suggested, "Let us sit here on the patio for our chat. I shall have a servant escort Mattan to another part of the mansion until such time as you desire to speak with him."

Bartimaeus was surprised by Devorah's quick initiative. He did not understand its meaning. Cautiously, he replied, "That is a good suggestion. The sun is warm and will be a comfort to us." Devorah summoned one of the house servants who led Mattan to another portion of the house. Once his footsteps could no longer be heard, Bartimaeus began the discussion.

"Nigrid said you are called Devorah and that you are a supervisor in the pottery factory under the Nigrid's administrative duties. Am I correct in this?" The blind cobbler's voice was casual, warm, and inviting.

He had quickly put Devorah at ease. "You are correct, Bartimaeus."

The blind mediator proceeded, "What are your main frustrations with Mattan?" Devorah felt relaxed and answered the same as she had earlier to the Nigrid, "His refusal to make a bona fide effort in learning the skills to be a potter." Devorah's voice softened a she quickly added, "But, Bartimaeus, Mattan and I have already resolved this issue. It has taken us three days to break through the barriers that caused us animosity. We have a better understanding of each other. We are well on the way to surmounting our initial impasse."

Bartimaeus tilted his head to one side as he listened to Devorah's account. When she had finished, the blind mediator responded, "This is good that you have reached this point without the need of my services. As such, is there anything you might want to ask me, Devorah, since I, too, am blind?"

Devorah leaned closer to the mediator. "Yes, there is, Bartimaeus. How long did it take you to become the skilled cobbler I've learned that you are?"

The blind cobbler took a deep breath before answering the question. "Initially one year to learn the techniques of tent-making. My mentor was pleased with my progress and said he felt I had the talent to progress to making shoes. At first I was reluctant because making a good fitting shoe is quite different than making a tent! I had inner struggles believing I could not accomplish such a feat."

Devorah let out a short laugh. "Indeed, Bartimaeus! It is exceedingly different and much more difficult. How did you begin the process?"

Bartimaeus sat back in his cushioned chair and felt the breeze that funneled through the patio archway brush over him. "My mentor sat me down and took my hands and led me through the process. At first I was quite frustrated because I obviously could not see what to do. He was patient with me and often repeated each phase of the process. Soon I made little advances. This encouraged me to continue and I was able to construct my first pair of shoes."

The breeze gusted for a moment and both Bartimaeus and Devorah sat relishing the freshness of the air. Before Devorah could speak, Bartimaeus continued with a laugh. "That first pair of shoes were not a good fit for man or beast, but I felt so glad at just being able to construct something more intricate than a mere tent! Within a short period of time I was able to make good shoes without the aid of my mentor."

Devorah listened intently. "Bartimaeus, you have given me great insight how to proceed with Mattan. I now realize I need to teach him about pottery as if I too were blind."

Bartimaeus beamed, "Devorah, that is the secret to being able to keep Mattan encouraged and motivated to continue. I don't know if he can be a skilled potter; only he will determine that. So long as you guide him in a manner that he will want to continue, you shall learn quickly about his talents."

The two talked amiably for some time, then Devorah suggested to her teacher, "If you don't have any more questions for me, I would like to take my leave and consider all that you have said to me."

Bartimaeus had no further questions and felt it would be very beneficial for her to plan how to proceed with Mattan. He gave her one more piece of advice, "Go slow. Observe Mattan and make this learning fun and satisfying."

Devorah reached out, touching the blind cobbler's shoulder and softly said, "Indeed I shall, Bartimaeus."

The blind cobbler remained seated on the patio enjoying the slight breeze as he waited for Mattan to arrive. During the interval, Bartimaeus regrouped his thoughts and devised his approach to his fellow blind man.

A house servant helped Mattan get seated in a cushioned chair similar to the one Bartimaeus was sitting in. The servant made sure Mattan's chair was positioned for conversation and comfort, directly facing the blind mediator for good audibility.

Bartimaeus initiated the conversation. "I know, Mattan, that you were not born blind. Tell me about your frustrations being totally without sight now?"

The blind shepherd was taken aback at the bold directness of the question. But because of Bartimaeus' understanding demeanor, Mattan relaxed and opened his thoughts to the stranger. The blind shepherd was pleased and surprised how easy it was for him to talk about his blindness with someone he hardly knew. He chastised himself for not initiating similar honest discussions with any of his family members, especially Iza.

Jumping right into the matter, Mattan spoke with an edge to his voice. "I'm angry at God for allowing this to happen. I was a fine shepherd, taking good care of my flock. I was married to a woman I thought God wanted for me. I'm angry that I can no longer be a shepherd and continue the traditions of my family. I'm angry that I can no longer support my wife. I'm angry because I don't foresee a future for me."

Mattan had to pause to compose himself. He bit the back of his right hand and breathed heavily. Bartimaeus heard his undisguised anger but did not argue about it.

With renewed vigor, Mattan continued his testimony to this mediator. "I'm angry with all the religious rabbis who sling fiery arrows at me and my family. A shepherd is not accepted by these religious fools, yet their words cause others to shun us, despite that we do them no harm. They say my sin is the cause of my blindness, yet they don't say what that sin is."

Again Mattan took a deep breath and Bartimaeus could hear his long exhalation of anguish. Bartimaeus waited quietly while the angry blind shepherd vented. Mattan loudly proclaimed, "I want to be a shepherd and only a shepherd!" Losing energy, he bowed his head into his hands and continued to lament, "I do not foresee anything good with this blindness."

A long intermission occurred as each blind man thought about what had just been revealed. Finally, Bartimaeus spoke, "Mattan, I fully understand your anger. You see, I, too, am blind. Have been since birth. I've experienced the same discrimination from the Pharisees and the rabbis. For a long time I wondered why God kept me alive."

Mattan was dumbfounded. Bartimaeus stopped to let his revelation sink in. After a moment the mediator went on, "My father was not only ridiculed, but banished from doing business with any Jew because of the stigma of their perceived sin that came into our home." With emphasis he proclaimed, "I, too, faced a future of being a beggar and an outcast spit upon by everyone. Mattan, I, too, doubted I could have a future."

Bartimaeus' words reverberated in Mattan's head. The blind shepherd sat motionless and silenced. Bartimaeus sensed Mattan's thoughts and queried, "Are you willing to attempt to construct a new life? One that obviously is far different than what you have had or desire, but nonetheless one than can be fruitful and give you dignity?"

Mattan raised his head and looked in the direction of Bartimaeus. The blind shepherd sighed heavily and answered, "Until I talked with Devorah and now you, my answer would have been no. You especially, Bartimaeus, give me hope. My new answer is yes, I'm willing to do what is necessary to live a new life."

The blind shepherd now became immensely more attentive to the words spoken by his blind counterpart. Bartimaeus went on, "My father had business dealings with the Nigrid and spoke with him about both his and my situation. The Nigrid took me into his custody, just as he has you, and put me with an accomplished tentmaker. As an apprentice to this man, I learned how to make tents. Later, my mentor promoted me to learn how to become a cobbler, which I am to this day."

Mattan took in this new revelation. Bartimaeus continued his life history. "In the beginning, Mattan, it was very frustrating to learn the techniques of making tents. I struggled but persisted, and finally became a cobbler. With time and patience, I have become adept at both. I earn a living and can provide for myself. God is the one who has made my potential become a reality."

Bartimaeus realized he needed to encourage Mattan to leave his despondency. "Mattan, it will be more difficult for you because you once had sight. Your frustration will be great, but the only way you can succeed is to let your hands become your new eyes. In doing this, your hands will be an avenue for all your senses to guide you in a new way of living." The blind cobbler emphasized, "What God has done for me, He can do for you, if you allow Him to do so."

Mattan bristled at that last comment and said, "Do not jest with me, Bartimaeus. I will not listen to such nonsense! God has forsaken me. I believe He ridicules me."

Not at all deterred, Bartimaeus explained, "God revealed to me what He had given me ever since birth. The ability to see through my other senses. You know what a blue sky looks like; I do not. Describe to me, Mattan, what a blue sky is?" Bartimaeus let this question sink into his colleague's mind, knowing it would be unlikely for him to answer. He quickly added, "It really doesn't matter that I don't know what a blue sky looks like. I can sense a sunny day by feeling the sun's warmth on my skin. Likewise, a wintry day makes my skin cold and the wind is harsh, biting, and strong. I know each season by the smells of the flowers, the grasses, and what the wind brings forth. I can tell the difference between the seasons by the chirping of the birds."

Bartimaeus grew more animated as he spoke. "These are the ways I can see. In many ways I appreciate more what God has created than those who retain their sight. I've never been angry with God, but truly can understand how you are. I do not tell you not to be angry with God, but only to let Him reveal His plan for you and show you how to see again but in a different way."

Mattan was still irritated, and launched a question he was sure would silence this fanatic. "Tell me, Bartimaeus, since you cannot see the work you are turning out, how do you know your work is really acceptable?"

The blind cobbler expected this question and had his answer ready. "I see with my fingers and my hands, Mattan. When I am given leather, I smell it and run my fingers over the hide learning its thickness, any scars, and other things that determine what I have to work with. I feel the old shoe and my touch tells me how to construct the shoe to fit the owner. Then I proceed with the techniques taught me by my mentor until the shoe is completed."

Somewhat quieted by Bartimaeus' reasonable and unruffled answer, Mattan listened with renewed interest as Bartimaeus concluded his explanation. "Once the shoe is completed, the buyer tells me how well it fits. Most are amazed that a blind man can create such a fine fitting and quality product. They pay me for my service. The money is quite acceptable but I enjoy even more the satisfaction that I can work and receive the respect of those who otherwise would shun me. This is how I destroy the bias against me. This is how God blesses me and keeps me out of the streets begging."

Bartimaeus laughed. "You see, Mattan, it's the customer who is really blind and not I. They are blinded by lies, rituals, and traditions until they encounter me and receive one of my shoes! Some remain blind, but most are changed when they see my skill level that they didn't believe possible. In this way those blind fools see God through me. He gets all the glory and I receive His blessing."

The blind cobbler's words jolted Mattan. His body tingled as he asked his mentor, "You say this can be the case for me should I learn to be a potter?"

"Most certainly, Mattan! Let me add, the Nigrid would not have placed you into the hands of Devorah, the pottery supervisor, if he thought you were not capable of overcoming the challenges involved. He does not want to humiliate you. He wants you to become a potter and show the blind, foolish Jews you have the right to worth, dignity, and respect."

Suddenly, the air felt heavy. Bartimaeus detected it was time to allow Mattan time to think about what had just been said. The sightless men sat facing each other, wondering what expression was on the other's face. One was physically blind but had insight and wisdom. The other was physically blind and was only just beginning to gain a new view of things.

Instinctively, Bartimaeus added a final thought that resounded with Mattan. "I must clarify something with you, Mattan. While I do not get angry with God over my blindness, I certainly do get frustrated at not being able to see. If it were possible, I would give all that I have to see the things you once saw."

Mattan cleared his throat and swallowed hard. "I believe you are sincere in what you say, Bartimaeus. My anger has consumed me and prevented me from understanding about the Nigrid's motives. You have taught me much this day about blindness and about myself. I resolve this day to accept the challenge before me. I do ask one thing of you, and that is, will you mentor me through this process? You, better than anyone, can provide what I need to continue."

Immediately Bartimaeus replied, "This I wholeheartedly will do, Mattan."

As the discussion between the two blind men was taking place, the Nigrid was on his way back to Jericho. The journey from Caesarea to the economic hub northeast of Jerusalem during that period of time was over seventy miles. It could be safely completed in two days. But the Nigrid chose to take a more leisurely pace and even stopped in Ephraim to conduct some personal business. He wanted extra time to ponder the words of Procurator Gratus; but he also wanted to allow sufficient time for the issue between Devorah and Mattan to be resolved. His paternal love for each of them was such that he did not want either of them to fall by the wayside.

Chapter 15

A mid-spring sunset of yellow mixed with lavender, crimson, and varying shades of purple chaperoned Nigrid to his mansion at the base of the hills that surrounded Jericho.

To the returning business administrator, he interpreted the sunset as a good omen that things had worked out well during his absence. He did not immediately announce his presence to Mattan after entering the mansion. The Nigrid had one of the house servants bring some food to his bedchamber where he could eat, then fall into his bed from the tiring journey.

Early the next morning, feeling refreshed, the administrator summoned Mattan to have breakfast with him. He was anxious to find out what had transpired among Mattan, Devorah, and Bartimaeus. The answer he sought did not disappoint. As Mattan was led on to the patio, Nigrid detected a change in his adopted nephew. Instead of walking lethargically and slumped, the blind shepherd stood erect and walked with purpose, guided by the servant. Mattan's facial expression was also transformed. The previous angry set of his jaw was replaced with a softness that now accurately revealed the youth of the blind man. Nigrid was pleased at the change and exhaled a sigh of relief, straightening his own shoulders to match his mood.

He called to his nephew, "Mattan, did you and Devorah reconcile your differences during my absence to Caesarea?"

"The blind shepherd joyfully exclaimed, "Indeed we did, Uncle! All is for the better. We now have a better understanding of each other and are ready to proceed with my lessons on how to become a potter."

The reassured administrator sat patiently watching his house guest, expecting there was more to come from his protégé. He did not have to wait long. "Uncle, I want to thank you for bringing Bartimaeus to us. He has given me much insight and showed me how my thinking was in great error. He is willing to help me in learning how become a potter and even more, how to live with my blindness. Naturally, he has learned a lot about overcoming many impossible things, and I want to glean everything I can from him."

The house servant appeared with food, causing a tasty pause in the conversation. When the servant had departed the patio, the comforted host fought hard to contain his excitement. "Are you sure, Mattan, that you are both physically and emotionally ready to undertake this challenge?"

Without any hesitation, Mattan insisted, "Most certainly, Uncle. In fact I wish to start this day."

The Nigrid's heart was racing at Mattan's declaration. "I am indeed pleased with your decision. Your learning shall begin this day, just as you wish. Now let us eat and enjoy this glorious new day."

One of the Nigrid's most respected house servants was assigned to be Mattan's guide. He would be present throughout his stay in Jericho. The man obediently followed his master's directive and took the blind shepherd to the pottery factory. Devorah was nervously waiting. She had spent much time preparing an improved approach for teaching Mattan the craft of pottery. In her mind, she felt ready to proceed. Her main concern was being able to communicate the techniques in ways that Mattan could learn and not become overwhelmed and despondent.

Mattan was equally nervous. He wanted to fulfill his vow to his adopted uncle and wondered if it would be possible. He was resolved to control his temper and hoped that Devorah would be patient with him.

When the two came together to begin the process, Devorah was the first to speak. "Mattan, I have taken to heart what you told me about your blindness, and I believe I have a method that will make it easier for you to learn the process of making pots." Mattan thought he detected nervousness in his teacher's voice and was relieved that she shared some of his uncertainty.

"I, too, have thought about your words, Devorah, and am ready to commit to your teaching." Mattan chuckled. "I believe we also are remembering the stern warning given to us earlier should we fail."

Devorah smiled at the truth, and acknowledged it aloud. "That is a good incentive for both of us. Now let us get started."

Devorah guided her student to the back of the small factory where she had set up a potter's wheel and chair. It was sufficiently away from the other potters to ensure there would be no interference. She was thankful for the available space, mainly to separate themselves from the piercing eyes of the other potters.

Gently, she assisted her experimental project onto the potter's seat. Then she took Mattan's hands and placed them onto a block of fresh clay that was on the wheel. She showed Mattan how to place his foot on the pedal that rotated the wheel and how to change speed. At that point she stopped.

"Now I want you to not turn the wheel, but let your fingers feel the clay," said the anxious teacher. Mattan did as instructed and concentrated as Bartimaeus had told him to do. The blind shepherd began moving his fingers through the moist mass that lay on the wheel. The clay was cool to his touch and he noticed the level of moisture associated with the special mud. To his amazement, Mattan liked the feel of the clay and he began to imagine the potential it offered to create something special.

Devorah took note of her pupil's movements without interfering. She realized it was more important for her to observe and to learn from what she saw. Mattan began to move the terracotta around with his hands. Seeing his interest, Devorah intervened and said, "Very good, Mattan. Now I want you to visualize in your mind the shape of a small pot you have used in the past."

Mattan let his fingers rest as he thought of a pot. This was harder than he expected, mainly because pots were associated more with women's work than that of a nomad shepherd. A familiar memory was of a cup he used at family meals. Within a few moments his fingers grabbed hold of the moist clay and slowly began to shape it into conformity with the simple shape he remembered holding in his hands hundreds of times. The nervous instructor watched her pupil's intensity as he moved the clay around. She did not interrupt, and after ten minutes of shaping and re-shaping. Mattan's first assignment was finished.

"That is the best I can remember. How did I do?"

Devorah spoke reassuringly, "For your first attempt, it is better than I expected. In fact, what you've made is better than some of the sighted students I've had."

Mattan grinned and with a relieved sigh asked, "Do we continue, or what comes next?"

The blind shepherd's comments surprised his teacher. "I see nothing wrong with continuing, but should you become frustrated, we shall stop." The lesson continued throughout the day until the instructor called a halt to the proceedings. "That is enough for one day. I am quite pleased with what you have done in your first try. We shall continue tomorrow." Inwardly, Devorah was more pleased with her own efforts as well.

As his servant guide led him back to the Nigrid's mansion, Mattan's thoughts were buoyed by Devorah's words of encouragement. A sense of accomplishment to associate things he could no longer see and bring them into reality brought a surprising feeling of satisfaction into his heart. He felt confident he could learn to be a potter—a good potter.

Once inside the mansion, Mattan asked to be led to the patio where he sat enjoying the final rays of the warm sun. He sipped wine while his thoughts reviewed the day. The blind shepherd made a secret vow to himself. He would work to be able to make some good, sturdy, workable pots for his family next spring when they made their annual stop at Jericho. He would push himself, as well as Devorah. He strained to remember different sizes and shapes of pots that were more familiar to his mother and sister than to himself.

When the Nigrid returned from his day's duties as chief administrator of Judea, he hurried to his nephew's side on the patio. He was anxious to find out how Mattan's first day of learning had transpired. He and Mattan sat under the patio cover to eat their evening meal as the business icon of Judea plied Mattan with questions. "Did it go well for you today, Mattan?"

The apprentice cocked his head in the direction of Nigrid's voice and cordially answered, "I felt I made progress. There are many, many challenges, but Devorah's instruction is very helpful."

"May I assume, then, that I shall not be told the two of you are attempting to kill each other over this process?"

Mattan tilted his head back and laughed, "Uncle, at this point the answer is definitely no. But..." and Mattan waved his finger in the air..."that does not mean that later Devorah may not become angry with my lack of progress. I fear she could be quite deadly should that happen."

Nigrid laughed and said, "Mattan, your changed attitude will answer that question. But I agree, Devorah could be quite an adversary should she become really angry." They laughed at the imagined scenario.

When he was alone in his room, the small man relaxed. He was very thankful that the touchy issue was in the process of getting resolved. He had promised Terach he would take care of his son and wanted to show the shepherd leader he was making good on his promise. Next spring would be the moment this would be revealed.

For the Nigrid, now he could concentrate on pressing matters associated with the finance administrator duties added to his list of responsibilities. He was thrust into the role of being the chief tax collector for all of Judea. Rome was expecting much from this position and should he fail, it could be very costly for him. He had to find a way to balance both administrative duties without losing ground, and in the process smoothly add to his own personal wealth.

The Nigrid had spent considerable time creating a schedule to perform both functions. He had to devote the majority of his administrative time as business administrator traveling throughout Judea and Samaria to make sure the variety of businesses were run properly. As chief tax collector he would continue Nicolas' method and have subcollectors at key cities and points along the trade routes to garner Rome's bounty.

He realized his life was in the midst of dramatically changing. All his life he had been ridiculed for his short stature. Rumors spread that his short stature was the result of his personal sin as well as familial sin. He had thus been shunned from an early age. Now as an adult he would be ostracized from Jewish society for being a tax collector and aiding Rome's accursed plundering of Judea. He was to become part of the despised of Jewish society. It didn't matter, he consoled himself, because he already was voted an outcast. His solace was the money he would receive from his authority over them.

The next morning at breakfast with Mattan, the Nigrid informed his protégé, "Mattan, my added duties of being finance administrator for all of Judea and Samaria will require a great deal of my involvement. Unfortunately, I will have to travel and as such not be able to spend as much time with you as I would like. I feel that your efforts in securing a new career will proceed well. Should you have any difficulties or problems, don't hesitate to let me know so that I can assist you."

The blind apprentice discerned the regret in his uncle's voice. The news also saddened Mattan. "I do not wish to restrict you from carrying out your assigned duties, Uncle. I have confidence this learning process will go well for me. I will have access to Bartimaeus who will keep me tempered when difficult times arise."

The Nigrid responded, "I'm glad you and Bartimaeus are becoming aligned. He is very knowledgeable and his personal experiences will be far more valuable than anything I can say or do for you. I hope it's possible the two of you will also become friends."

From that day on, lengthy periods elapsed before the uncle and nephew were able to share moments together. Both were caught up in matters of great importance to each of them, and time passed very quickly.

The middle of spring gave way to the wave of hot summer months, which eventually succumbed to the inevitable cold, rainy winter. Amid fluctuations in the weather-dominated seasons, Mattan remained unfaltering in his quest to become a potter. There were times he and Devorah had clashes, primarily as a result of Mattan's frustrations; but each occurrence was resolved amiably. The working arrangement between the two developed into a genuine friendship. They enjoyed a more relaxed relationship as they discovered each other's personality quirks and habits.

Each passing day, Mattan and Devorah's bouts of disagreement became fewer and were replaced with kindness towards each other. One day, Mattan was fumbling at the potter's wheel when Devorah placed her hand on his as a guide. Contrasting with the coolness of the clay, Devorah's gentle touch warmed more than the apprentice's hand. His heart began to thaw and he allowed emotions to return that had been stolen by his blindness.

Devorah found herself lingering as she touched Mattan's hand. Inside she felt a warmth she had not experienced in quite some time. The instructor blushed at her thoughts toward this blind shepherd and was glad he could not see her pink cheeks. Each time she looked at his face, her heart skipped a beat. The heat of the summer was becoming matched by the warmth the former antagonists were feeling toward each other. By early fall, neither Mattan nor Devorah attempted to hide their fondness for the other.

One night while sitting alone on the patio, enjoying the cool evening breeze against his body, Mattan reflected on his growing feelings towards Devorah. He compared his newfound feelings for Devorah with what he had felt earlier for Iza. He chuckled at how young the two were then, and how the love he felt now was vastly different.

His main thoughts were full of hope that Devorah felt the same way about him. He reminded himself to be cautious around Devorah. He did not want to irritate her or do anything that could possible derail the growing love in his heart for this woman who excited him so much.

That same evening Devorah paced back and forth in her room. Her fingers played continuously with a long strand of her dark hair. Her thoughts were centered on the blind shepherd under her tutelage. Her thoughts were swinging like a pendulum. At times she chuckled at how the stalwart young man would act like a child throwing a tantrum when she disciplined him at the potter's wheel. Moments later, though, he would be giggling at the process, enjoying the cool clay slipping between his fingers, and how he was able to perform a new task.

Devorah was deeply touched by how earnestly he worked to develop his new skills. What caused her torment was hoping their newfound fondness for one another was not an illusion. The distraught woman pulled at her hair as she paced and wondered. Her longing to know Mattan's feelings made her feel as if she were going mad. She resolved to control herself when around him.

It was also during this time that Mattan and Bartimaeus became close compatriots, freely sharing personal and meaningful matters as brothers might. Mattan no longer felt alienated, lost, hopeless, and without purpose. He still longed for his family, but he was content and appreciated more each day his surrogate family of Bartimaeus, Devorah, and the Nigrid. Even so, in the midst of his adjustments, the blind shepherd was still plagued by his unrelenting dreams of evil eyes of the enemy and soothing eyes of the infant from long ago.

During the last of the Jewish pilgrimage feasts, the Feast of the Tabernacles, Procurator Valerius Gratus seized the opportunity to implement his plan of keeping the Jews appeased while under Roman rule. It was the duty of the procurator to travel from Caesarea to Jerusalem to attend the major feasts that required animal sacrifice at the Temple.

Gratus was to observe the activities during these feasts and report his findings back to Rome, as well as to the Legate governor in Syria. This information went towards informing Rome how to handle the peculiarities of the Jewish people. Gratus most reveled in how the Jewish religious leaders kowtowed to him, seeking favor. Such fussing enhanced his already sizable ego.

On the final day of the Feast of Tabernacles, Procurator Gratus sprang his plan on the Jewish Sanhedrin. He called for an assembly of the main ruling body. He gave no details why such an unusual event was to take place. The ruling despot made sure he appeared in his finest Roman attire to make the despised Jews feel their inferiority. The religious legislature muttered among themselves until Gratus made his grand entrance into the Temple meeting hall.

Gratus strode into the hall with great pomp wearing a new toga that depicted his status and rank within Roman hierarchy. He moved deliberately and regally, making sure his first impression of power and control on the Sanhedrin membership would also be a lasting impression. The Roman bureaucrat surveyed the perplexed expressions directed towards him. He was delighted at their reaction.

Without fanfare, Gratus announced tersely, "This day marks a significant change in your servitude to Rome. From this day forth, I will continue to appoint the high priest of this religious congress. You shall not submit the names of any candidates to this position. Nor shall you confer among yourselves as to whom you believe is best qualified for this positions." Anticipating a shocked reaction from the Sanhedrin, Gratus paused to allow his announcement to sink into the minds of the Jewish religious leaders.

Shouts came forth from the membership and chaos erupted. Gratus simply looked over his shoulder to his aide who opened the doors of the hall to allow twelve heavily armed soldiers to rush forth. Shouts of resistance became murmurs of dismay at the sight of the military enforcers and their drawn swords. Both the Pharisees and the Sadducees cowered backward at the military's implication.

Silence quickly returned to the hall, and the procurator continued with a heartless smile, "Annus ben Seth is no longer your high priest. I now immediately appoint Ishmael ben Fabus as the new high priest. He shall serve in this capacity until such time as I deem a replacement is warranted." Seventy-one sets of fearful eyes stared at the Roman policy enforcer in disbelief. One set of unblinking eyes stared back at Gratus in contemplation; it was Annas who showed no emotional signs at his forced resignation. However, inwardly, Annas' mind was calculating this turn of events. He silently vowed to retaliate, but for now he would find out more from this Roman dog.

Annas stood to take control of his fellow Sanhedrin members and to confront his Roman adversary. The seventy-one sets of eyes shifted their focus to their leader. "Procurator Gratus, as you would imagine, this announcement is a great shock to this holy assembly. This has never been done before, not even during the reign of King Herod. He listened to the pleas of the Jews and appointed one who was a true elder, complete with wisdom, piety, and leadership capability. King Herod took time to evaluate the candidates deemed worthy of the high priest position."

Annas feigned adjusting his high priest special garments. All eyes and ears were his, including those of Gratus, who bristled at his impertinence. "The position of high priest requires special gifts because it is the high priest alone who can enter the Holy of Holies within this Temple to commune directly with God. This spiritual fact cannot be denied nor overlooked." Rising to his full height, the dethroned high priest ended, "Rome's ruling emperor, the mighty Caesar, has personally permitted us to continue our holy traditions."

Gratus' eyes narrowed at this insult to his authority. He held up his right hand and loudly proclaimed, "Annas, I am quite versed in your religious customs and do not need a lesson at this time. My ruling is final and I alone will decide who will be in charge of your religious conclave. You may complain to Caesar, if you will; but rest assured, he will allow me to govern you as I see fit and deem necessary!"

When he finished, Gratus immediately turned and quickly strode out of the hall, followed by his aide and the armed soldiers. The Roman procurator was pleased with himself for not allowing the rambling religious moron to take control from him. He had expected negative reaction to his permanent decree, but would not tolerate being swayed by a vain religious hypocrite.

With his monumental command now invoked, Gratus settled into his carriage for the long journey back to Caesarea. Along the way he would have plenty of time to anticipate any new moves by the pathetic religious leaders to attempt any modification to his takeover and control of the Sanhedrin.

Little did he know, this upheaval occurring in the fall of 15 AD, would prove to be impactful to events that would occur 33 years hence. The decision by Gratus would factor into the Great Jewish Revolt, resulting in the total destruction of Jerusalem and the Temple.

Chapter 16

The following spring marked a momentous turn in the lives of Mattan, his family, Devorah, Bartimaeus, and the Nigrid. There were joys mixed with surprises and letdowns. Their lives were being lived in the world's most impactful century.

One week prior to the Passover celebration, Mattan's family arrived and set up camp on the northwestern part of Jericho. The family hurriedly got everything in order, particularly because they were anxious to spend time with Mattan. The stress of separation from loved ones in the case of Mattan's family was especially so because of their realization their son and brother was no longer a shepherd. Their long separation had heightened their eager anticipation for the family reunion.

Terach met with the Nigrid who quickly sensed the shepherd leader's anxiety. "My friend, what makes you anxious like a lost lamb searching for its mother?"

The patriarch of the nomadic clan confessed, "My friend, I and the rest of the family are longing to reunite with Mattan. It has been a very long year. Our shared concern has been building for quite some time."

The Nigrid smiled and threw his hands out in a wide open gesture, saying "Mattan is making his adjustments with a positive attitude. As we speak, he is at the pottery workshop constructing products to be sold in the marketplace." The business icon leaned toward his colleague and asked, "Would you like to go to the workshop and observe your son working?"

His question startled the nomad patriarch, but he recovered quickly. "You say Mattan is now a potter? I never would have imagined such a thing." Terach searched his friend's face for any sign that this was some kind of a joke. Seeing only the friendly twinkle in his friend's eyes, the nomad shepherd declared, "Oh, Nigrid. This would be most pleasant. Is it possible for the rest of the family to join us?"

Smiling at his guest, Nigrid replied, "Of course, Terach! The workshop is close to where you have established your base camp. We can pick up the rest of the family on our way."

Fifty percent of the workshop was devoted to the kiln and benches for the greenware that had sufficiently dried and was ready to be fired. The remainder of the workshop was divided into sections where the potters were set up. The family was instructed to remain very quiet in their observation of Mattan. This would allow them to see their son and brother developing his newfound craft.

Terach and the family eagerly scanned the workshop with eight potters all engaged in various stages of making a different type of pot. One potter obviously stood out from among the rest. They quickly recognized Mattan despite his change in clothing and the dirty residue of clay on his arms and work tunic. There was a dark-haired woman sitting next to Mattan. The woman was intently studying the apprentice potter's hands and movement.

She had him halt the spinning wheel, place his hands in a different position and restart the wheel. After watching for a brief time, the family was amazed. Mattan stopped the turning wheel and sat back listening closely to his instructor. He nodded his head in understanding and the woman stood up and took the finished pot to the curing area. When she returned, she noticed the Nigrid and the group with him.

The pottery business owner signaled the woman to silence and she sat back down next to her pupil. Another slab of clay was placed in the center of the wheel. Words were exchanged between instructor and pupil and the wheel slowly began to turn.

Mattan's family saw his attention to the woman and thought they detected something more than just student to instructor relationship. His face beamed when Devorah spoke and his features softened. Channah leaned towards her parents and quietly whispered, "Mattan is in love. Isn't it wonderful!"

Beulah placed her hand over her daughter's mouth and whispered back, "The woman is also in love with Mattan! Observe how her eyes search his face when he speaks to her and how she touches his shoulder with hands of love." Beulah happily sighed and added, "God's grace is upon them. It is merely a matter of time before they wed. But Channah, do not speak of this to either of them. It is not our place to do this." Channah nodded her head, though she knew it would be hard to keep still.

Mattan's hands moved in concert with the shape the apprentice was visualizing. Coinciding with the turning wheel, Mattan moved his head side to side, manifesting a habit he had developed after his blindness. It was as if there was a rhythm to his work. As the wheel turned, the slab of clay began to take on a graceful shape. The more the apprentice moved his hands, the more his mental image became revealed on the potter's wheel. His intensity and concentration was evident from head to toe. Periodically, his head stopped swaying and he looked down as if inspecting the creation enfolded in his hands.

This time the instructor remained silent throughout most of the process, as she watched the pot take form. Twenty minutes into the process, the pot was finished. Again, the woman carefully lifted the finished piece and carried it to a drying bench. When she returned, the Nigrid motioned for her to bring Mattan to the group. The woman nodded and told Mattan to stop. She gave him a piece of material to wipe his hands, and then guided him to the astonished wide-eyed onlookers.

"Mattan, I've watched you work on the last two pots and am quite pleased with the finished product. They will bring a good price in the marketplace," said the Nigrid, "It is time for you to take a break from your duties. There are some people who wish to speak with you." The Nigrid motioned for the family to relax and greet their loved one.

Per Jewish custom, the patriarch of the family was the first to speak. "My son, my son, I am very proud of what I've seen you accomplish this day. I had no idea this would be possible."

Mattan's face registered shock and complete joy at hearing his father's familiar voice. It was a much longed-for moment. They embraced with strong arms and claps on the shoulders, greeting one another in a torrent of words. Catching his breath, Terach suddenly realized Mattan did not know how large his audience was. He announced, "My son, we are all here." Then the joyful scene was repeated all over again with Beulah and the others grabbing their beloved son and brother, nearly knocking him off balance in their elation.

Channah had been hanging back, unable to penetrate the wall of her brothers' broad shoulders. Given the opportunity at last, she stepped forward and tightly hugged her dirty brother. She could only speak Mattan's name over and over; but her sobs relayed what was in her heart. She clung to Mattan tightly and the apprentice reciprocated her love, laughing softly.

Devorah had moved to the side, taking in the initial family reunion. The emotion displayed by the shepherd family touched her deeply and she fought hard to hold back empathetic tears of joy. The Nigrid beamed and he, too, became emotional at the drama playing out in front of him. "I...I believe your work day is complete, Mattan. Clean up and come with us back to my mansion. We have a great celebration planned." The Nigrid saw Devorah's appreciation and quickly invited her to join in the celebration.

The special dinner celebration was as festive as any Devorah had ever encountered. There was much laughter and smiles all around. The female pottery supervisor enjoyed the party, but she felt like an interloper and refrained from joining the revelry. Devorah's eyes again moistened as she witnessed Beulah and Channah clinging to Mattan while Terach sat proudly, hardly taking his eyes off his youngest son.

When the merrymaking had tapered off, Terach took control and made a serious announcement. "My son, there is much to be happy and thankful for. But always in life, joy is mingled with sorrow from time to time. I must inform you that last fall when we returned to Bethlehem, Iza petitioned for divorce. Nadan and I thoroughly evaluated the situation and agreed it would be the best for her."

The echoes of laughter and merriment ceased, and all eyes were on the blind shepherd. The festive room was eerily quiet to the point of discomfort. Mattan felt the stares and imagined the concern that accompanied them. He hastened to ease their discomfort. "This is not a total surprise to me, Father. Iza and I briefly talked about this when I stayed behind here in Jericho. She was so unhappy that I did not want to burden her, especially not knowing what lay ahead for me."

Mattan sighed, turning his head back and forth in an effort to include everyone in the room. "I hope she is doing well. There is no malice or anger in my heart. She is entitled to a good life." Beulah gave her youngest son the words he sought. "Iza is in process of adjusting to her situation. Some of the self-righteous Jews, led by the rabbi there, attempted to scorn her, but Nadan effectively put a stop to that insanity. There is nothing for you to be concerned about."

The apprentice potter looked relieved. "Rest assured, all of you, that I am reconciled with not only the divorce but that Iza is making strides to reclaim her life. I have no doubt she will remarry into a good family."

Devorah listened to this exchange very closely. Her own circumstances allowed her to empathize with both Iza and Mattan. She now had greater respect for Mattan and his family. It was difficult for her to refrain from longing to be a part of this noble clan.

At the end of the evening's social soiree, Channah took Devorah aside. Confronting her, the young woman demanded, "Devorah, tell me truly, how is my brother emotionally adjusting to this new life?"

The dark-haired widow saw Channah's desperation in her questioning eyes, and gave as honest an answer as possible. "In the beginning we had grave issues I believed could not be overcome. The Nigrid counseled us and now we have a better understanding and respect of each other." Devorah assured her, "Mattan has the talent to become a very skilled potter. All that is needed is time and practice. I have no doubt he will continue to improve. His attitude is his best weapon in this adjustment."

Channah kept her intent focus on Devorah's eyes. When the supervisor finished, the young Jewish woman said in a much softer tone, "I observed how you worked with my brother today and am pleased one such as you is his instructor and mentor." Satisfied, Channah ended the interrogation and the two women resumed their places with the others. Both women felt relief after the exchange, and had a desire to become friends.

The Nigrid made sure the remainder of the week was devoted to the reunion of the nomad shepherd family. He perceived the family needed to share their hearts and emotions with each other. He informed Devorah that Mattan would not be at the workshop until after the family resumed their trek south with their flocks. The disappointed supervisor went back to her normal duties. Devorah would have preferred to be a part of the tender and joyful interactions of the nomad shepherd family.

At the end of the Passover Feast, Terach and Nigrid had one last meeting. "My friend, my heart is greatly thankful to you for this time with my son, and most importantly for your assistance to him to gain a new and meaningful life. I also wish to say that I have no doubts about your choice of a new career for Mattan. You are a true friend."

Nigrid was overcome by Terach's praises and he was unable to maintain his usual stoic manner. He grabbed Terach and hugged him tightly, saying, "Terach, I consider your family as my own and am content and humbled by your words. Since we first met, you have treated me with respect when others only ridiculed and spat upon me. I will always be grateful and value our relationship."

The conversation turned and the newly-promoted Roman administrator detailed his new position to his best friend. "Terach, I want you to know that as the chief tax collector for all Judea everyone will hate me. I don't want you or your family to be part of their hatred. I will understand should you elect to curtail involvement with me."

Terach gave his surrogate family member a quizzical smile and replied, "My friend, you shall remain my friend for life. Your pain is my pain and your joy is my joy. Nothing and no one can ever change that."

The Nigrid's legs nearly buckled hearing such affirming words spoken to him. He desperately needed and wanted this sense of love that had eluded him the majority of his life. Neither man said anything, but the looks they exchanged spoke volumes of the depth of their relationship and mutual respect.

Nigrid made a point of watching his adopted family head slowly southeast along their spring route. When the procession was out of sight, the Nigrid went back to his normal routine, but with a new softness in his heart. He murmured to himself, "Why must life be interrupted by sadness and troubles?"

While Terach and his family made their way south, Annas was having a secretive meeting with a scribe named Tertullus, a lawyer for hire, one whom Annas trusted. The high priest explained how Gratus was now going to appoint the high priest and had officially removed him from office.

"What advice do you wish from me, Annas?" asked Tertullus.

"I want you to give me your view of how I plan to deal with this imbecile Roman son of a pig!" exclaimed Annas.

The lawyer for hire was amused how the high priest chose cursing words for the dominant controllers of most of the known world. For the next fifteen minutes Annas laid out his plan to the hired lawyer. Tertullus was known for his wit and interpretation of both Jewish and Roman law. When Annas finished, Tertullus was quick to respond. He did not mince words. "It's obvious you understand this change in procedure of appointing the high priest is not going to be revoked." Tertullus' eyebrows rose as he paused and leaned towards the high priest for emphasis and clarified, "Your plan to minimize further interference by the procurator is not valid, Annas. Rome will do anything it deems necessary to maintain order in Judea. You put yourself, the Sanhedrin, and all Jews in harm's way."

Annas was disappointed by the lawyer's comment but let him finish. The lawyer continued, "You are a man of intelligence, Annas. Be clever first in dealing with this Roman pig. Let him believe you acquiesce to his ego. Once you solidify that issue, you can find ways to chip away at his controlling ways." The lawyer cupped his hands together and continued, "As your submissiveness sways Gratus, your dealings with the Sanhedrin will allow you to control them as well. Do not deviate from this procedure, otherwise everything you wish to attain will be lost."

Tertullus could see the high priest's eyes darting from side to side as he considered his options. Annas' set jaw showed he was processing the advice given him. "Tertullus, It is most difficult for me to do as you recommend. However, I agree with your advice. I shall immediately begin to construct my next move with that street dog Gratus."

The high priest produced a small pouch filled with money to pay the lawyer. Tertullus was not cheap, but his fee was well-earned for his highly-valued advice. Annas immediately summoned his ornate carriage and left Jerusalem for Caesarea where he would confront Gratus with a most unusual proposal.

Upon the completion of the two-and- a-half-day journey, Annas was informed by Gratus' secretary the meeting between the two authorities would be restricted to no more than ten minutes. Annas was jolted by this announcement and immediately began to mentally change how he would proceed with the Roman procurator. He realized this short meeting was one of Gratus' ways of retaining dominance.

Annas was led to Gratus' office where he was assigned to a chair placed directly in front of the procurator's desk. Gratus' face displayed an unflinching sternness. Annas could tell the Roman disliked him, and the feeling was mutual. Only Annas opted to camouflage his hatred towards the Roman, as advised by Tertullus.

"You have little time, so tell me what brings you to me?"

Annas immediately revealed his proposal. "I believe I can provide you a means by which you will have full cooperation from the Sanhedrin and thereby eliminate any threat of reprisal against you and Rome." Annas briefly paused to gauge the procurator's reaction. "That is, if you are interested. If not, our meeting is finished and I will return to Jerusalem and the events will play out."

Gratus inwardly bristled at the ploy of this obstinate Jew, but did not take the bait. "I really don't see how you can help me, as you say, in stemming any revolt by you Jews. Rome is the most powerful force and you are its inferior subjects. As such, you and your people must remember to remain obedient to us in every way, otherwise we shall stomp you like stepping on a bug."

The Roman authoritarian let his words sink in. He waved his hand in disdain. "Quickly inform me of your grandiose idea. I tire of your presence."

Annas stifled his anger and made his pitch. "You do not fully understand how the Sanhedrin influences the Jewish people. The high priest dictates the religious, social, and cultural direction the people take. There are two main bodies that comprise the Sanhedrin—the Pharisees and the Sadducees. The Pharisees do not wish to conform to Roman rules. The Sadducees, on the other hand, are more willing to compromise and cooperate with you. I have control of the Sadducees. As such, I can supply you a list of the Sadducees willing to cooperate with you and influence the people to do the same. The people will be influenced by us."

The high priest was proud of how succinct his brief presentation was going. He added the finishing touch. "It will take you a long time to learn who is of which group. I already know this. Simply put, I can make your choice of high priest much easier and guaranteed not to cause the people to revolt."

Gratus placed his right index finger up against his cheek and stared at the Jew without blinking. His thoughts were how this official was willing to sell out his own governing body for personal benefit. This he easily understood, being like-minded, himself. There was some merit to what the high priest said.

Time was a key ingredient in maintaining obedience of these impertinent Jews. Besides, any uprising would be handled quickly. In some ways Gratus hoped for an uprising, simply because it would make his job much easier and lessen the time he had to spend with these obstinate creatures. Aligning with this hypocrite could result in the promotion Gratus sought.

With his finger still against his cheek, Gratus nonchalantly stated, "Leave the names of those you recommend with my secretary. I shall decide later today if I want to align with you. Now leave. Our meeting is over."

After leaving the chosen names, Annas descended the steps of the procurator's mansion and stepped inside his coach for the ride back to Jerusalem. He was not disappointed how the meeting with Gratus had gone. The high priest was sure that the Roman would heed his proposal; he had nothing to lose and much to gain. It was simply a matter of perception and control.

The meeting lasted twelve minutes yet would impact the Sanhedrin for the next fifty-five years. No member of the Sanhedrin ever became aware that Anna's deal struck with the Roman Empire and this assigned procurator would become de facto policy.

One week after Annas returned to Jerusalem, notification came from Gratus' messenger that he had chosen Ishmael ben Fabus as the next high priest. Fabus was one of the Sadducees on the list supplied by Annas. He was also a person Annas could control. Everyone was happy.

Annas was 36 years old when he was deposed by Gratus who made it a point to replace the high priest position once a year. This was a deviation from the original agreement and demonstrated how deviously Gratus maintained control. Annas, or Ananias as he was often referred to, seethed at the one-year appointment policy. He complied, but made sure each recommended name was one of his sons. In this way Annas remained the most influential political and social power over the Jewish governing body as well as the nation. He effectively solidified the position of high priest not only for himself but for the Sadducees as well.

From AD 15 to AD 18 events in the lives of the Judeans remained normal, with a few notable exceptions.

There was a series of marriages, the first one being Iza's to the son of a business magnate who had a small fleet of ships that transported Egyptian grain and imported spices to Rome. When notified that his ex-wife had remarried, Mattan informed his family that he was glad she had found someone better suited to her and her family's liking. Mattan's family was greatly relieved at how calmly he reacted to the news and felt it was a good sign of the healing going on inside of him. It also assured them his new life was a positive change.

The second marriage was Channah's, which impacted the family greatly. Because she was the youngest child and the most protected by her parents and her brothers, her marriage partner would be carefully chosen. And he was. Her dominant personality was such that Terach and Beulah were glad she had a husband to deal with her directives and demands. Mattan was saddened he could not be present for his sister's union. He missed the annual reunions with her during the Passover Feast.

Terach had been approached by one of the owners of a series of land caravans who had a good relationship with the nomad shepherd leader. The businessman's son was of strong character and Terach had no objections in arranging his daughter's marriage to the son. The newlyweds made their home in Emmaus that was part of the ridge route trade bridge connecting the two main trade routes of Palestine.

The ridge route trade ran along a range of mountains that extended from Shechem in Samaria, south past Bethlehem. At Emmaus the route connected the western, coastal Via Maris trade route with the eastern King's Highway trade route that went all the way north past Damascus to Antioch.

Channah's husband was the administrator for his father. He scheduled trade caravans between the two main routes. It did not take long for his assertive young bride to adapt to life in a bustling community. However, even the busyness and demands of her new married life didn't erase Channah's longing for her family, especially for her favorite brother Mattan.

The third marriage was that of Bartimaeus to a woman whom the Nigrid assigned to be his guide and servant. Her name was Hadassah who had an engaging personality similar to her new husband's. Originally she had been sold into slavery by her Jewish father to the Nigrid as payment for money owed. The Nigrid put her to work in one of his cobbler workshops where she earned a reputation of being an honest and capable worker. Her business sense and affable manner had brought more business and various hides to the workshop.

Hadassah and Bartimaeus were of the same age, which was unusual for Jewish married couples at that time. In the majority of cases the husband was at least seven years older than his wife. The Nigrid felt that Bartimaeus needed someone to assist him in daily life and thought Hadassah was well-suited for the position. He did not realize his business decision would result in matchmaking until both Bartimaeus and Hadassah approached him about marriage.

Because neither the husband nor the bride had family to perform the traditional rituals of arranged marriages, the Nigrid assumed this position and agreed to the union. The ceremony had attributes of traditional Jewish unions but without any involvement of any rabbi.

The marriage did not diminish the relationship between the blind cobbler and his colleague Mattan. In fact, their friendship solidified and grew over the years with continued openness in sharing on many levels and about many things.

Because Jericho was a bustling hub of commerce with influences from many parts of the world, the issue of a blind man being a cobbler and also married did not have a negative impact on the residents of the city. The union between a blind cobbler and a former slave was just part of the accepted culture of Jericho. This was a far cry from the Jewish way of life. Jericho was always regarded as a secular heathen city by the Jews who nonetheless engaged in various business activities with merchants and vendors based there.

In AD 18, two years after the marriage of Bartimaeus and Hadassah, a fourth marriage took place, much to the delight— and relief—of everyone involved. It was considered long overdue when Mattan finally took Devorah as his wife.

It had been a gradual process that was influenced by the annual reunion of Mattan's family during the Passover Feast. Devorah was always included and the family became very fond of her and hoped she and Mattan would come to love each other. Channah, during these Passover reunions, would periodically chide Mattan about not taking Devorah for his wife.

The process of Mattan's letting go of his fear that Devorah wouldn't want to marry a blind man was initially a major hurdle for him to overcome. Memories involving Iza and her family weighed heavily upon him, reawakening fears of rejection and insecurities. But the more he was around Devorah, the more he realized he could no longer hide his fears. He prayed to God for His wisdom, strength, and help, and the Almighty did not neglect to answer Mattan's plea.

Mattan finally took the initiative one day in the fall. He and Devorah were conversing during their meal break when the new potter shyly took Devorah's hand and squeezed it gently. He simply and clearly declared his love for her and his desire for her to be his bride. "Devorah, I must speak to you of what's in my heart. Each time I hear your voice and feel the touch of your hand, I get weak. I've come to realize how much I love you and desire that you would be my wife." Mattan stopped and cleared his throat. "I hope I haven't offended you."

Devorah scanned his face with loving eyes and saw a wonderful mixture of eagerness, anxiety, and deep earnestness as Mattan entreated her. "Mattan," she assured him, "You indeed are the love of my life. You have been for some time and it's been difficult for me not to speak of my feelings to you." She took his hand in hers and placed it against her cheek and said, "My answer is yes and I only wish you had eyes to see the happiness on my face."

After notifying the Nigrid of their plans, the business magnate congratulated himself for the second time on his success as a matchmaker. He sent a personal messenger to catch up with the nomad shepherd leader announcing the news. In turn, Terach delighted Channah with the update. When Terach and his flocks arrived at Jericho early that spring, Channah and her husband made their way to Jericho as well. It was a long-awaited event no one in the family would miss.

Nigrid, the unintentional matchmaker, did not inform either Devorah or Mattan that he had contacted Mattan's family. He stalled the engaged couple with a convincing ruse he was quite proud of creating. Executing his clever plan, the Nigrid, with great regret, told Mattan that his family would be late arriving in Jericho. He insisted the wedding should not be postponed but should proceed as planned. However, unbeknownst to Mattan, it was now the second day after his family's arrival in Jericho, and all things were ready to unfold.

A disappointed groom and bride waited in the Nigrid's garden area for the Nigrid to perform the ceremony. The Nigrid's secret became known in the stillness of the moment. As the wedding was about to begin, Terach and the family dramatically made their entrance to the great surprise of the subdued couple. A familiar booming voice reverberated, "Nigrid, wait! This marriage must include Jewish tradition!"

Recognizing his father's voice, Mattan let out a shout of joy, "Father! You are here along with my mother and my brothers?" Terach let each family member speak for themselves as ecstatic tears cascaded down Mattan's and Devorah's shining faces.

Suddenly, a new sweet voice rang out. "Am I not allowed to participate in my brother's marriage and give him my well wishes?" It was Channah. She burst forward and gave Mattan a tight squeeze. The elated sister did the same with Devorah and whispered in her ear, "You look lovely." Channah and her husband had arrived from Emmaus two days earlier but were secretly sequestered by the slightly devious matchmaker.

Now each member of the family had to wipe tears of joy from their faces as they witnessed Mattan's and Devorah's love and beaming smiles. Even the Nigrid slyly wiped away his own tears.

Terach approached the diminutive matchmaker, seeking the traditional permission for Devorah to become Mattan's wife. Because Devorah had no family, the Nigrid had happily assumed the role of her surrogate father. The dowry was given to Devorah, and the proud surrogate father ceremoniously declared, "I agree to this marriage."

Mattan repeated the same vows that he had spoken earlier when marrying Iza, but without the slightest thought of that great disappointment. His focus was on the love of his life, beautiful Devorah, the woman who had captured his heart forever. The celebration was wildly enthusiastic and lasted throughout the entire time the family was in Jericho.

When it was time to return to daily life, the seasonal trek south for the nomad shepherd leader and his family would be both happy and sad. The entire entourage was euphoric for the newlyweds, but saddened to leave when they had to end their sojourn and head for the grassy plains.

After a prolonged farewell, the Nigrid surprised the newlyweds. Judea's chief administrator took the newlyweds on a short journey close to his mansion. Relishing yet another secret, he did not speak until they reached their destination. "My beloved adopted family, I have secured this house for you. It is yours so long as you live here in Jericho."

Devorah gripped her new husband's hand tightly and trembled. Never had she dreamed this would happen to her. Overcome with gratitude, she grabbed her adopted father and put her arm around his shoulder saying, "Thank you so very, very much. It is a wonderful gift. We shall enjoy it until such time we are carried out to be buried."

Mattan was stunned by the announcement and chimed in, "Uncle, your love for us is great, but not as deep as what we have in our hearts for you."

Chapter 17

The year AD 18 also marked a dramatic grievous change in the life of the Nigrid. It was the beginning of his being overtaken by pride, arrogance, and control, all the elements that had resulted in the devil being cast forever out of heaven and away from relationship with the Godhead. Unlike the devil's forever fall, the Nigrid's fall from benevolence to malevolence would last only fifteen years.

With the consolidation of administrators in Judea, the Nigrid was the sole head over business matters and finance. This meant he had complete authority over the tax collection system throughout Judea and Samaria. There was a tremendous amount of money to be had, and the promoted civil servant of Rome soon saw irresistible opportunities whereby he could extract additional tax revenue from all the inhabitants of the land.

One of the early tax changes enacted by the opportunist was an export tax on all goods sold by merchants of Judea and Samaria. Tax collectors were stationed at strategic points along the two main trade routes and all the western port cities of Judea. No land caravan or cargo ship could escape the clutches of the tax man. In addition to the export tax, a toll tax was imposed on all the main roads throughout Judea and Samaria. Only a few favored caravans from Egypt, Damascus, and Antioch received an exemption. These favored caravans transported goods produced by the Nigrid's personal businesses.

Three additional taxes were imposed on the Jews and the Samaritans over the next three years. As much as he wanted to implement his entire tax scheme at one time, the Nigrid chose to instigate the taxes over time so as not to cause an outright rebellion by the Jews, which would irritate Rome and would certainly result in his dismissal.

The final taxes included sales tax on all food bought or sold in the marketplace. Increased income tax from one percent to two percent of the yearly income of individuals as well as businesses. And naturally, inheritance taxes.

Revenue from these new taxes accounted for an unconscionable increase of nearly fifty percent personal income for the Nigrid and fifty percent for Rome. Procurator Gratus was very pleased how the ambitious tax collector was able to accomplish such a feat. Of course, Gratus took full credit when Caesar took note and commended this large increase.

While Gratus and the Nigrid were enjoying their newfound wealth, the excessive tax burden gave rise to the Zealots who to that point were only a minor faction within both the Romans and the Jewish religious leaders.

By AD 25 as the various taxes grew, and the ire against the new taxes grew with them, increasing in both Judea and Samaria. The Zealots were able to recruit more to their cause throughout the entire regions of Judea and Samaria. The Zealots vehemently opposed paying the taxes levied by Rome and enhanced by the Nigrid.

The majority of Jews refrained from following the Zealots' dangerous example because the moderates of Jewish society felt they were not severely impacted by the various forms of taxation. Most of these people were able to circumvent the majority of the total tax levy and so continue their daily lives. Only the poor became staunch advocates of the Zealots. Since Rome's taxes did not interfere with the Jewish religion's tax structure, the religious leaders remained mum on the subject.

In AD 26 Gratus was recalled to Rome and replaced by Pontius Pilate who was a very cunning and astute manipulator. On his initial visit to Jericho after assuming his procurator status, Pilate met with the Nigrid at the Judean administrator's mansion.

Pilate was always direct and did not mince words. "Nigrid, Rome is very pleased with the increase of tax revenue you have garnered. However, I want to propose increasing some of these taxes another five percent."

The Nigrid earlier had learned about Pilate and was on guard as the conversation ensued. The chief tax collector had his own plan on how and when to increase taxes and his personal percentage. He was interested to compare what Pilate had in mind. He decided to be coy and probe Pilate's mind and intentions. He proceeded cautiously.

"Raising taxes more at this time is not wise, Procurator. The Jews are at a point that I fear additional increases will incite them to riot. Did not Gratus inform you how this sect known as Zealots is increasing in number and popularity among the Jews?"

Pilate held his head erectly in a regal fashion. He made sure his posture and personal appearance not only reflected his position of authority, but also evoked a sense of fear in his audience, whether an audience of only one or many. "Gratus did mention this to me, but he is a weak man who does not understand how to govern," he scoffed. "In addition, he is prone to lying about many things. That is why Caesar has recalled him to Rome." Pilate then gestured with his hand for the Nigrid to resume his part of the conversation.

"What types of tax increases do you propose, Pilate?"

"Increases on the exports, tolls, and food bought and sold in the marketplace." With a stern command Pilate finished, "No more than five percent in each case." The new procurator shot steely eyes at the civil servant and said, "There shall be no additional levies that will add to you or your henchmen's personal coffers. Should I learn of such additional increases; you and the subordinate collectors will be scourged."

The Nigrid shuddered at the thought of being scourged. Roman torture methods were well known throughout the region. The disconcerted tax man perceived this order to be a test by Pilate to learn if the Nigrid could be trusted. He answered evenly, "Your command will be obeyed, Pilate. I do request that favor be granted to me on those businesses I have inherited from King Herod." Pilate knew the Nigrid had confiscated Herod's businesses after the king died. It did not matter to Rome so long as the products from the businesses went to Rome first. The related tax money was of no consequence to Caesar. It was considered just a part of doing business in this province.

"It is granted, Nigrid, "he announced magnanimously. "Now, one last matter to discuss. I want to implement spies throughout both Judea and Samaria to learn of this Zealot sect's plans as well as to identify who they are. At this point I want only to monitor them, unless, of course, they commit a serious crime against Rome. Do you have people who can do this?"

"I can recruit such people. They will come from the ranks of the Jewish moderates. They are the easiest of the three separate classes of Jewish society. This shall be no problem."

At that, Pilate stood up, thereby ending the conversation. His steely gaze remained focused on the near dwarf-sized man and he turned and departed the mansion. The worried Nigrid breathed a sigh of relief. Calling for some refreshment, the anxious tax man sat on his softly covered couch and stared at the smooth marble patio floor. For quite some time he reflected on the true meaning of the conversation with the new procurator.

Pilate immediately left Jericho and traveled southwest to Jerusalem where he met with the high priest Caiaphas. The procurator's mission was to implement his second phase of dealing with the Zealot sect.

Caiaphas was confident he could control the new Roman dog—governor over Judea—and do it much better than his counterpart in Samaria. The high priest was festooned in his finest garments and sat on his throne to receive Pilate.

The Roman authoritarian remained expressionless when first introduced to the Jewish high priest. He was not impressed with the garments or the pomp. Pilate rejected the hard-seated chair in front of the high priest's throne. Instead, he stopped approximately fifteen feet away. He stood in regal stance, making sure his toga prominently displayed his official stripe of position.

True to his nature, Pilate wasted no time. Because of his chosen distance from the high priest's throne, Pilate significantly raised his voice knowing it would ricochet and echo in the room. "Caiaphas, it is my understanding from Gratus that you have a special arrangement to make sure your governing body will remain friendly towards Rome. Do you intend on continuing with this agreement?"

The Jewish high priest was somewhat deflated by Pilate's undisturbed demeanor and the resonating voice bouncing off the walls of his vaulted chamber. He witnessed how the Roman stood with confidence, and had a commanding voice. It was evident this Roman was unlike the weak Gratus.

Attempting to save some face, Caiaphas summoned equal strength into his own voice. "I am willing to continue so long as you do the same, Procurator."

Pilate exhibited no emotion and went on to his main purpose. "The rise of the Zealot sect can cause you great and harmful difficulties with Rome. I want you to instruct your rabbis to obtain information concerning this sect and those who follow them. When you receive word of the identities of these followers and their intended plans, immediately notify the garrison commander here in Jerusalem. The military will do what is necessary to quell these rebels."

The echoes filled the great hall and Pilate began to be annoyed by Caiaphas' delay in agreeing to the command. Finally, Caiaphas responded with a submissive tone, "I shall immediately notify the rabbis of this directive."

Pilate quickly ordered, "Caiaphas, my command is for all the rabbis throughout Judea and not just those here in Jerusalem. Am I understood on this matter?"

Caiaphas gestured with his left hand and said, "It is understood, Procurator."

Pilate gave one final ominous directive, "And Caiaphas, don't do anything stupid and hide the identities of these rebels from me." Briskly, he turned and marched out of the great hall. The meeting was over and Pilate was relieved he could now return to Caesarea, which was more to his liking than these bearded imbeciles who practiced strange rituals. He was quite pleased how easy it was for him to intimidate both the tax man and this hypocrite religious leader. In his mind he thought, "Such weakness."

As predicted by Pilate, the new tax increases went into effect with a minimum of rebellion. The moderates remained complacent, but the poor grew in outrage and more vocal in their protests. As for the Nigrid, the Jewish nation resented him, held him in contempt, and labeled him a traitor to his fellow Jews. The same went for the subordinate tax collectors located throughout Judea and Samaria. The Nigrid was no longer referred to by his title that meant benefactor, but by his Jewish name, Zacchaeus. Each time his name was uttered by the Jews it was with venom and total disdain. Now, only foreign businessmen called him Nigrid.

The Jewish religious leaders led the protest and ostracized him from all participation in Jewish rituals and synagogue attendance. This was merely a show, because Zacchaeus had been eliminated long ago from proper Jewish society due to his dwarf-like size. The cold shoulder proclamation by the religious hypocrites meant nothing to Zacchaeus' hardened heart. It merely amused him and increased his resolve against them.

His exposure and exclusion from Jewish society did not have a negative impact on his relationship with Terach and his family, especially Mattan and Devorah, and also Bartimaeus and Hadassah. He treasured their friendship and vowed to continue to care for them. His heart especially ached over the fact neither couple could produce heirs. This added to the Jewish leaders' list of reasons for blacklisting them.

In AD 33 forces came into play that began the spiraling down of the Jewish society and reducing the power of the Sanhedrin. By that time Pilate and Zacchaeus had increased the tax base more. The effect was the Zealot sect gained support and power from the disgruntled downtrodden. Under the leadership of John of Gischala, a member of the original group that revolted against the Romans in Galilee, the Zealots flexed their might and became more violent.

John of Gischala had successfully escaped the Romans in the Galilee uprising and settled into obscurity in Jerusalem, always mindful of resurrecting the sect. The Romans played into his hands, making it easy for him to recruit members. Their tax greed was sufficient fuel to kindle the embers of the dormant sect.

One of the early Zealots, a former nomad shepherd, had risen above the others and exhibited both leadership skills and a fierce warrior demeanor. His name was Jesus Barabbas. John of Gischala assigned Barabbas and twelve hand-picked warriors to the territory that encompassed Jericho west to Jamnia and back east to Emmaus and Qumran at the northern tip of the Dead Sea. Jesus Barabbas and the numerous other sect cells were instructed to rob the land caravans, and harass those Jews who aligned with the Romans. Jesus Barabbas relished this new assignment. The former nomad shepherd conducted numerous raids and became well-known to both Jews and Romans. In fact, a bounty had recently been placed on his head, along with other known sect leaders.

In the early spring of AD 33, three weeks before the Passover observance, Jesus Barabbas was captured by the Roman military outside of Emmaus. The rebel robbed a caravan making its way west through the ridge route trade bridge. In the skirmish, the bandits killed the small contingent of Roman soldiers who accompanied the caravan. A hidden troop of Roman cavalry archers intersected the bandits, all of whom were killed, except Barabbas.

The rebel was taken into custody and returned to Emmaus where he was transferred to a second patrol of Roman soldiers who took him to Jerusalem and the Roman garrison. During his initial incarceration, the Romans exacted their revenge on Jesus Barabbas' body making sure they did not cross the line to kill him before his public trial.

The garrison commander ordered Barabbas beaten. Bloodied, fatigued, and almost unconscious, Barabbas was interrogated by the commander. "Tell me, you Jewish pig, how did you know of the caravan?" Jesus Barabbas remained silent, painfully gasping for breath. The commander got close to the bandit's swollen, puffy and bloodied face and hissed, "Who is your leader?" Jesus Barabbas looked at the Roman with his only open eye and spat a bloody glob into the man's face.

Immediately the commander struck Barabbas along the side of the head, rendering him unconscious. The commander quickly wiped the spittle from his face. He instructed the guards to keep the prisoner chained upright, preventing him from lying down. Jesus Barabbas remained in this position for several days. He was given no food and a minimum of water. The commander wanted to inflict maximum punishment on the rebel before his trial date.

A carrier pigeon note sent to John of Gischala soon after Barabbas' capture put the bandit leader on high alert. The Zealot commander immediately initiated a series of disruptive raids. The sky was filled with carrier pigeon missiles to all regions of Judea ordering the raids. Gischala also sent a message to his counterpart in Samaria, who began his own attacks against the Romans stationed there. It was hoped word of these raids would disrupt the Romans from their torturous treatment of Barabbas.

Within hours of receiving the orders to disrupt and kill any Roman soldiers or Roman sympathizers, the raids were carried out with enthusiasm by the Zealot rebels. As hoped, reports of the impact of these raids were sent to Jerusalem and the garrison commander.

The commander stood looking at the unconscious prisoner hanging limp and unconscious from the shackles around his wrists. The Roman was confident the Zealot rebel would confess the information concerning the rebels. The anti-Semitic Roman, nonetheless, was impressed at the resolve and defiance of this hated Jew.

With arms behind his back, the Roman commander waited silently for Barabbas to awaken in order to resume his torture. Suddenly, a soldier burst into the prison cell and whispered words into the commander's ear. This caused the startled Roman to recoil as he stared into the messenger's face. He dropped his barbed whip and rushed out of the prison cell, running to his office on the other side of the walled fortress.

For the time being, the torture of Barabbas would have to be postponed.

At the same time of Barabbas' imprisonment, a Jew from the town of Nazareth was making his way towards Jerusalem for the Passover observance and also his destiny. Throughout his route a multitude of curiosity seekers as well as admirers and followers joined him and his twelve apostles. The various spies of both Pilate and Zacchaeus took part in this procession and sent word via carrier pigeon to Jericho and to Caesarea. The two recipients of the breaking news had different reactions.

Zacchaeus was interested because of news how this Jesus of Nazareth was gathering many followers and that he had performed miracles of raising the dead as well as restoring sight to the blind. The chief administrator of Judea thought about intercepting this Nazarene and paying him to restore the sight to both Bartimaeus and to Mattan. To the diminutive Jew, everyone had a price; it was merely a matter of determining what that price was. In many instances, it was other than money. Zacchaeus was intrigued to think what this Nazarene's price would be.

Pilate was finalizing plans for his trek to Jerusalem for the mandatory appearance of the procurator at the main pilgrimage feast of the Jews. There would be hundreds of thousands of Jews from throughout Judea congregated in Jerusalem for this festival. It was the duty of the procurator to amass sufficient troops to keep order during this festival week. It was a duty Pilate, like all the procurators, disliked immensely.

The disturbing and alarming news of the Zealots' raids throughout Judea and Samaria gave Pilate cause to rethink his position on this festival involving such a mass of humanity. Pilate conferred with his secretary. "Janus, you have knowledge of these people. What thoughts do you have about this situation involving the timing of the raids to coincide with this ridiculous festival we must attend?"

Janus had several ideas. "It could be a signal that these Zealots intend on disrupting this festival and potentially doing you harm because they know you must attend as part of your duties. The Jews are quite open about their hatred for us Romans. Such an attempt on your life would be within their reasoning."

Pilate sat in his office chair, staring at his secretary. Janus' words caused Pilate to frown. His eyes narrowed as he pictured the scenario depicted by his trusted ally. Janus went on to correct his first statement, "Personally, I believe two important factors preclude these raids as signals of intended harm to you."

The newly appointed procurator sat back in his chair and cocked his head at Janus who explained, "First, these raids are by this sect that has limited support among the Jewish elites, especially their religious leaders. I perceive these leaders desire to learn more about how you plan on carrying out your duties before they attempt to take your life. Second, this religious festival is very important to these people and they are obligated to observe it in prescribed rituals. A disruption to their set of rituals would be very bad for the religious leaders."

Pilate placed both hands on the arms of his ornately carved chair and pursed his lips. "Janus, I agree with you. This brings us back to question why the Zealot bandits are conducting these raids at this particular time. What could be their motive and their objective?" The Roman procurator would not find out the answer to that question until he arrived in Jerusalem and spoke with the garrison commander.

Zacchaeus came up with a plan of his own to make sure his blind tradesmen would have access to the Nazarene. The year before the Passover event, the business administrator had dispersed his own spies concerning the Zealots. It took some concentrated persuasion to get his adopted family members to assist him. Finally, each man agreed so long as it did not take up much of their valuable time and all they had to do was acquire information.

Zacchaeus was elated the two men would become part-time spies. He requested that both Bartimaeus and Mattan position themselves separately at different key spots where they could acquire important information for him. Almost immediately, the blind duo was able to supply Zacchaeus much valuable information.

Now Zacchaeus would utilize his stalwart agents in his bigger scheme for them to encounter the Nazarene healer. He did not wish to tip his hand and potentially create difficulties. He knew that Jesus of Nazareth would be traveling through Jericho on his way to Jerusalem for the Passover. From Galilee, this was the quickest route to Jerusalem. Zacchaeus figured it was merely a matter of timing to achieve his purpose.

In Jerusalem, the garrison commander had to completely alter his plan for the captured Jesus Barabbas. The frequency of the Zealot raids and their impact forced him to address the matter with his full attention. As such, the rebel fighter was left alone in his prison cell. The garrison commander instructed that Barabbas be kept hanging by his arms and given only minimum food or water.

The garrison commander knew that his superior, the procurator, would be in Jerusalem for the Jewish religious event. He did not want to incur the wrath of Pilate by failing to quell these disturbances that could expand into Jerusalem. The commander felt the intense pressure of the situation. He dared not anger Pilate. Consequences would be similar to that of the imprisoned Jesus Barabbas.

The warm springtime weather of nearly 80 degrees brought out the aroma of various spices, balsam, dates, and perfumes grown in the area that heralded the arrival to the fenced city of Jericho. Abundant tall palm trees acted as sentinels for all who came to the chief city of commerce in the region. Spring flooding had subsided, making the trek less dangerous.

There were several new ongoing construction projects that signified the prosperity of the city. As time drew closer for the beginning of Passover, Zacchaeus increased the daily reports from his moles as to the progress of the Nazarene and his group of followers. One message caused Zacchaeus to clap his hands together in glee. The faith healer would arrive in Jericho tomorrow.

Zacchaeus met with both Bartimaeus and Mattan to give them his instructions. All they had to do was wait and listen for the sounds that would announce the Nazarene's arrival.

The night before their assignment, Bartimaeus and Mattan spoke about the miracles the faith healer had performed. "In my heart, Mattan, I believe this Nazarene has divine power, and not demonic, as the Pharisees and rabbis say." The blind cobbler then confessed his private thoughts. "I have confidence this healer could restore our sight, should we make his presence."

Mattan concurred with his blind friend, "I have the same thoughts, my friend. I know that Zacchaeus has given us instructions for what he wants, but I believe there could be an opportunity for us to seek him out that he could heal us." Mattan stroked his beard and added, "We have nothing to lose and everything to gain, but we must be alert and act quickly."

The men were in agreement that following what Zacchaeus wanted, they would do all within their power to get the attention of the Nazarene. Devorah and Hadassah said they would accompany their husbands and assist in getting the attention of the man named Jesus. The women longed for a return of sight to their husbands not only for the men's benefit but for selfish reasons, as well. Each woman wanted their husband to be able to see them and share visual experiences that would surely enhance their communication. How often they spoke with a twinkle in their eye or a quiet smile that their husbands never saw and couldn't hear. And, oh, how they hoped their husbands would find them attractive.

Very early the next morning the group hastened to the spot in the road as directed by Zacchaeus. The women stood back while the two blind agents sat patiently waiting for the arrival of Jesus and his followers. They felt the early morning chill, but their emotions also played a part in their shivering.

The sun rose in the early morning sky, bringing its warming rays to comfort the two blind men and their nearby wives. Within an hour they heard the first sounds of an approaching group. The blind men's trained senses informed them it was a very large group by the sound of the thudding footsteps, the voices, and the breathing from the travelers. There were jumbled noises but they could not detect the sound of the faith healer's voice.

Both men tensed in anticipation. With each footstep and growing clarity of the conversations from the travelers, the two spies felt they would soon get what their employer wanted.

The huge crowd was very close. A couple of the men in front of the procession approached the two blind agents saying, "You, beggars, make way for Jesus of Nazareth. Do not impede his journey with your lowly presence." The front men attempted to push the blind beggars off to the side of the road.

To their surprise, the blind men jumped up and resisted their efforts. The ruckus garnered attention at the front of the human caravan. Bartimaeus and Mattan became aware of someone important moving forward. The anxious blind men concluded that Jesus was very near and Bartimaeus flailed his arms as defense against the restraining efforts of the men associated with the healer. He shouted, "Have mercy on us, O Lord, thou Son of David!"

Several more of the multitude came and warned Bartimaeus and Mattan to be quiet. Instead, the blind men cried out together even louder, "Have mercy on us, O Lord, Son of David!" Aided by adrenaline at a fever pitch, both blind men forcefully resisted the efforts of those who claimed to be disciples to the Nazarene.

The huge procession stopped in response to the pleading of the blind beggars. Those in back who could not see what was taking place murmured and demanded the convoy continue. In unison they attempted to push those ahead of them onward but to no avail.

All eyes at the front of the procession were on the faith healer, and on the spies sent by the high priest. Jesus purposefully made his way to the front edge of crowd. Casually, he stopped and listened to the words shouted at him by the desperate men. His face was calm and his eyes conveyed deep interest at the near hysterical pleading words spoken to him.

Jesus of Nazareth motioned for the two blind beggars to be brought to him. As both Bartimaeus and Mattan were escorted towards Jesus, their wives hurried to witness what was taking place. Each woman's heart was pounding feverishly. They successfully pushed their way to the front of the crowd that now encircled Jesus and the blind beggars. The Nazarene kindly spoke to each man asking, "What do you want me to do for you?"

In unison the blind men cast their cloaks aside, a significant sign to all Jews. The gesture meant they were giving up everything to receive the blessing that could come only from God. Together they passionately replied, "Lord, that we may receive our sight!"

So Jesus had compassion on them and stepped towards them. He reached out with both arms and gently touched each man's eyes, caressing all around the eyes with his hands while speaking. In a voice of great love and compassion, he said, "Receive your sight, your faith has made you well."

Jesus released his fingers from their eyes and smiled warmly. All eyes, especially those of Devorah and Hadassah, were focused on the two blind beggars. There was a hushed silence and even the nearby birds stopped chirping. God's creatures instinctively knew the significance of the event that was ordained by their Creator.

Everyone closest to Jesus and the blind petitioners watched as the blind men's eyelids flickered and widened. The heads of the blind men moved side to side and each slightly staggered and repeatedly blinked. The crowd remained breathless as the miracle unfolded.

First, Bartimaeus lifted his head and peered in the direction of Jesus. He gasped, broke into a wide smile, giggled, and began to cry. He quickly dropped down with his shoulders shaking and knelt at the feet of Jesus who quietly reached down and brought him back to his feet. Bartimaeus continued to sob tears of joy and thankfulness. He looked into the benevolent face of the loving Lord and peacefully uttered, "This is the first time in my entire life I've been able to see. It is a wondrous thing!" He grabbed Jesus' hands and held them tightly, repeatedly kissing them, saying, "Thank you, thank you, thank you!'

While Bartimaeus gave thanks to his Lord, Mattan gazed at the ground, and for the first time in seventeen years recognized dirt that had once seemed so common to his eyes and he had often disregarded. What a glorious event now to see it once again! Was he dreaming? The impact caused tears of astonishment and gratitude to stream down his face. He vowed never again to take anything for granted or think of it as commonplace. He lifted his head and watched his close friend's interaction with Jesus.

Still smiling, Jesus gently moved away from the unrestrained Bartimaeus and stepped closer towards Mattan. As Jesus approached him, Mattan's newly sighted eyes latched onto those of the Nazarene. They seemed like magnets that refused to allow Mattan to peer elsewhere. The Nazarene came face-to-face with Mattan and stopped a mere six inches from him, smiling. The former blind man gasped and exclaimed in awe, "It is YOU! You are the baby Jesus I first saw back in Bethlehem, in a manger. You are Jesus, the young child I visited so long ago. It truly is YOU!"

Jesus smiled warmly at Mattan and embraced him. Mattan would not release Jesus from his devoted embrace until Bartimaeus joined them. Jesus leaned forward and softly spoke into each man's ear, "Follow me." He released his newfound followers and stepped back. He gave them one last look of love, smiled warmly, then proceeded on the road towards Jerusalem to prepare for his bout with evil.

As the multitude followed Jesus of Nazareth, the two recipients of Jesus' miracle remained fixed on the side of the road, staring at the departing Messiah until he was out of sight. Then they turned and faced each other. Smiles of astonishment spread over each man's face. Bartimaeus put his hands on Mattan's shoulders and kindly said, "What Jesus said to us does not mean merely to follow him to Jerusalem. It's much more. I believe he means for us to totally give our lives over to him."

Mattan peered down the road at the mixed crowd, then at Bartimaeus, and replied, "I agree with you, my friend. I suspect this will prove to be more difficult than either of us realizes."

Bartimaeus grabbed his friend's shoulders and forcefully turned Mattan towards him, booming, "So this is what you look like! What a sight you are for me!"

Mattan in turn tightly grabbed Bartimaeus and laughingly reciprocated, "I've often wondered what you look like, as well. I'm glad you are not ugly, otherwise I may ask Jesus to make me blind again!"

At that time both Devorah and Hadassah came close to their husbands. Cautiously, Devorah looked into the eyes of Mattan and delicately uttered, "I am Devorah, your wife." Mattan stood motionless as he tilted his head and gazed into his wife's glistening eyes for the first time since they met. The now sighted potter stood mesmerized for a brief moment, then reached out and drew her close to him. He tenderly kissed the side of her cheek and proudly stated, "You are beautiful. More beautiful than what I had envisioned." Tears ran down the cheeks of the couple and they embraced reverently, straining to grasp all that had just happened.

While Devorah and Mattan clung to each other, Hadassah tentatively stood in front of Bartimaeus and timidly said, "It is I, Hadassah, your wife." Bartimaeus immediately took her hands into his, squeezing them tightly and grinned. "You are the first woman I've seen in my life. You are beyond what I ever imagined. You are my vision of loveliness!" Wrapping his arms around her, he bundled her up and held her as if she were the most precious armload of goods he had ever held. And indeed she was.

A lone figure hidden nearby witnessed this exchange and a lump formed in his throat as he fought to contain his emotions. His short legs crumbled and tears ran down his face. It was as he had hoped it would be and he was overjoyed for his loved ones. Zacchaeus shifted his eyes south as the multitude was slowly marching down the road.

The diminutive man quickly ran parallel to the multitude. As the group swerved around a bend in the road, Zacchaeus went straight over the knoll to get ahead of the marching throng. His curiosity to see the miracle worker gave him extra adrenalin and he was able to get sufficiently ahead of the approaching mob.

Hurriedly, he climbed up the branches of a sycamore tree that was close to the road and often used by weary travelers as a rest spot.

Feeling sufficiently hidden among the leaves, Zacchaeus looked down as the swarm drew near beneath his perch. Once again the crowd had resumed different conversations including two who were talking with the miracle worker. Zacchaeus was able to identify Jesus of Nazareth and he scrutinized the man so many were following. He was amazed how common this man of repute looked and carried himself. Nothing like the rumors about him, most certainly about him being the promised messiah.

Suddenly the Nazarene stopped walking and held up his hand to interrupt those with whom he was talking. The Nazarene peered up into the sycamore tree pointing to the hidden observer. Raising his voice, Jesus addressed the tax collector, "Zacchaeus, make haste and come down, for I must stay at your home."

The tree climber was startled and nearly lost his grip on the branch holding him aloft. He was perplexed. First, that this Jesus of Nazareth knew his name because the two had never met. Second, that a man of such renown would seek to stay with the likes of one so despised by all of Jewish society. Wondering at all these things, Zacchaeus did as instructed and scurried down from his tree perch.

When many in the crowd recognized him as the chief tax collector, they loudly and angrily complained about Jesus, saying, "He has gone to be a guest with a man who is a sinner." Jesus and Zacchaeus paid no attention to the murmuring mass and made their way to the Judean business administrator's mansion. The twelve apostles closest to Jesus followed a discreet distance behind.

The throng of humanity turned aside and went their separate ways. Many were heard saying, "Enough of this Nazarene who mingles with such low lifes." Others who proclaimed to be disciples to the Nazarene waited by the sycamore tree for their teacher to return.

Once inside his abode, Zacchaeus summoned a servant and ordered him to quickly fetch the two couples who were the recipients of the day's miracle. Next, he called his subordinate tax collectors to also come to his mansion. They were in Jericho for the impending Passover observance and business meeting that took place afterward. Because the guest list was large, another servant scurried to the marketplace and purchased prepared lamb and fish to supply the hungry guests.

As the great feast was prepared, Zacchaeus and the rest sat around the guest of honor. Jesus of Nazareth spoke many kind, yet strong words of truth that moved the hearts of everyone in attendance.

No one interrupted Jesus and all were deeply touched by his words of divine wisdom. On occasion the heavenly preacher's words impacted his audience to the point they were speechless. None more than their host, the hated tax collector.

Just before the feast was served, Zacchaeus stood and announced in a choking voice, "Jesus, I feel the impact of your words deep within my soul and am ashamed for my actions." Visibly shaken, Zacchaeus nearly fell for the second time that day. He looked humbly into his guest of honor's eyes and resolutely stated, "Lord, I shall give half of my goods to the poor; and if I have taken anything from anyone by false accusation, I will restore fourfold!"

The room became very hushed. The twelve apostles looked in amazement at the dwarf-like man. To them this demonstrated what Jesus had taught about being repentant. Truth had come to life for not just the twelve, but also for the others in attendance. Zacchaeus' eyes were moist with emotion as he made his vow. He was transfixed with joy as he stared at Jesus of Nazareth, now his Lord, the one he would follow from now on. The small man realized he was free, released from years of bondage. Despite his unchanged small frame he felt as if he were ten feet tall. The reborn man felt completely new inside.

The quiet contained within the great room broke apart as the doors swung open and servants brought forth a lavish meal. Before the meal commenced, Zacchaeus and the two couples privately made the declaration that was now in their respective hearts that Jesus of Nazareth was their Lord and Savior.

Very early the next morning, Jesus of Nazareth and his twelve apostles returned to the road that headed to Jerusalem for the upcoming Passover feast. They met the waiting disciples at the sycamore tree along the road and the journey resumed down the winding dirt road, the ribbon that guided Jesus of Nazareth, Messiah, to his destiny.

Chapter 18

The same day that Jesus of Nazareth and his reduced entourage left Jericho for Jerusalem, Zacchaeus prepared for his annual dinner with Terach and his family. This year would be a very pleasant surprise for them. The business administrator of Judea had a special plan for the nomad shepherd and his family.

In addition, the chief tax collector worked on his plan to implement the vow he gave Jesus of Nazareth. It would require an in-depth study and calculation, but the spiritually changed man had no reservations about accomplishing his monumental task.

The easier of Zacchaeus' plots began as expected when Terach and his family, which now included the husband of Channah, arrived at the host's mansion. He had purposely instructed both Devorah and Mattan to arrive late for the celebration dinner.

Terach became nervous as the time lengthened for Mattan and his wife to arrive for the dinner. "Zacchaeus, why are Mattan and Devorah not yet here? Your dinner will begin soon and it's not like them to be this late."

Zacchaeus assured his chief guest that the couple would arrive before dinner was served. Just then, a servant ushered Devorah into the dining room. Terach, Beulah, and the rest of the family had raised eyebrows. Devorah was always on hand due to being Mattan's guide. He could not function alone. The raised eyebrows also reflected thoughts of concern.

For her part, Devorah acted nonchalantly as she greeted her adopted family. Terach took the lead in addressing the obvious question. "Devorah, where is Mattan? Is he ill that he is not able to attend our annual dinner?"

Before Devorah could answer her father-in-law's questions, a hearty voice from the dining room doorway exclaimed, "My family, I am here and in good health!" All eyes turned toward the voice and witnessed their blind shepherd moving casually and easily in their direction, avoiding all obstacles in his way. He was grinning from ear to ear.

Mattan specifically came to where his father stood, who now had a quizzical expression on his face. The senior nomad shepherd watched his youngest son's advance until Mattan stopped just in front of him. Something was different. Terach's eyes darted back and forth questioning what was taking place. Mattan teased him, "Father, I see your beard is getting gray as is your hair."

At those words, the quiet room exploded in a succession of gasps from the assembled family members. Terach stood and realized for the first time that his son's eyes now sparkled and reflected life and not the dullness of blindness. "You...you...can see me?" Terach choked out the words.

"Father, I see you most clearly!" Mattan joyfully exclaimed. He turned and surveyed the shocked expressions of his entire family whom he had not seen for so long.

The once blind shepherd dashed to his mother and gave her a kiss on her cheek. Next, he embraced his younger sister Channah, who always seemed to burst into tears. This time was no exception. Finally, Mattan extended heartfelt greetings and embraces to each of his three brothers. Devorah and Zacchaeus with misty eyes stood to the side watching the reunion.

During and after the sumptuous dinner, Mattan and Devorah relayed the details of how Jesus of Nazareth restored sight to both Mattan and to Bartimaeus. The family sat in awe.

Terach wanted to know more. "Throughout our route, word came to us of this faith healer from Galilee. It was said, he even raised the dead to new life. The rabbis conditioned the Jews that this man was demon-possessed. Do you perceive this to be the case, Mattan?"

"I do not, Father. Why, I recognized the eyes of this Jesus to be the same as the infant Jesus we viewed in the manger when I was but a mere boy! He verified to me it was him. I believe him to be the promised messiah, not just with my new sight..." and Mattan paused to select the right words, "...but with my heart."

Awe filled the room. Terach leaned towards his now sighted son. "I believe your words, my son." The patriarch of the family turned so all could see and hear what he had to say. "Many have proclaimed this Jesus to be the promised one. It is one thing to heal and to raise the dead; it is quite another to lead the Jews out of bondage as we have been taught to believe. My question is, will the religious idiots in control receive Jesus as our Messiah?"

The remainder of the evening was devoted to give and take on the subject of the promised messiah with no definitive conclusion. One item that was unanimous centered on how the family would spend the Passover week with their now sighted son. Zacchaeus took matters into his hands and declared Mattan would have a holiday from his normal work routine making pots. The reformed tax collector also shocked his guests with his promise made to Jesus of Nazareth.

"This is most unusual for you, or anyone in your position, Zacchaeus," said Terach. "I am most surprised at your vow. Do you really believe what you intend on doing can come about?"

Zacchaeus replied in humble sincerity, "Indeed I do, my friend. It will take time and planning, but I've begun the process this day."

Terach asked, "Will this not cause you considerable problems with Pilate because you will be giving back taxes?" Zacchaeus shook his head no. "It will not. Because what I intend on returning is the excess I took when collecting the taxes. The money will come only from my own treasury." Everyone in the room was astounded at their friend's declaration.

Channah spoke up boldly, "Zacchaeus, this is a great testimony to the impact this man Jesus of Nazareth has had on you. It bodes that the rest of us should consider becoming followers of this one who could very well be the promised messiah." Everyone in the room agreed with the young woman.

Zacchaeus quickly agreed. "Channah, there is no doubt in my heart that Jesus of Nazareth is indeed the promised Messiah!"

Very early in the morning of the same day Jesus of Nazareth arrived in Jericho, Pilate and his larger than usual force began their journey to Jerusalem via the Via Maris trade route that ran through Caesarea south into Egypt. The procurator's route would initially go south at Jamnia and turn east to Emmaus along the ridge route trade bridge, finally ending at Jerusalem.

This would be Pilate's seventh attendance at the Jewish Passover observance. Each time he detested having to perform his duty as procurator to honor the Jews' religious ritual. This particular event had an extra twist in that Pilate had to address the issue of the Zealot raiders. It was a big problem that he must resolve, otherwise Rome would replace him.

As a show of strength and as a precautionary measure, Pilate summoned the entire 12th Legion of Roman military might to accompany him to Jerusalem. Of the twelve thousand soldiers, six thousand were mounted archers, four thousand were battle-tested infantrymen, and two thousand were experienced spear throwers. In addition, there were one hundred wagons of replacement arrows and spears for the specialists.

It was a massive exhibition of Roman military might, intended for service and not merely to parade. Pilate wanted this very battle-tested legion on hand should the Zealots attack Jerusalem or the surrounding smaller towns. Pilate hoped the presence of a mighty fighting force would compel anyone with knowledge of the Zealots to come forth with valuable information to be used against the religious fanatics.

Pilate and his wife, Claudia Procula, rode in an ornate carriage positioned near the front of the phalanx of men and horses. Their forward position was to protect them from the massive dust that filled the air from the feet and the hooves of so many travelers.

The fifth Roman procurator to Judea enjoyed the time with his wife, whom he often consulted concerning matters of state. "Claudia, tell me your thoughts concerning these Jewish religious rebels and their numerous attacks."

Claudia dabbed her brow with a delicate cloth. The springtime heat and the confined carriage caused her discomfort. This was among several reasons she, also, detested going to the Jewish festival. "Obviously, the increased tax structure is at the root of this rebel faction." Claudia wiped away perspiration from her neck. "Also, husband, their insidious religion causes many to put aside good judgment. They act in ways that defy practicality. This is what appears to be the case, at least on the surface. There very well could be another motive in their actions." Claudia Procula did not like discussing this subject under the circumstances with the heat and the dust. She longed for completion of the dismal journey.

Pilate relaxed in the fine cushioning of the carriage seating. "You confirm my thoughts and are correct, Claudia, about another motive. I believe once I interrogate the garrison commander in Jerusalem, that motive will be revealed."

No further discussion of the topic occurred during the two-and-a-half-day journey to Jerusalem. The speed of the trek was in accordance with Roman military tactics to get to a battle site quickly. As such, Roman infantrymen were trained well and in excellent marching condition. Part of the incentive for the infantrymen and other Roman fighters was the thought of engaging an enemy in deadly battle and enjoying the spoils afterwards. To make the journey faster and easier, the Romans had worked to greatly improve all the main roads, especially those of the trade routes.

Immediately upon their arrival in the Jewish capitol, Pilate summoned the garrison commander to the procurator's quarters. The garrison in Jerusalem was constructed on the ground floor with rooms for the soldiers, the armory, and the offices of the officers. The entire second floor was devoted to the procurator, the garrison commander, and any dignitaries of Rome. The top third floor was divided into prisoner cells and interrogation rooms. The higher level was designed to thwart potential prison escapes.

The second floor was lavishly decorated much to Claudia Procula's delight. The room most sought by Claudia was the bath, which she hurriedly utilized while Pilate spoke with the Roman commander.

Pilate began his interview of the commander immediately. "Commander, what can you tell me about these irritating raids?"

The garrison commander anticipated his superior's question and knew he must not hesitate or vacillate in any way. "They are at the behest of John of Gischala, the Zealot leader. We captured one of his subordinate leaders, a Jew known as Jesus Barabbas. He is above us in an interrogating cell. I have questioned him, but he has not revealed any information about himself or the Zealots. I intend to bring this information forth, with your permission."

Pilate's mind was processing what the Roman official spoke. As was his custom, Pilate stared at his underling with penetrating eyes. The effect made the Roman military officer uneasy, just as Pilate intended. "Are you saying these raids began soon after the capture of this Jesus Barabbas?" The commander tried not to look sheepish as he admitted this was true. Pilate rubbed his hands together while thinking for a moment. Then he instructed his minion, "Do not interrogate or torture this bandit any further. Now, report to the legion commander for your instructions." When he had finished, Pilate waved away the Roman soldier with his hand.

Once the garrison commander had left the room, Pilate summoned his secretary, Janus, for a conference. "I believe I have found the reason for these Zealot raids, Janus. They stem from the capture of a Zealot leader named Jesus Barabbas. I believe these raids are to protect this prisoner from torture and revealing the religious fanatics' next move. Tell me your assessment."

Janus puckered his lips briefly and said, "It is probable these Zealots intend on making additional strikes against our forces. However, I do not believe it will happen until after this religious ritual that means so much to them. Prepare for a battle after this religious festival, Pilate."

The procurator arched his back and his eyes reflected pleasure at his secretary's assessment. "I've instructed the legion commander to disperse his troops completely around the city. They shall remain in place throughout this ridiculous event. The legion commander is prepared for any attack that may ensue once this religious observance is finished. I believe we shall be well prepared, Janus."

Jerusalem remained calm the next four days, allowing Pilate to relax with his wife. Rarely did they venture outside the garrison's headquarters. On the fifth day, another highly volatile powder keg with a short fuse confronted the Roman procurator.

The Jewish leaders had arrested a Jew named Jesus of Nazareth on charges of blasphemy against their religion. The punishment for this religious crime ranged from scourging to death. The death penalty could not be enacted because only Rome could permit such action. Rome's policy of death seldom included religious actions because Rome was so polytheistic and encouraged all religions, as long as they did not incite riot against Rome.

Caiaphas and Annus and other leaders brought Jesus of Nazareth to the garrison and petitioned Pilate to allow the death of the one they accused of blaspheming. Pilate listened intently to the charges and noticed the accused had been horrifically beaten. This was permitted by Roman law. "I must personally question this man to determine if your charges merit such action. Leave me to do my work." The disgruntled accusers left to join the crowd in the street below.

Pilate shifted his attention to the bloodied Jew. He majestically walked around the weak and beaten Jew before him. The Roman enforcer stopped in front of Jesus and looked at the suspect with puzzled eyes but a placid demeanor. After studying the personage of Jesus of Nazareth, Pilate asked in a staccato voice, "Are you the King of the Jews?"

The defendant lifted his head and looked into the face of his prosecutor. In a low voice he only said, "It is as you say." The monotone voice of the accused shocked Pilate and caused him to take a step backward. Before Pilate could utter another word, the gathering of the crowd prompted by their religious leaders in the street erupted, creating a deafening and irritating noise. Pilate went to the window and peered down at the mob. Quickly, he held up his hand to silence the rabble of Jewish fanatics. A pronounced scowl was frozen on his face and his eyes squinted in anger. His appearance, aided by heavily armed soldiers, subdued the mob.

Now that the room was quiet again, Pilate said to Jesus, "Do you answer nothing to these fanatics and their charges against you?" Pilate gestured toward the angry throng and turned back to Jesus adding, "See how many things they testify against you."

Pilate waited for the indicted one to defend himself, but Jesus remained mute. Pilate stepped closer to the defendant, cocking his head and peering deeply into Jesus' face. Pilate's eyes were no longer squinting, but wide in searching for explanation. His facial muscles were relaxed and his lips slightly parted.

There was no reaction from the accused religious rebel. From behind him the Roman procurator heard a loud voice from outside say, "He stirs up the people, teaching falsehoods throughout all Judea, beginning at Galilee."

Hearing the word Galilee, Pilate stood motionless, stunned. He raced to the window asking the anonymous voice if indeed this Jesus was from Galilee. The reply that drifted upward toward the window and beyond to the heavens was affirmative.

With a sigh, Pilate again raised his hand, demanding silence from the anxious rabble. Silence immediately took place and in an emotionless voice Pilate declared, "Since this man is from Galilee he must first be interrogated by Herod Antipas. After this, a decision will be made concerning your demand. Now leave this place until such time as I recall you."

A relieved Pilate breathed a sigh and ordered the Roman guards to take the weak and weary Jew to Herod's quarters since he also was in Jerusalem for the Passover event.

During the time the religious prisoner was with Herod Antipas, Pilate conferred with both his wife and with his secretary about the matter. "This case obviously does not merit Rome's death penalty. His crime is religious in nature and as such is of no consequence to Rome. The question is, what is sufficient punishment for this religious rebel?"

Claudia Procula implored her husband, "Have nothing to do with that just man. He is innocent of the charges levied against him." Then in a strained voice she added, "I...I have suffered through several dreams because of him. I have a bad feeling because of him."

Pilate noted the fear in his wife's voice, but solicited the comments of his secretary before addressing Claudia Procula's concern. Janus stated, "What Herod Antipas discerns will determine the man's fate. You know full well, Pilate, Herod Antipas may take this decision away from you."

The procurator with the power of life and death surprised his confidants with another perspective. "It is as you both say. I also must take into account the unrest that spreads throughout this region. It is at a point of eruption that could result in revolt by these Jewish dogs." Pilate thoughtfully paused and finally pronounced, "I believe there is a way to placate these religious perverts."

Both Claudia and Janus looked on perplexed, waiting for Pilate to unveil his plan. Their wait was brief. "If I determine this Jew to be innocent and release him, the leaders of the Sanhedrin will assassinate him under our eyes. This will make us look very bad, especially considering the amount of force we have in the city. It could give these bearded fools incentive to create more problems for us later."

Janus now fully concentrated on the evolving plan of his employer. He was anxious to hear the rest. Pilate complied with his secretary's thoughts, "These despicable religious partisans are so obsessed with this man. I believe they can easily be swayed to carry out my plan." Pilate stood up and motioned for his listeners to follow him. He walked to the balcony and threw open the curtains, but stood back from the window opening in the shadows. He gestured for both Janus and Claudia to look below. The mass had not dissipated as ordered and remained nervous and eager for the rendering about the man they so wanted to kill.

"See how the leaders of the Sanhedrin gather their stooges below us." There was disgust in his voice. As the trio looked down, it was evident a crowd of nearly four hundred men were shuffling below. Pilate pointed out the faces of those who earlier had dragged Jesus to him. "I fully believe these conniving priests have paid these men to protest against this Jesus of Nazareth. It is a show to convince me of their power."

Pilate let out a small laugh. "They are so predictable to me. They have power only in their own minds. Yet I shall give them cause to hope they believe they can influence my decision." With a broad smile, Pilate looked at his confidants and elatedly chimed, "They shall get what they want, and I shall get what I want and they will never realize how duped they were."

Janus looked on with amazement. He knew Pilate to be cunning and hard-boiled, but now he was about to witness how cold-blooded his employer could really be. It made him shudder.

It was still early in the morning of the day the Passover event was to begin. Pilate looked up into the earlier morning sky with the sun barely over the horizon. He was not pleased to have his usual first meal of the day delayed due to the issue of the accused blasphemer. He hoped Herod Antipas would not take too long in coming to the same conclusion as Pilate had. Within minutes of his thinking, Herod appeared with the accused Jew who now had received a second beating at the hands of Herod Antipas. The second beating of this accused Jew had a great impact on the hungry Roman.

Herod Antipas nonchalantly informed his Roman supervisor, "I have found this man to be without blame to the charges brought by the leaders of the Sanhedrin. Do as you see fit, Pilate." Rising to his full height, Herod Antipas continued, "Considering all aspects of this case, plus the fact you are responsible for controlling all religious festivals, this matter rests in your hands."

Pilate shot a glance towards Janus that included a slight smile at the corner of his mouth. "Very well, Antipas. I shall inform the crowd below. But first I want the Zealot bandit Barabbas brought to me now." This command startled Janus, Antipas, and Claudia, who all remained in the room.

It took only a few minutes for the guards to shove Barabbas towards the man who held his fate in his hands. Janus stood sufficiently back of Pilate so as not to interfere with what the procurator judge was about to do.

The Roman secretary noticed how the early morning light filtered into the room creating streaks of yellowish bands that highlighted and softened the red drapes surrounding the balcony windows. It also made Pilate and the two accused men silhouettes, gray and without detail. Janus thought it fitting the two accused prisoners were without detail and gray. To the Roman it symbolized their fate.

Pilate had the two rebels stand on each side of him. Jesus Barabbas to the left and Jesus of Nazareth to his right. Both men were badly bruised, bloodied, and slumping with heads hanging down. The Roman judge made sure neither bloodied man was close enough to stain his fresh new toga. Pilate stepped towards the balcony and stood at full attention. A loud uproar rose up from the assembled rabble and penetrated the judgment room. They salivated at the thought of their hoped-for judgement.

Janus could tell how much Pilate enjoyed the show. The Roman stood regally with his left hand near the broad stripe on his toga. The toga was fresh rich linen reserved for those of the upper class. Pilate made sure those below saw his attire as well as his royal countenance.

Claudia, on the other hand, had moved away from the spectacle. Her stomach could not tolerate the sight or what was about to take place. Her breathing was shallow and uneven, and her body became rigid with tension. But even in her dread, her ears were reluctantly alert to hear the rendering by her husband.

The guards quickly pushed both accused Jews out to the balcony to join Pilate. The crowd let out a second roar. With pomp and fanfare, Pilate looked down and addressed the mass of Jews he so hated. "With great respect to your holy observance, I participate in this special occasion by asking which of these two criminals do you want released as part of your ritual observance?"

With that Pilate extended his left hand towards Jesus Barabbas saying, "Do you wish the release of this man Jesus Barabbas who is a convicted murderer and inciter of treason? A bandit who has caused you much grief and retaliation from Rome?"

Dramatically and without hesitation, Pilate pointed towards the other accused and said, "Or do you wish me to release this Jesus of Nazareth whom you convict of blasphemy? A crime not recognized by Rome." At that point Pilate stopped and waited for the response he expected.

Annas and Caiaphas as well as other leaders of the Sanhedrin were taken aback at having an option for them to consider. Their focus on Jesus of Nazareth blinded them to the law that bound the Jews and the Romans together. During the Passover feast, either the Jews or the Romans could make a show of good faith by acquitting a criminal. Only one could receive this reprieve and it had to be a capital offense to be considered.

The religious leaders realized the people could ask for Jesus. To stop this from taking place, Caiaphas initiated the answer against releasing Jesus. "Give us Barabbas!" he shouted. He looked at his henchmen and motioned for them to join him. In unison, the paid protesters echoed the urging of Caiaphas, "Give us Barabbas!"

"Then what of Jesus of Nazareth?" Pilate prompted the mob.

Annus shouted vehemently, "Crucify him! Crucify him!"

The hired demonstrators joined Annus with fists raised towards the balcony, and thundered, "Crucify him! Crucify him!"

Pilate remained expressionless as he looked at the disgusting mob. He let them continue their fervent venting. The Roman governor simply watched this horde of idiots, wondering at their height of emotion.

The judge feigned ignorance, asking, "Why, what evil has this Jesus of Nazareth really done?"

In answer the throng of angry voices again screamed, "Crucify the man!" There was no reasonable response given for such a punishment.

Pilate finally raised his hands to silence the mob. He turned to a servant who produced a small basin filled with water, which he placed before Pilate while presenting the judge with a small towel. Pilate looked at the basin and raised his hands to silence the madmen below.

In a commanding voice, Pilate shouted his decision. "Very well. In accordance with the agreement Rome has with your nation, I release Barabbas to you." With those words the guards grabbed both arms of the weak bandit and pulled him away from the balcony. Janus observed that while he was pulled back, Barabbas lifted his bruised head and glanced over at his counterpart who stood motionless, head hanging down. Jesus Barabbas remained focused on his replacement for death. Wonderment and disbelief at his fate etched his bloodied face.

Janus turned to Pilate who with great fanfare dipped his fingers into the basin containing water. Slowly he withdrew his wet hands, grabbed the towel and loudly proclaimed to the crazed crowd, "I am innocent of the blood of this just man! You see to it." At once, Pilate turned his back on the crowd as another rush of glee flooded the street below.

Out of sight of the mob, Pilate issued another command to the assembled band of guards. "Take this man to the Praetorium and scourge him before ushering him to the cross.

239

Make sure he remains conscious for the trip." The guards roughly removed Jesus of Nazareth from the balcony and took him to carry out Pilate's order.

At this final decree, Claudia shook in disbelief. In an instant she realized the reasoning for Pilate's order of scourging. Death by crucifixion was one of the more horrible deaths any human being could incur. It usually took three days for the condemned to die. Three of the most agonizing days of physical pain. Pilate's order for a third severe beating meant the condemned Jew would be so weakened he would probably die within hours of hanging on the cross. Claudia's body relaxed, her breathing returned to normal, and her emotions were now oddly peaceful, believing that at least the suffering would be shortened.

After hearing Pilate's words, Claudia quickly turned to face the man she had shared her bed with so many years. Tears rose in her eyes. She was pleased that Pilate remained true to his inner belief of being fair. She knew Pilate shared her same compassion over injustice to the innocent and didn't enjoy the scene that just transpired.

Pilate gracefully joined the trio that had presided over the death sentence, Claudia, Janus, and Herod Antipas. Looking directly at Janus with a sarcastic smile, the conniving procurator commented, "That is how to convince the delusional they are sane."

It was only one half hour past the usual time for Pilate's morning meal. He instructed breakfast for three and the trio sat down to enjoy a succulent array of food. Jesus of Nazareth meanwhile was taken to his cross. Pilate never revealed his inner emotional state of having to put an innocent man to death in the most horrible manner possible.

As they ate, Pilate spoke to his guests, "Now we wait to find out how well this ploy works concerning the Zealots. I do not anticipate much of a delay." Herod Antipas looked on with bewilderment; he had no knowledge yet of Pilate's scheme.

Pilate explained to Antipas how the release of Barabbas would impact the Zealots' raids. "I have instructed the garrison commander to monitor this Barabbas' activities. Soon he will make contact with the other rebels and when he does we shall be close by to capture the lot. This Jesus Barabbas may be a free man, but his compatriots are not. Besides, it will be but a short time before this Jewish rebel commits another crime against Rome and we shall have him back."

Quite pleased with himself, Pilate enjoyed the rest of his meal. Claudia Procula yearned to uncover the more compassionate side of her husband but she remained silent. Inwardly, she retained the feeling that the Jewish so-called blasphemer would somehow have an effect on their lives.

Jesus was hung on a cross between two thieves. It was only hours before the Sabbath beginning of the Passover. The Passover observance by Jewish religious tradition mandated that any criminal sentenced to crucifixion must be officially declared dead and removed from the cross prior to the Sabbath. To ensure a quicker death as the Sabbath approached, the Jews asked Pilate that their legs might be broken and that the bodies might be taken away. The legs of the thieves were broken to hasten their death, but Jesus of Nazareth did not have his legs broken. The Roman centurion assigned to his execution saw that Jesus was already dead, and the action wasn't necessary. However, the centurion thrust his spear into Jesus' side, an action which was later noted to have fulfilled a prophecy written about the Jewish Messiah hundreds of years beforehand.

An unlikely observer to this crucifixion scenario was the physically weakened Jesus Barabbas. The reprieved criminal had been taken by several of his fellow Zealots to a safe place where his wounds were attended. Despite the wishes of his comrades, Barabbas had demanded to go to the site of the crucifixion. Painfully and slowly he made his way to the hill area were the execution was to take place. Along the path, his fellow Zealots supported and steadied him and even carried him when he came close to passing out.

At his destination, Barabbas stood far back from the small group of people that consisted mostly of women who gathered to witness Jesus of Nazareth's death. There were two designees of the Sanhedrin assigned to witness the much sought-after death of the so-called religious rebel. Barabbas wasn't sure, but felt he could see a couple of the close followers of Jesus.

His swollen, beaten eyes made it difficult for him to see clearly. The Zealot bandit had strange feelings of turmoil within. He inched closer to where Jesus of Nazareth and the two thieves hung on the wooden beams. His limited eyesight caused him to squint and his head hurt from the effort, yet he persisted.

It was more than remorse that flooded through Barabbas at the sight of Jesus hanging on the cross flanked by two criminals also ending their life's journey on a piece of wood. Barabbas knew both of the men, but his focus was on Jesus.

The more he looked at Jesus, the more he felt change happen within his heart. He felt the conviction of the Holy Spirit. Tears ran down his cheeks as he watched the promised messiah slowly die, nailed to the wood. He hung his head in shame. Within a short period of time, Barabbas' head lifted at the sound coming from the lips of his dying Savior. The Zealot bandit was close enough to hear Jesus of Nazareth's final declaration, "It is finished."

At that very moment Barabbas placed his hands over his wounded and puffy eyes. His breathing was labored, but he morosely muttered, "If you, Jesus of Nazareth, are the promised one I have been taught would come, have mercy on my soul."

Jesus Barabbas then felt a strange warming throughout his entire body. It was vastly different than that of a fire on a cold winter's day. His skin tingled and he felt very refreshed. His plea had been heard and his name at that very moment was recorded in God's book of life.

Barabbas painfully returned his gaze to the cross and the centurion on duty who stood peering up at the now lifeless body. The centurion ordered the troops who were on guard throughout the proceedings to take the body down. The two other criminals remained to finish out the last minutes of their death penalty.

Back at the garrison headquarters, a member of the Sanhedrin, one Joseph of Arimathea, had petitioned Pilate for the body of the purported blasphemer. Pilate did not care what happened to the body and waved off the request with his hand saying, "I have no issue with your request, but do it as soon as this man dies."

When Caiaphas and Annas learned that their nemesis was dead and had been placed in a sealed tomb, they quickly sought out Pilate. "Sir, we remember while this traitor was alive he said that on the third day he would rise."

Pilate looked at them with a perplexed expression. "What do you mean he will rise? ...rise from the dead?"

Annas was quick to reply, "Yes, yes. We strongly advise that the tomb be guarded until after the third day, lest his disciples steal the body and say that he is risen from the dead. This impossibility could further cause trouble for you by the Zealots seeing this as a sign to continue their murderous ways."

The frustrated procurator scowled, and shot a hard glance at the high priests, "You shall have your guard. I will order several soldiers to remain at the tomb until this so-called threat is dissipated. Now go."

Annas accompanied the guards to the sealed tomb and inspected the burial site, satisfied all would be well. He spoke to the assembled guards, "Should anyone come here, notify me immediately before you notify your superiors. This is a matter of Jewish law first."

The soldiers scoffed at the instructions. "Surely this man knows that if we let such a thing happen, Rome would have our heads. We have sealed the tomb."

On the third day, Annas' heart sank. A representative of the guards informed him the tomb had been opened and the body was gone. Annas questioned the soldier repeatedly and harshly. Each time his anger grew more pronounced. He convened with Caiaphas and several other trusted Sadducees. After a short time, Annas reappeared before the soldier with a bag.

"You have done well, notifying me before you do your superiors. In gratitude, here is money to divide with the other guards. It is yours so long as you say that the man's disciples came during the night while you slept and stole him away. Do you understand my instructions?"

The soldier stared wide-eyed at the large bag of money. He looked up at the benefactor and quietly said, "I understand. It shall be as you say." Annas handed over the bribe and the soldier left.

Suddenly it was necessary that Annas, Caiaphas, and the other Sadducees plot how they would relay this disturbing news to the rest of the Sanhedrin. The soldiers also discussed the matter of the disappearing body and divided up the money. It was a sizable amount for each man, six months of regular pay. They realized the money would do them no good should they relay the tale instructed by the Jewish high priest.

"Our centurion and even the governor will easily see through this ruse. If they think we slept while on duty, we all shall be killed for that is a death offense." The other guards concurred and one of the group said, "It is better for us to speak the truth about this matter." They agreed only one would inform their superiors of the disappearance while the others remained at the scene, lest anyone disturb it and cause the investigation to become muddled. They also agreed to keep the money and not tell their superiors about their windfall.

Pilate and Claudia were having their morning meal when Janus interrupted with news of the disappearing body. Pilate briefly closed his eyes, then looked up at Janus and sighed, "How can this be? What happened to the guards assigned to the tomb?"

Janus offered, "Details are not available at the present moment. Their centurion is investigating and will let you know when he is finished."

The disgusted prefect of Judea again sighed heavily and dismissed his secretary with a weary wave. Claudia looked at Pilate and said with a fearful voice, "My feeling toward that Jew was one of apprehension. Now it has come to pass. He haunts us and disrupts our lives. My husband, I do not believe this Jew to be human. Please be very careful in how you handle this matter."

Pilate examined Claudia's fearful face, then leaned back in his chair and said, "Control yourself. There is a logical explanation and I shall learn of it."

On that fateful day after Jesus' death, Mary Magdalene, who first witnessed the open tomb and the directive of the angel to tell the apostles, was stopped short of her destination. There stood the risen Christ in front of her. His radiance warmed her heart and she immediately fell at his feet and worshipped Him. Lovingly, He instructed her to tell His apostles to go to Galilee when He would meet with them. The eleven apostles did as instructed. On their way they stopped in Jericho and relayed the news to Zacchaeus, Mattan, and his family.

Earlier, news of Jesus' crucifixion had quickly made its way to Jericho. The majority of residents and travelers paid little attention to news about a Jew being sentenced to death. But it had great impact on those who recently had their lives changed by the now deceased healer. There was deep grief, mourning, and confusion in the hearts of the newly saved.

Zacchaeus had Terach and his family, along with Bartimaeus and Hadassah, come to his mansion to discuss the new development. Zacchaeus was the first to broach the topic. "I have been informed by Jesus' apostles that He has risen from the grave and is alive!" The short, dumbfounded administrator waited for his audience to grasp the astounding news. He then asked, "Shall we believe what these apostles say, or could it be they are touched in the head with such grief they know not what they really say?"

The great room that served to entertain guests was eerily silent. Eyes darted from one person to another expecting someone to answer the question. Lips were puckered, slight frowns formed, eyebrows showed various expressions, and each listener was deep in thought, vacillating between hope and skepticism. After several long moments, Terach replied, "Jesus of Nazareth has performed many miracles, including raising some from the dead. Is it not possible he can also raise himself from the clutches of the grave? His power is extraordinary and not of this world." The nomad shepherd took in a deep breath before concluding, "Rising from the dead is clear evidence Jesus indeed is the promised Messiah."

Again there was a long silence as the group pondered Terach's insightful words. The realization that Jesus was the Messiah had differing effects on these new converts. Bartimaeus was the first of the group to speak. "At the time he restored both Mattan's and my sight, he said we should follow Him. I, I wondered what He meant by those short words. His rising from the dead is part of this... but I don't know what to do." Bartimaeus looked around to his fellow stunned friends, waiting for comment.

When none came forth, Bartimaeus added, "I believe we should wait until such time as we receive instruction from His apostles. At that time we will have insight how to follow Him."

They would not have to wait long.

Chapter 19

As Zacchaeus and his guests pondered Bartimaeus' suggestion, a new voice was heard just behind them. It was that of the Risen Christ! "My friends, I come to you with good news. But first, do you have anything that I may eat?" The dumbfounded gathering could only stare at the personage standing before them. Finally, Zacchaeus fumbled around and offered the Risen Christ some bread dipped in fish sauce.

Every eye was riveted on the Risen Savor as he ate what was given Him. Mattan was the first to ask the obvious question, "Jesus of Nazareth, is it true you were crucified three days ago in Jerusalem?" Christ Jesus answered, "It is true. I was laid in a tomb until the third day when the Holy Spirit came for me. Now I have come to you saying 'Believe in Me, that you may have life eternal. Sin can no longer have its power over you!'"

The group fell to their knees in awe and bowed their heads, completely overcome. Then Christ instructed them, "Arise, for the Holy Spirit will come to dwell within you until the end of the age. You have seen me. Touch me and know that I am real." Each one did, weeping for joy. Then Christ said, "Now, follow Me. Go forth and give the good news of eternal salvation to those whom you encounter."

With that instruction, the Savor of mankind, the Messiah, disappeared from the room. Each member of the group was stunned. They looked around but there was no sign of Christ. The manner of His disappearance was not of this world. All eyes stared at the vacant space where Christ had just stood. There were no words. Their astonished faces were elated.

Zacchaeus was the first to speak. "Do all of you share the same feeling deep within that something real has changed us?" Each member of the esteemed group spoke of their similar feeling, but had difficulty explaining what was taking place within each of them.

The business administrator and tax collector of all Judea surveyed his friends' faces and knew they concurred with him. He suddenly proclaimed, "I know Jesus is the promised one, and I will follow Him for the remainder of my days!"

Zacchaeus' words were echoed by everyone in the room. There was an influx of joy words could not explain; each person felt exuberant giddiness unlike anything before. They hugged each other in excitement. Terach uttered words of caution. "Christ has commanded us to follow Him; but I fear this will not be without complications and conflict. The forces against Him will now be against us, as well."

At that moment, one of Zacchaeus' servants announced someone was seeking his presence. Zacchaeus left the room and within a few minutes returned with none other than Barabbas. The Zealot bandit, now a free man, relayed his story of witnessing the death of his Lord and Savior and the impact it had on him. His audience was spellbound.

Barabbas had moist eyes as he declared, "I tell you this because my life is forever changed and I will no longer be a member of the Zealots. I devote my life to doing what Christ Jesus wants me to do."

The group of devoted converts surrounded the humbled man, and shared their own declarations to follow Christ Jesus no matter what the cost. A great celebration followed.

Three months later, another miracle descended upon the former blind men. Hadassah and Devorah announced they were pregnant. Prior to the miracle event of their husbands regaining their sight, the two women were deemed barren and had become resigned to their fate. Another miracle had taken place and its source was not overlooked by the joyous family members.

On the next Passover observance, Terach and Beulah were on hand for the birth of their first grandson. Zacchaeus became the surrogate father to Bartimaeus and enjoyed the double blessing in his friend's new family—twin boys.

Over the course of the next three years, Devorah delivered two more sons to Mattan. "God's grace to us is beyond compare. I'm humbled to receive such love," declared Mattan after the birth of his third son.

The fathers of the expanding clan continued their livelihoods, producing fine quality goods while still finding ample time to participate in the growth of their beloved brood. During this joyous time, the two couples also made a concerted effort to carry out Christ's command to spread the good news. The plethora of lost souls that came to Jericho made it a perfect place to evangelize.

Shortly after the news of Christ's resurrection, Zacchaeus informed Pilate of his vow to return money to anyone whom he defrauded. This news took the Roman procurator by surprise. "You believe in this man that much, to deplete your treasury?" Pilate gasped.

"I do, Procurator," said the chief tax collector. The befuddled Roman stared intently at his tax collector. It was not often Pilate was rendered speechless.

Pilate considered Zacchaeus' words, then flatly stated, "Since you have established a contract with Rome to be its business administrator and chief tax collector, you may continue in this capacity until such time it is determined you are not acting in Rome's best interests."

The perplexed Roman studied the civil servant's face carefully, and asked, "Do you intend on adding twice what Rome requires in tax money to your own coffers?"

Zacchaeus emphatically shook his head. "I shall collect only what Rome demands."

The Roman procurator doubted the sincerity of Zacchaeus' words, but over the next three years witnessed the truth in what the chief tax collector had declared. In AD 36 Pilate was recalled to Rome due to his harsh dealings with the Samaritans. He and Claudia were very happy to put their Judean experience behind them. Their encounter there with Jesus of Nazareth was the one event they both remembered, and it remained an inexplicable event they would periodically discuss for the rest of their lives.

Between AD 33 and AD 36 Bartimaeus, Mattan, with their wives, went about witnessing and evangelizing to the lost souls that lived in Jericho and the surrounding villages. The foursome was eager also to engage the many travelers who frequented the commerce hub. "We have a wealth of opportunity right here. So many lost souls to share Christ Jesus with! I do not envision a drought of lost ones to tell our stories to," said Hadassah.

It was a busy time for the new evangelists. The women had young children to raise while the men remained employed in their respective crafts. Devorah left her position in the pottery mill to raise the sons she had longed for but felt never would become a reality. She and Hadassah spent an average of two days per week together building their friendship.

Zacchaeus made good his vow to Christ to refund those whom he defrauded. It was impossible to return the extorted money directly to each person but the new follower of Christ found a way to fulfill his vow to his Savior. In several towns, including Jericho, throughout his domain, Zacchaeus established the world's first community centers. These outlets became sources of food, clothing, and when needed, shelter for the disenfranchised and poor of the region.

Needless to say, his actions were a popular topic among the residents throughout Judea and Idumea. The Samaritan leaders remained hostile to the chief tax collector mainly because he was a Jew associated with the Sanhedrin and Jerusalem. But the Samaritan people were quick to accept his generosity.

In AD 37 Bartimaeus and Mattan were immersed in evangelizing in Jericho. Bartimaeus became involved with a small group of Jews who were traveling to Jerusalem. The former blind man was passionate as he spoke the good news about Christ Jesus, telling his own experience with the Son of God and how Christ had given him his sight. There were approximately 20 in the group, and the majority listened with awe.

Two young Pharisees interrupted Bartimaeus at different times and inserted points of the Torah book of law that seemingly refuted the simplicity of Bartimaeus' message. Skeptical expressions appeared on some of the faces in the crowd, while others listened intently. One traveler in particular was keenly observant. He was dressed in traditional Jewish work clothing, blending in with the others.

The traveler's eyes narrowed as the Pharisees spoke and at times ridiculed Bartimaeus' belief in the blasphemer who had been convicted and sentenced to the cross. "If this Jesus you speak about is the promised messiah and the Son of God as you say, why didn't he keep himself from the cross? And why isn't he here to convince his so-called people he is the promised savior?

Bartimaeus attempted to answer these and other questions of doubt but did not fully succeed. The lone traveler took note of the former blind man's disposition, but kept still in the shadows. His eyes revealed disappointment and criticism.

When the novice evangelist could not effectively rebuke the Pharisees, the crowd dispersed and the lone traveler heard their murmuring. The traveler approached the dejected follower of Christ. His stature was short, but he held his head erect and looked Bartimaeus in the eye. "Do not be disheartened. You speak truth, but you need teaching how to deal with these religious hypocrites."

Bartimaeus looked at the unprepossessing stranger. He asked, "Who are you? How is it you can teach me the right way to speak of Christ to these people?"

Without answering the question, the bearded traveler replied, "Where do you live? I will sup with you and teach you."

Bartimaeus was skeptical, but he gave directions to the stranger and suggested, "I have friends who would also greatly benefit from your teaching. Can they also learn from you?"

The traveler assented. "They may come. It is important for all followers of Christ Jesus to know how to deal with the unsaved and the hypocrites of religion." On that note, the he left and went on his way into the main part of Jericho. Bartimaeus hurried to inform both Mattan and Zacchaeus of the opportunity to meet with this intriguing man.

When the stranger entered Bartimaeus' and Hadassah's home, he was greeted by staring eyes and solemn faces. Zacchaeus penetrated the uncertain atmosphere with the obvious question, "You are a stranger to Jericho, but I see by your clothing you are a Jew. Where are you from?"

The stranger slightly bowed and said, "First, I wish to thank you for allowing me into your home. I am Paul and I come from Tarsus."

Zacchaeus' eyes widened, "Are you the one also named Saul, the Pharisee who persecutes those who abide by the teaching of the Son of God?"

Paul was prepared for the challenge. He nodded his head and contritely answered, "That *was* I. But when I traveled to Damascus to arrest followers of Christ Jesus, Our Lord blinded me for three days and convicted me of my sin against Him! He moved deep within me and gave me the indwelling of His Holy Spirit. Now I travel to give the gospel that He alone is the Promised One, the Savior and only Son of God."

The group was astounded to learn the identity of this man about whom they had heard much to fear. He was reviled by all followers of Christ. Paul had the same status among the pious Jews as nomadic shepherds and other outcasts of Jewish society. Bartimaeus boldly spoke up. "How are we to know you are sincere and not here to do harm to us?"

Paul answered earnestly, "After three days of blindness and captive to Christ, I went into Arabia for three years and received His teaching, wisdom, and direction directly from Him. I now live to only speak the truth that He is the promised Savior. I do not speak to please men, for if I still pleased men, I would not be a bondservant of Christ."

Persuaded, Hadassah broke into the interrogation and extended her invitation, "Please come and sit down. We shall eat in a few minutes. Tell us more." Paul looked at his hostess and did as she requested. The others followed the transformed traveler and encircled him with their chairs at the dining table. Their economic status was such they did not have the luxury of reclining couches while eating.

"I return from Jerusalem where I met with Peter and the Lord's half-brother James. For fifteen days we talked at length about Christ and the gospel. They have concluded I am who I say I am and accept me as one of His own."

Mattan started to speak, but Zacchaeus held up his hand to quiet the former shepherd. "I doubt you, Paul, for now. I have many contacts in Jerusalem who can easily verify the truth or deceit of what you speak. In the meantime, you told Bartimaeus you can assist us in dealing with the Pharisees and rabbis who discredit what we say. How can you do this?"

Before the guest could begin, Hadassah announced it was time to eat. She and Devorah placed the meal on the table and Paul took a piece of the bread and gave thanks to God. Then they proceeded to eat and listen to the evangelist.

Paul needed to first address their skepticism. "I welcome your scrutiny, Zacchaeus. It is necessary, and you will find everything I said is true." Paul put down his bread and began to instruct them from his personal experience as a Pharisee. "Do not attempt to argue with these Pharisees. They are purveyors of deception and are religious hypocrites. They will entice you into points of the law they teach and will trap you because you do not have knowledge of the law the way they do."

Mattan broke in, "I have such knowledge."

Paul blinked at Mattan in disbelief. "How is this so? Pharisees can read while the majority of Jews cannot. The ability to read is regarded as a great weapon of control for them."

Mattan answered, "When I was a young shepherd boy, my father Terach would read to me and my family from the scriptures in the Tanakh/Torah. He and my mother taught me and my siblings how to read. After each of us learned to read, I continued to read on my own before I became sightless. I remember much from those readings. Not being able to read the scriptures was part of my anger at being blind."

Paul quickly interjected, "I do not speak of the book of scriptures. I speak of the Pharisees' Book of Law, the Talmud. It takes scripture and combines it with their man-made laws. This perverts God's word and is impossible for any man to follow." Paul chewed a bite of his food, giving them time to absorb the ramifications of this revelation. "The Pharisees and the rabbis teach only the Talmud."

Mattan put his hand to his beard while taking in Paul's words. Paul went on, "Speak only of the gospel and how it was Christ, not man, who restored your sight to you. Tell the people your personal experience with Christ. This cannot be disputed by the religious hypocrites, for they only can argue their law." To emphasize his point, Paul clearly explained it a different way, "Do not argue religion. Speak only about having personal relationship with Christ. This supersedes all religion. This the people will hear."

Eating the evening meal was leisurely as the group became more enthralled by Paul's teaching. Sometime later, the bondservant to Christ said, "It is late and I am tired. I must go and rest. We can meet again tomorrow." His captivated listeners quickly agreed to continue learning more.

The Apostle of Christ stayed with the followers of Christ for two weeks, each day relaying to them in depth the teachings of their Savior. Finally it was time for Paul to leave. On the last evening with them, the Apostle concluded his mentoring with words of encouragement and exhortation.

"Brethren," he tenderly addressed them, "Bear one another's burdens and so fulfill the law of Christ. Your efforts in giving the gospel will be met by those willing to receive Christ and those who are not. Do not be dismayed when some of the lost reject the gospel. They do not receive because their hearts are of this world and they reject the efforts of the Holy Spirit to soften their hearts."

Paul spoke more softly, "Be gentle with all and do not allow pride to deceive you into thinking you are something, lest the Holy Spirit convict you of your wrongdoing. You have been saved by grace through faith and not of your own doings. Remember you are His workmanship, created in Christ Jesus for His good works, which God prepared beforehand that we should walk in them."

As the humble mentor and teacher of God's Word stood in the doorway of Bartimaeus and Hadassah's home, he turned back to his mentees one more time. He saw how earnestly they desired to serve their risen Savior. He smiled affectionately and said, "My brothers and sisters in Christ; let you who have been taught be a teacher to those who need. In so doing, each will receive the blessing of the Lord God and build your treasures in heaven. Remember, whatever you do, do it in the name of the Lord, for it is Christ Jesus whom you serve."

For several days after Paul's departure, the disciples of Christ rehashed what they had learned. "Paul has been a blessing to us and now we must put into practice all that he has given us," Devorah commented. A chorus of agreement rang out and they encouraged each other to begin doing the works that would honor and glorify Christ.

One day, Bartimaeus met another gathering of travelers passing through Jericho. He described in detail how Christ gave him sight that he never before had enjoyed in his life. His words were passionate and resounded in the hearts of the listeners. When the former blind man began to give the gospel to the lost listeners, a Pharisee began to heckle Bartimaeus and dispute the gospel.

This time, remembering Paul's inspired teaching, Bartimaeus remained steadfast and unwavering. He did not debate the law, but referenced scripture. The Pharisee arrogantly interjected how scripture was enhanced by the Oral Torah because of the changing times and the need to be more pure. He said it was necessary to add these laws because of the Roman influence that was meant to degrade the Jews' faith.

The Pharisee finished and stood with a proud look of victory over the new disciple of Christ. He puffed out his chest and looked haughtily at the evangelist. In a calm voice, looking away from the Pharisee, Bartimaeus said to the people, "If you accept part of the Pharisees' law, you accept it all and become a slave to it and to them. In so doing, you lose relationship with Christ. You fall away from God's grace that was given to you by His Son's death on the cross."

Feeling the power of the truth, the evangelist moved among his listeners saying, "When you have relationship with Christ, you don't need man's law. Christ is above man's law. He simplifies all through the power of the Holy Spirit who indwells you until the end of the age. It is the Holy Spirit who will counsel, guide, and direct your ways. In this way, you truly follow Christ. Christ alone is the way, the truth, and the life."

The Pharisee was taken aback by Bartimaeus' words and knowledge of scripture. Each time he attempted to entice the evangelist into debate, Bartimaeus effectively rebuked him. Finally the evangelist asked the religious hypocrite a question, "You say you know the scriptures and how the ancient prophets foretold the coming of the promised one. Then answer me this. When is the promised one to come; where will he begin, and how will he lead the Jews out of bondage?" Bartimaeus paused momentarily, then added, "And what type of bondage will the Messiah destroy?"

All eyes shifted their attention to the Pharisee who was perplexed by the evangelist's questions. The religious leader fumbled his words and had no real answer to the questions. Bartimaeus completed his challenge with fervor, "How then can you say that Christ Jesus is not the Messiah?" The Pharisee had no answer, but stared at his adversary while he thought furiously for a rebuttal.

Bartimaeus shifted his attention to the crowd. "When you take that step of faith and ask Christ into your heart, you will know firsthand that He truly is the Messiah, Lord of Lords, and King of Kings." The faces of the crowd showed they were pondering Bartimaeus' words.

One member of the gathering spoke, "You speak with power and thoughtfulness, Bartimaeus. There is much to ponder."

The evangelist breathed a sigh of relief and said, "Ponder my words which are the truth spoken by Christ Jesus. Then compare them to the misery the Pharisees' Laws cause you." He pointed at the disheveled religious advocate and stated, "Their law is confusion that leads to damnation; but Christ leads to everlasting life."

Since life after death was a common topic among the Jews and heathens of different religions, Bartimaeus' words served to provoke many to convert from religion to a personal relationship with Christ. Over the course of another month, Bartimaeus encountered several other Pharisees, and each time he did as his mentor Paul instructed. Many came to Christ. The Pharisees merely listened, but did not attempt to engage Bartimaeus in debate.

During this time, Mattan also had opportunities to put Paul's teaching into practice. On one occasion, the potter had a table of his wares setup for sale in the marketplace. Word had circulated that he was the blind shepherd who became an accomplished potter. People gathered around him and queried how he was able to make such fine pottery.

Mattan detailed how he became blind and his initial difficulties in learning how to throw pots. He did not hide the struggles and frustration he had encountered during the learning process. Many were enthralled as he depicted that momentous day when Christ stopped and had mercy on him by restoring his sight. "I felt so hopeless that when I heard the faith healer from Nazareth would be passing through Jericho, I knew I had to beseech him and ask for healing." Mattan also told how he saw Christ for the first time as a baby who lay in a manger. And how he looked into his compelling eyes and never forgot them.

In telling that memorable event, Mattan recited the prophecy of the ancient ones and how the angels heralded that the baby was the messiah. He recounted how Christ had asked Mattan to follow Him. "Christ invited me to give my whole heart to Him. I know He is the Messiah and the Son of God sent to redeem all of those who trust in Him and give Him their heart and soul."

The former blind shepherd gave the people gathered around his table a passionate commentary. "Many times I've asked myself, why did God restore my sight? After all, I am a shepherd. One who is regarded by the rabbis and the Pharisees as despised and not allowed to participate in Jewish rituals. Shepherds and others are deemed unworthy to sit in the synagogue." All heads nodded, knowing this to be true. Even among this group were some who were also deemed unworthy by the religious leaders of Judea.

Mattan went on, "If the Pharisees and the rabbis are right in their dictates, why would Christ show compassion on me, restore my sight, and ask me to follow Him?" Eyes focused on the speaker, waiting for his answer. Pharisee spies in attendance became uncomfortable and looked down, but were anxious to hear the evangelist's answer.

"It's because Christ has such love for me and values me that He wants to have eternal relationship with me," thundered the evangelist. "It's not because I keep the Law that the Pharisees demand I should obey. It's because I trust in Him completely. My faith is in the true Son of God and not any man-made law that says I am unworthy. Unworthiness is what the Egyptians taught our forefathers during the time of our bondage in Egypt."

There were gasps among the gathering as they realized Mattan's words were indeed true. Simultaneously, the Pharisees in the group looked at each other and eased away from the group.

Mattan took note of this, and stopped them with a thunderous voice demanding, "You there, you Pharisees! Tell these people I am wrong." The cluster turned their attention to the religious followers, waiting for an answer. The Pharisees merely held up their hands in defense and signaled no desire to participate in the dialogue. Hastily, they retreated.

Mattan returned to his personal testimony. "My faith is the same faith that Abraham had. Abraham was a mighty shepherd whose faith made him right with God who told Abraham that all nations will be blessed because of his faith." The potter evangelist paused and looked deeply into the eyes of the small group. With a soft and earnest voice he declared, "Abraham's faith can be your faith. All you have to do is give your heart and soul over to Christ."

All Jews revered Abraham, as did other nations of the time. Mattan's reference to Abraham and God resonated deeply with the gathering. The majority of the crowd responded to the invitation place their faith in Christ Jesus, the resurrected Son of God. They either stood or knelt, and implored God's only Son, the Savior of the world, to come into their lives.

One day, Devorah and Hadassah went down to a section of the river where many Jewish women washed the family clothes. A group of women were huddled together, washing and conversing. A separate woman some thirty feet away was also washing her clothing. "I foresee the Jewish women casting condemnation on the one by herself. She looks so sad." Devorah felt compassion for the lonely soul and suggested, "Let us see if she is willing to engage with us."

The lone woman glanced with suspicion at the two newcomers to the river's edge, but did not speak to them. Devorah and Hadassah smiled at the woman and proceeded with their washing. Devorah began to talk to the woman in friendly small talk, until the woman began to respond. She finished her wash, gathered up her clothes and looked at Devorah saying, "Perhaps we shall speak here again. I usually try to come when no one is around." Gesturing with her head she said, "They view me as unclean because I am a prostitute." She waited to see if this announcement would repulse the women who seemed to care about her. She fixed her gaze on Devorah and said, "Maybe you also will determine me to be unclean. If so, I won't bother you."

She took a few steps to leave, and Devorah reassured her, "I do not see you as unclean. You are a woman in need to do her laundry. I enjoy talking with you. Tell me when you will return here."

A surprised expression brightened the woman's face. Cautiously, the woman shifted her laundry and answered, "Every Tuesday about this same time." With that, she hurriedly left the bank of the river.

Hadassah smiled at her friend and said, "Devorah, I anticipate we shall be coming here at the same time as that woman. Obviously, you feel compelled to minister to her."

Devorah watched the woman leave and softly answered, "Yes. I feel I must talk with her. I believe it's the Holy Spirit directing me."

Over the course of the next month, Devorah and Hadassah met the woman at the riverbank and engaged in casual conversations. The other Jewish women looked on in contempt, but the threesome paid no attention to the self-righteous gossipers.

The woman revealed how she was divorced by her husband and was forced to provide for herself. She had no family, and because of the limitations imposed by the Jewish culture, felt becoming a prostitute was her only means of survival. "There are times I question my desire to even live. Once I was respected and accepted within Jewish society, but no longer." She hung her head and uttered, "Deep within me, I no longer have feeling or life. I go through the motions from one day to the next. From one man to the next. Why do you befriend me, one who is tainted and admits to being a prostitute?" asked the woman.

Devorah simply replied, "I like you. In God's eyes we all are sinners in need of His grace."

The woman stopped her washing and searched Devorah's face. "Are you both part of the Way I have heard about? Your answer is not that of Jewish precepts."

Hadassah nonchalantly confirmed the woman's suspicions. "We do follow Christ Jesus and not the Jewish law."

"There is a difference about the two of you. At first I was uneasy with you, but you treat me as if I were like you." The woman briefly hesitated. "I have heard many tales about the founder of this Way. Tell me more about this man, and why are you bound to follow his teachings?"

Hadassah gladly told the woman about Jesus, and the love and grace of God. Then Devorah took over. "I, too, was forced to fend for myself because I was barren, like Hadassah. Zacchaeus befriended me and gave me a position in his pottery workshop. He helped me retain my self-respect. I now know it was Almighty God who directed my path to cross with Zacchaeus. God works in ways we do not always understand."

The woman slightly tensed. She was about to confess a secret that plagued her. "I have something to tell you that very few people know about me." The woman looked around and quickly spoke while she had the courage to do so. "Some years ago I had an abortion." She stopped to gauge their reaction. They merely listened without any sign of contempt. The woman continued, "It occurred within one year after I became a prostitute. Obviously, I did not want the burden that a child brings, much less my lowly status."

The woman stopped in an effort to control her emotional turmoil. At that juncture, Devorah took hold of the woman's hand and softly said, "Please continue. We are not here to condemn you."

The woman heard the sincerity in her voice and was encouraged. She proceeded with her narrative. "Being outcast by the Jewish religious leaders, I could not go to a rabbi or anyone else for spiritual help. Since listening to both of you and hearing about this Jesus, I've been plagued by my memories and guilt over what I did." The woman hung her head and blurted, "Can I be a follower of Jesus after what I did?" The woman's defenses were gone. She looked skyward and wailed, "I feel unworthy and unacceptable."

Devorah placed her hand on the woman's shoulder and gently said, "God loves you and cares deeply for you. Christ knows about your abortion and He is saddened." The woman looked at Devorah with confusion until Devorah continued. "The fact you are deeply remorseful in your heart is a sign that you are ready to be released from your torment of guilt."

The woman exhibited signs of hope and Devorah smiled before explaining. "Once you ask Christ into your heart without reservation, He cleanses you of your guilt, and all your sin is forgiven. His Holy Spirit comes to dwell within you and protects you from any demonic attempt to keep you in bondage to your emotions."

Hadassah watched the reaction of the woman and her heart jumped for joy when she saw the woman relax and truly listen to Devorah's salvation message.

Devorah softly went on. "All Christ asks is for you to trust in Him alone. Surrender your will to His and follow His commands. He promises to always guide your path and your days." The prostitute listened carefully but did not know what to say. Devorah and Hadassah watched the lost soul as she contemplated their eternal life-saving message.

The woman squeezed Devorah's hands that had gently held them throughout her salvation plea. As she did so, she raised her head skyward once again. This time she proclaimed, "Christ Jesus, I need You! Help me stop my wicked ways!" With that, tears of joy welled up and slid down her face in a steady stream. She could not contain the freedom and ecstasy that flooded her entire body.

Her two friends witnessed the salvation of the lost soul and raised their hands towards the heavens, verbally praising God for this milestone moment. They hugged the new convert and the three basked in this unforgettable moment.

Devorah then suggested an idea that would change the tainted woman forever. "Meet me tomorrow at the pottery workshop. I shall make a position for you and personally teach you to become a potter. Will you do this?"

The astonished prostitute stuttered her gratitude and agreed to meet with Devorah.

At the pottery workshop, Devorah did exactly as she had promised the fallen woman. Within several months, the former despairing prostitute became revitalized and regained her self-worth.

One day, Devorah met with the new potter and congratulated her on the progress she was making. "There is more to my life than learning new skills," the novice replied. "More importantly, I've vowed to give Christ all glory and honor for His blessing me with these new skills. And you."

Several days later, Hadassah was approached by a wife of one of Christ's followers. The woman was in deep anguish over the death of her five-year-old son. The mother and her husband were recent converts to the Way, but the loss of their son was having a deeply negative impact on their walk with Christ.

The emotionally and spiritually tortured woman requested a meeting with Hadassah concerning her emotional situation, and Hadassah arranged a meeting as soon as she could.

The mother was tense and her anger erupted like a volcano. "Where is God in my time of trial and why did he allow this to happen?" Not waiting for any reply, the mother continued her accusation, "The Jews insist the cause of my son's death is due to sin in our house. But they do not identify this sin or how it came about. Members of the Way have no answers for me. I feel abandoned and without hope." Her undisguised anger began to dissolve into a bottomless pit of grief.

With tears in her eyes, the mother detailed how her son died. "He became ill, vomiting, and had dreadful diarrhea. Day by day he was in great pain...soon he died in my arms, crying." Remembering that moment all too vividly, she convulsed into sobs, reliving her loss and confusion. Hadassah sat quietly and gave her plenty of time to expel her wracking sobs. The grieving mother refocused on Hadassah with puffy, red eyes and confessed, "I'm angry at God. Why did He allow a child who barely got started in life to die the way he did?"

Hadassah waited for the distraught mother to pour out all that she needed to say and to voice her complaint. When she had run out of words, the mother slumped, exhausted from the release of her mountain of emotions.

In a calm and straight-forward voice, Hadassah said, "I will not give you words that only anger you more. That would be very unkind. I, too, suffered through what you now do. Shortly after Bartimaeus and I were married, I was with child; but he died four years after birth. I was very happy God blessed me with a child, especially a son for Bartimaeus. I believed our son was a gift and a blessing for Bartimaeus' life of blindness. It never entered my mind something like death would be allowed by God to remove such a blessing. I went into a dark desert with my anger. It took a while before I could hear God's voice to me." Hadassah stopped to take a deep breath and recompose herself before counseling the young woman, "Do not let your anger towards God lead you into sin. He understands how you feel and will comfort you during this time. Be angry if you will, but do not forsake the Lord."

The devastated mother wondered how she could receive any comfort. She had a quizzical expression on her face. "When did God comfort you?"

Hadassah said, "When I became so weak from anger and could not lash out at Him any longer, He spoke to me through

His Holy Spirit. Only then could I hear His voice. I had to surrender my will and emotions completely to Him before my ears and my heart were open to listen to Him."

The grief-stricken mother queried her new comrade in suffering, "Are you still angry with God?"

Hadassah mildly shook her head no and explained, "I have experienced His compassion for me that replaces all anger. I still lament the death of our son and always will; as you will also your son. He was of my flesh and blood. I believe in my heart that when I die I will reunite with him in heaven. I truly believe this every day God gives me breath."

The distressed mother looked away for a few moments, pondering her counselor's words. She gathered her thoughts and turned back to Hadassah. "How long were you angry at God?'

Hadassah gently answered, "Too long. The devil twisted my mourning into thoughts of anger at God. This persisted several years until I let go of my pride, arrogance, and control, and allowed God to comfort me as only He can."

The spiritually confused woman dropped her eyes and pursed her lips. "Hopefully, in time God will do for me what He has done for you." Then her expression hardened. "But now I am not ready to do as you say."

Hadassah looked at the grieving mother and only nodded her head, understanding that grief is a deeply personal thing and cannot be rushed or formulized. But she wasn't pessimistic. Hadassah continued to minister to the agonizing mother for two more years, helping her to come to terms with Almighty God and His mysterious ways that are hard to understand. God's love would break spiritual ground that religion could never achieve.

Chapter 20

Zacchaeus had a surprise visitor. Jesus Barabbas came to the reformed tax collector's mansion and requested an audience with his former business colleague. A servant led the pardoned murderer to Zacchaeus' office. In a startled voice the business administrator proclaimed, "Barabbas, it is you! I've wondered what became of you after Pilate released you! Where have you been?"

Jesus Barabbas' shoulders drooped and he looked down as he gave his answer. "Thinking about how Christ Jesus took my place on the cross has stayed with me all this time. It has been very difficult to accept. When I close my eyes I see him standing next to me, beaten, and with the crown of long thorns stuck in his head and his face battered from the beatings."

Barabbas' voice quivered as he continued, "I watched him die on the cross, Zacchaeus. I saw the Roman soldiers take his limp body down and give it over to one of the members of the Sanhedrin and his servants."

Zacchaeus felt his stomach tighten as he listened to Barabbas give his account of Christ's trial and death. The convert's watery eyes plainly revealed the gravity of conviction that now controlled the Zealot bandit. Jesus Barabbas lifted his head and met Zacchaeus' eyes. "I have gone into the hills alone, contemplating that day and Christ's death. Even my family did not accompany me."

Then Jesus Barabbas relayed an event that brought a holy shiver to the converted Jew administrator. "I escaped Jerusalem and made my way to a cave close to here. While I sat by my fire, suddenly a figure appeared on the other side of the fire facing me. He called out my name in a voice that was powerful, but also soft, loving, and kind. The flames jumped up and made it difficult for me to recognize who the man was. When I asked his name he told me, 'It is I, Christ, and I want to sup with you.'"

Barabbas waited for Zacchaeus to comprehend what happened before he continued.

"He produced food which we cooked over the fire! He sat next to me and we began to talk about our shared pain and beatings from the Romans! Only he also received a beating from Herod and also the Sanhedrin. I told him about being present at his death."

Barabbas' voice became more emphatic. "He told me about fulfilling the prophecy and that with his death, now I could be cleansed and forgiven to enter eternal life with him! His words pierced my soul. He asked me to follow him; that he would never forsake me and be with me until the end of the age."

In a louder voice Barabbas exclaimed, "I told him I would follow him and be his disciple! Then he vanished! I stood up and searched for him, but he was gone... yet I did not feel alone. There was a warmth and a presence within me. I did not know what happened; but I tell you, Zacchaeus, I knew in my heart I was different."

Zacchaeus motioned for Barabbas to have a taste of the wine that the servant had placed before them. As Barabbas drank, Zacchaeus disclosed, "I felt very much as you did, Barabbas, when Christ asked me to follow him the day he restored sight to both Bartimaeus and Mattan and had supper with me and my subordinate tax collector—right here in this house!"

The reformed tax collector confided, "Christ appeared to me, too, after His resurrection and said that He had risen from the grave and told me He would be with me forever!"

Jesus Barabbas sat stunned as he listened to Zacchaeus. But before he could ask his host a question, the business administrator convert to Christ said, "I believe in my heart every word He said to me, and you should believe what He said to you, Barabbas. I do not fully comprehend what He wants me to do. I only know whatever He asks of me, that I shall do."

Barabbas interjected, "I have heard much about you, Zacchaeus, these past few years. The people throughout all of Judea and Samaria comment how you have given back money to them and how you no longer take extra tax money from them. They know it is because of your commitment to Christ, but many still do not believe He is the Messiah. They think you are insane or possessed!" Barabbas gave a short laugh. "But I know better, and that's partly why I've come to you this day."

Zacchaeus raised his hand from the table. He pointed toward the ceiling and said, "I know what you speak about, my friend. Despite the many naysayers, there also are those who meditate on my actions and seek Christ. These have proclaimed Him to be the Promised One and now follow Him as you and I do. The numbers are growing. But tell me, what other reason prompts you to visit me this day?"

Jesus Barabbas shifted in his seat and professed, "I have had a meeting with John of Gischala and informed him I no longer am a Zealot, or a leader of one of his bands. He was taken aback by my decision. He said the Zealots were needed as the Romans were increasing their abuse over the Jews. I told him I must follow only what Christ wants me to do. He was very angry with me, so I left before matters turned worse."

Jesus Barabbas then gave Zacchaeus a warning, "There is more, Zacchaeus. John of Gischala and the other Zealot leaders are wary of you and your actions. They believe you are deceiving them and that you and the Romans will take more away from them." The reformed rebel sternly went on, "Beware, Zacchaeus. Your safety is threatened."

Zacchaeus nodded to his visitor and replied, "I know how the Zealots think and how they influence the minds of the Jewish people. I also know how the Sanhedrin uses the rabbis throughout all of Judea to discredit me. It makes no difference, Barabbas, because I know what is in my heart and I will continue to do what I vowed to our Lord."

"That is how I feel, Zacchaeus. I no longer can go the way that used to please me. I get satisfaction and feel content each time I do what I know Christ wants of me." The converted bandit then revealed his plans, "I will leave Jericho and catch up with Terach and reclaim my flocks. Along the route we take, I will go into the towns and give the gospel of Christ and tell the people the truth about Him and how He has changed my life."

Jesus Barabbas spent that night with Zacchaeus and left early the next morning, heading south towards his destiny. At Beer-Sheba, Barabbas took possession of his flocks from his friend Terach. Similar to the time spent with Zacchaeus, Barabbas repeated his testimony about the trial, witnessing Christ's death, and the encounter he had with the Lord that night in the cave.

Terach and his family were awed by Barabbas' depiction of events. When Barabbas had finished, Terach told how he and the family had also accepted Christ as Savior. "Barabbas, as followers of Christ Jesus, our lives in some ways remain the same. We shall continue to be despised and ridiculed by the Jewish leaders and their influence on the people. The big difference is that we must remain steadfast in allowing those lost in religion to see and hear Christ through us."

After the flocks had been divided and Barabbas resumed control over his sheep and goats, the former Zealot bandit and murderer was ready for his new life. His family was thrilled to leave behind the life of uncertainty and fear that had consumed them while they were part of the Zealot cells.

The night before the nomad shepherds were to depart the region, Barabbas confronted his long-time friend and confidant. "Terach, I must tell you that my family and I will not be traveling with you to the winter pastures." Terach had experienced several surprising moments during his association with Barabbas, so the nomad shepherd leader was somewhat ready to be surprised over whatever announcement Barabbas was about to make.

"My wife and I have talked about how our life has been these recent years. We have come to the agreement that we shall remain here in Beersheba year round." Jesus Barabbas waited for this announcement to sink in.

His excited emotions got the better of him, so Barabbas quickly continued, "There is plenty of good pasture throughout this region. I can feed my flocks and not destroy food for yours when you pass through on your way to the wintering grounds. I will have to adjust the size of my flocks to this land, but I do not fear any loss of income."

Terach sensed that Barabbas was hoping for approval of this major decision and he did not hold back his evaluation. "I can understand your decision, my friend. This land is vast, with plenty of nourishment for both our flocks. But tell me, how do you intend on selling your products if you do not utilize the Jericho market?"

Breathing a sigh of relief, Barabbas answered, "Twice a year I will go to Gaza and sell what I have to the seafaring merchants who use the port there. I know several businessmen in Gaza and know they will give me a fair price for my goods."

Terach recognized this as a sound plan. "The sea merchants will take your goods directly to Rome where the demand is great. I have no doubt you will be able to obtain a fair price, especially if you call upon the Lord for his guidance." The senior nomad shepherd reluctantly confessed, "My friend, we are getting to that age when it is more difficult to do what came so easily when we were young. I, too, have given thought about becoming settled in one place, but the life of the nomad remains strong in me to continue doing what our forefathers did."

That next morning Terach and his sons initiated the movement of the flocks westward.

In AD 40 the mentally deranged Roman Emperor, Caligula, obstinately set the wheels in motion for a future Jewish revolt. The Roman ruler's desire for total control over the Jews led to his decision to turn the temple at Jerusalem into his imperial shrine complete with an enormous statue of himself in the guise of the Roman god Jupiter.

Caligula's decision was to finally force the Jews into accepting the Roman practice of worshipping many gods. No Roman emperor prior had been able to accomplish this task. Caligula fashioned himself to be the one capable of such a monumental quest. The Sanhedrin and the Jewish people overwhelmingly rejected Caligula's forced attempt.

The idol statue was being constructed in Sidon and protected by Roman infantrymen. In addition, two legions of infantrymen and mounted archers were assigned in Galilee to transport the idol statue to Jerusalem and make sure it was placed in the temple.

Tensions were at an all-time high throughout Judea. Zacchaeus was gravely perturbed and met with Procurator Marullus concerning the situation. "Marullus, you must use your position of authority to convince Caligula that his actions will have grave consequences throughout all of Judea. The resulting rebellion by the Jews will halt all trade route traffic. All goods bound for Rome will stop or have to take the more dangerous northern route."

Marullus informed his peer, "Zacchaeus, I have notified Legate Publius Petronius of this very probability. From his position in Syria, he knows full well the dire consequences of Caligula's demented mind."

The appointed procurator slightly shook his head and uttered, "Unfortunately, word from Petronius is that Caligula will not be dissuaded from putting his grotesque image in the temple. Petronius is preparing for all-out war with the Jews. We both should prepare for this, as well."

As word circulated throughout Judea about the statue, the Zealots did their own preparation for battle against the Romans. The Zealots met privately with the Sanhedrin high priest Theophilus ben Ananus, a son of Caiaphas who had been appointed high priest by Marullus.

In that meeting, the Zealot leader John of Gischala was clear that should the Sadducees continue to appease the Romans by conforming to their rules, each member did so at the peril of their own death. Gischala simply stated what he would do, and left the great chamber room in the temple. It was a promise that the Jewish leader fearfully knew would be carried out.

The stalemate took a decided turn for the better when Agrippa I opted to intervene. He personally went to Rome and met with his long-time friend and drinking buddy Caligula. With little fanfare or debate, Agrippa convinced Caligula not to follow through with his statue plan. Work on the statue stopped and the two legions of Roman soldiers left their Galilee station and returned to the region's main garrison in Antioch, Syria.

Tensions eased somewhat throughout Judea. In Rome, the Senate had had enough of Caligula and the emperor was assassinated by a group under the leadership of Claudius who, in turn, became the new Roman emperor. This change in leadership caused the Jews and the Samaritans to relax. The group that did not relax was the Zealots, who maintained their rebellious ways.

In appreciation of his efforts in averting a major uprising, Agrippa I was designated the new procurator over Judea and Samaria. Taking advantage of the situation, Agrippa I convinced his benefactors to name him king over the entire region.

Despite the apparent return to peace, Caligula's action, although thwarted, served to create a churning molten lava pit in the minds of the Zealots and many of the ordinary Jewish people. The Sanhedrin, led by the Sadducees, returned to their earlier practice of appeasing the procurator of Judea.

On his annual stop at Beersheba, Terach discussed recent events with his lifetime friend Jesus Barabbas. "Terach, I can tell you this situation is not over. John of Gischala will do all that he can to recruit new members into his army. Gischala will prepare for a new opportunity that will allow him to create open rebellion against both the Romans and the Sanhedrin. Gischala will strike with great force." Barabbas emotionally pounded his fist into his open hand, dramatizing his point. "It will be a revolt of such magnitude that no one in our time has seen before."

As the former Zealot spoke, his firm voice emphasized his belief. This resonated with Terach, who quickly grasped the seriousness of the issue. He chimed in, "When I was in Jericho for the Passover and talked with our friend and brother in Christ, Zacchaeus, I learned that he and the Roman authorities are also quite concerned. They all believe that either the Jews or the emperor will do something to trigger a catastrophe event." The senior shepherd leader's tense expression relaxed somewhat as he realized, "Of course we must retain our hope in Christ Jesus. Only He will guide us through whatever tribulation will take place."

The two discussed how Barabbas had confronted several Roman spies. The reformed rebel reported that men had been sent to observe his actions to determine if he were still a member of the Zealots. Barabbas tapped his fingers and tersely said, "The pigs were dubious and did not believe me. I know they will continue to spy on me and my family. It's possible any insurrection by the Zealots will have a negative impact here on me."

Terach was shocked at Barabbas' revelation, yet he knew there was nothing either he or his fellow nomad shepherd could do to change the Romans' mindset and actions. This was a test of their trust in Almighty God.

They discussed other items and shared their thoughts and concerns, so like what they used to do in their younger days while traversing the entire region of Judea. Only these days the topics were far more weighty.

Finally, their visit had to end and Barabbas asked Terach, "Are you in good health, my friend? I detect you may have troubles."

Terach assured Barabbas he was fine. "I may be slow, not as strong as in the days of my youth, but I can still perform my daily tasks and I give thanks to Almighty God for each day that He gives me to do such things."

In AD 45 a milder than normal weather pattern swept through Judea. The warm winds blew in bacteria and pollens that normally would be killed during the colder winter months. It was late summer and many people in the region came down with fevers, flu-like symptoms, and diarrhea. Travelers making their way along the two main trade routes also became carriers of different ailments. The two main portions of Jewish society that were hardest hit were the very young and the old.

For several weeks both Terach and Beulah had exhibited symptoms of this strange illness. Each day they grew weaker, much to the concern of Gavriel and his two brothers who now had taken over management of the flocks. When the traveling small town reached the outskirts of the walled city of Beersheba, they made their customary camp. Gavriel sent his brother Amram to Barabbas with the anxious news about Terach and Beulah.

Barabbas quickly responded, "I know the doctor here. He is good and has dealt with this strange ailment. I shall send him to your camp. Go tell Gavriel and Eiton I will accompany the doctor." Within two hours Barabbas and the doctor arrived at the shepherd encampment. The doctor immediately looked in on both Terach and Beulah.

The physician administered compresses and ordered herbs to be ground into a tea mixture, which was repeatedly given the elderly couple. For ten days the doctor returned every day to his new patients. During that time, Barabbas remained with his closest friend. "Tell me, doctor, do you see any improvements in my friends as they endure this affliction?"

The doctor shook his head no and said, "Whatever this ailment is; it is strong in both your friends. We should know within the next few days if the illness will weaken."

Four days later, both Terach and Beulah succumbed to the illness. Gavriel, Amram, and Barabbas were at the couple's bedside when earthly life departed their bodies. Both Terach and Beulah had sensed death was imminent and were prepared. Terach had called Gavriel to sit next to him where he instructed his eldest son how to divide his estate.

After Terach's conference with Gavriel, he had called his best friend Barabbas to sit by him. "Barabbas, we have enjoyed many days together and experienced much during our lives. The time has come for both me and Beulah to be with our Lord. Thank you for being my friend."

Jesus Barabbas looked over at the frail shepherd and choked out, "Terach, I consider you to be my brother. You have been faithful and kind to me and my family. I shall miss you, my brother, but look forward to the day we are together in heaven." Barabbas had clasped his dying friend's hand tightly while he spoke. Having said what he longed to, he released his grip, stood up, and left the shepherd's tent.

Terach turned to his wife of nearly sixty years and gently held her hand in his. He smiled warmly at her and his eyes moistened with grateful emotion. "God blessed me greatly making you my wife. I cherish the time we have had together and look forward to sharing eternity with you." Beulah weakly returned her husband's smile but was too weak to speak. The expression in her eyes spoke clearly of the love she had for her husband.

Terach's eyes remained on the love of his life when he softly breathed his last breath. One hour later, Beulah joined him in heaven.

As the oldest son, Gavriel was in charge of the funeral of his parents. Because the clan were converts to being followers of Christ, they were not afforded normal Jewish funeral rituals. Any Jew who converted to following Christ Jesus' commands was considered a heathen and forfeited all Jewish recognition and involvement in the culture. Converted Jews could not be buried within one mile of any Jewish community. All this was expected and did not matter to the nomad shepherds who were ostracized from all Jewish rights of citizenship.

Gavriel's wife and her two sisters-in-law took charge of preparing the two bodies for burial. Each was thoroughly cleaned and wrapped in a simple, plain linen shroud. Barabbas' wife assisted the women and informed Gavriel and Jesus Barabbas when the couple was ready for their final rites.

Caves were often used for entombment sites, but the area surrounding Beersheba was not suitable as a final resting place. Thieves eagerly looked for signs of entombments to steal any items of value placed with the deceased. In addition, predators would use the caves as dens and devour the corpses.

Since all funerals are culture-based, the Roman practice of cremation was selected as the method of dealing with the dead couple. Jesus Barabbas and Gavriel had the necessary wood stacked and ready for the service.

As the family gathered around the fire, Barabbas commented, "It matters not how this loving couple are honored in death because their souls are alive and united with our Savior Christ Jesus." The family looked towards Barabbas, nodded their heads, and paid tribute to the couple who now resided in heaven.

After the ceremony, Gavriel and his two shepherd brothers broke camp and headed the flocks towards Gaza.

Before leaving Beersheba, Barabbas assisted Gavriel in sending notification of their parents' death to Channah who resided in Emmaus and to Mattan back in Jericho. Carrier pigeons completed each journey in just under two days.

When Gavriel and the flocks departed Beersheba, Barabbas mounted his trusty horse and made his way ahead of his own flocks and came to a small hill where he went to God in prayer and fasting over the death of his long trusted friend and brother in Christ.

Despite the distance between them, Channah and Mattan had a similar reaction to the news of their parents' death. In each one's separate location, the two siblings gathered their respective families and gave God prayers of praise for their parents and that they now were with Him in heaven.

In the case of Mattan, Zacchaeus also participated in the loss of a trusted friend and business associate. For two weeks afterwards, both Channah and Mattan were numb as they adjusted to the inevitable fact of death that accompanies life on earth. A combination of warm memories and sorrow for lost earthly contact would remain with them and their other family members the remainder of their lives.

Chapter 21

During Emperor Claudius' fifth year of reign as Caesar, a three-year famine occurred in Judea beginning in AD 45 until AD 47. Famines were greatly feared by common people, as well as those who ruled over them. There was no way of knowing how long, to what extent, or why such events took place. Fear was universally experienced regardless of age, gender, or rank.

For the common man, it was fear of survival and fear of witnessing family members, especially young children, die from lack of food. Rulers' fear was a more callous one, fearful that prolonged famines would cause uprising that could topple their regime.

Claudius encountered his first famine during the initial two years of his fourteen-year reign. The earlier famine was centered on the city of Rome. It had potential to bring his rule to a crashing halt, but he was astute enough to take proper measures to minimize its impact.

A combination of weather factors and conscription of the small farmers in the region into the military were the main reasons for the famine. Despite the fact many of the elite wealthy citizens and businessmen of Rome took over these small farms, there was insufficient manpower to do the daily work. As a result, crops failed and the land became fallow.

Rome had already been involved in importing much of their grains, herbs, spices, and other goods from foreign countries, especially Egypt, prior to the famine. With the logistics already in place, directives were issued for larger supplies to be sent to the ever-hungry populace of Rome.

Judea with two of the major land trade routes plus six port cities made the region a prime source of supply for Rome. Now that the entire Judean region was experiencing the first phase of its famine, caution became the watchword for Claudius.

As part of his duties as chief business administrator over Judea and Samaria, Zacchaeus sent a communiqué to Rome informing them of the early phase of the famine. Within a week of sending the alarming news to Caesar, Zacchaeus was petitioned by the garrison commander for more detailed information. "Zacchaeus, Caesar is concerned about this news related to the famine. Tell me why you believe this shortage will become so impactful. What you say will be sent to Caesar, plus will provide me information how I should proceed here."

The diminutive administrator began to describe the crisis. "Commander, I monitor both Judea and Samaria on a regular basis. There are many informants I utilized to provide me much needed information on what is taking place throughout the entire region. In this way, I can assess what decisions must be made to maintain control over the business affairs."

The commander listened thoughtfully until the chief administrator finished. "So, what are your conclusions?"

Zacchaeus elucidated, "Crops from the northern part of Samaria to the southern border with Negev are suffering from blight. It is such that this year's production will be less than half the normal harvest." He was glad to see the commander's concern grasped the seriousness of his report. "It is not because of lack of water. It is not because of locust. It is something in the air that invades all of Samaria and Judea. No one is able to tell me exactly what the reason is."

The commander became pensive and placed his hand under his clean-shaven chin. He looked down at the tabletop for some time before engaging with Zacchaeus. "Do you know how full the store-houses are with grain?"

Zacchaeus knew the answer. "In Samaria they are three-quarters full. Throughout Judea, less than that. I estimate just over half full."

This time the commander let out a sigh that was more of a groan and he sat back in his chair and looked at Zacchaeus with genuine dismay. "This does not bode well for this region or for Rome. More grains will have to be imported from other areas. This will require both ships and land caravans." The commander grimaced and stood up to leave. "You have done well, Zacchaeus. I only hope this does not get worse or last for any length of time. It would be disastrous for everyone concerned."

Zacchaeus agreed and asked the main question that required an immediate answer, "How do you want me to proceed?"

Rising to his full height, the commander instructed as clearly and authoritatively as he could, "Do not make the grain available to anyone in either Samaria or Judea until I receive word back from Caesar. I will deploy troops to safeguard these storehouses to prevent looting. When I receive word from Rome, I will convey the decision to you."

One week later, Zacchaeus cringed when he learned of Caesar's decision. Only one-third of what currently was available in the storehouses could be sold throughout the region. The remainder was to go to Rome. He knew should the grain shortage continue into the next growing season, two-thirds of the harvest would go to Rome and the remainder would be sold throughout Samaria and Judea. There would be insufficient amounts to feed both Samaria and Judea. The inhabitants would become collateral damage and forced to fend for themselves.

In the second year of the famine there was much clamor and discontent for the short supply of necessary grains. The Legate of Syria dispatched more troops to assist the garrison commanders in Samaria, Jericho, Jerusalem, Beersheba, Joppa and Caesarea. Claudius was intent on keeping order.

In the third famine year farmers who attempted to horde their harvest were beaten by the Roman troops. All harvest was confiscated. Businessmen who made overtures to buy or sell grain and other crops through the black market were severely beaten and their goods seized.

Zacchaeus told his many tax collectors located throughout the region to be watchful of such activities. The efforts of the field tax collectors made many of the Jews and Samaritans angrier at both the tax agents and Zacchaeus. These officials of Rome were hated by all, and the garrison commanders had to provide them protection.

One evening when Zacchaeus invited the families of Mattan and Bartimaeus to his house for dinner, he confided, "The situation concerning this famine grows worse each day. Farmers and businessmen who hold back on the grain and other crops are growing in numbers, as does Rome's retaliation. Some have been executed to set an example; but others rise to take their place."

Mattan asked his host, "What do you hear from the nomad shepherds who journey throughout Judea?" Zacchaeus softly answered, "The grasslands are not impacted by this famine, especially surrounding Beersheba west to Gaza and as far north to Joppa."

Anticipating the cause for Mattan's question, Zacchaeus continued, "Fear not. Your family, Barabbas, and most of the nomads are not in danger of losing their flocks. On the contrary, when they bring their animals here or at other markets in Judea, they will sell their sheep and goats and the cheese for a premium price. I have notified the garrison commanders of probable trouble with bandits who would rob the shepherds. Rest assured, they all will be protected as much as possible."

In AD 47, hunger plagued the regions of Samaria and Judea. A prophet named Agabus was in Antioch telling the people of the greatly feared famine. Among those who heard the prophet were a disciple Barnabas and the Apostle Paul. The two had spent one year teaching in Antioch, and many of the area's lost souls had converted to following Christ Jesus.

The two ministers approached the followers about giving aid to the followers of Christ in Jerusalem and the surrounding area. The new disciples of Christ gave money according to their ability. Paul and Barnabas were elected to take the contribution to Judea and give it to the elders there.

All Jewish converts to following Christ were subjected to having the Jewish leaders and their henchmen confiscate their goods. Adding to their trials, these converts were deprived of making a living within Jerusalem. Rabbis in main towns and cities throughout Judea were also instructed to persecute any Jew who left the Jewish religion.

Paul and Barnabas carried the contribution which consisted of money in two pouches. Animals and perishables could not be transported the distance from Antioch to Jerusalem because they would spoil. The animals would be too difficult to handle, especially since there were only two men making the journey.

The pair procured mules to speed the relief mission and they arrived in Jerusalem in short order. Portions of the money were given to the elders of the church cells, not only in Jerusalem but also in the surrounding area including Bethlehem, Emmaus, Herodium, Tekos and Hebron. There were sufficient funds that grains could be purchased from the trade caravans that passed through along the two main trade routes. Terach's sons and Barabbas also changed their normal routes and provided the people of Masada, Arad, Beersheba, Gaza, and north to Joppa with animals and their by-products at a fair price. Other nomad shepherds sold their animals and cheese at premium prices.

With nearly all the monetary resources depleted, Paul, Barnabas, and another disciple John Mark made their way north. Their first stop was at Qumran where the weary travelers stayed with like-minded followers of Christ. Early the next day, the trio set out for the final leg of their relief mission to Jericho.

It was late fall in Jericho. Often the days were marked by cold winds coming out of the northeast. Many days, rain accompanied these winds making it difficult for any kind of travel. On one such cold, blustery day, Mattan stood in front of his tent where his pottery was sold, speaking about Christ to many who had braved the inclement weather to hear his words. There was no shortage of curiosity seekers wanting to hear Mattan's incredible litany of events leading to his accepting Christ's forgiveness of sins and invitation to eternal life.

The listeners huddled together in an effort to block the chilling wind from weaving through and around the onlookers. One person remained in the back of the crowd, seemingly unconcerned about the effects of the cold wind. The shrouded figure stood motionless and quiet, not asking questions as others in the group did. His eyes went from one person to another and settled on the main speaker, Mattan.

The message rolled off Mattan's lips in eloquence, conviction, and passion. The motionless figure observed several in the crowd as they began to sob, while others raised their hands and their heads toward the heavens. At the end of the speaker's presentation, several members of the group knelt down, and Mattan went to each one and quietly spoke. The observer noted Mattan whispered into the ear of each person, after which the individual would nod their head and speak something the shrouded figure could not hear.

After the last individual stood up and left, the stranger approached Mattan who waited, not recognizing the faceless person. When the mysterious figure got to within several feet of Mattan, he raised his head and smiled broadly. It was the Apostle Paul!

Once Mattan saw his mentor and friend, he opened his arms wide and embraced the heavily cloaked apostle of Christ. "Paul, it is so good to see you! What brings you to Jericho, especially this late in the year?"

The apostle reported the trip he and Barnabas had made to dispense money to the elders of the church cells.

"Praise the Lord for your efforts, Paul! All of Samaria and Judea are suffering greatly from lack of grains and other crops.

There is much hardship in the land. Of course, the Jews withhold any available grains and other food from us followers of Christ. It has been very difficult, especially for those who live in Jerusalem," Mattan admitted.

The two men stood for a few minutes next to the tent lined with pottery until the first drops of rain began to fall. "Paul, please join Devorah and our family tonight for dinner. I shall inform Zacchaeus and Bartimaeus, as well. They all want to spend time with you."

The apostle of Christ's eyes twinkled with the thought of reuniting with his mentees. "I shall be delighted to eat with all my friends. It has been fourteen years since we last were together. On this trip I have a fellow disciple named Barnabas with me and a young man named John Mark who is traveling back to Antioch with us."

Mattan quickly adjusted the plan, "In that case, we must meet at Zacchaeus' home because it is more spacious. He will not object and I know he is in Jericho. We all shall enjoy your company, my friend."

The rain pelted down harder, and the two separated. Paul returned to meet up with Barnabas and John Mark. Mattan hurried to the home of Zacchaeus with his delightful news.

At dinner that evening there was much levity among the group and much to share about events that had taken place over the last fourteen years since Paul's last appearance in Jericho. The guest of honor looked at his friends with love and respect. "Earlier today, I watched both you, Mattan, and Bartimaeus as you witnessed to different groups of travelers. I must commend you on your spiritual growth. The Holy Spirit has been working within you. Each of you has progressed greatly in giving the gospel. I am sure many have come to receive Christ's gift of salvation after listening to you."

Paul addressed Zacchaeus, "I am thankful how you have remained faithful to your vow to our Lord Jesus. People throughout all of Samaria and Judea have benefited from your repentance. Your personal dealings with leaders of these caravans have given needed food and supplies to Christ's children. You truly are letting many lost souls see Christ through His obvious changes in you."

Throughout the evening the group queried their guests about their evangelizing throughout Antioch and Paul's efforts in his hometown of Tarsus. They were amazed at how many people were repenting and turning their lives over to Christ. One of the final topics of the evening was introduced by Barnabas stating that when the trio returned to Antioch they would resume efforts to procure more money for another trip to assist Christ followers. "Only our Lord knows when this famine will cease. Until such time, we must do all that is possible to assist our brethren here in Judea and Samaria. We will return."

There was much insistence from Paul's mentees for him and his companions to remain in Jericho for an extra period of time. The weather became the deciding factor. A large winter storm created harsh conditions for traveling, and so Paul and his cohorts remained with Zacchaeus for nearly a week. During the week, Paul and Barnabas gave some instructions to the Jericho evangelists.

When the storm's impact lessened and bright blue skies once again returned to Jericho, the traveling evangelists bade farewell to their hosts and resumed their journey back to Antioch.

The combination of fellowship and Paul and Barnabas's teaching, plus getting to know the young John Mark, buoyed the spirits of Paul's mentees. With renewed verve they went about witnessing and evangelizing to those who not only lived in Jericho but also to the many travelers who stopped at the oasis during their long journeys. With each effort there were converts who then took Christ with them along their way.

Per Paul's instructions, the evangelists made sure they showed Christ's love to every sinner. It was manifesting Christ's love that swayed many lost souls to first listen, then act, on accepting Christ as Savior.

On one such occasion, Bartimaeus was witnessing and teaching a group of lost souls on the Sabbath. Word of this reached the ears of one of the young Pharisees who was stationed in Jericho. The young man approached Christ's disciple and listened to Bartimaeus' words.

With great pomp and ceremony to impress the crowd, the Pharisee approached Bartimaeus. "You are a Jew, are you not?"

Bartimaeus looked intently at his inquisitor, braced himself, and replied, "Indeed I am."

The young Pharisee shot out, "Why, then, do you commit sin by teaching on the day set aside to obey God?"

Bartimaeus peered intently into the young man's eyes. "Because these lost souls are in need of hearing the gospel given to His followers."

The young Pharisee roughly asserted, "It is against the law to do such a thing. Only the rabbis can do such teaching, or a Pharisee such as myself. The law says teaching is to take place only on the Sabbath and in the synagogue. You are not qualified to teach, especially about the blasphemer who was put to death for his insolence."

The young Pharisee postured defiantly. His face hardened as he awaited a response from his religious adversary.

Bartimaeus calmly looked at the young man. He took a deep breath before he answered, "Do you not teach that on the Sabbath should one spill something, it is not to be cleaned up until the day after?"

The surprised Pharisee said, "That is the law."

"Do you also teach that should you pick something up in one hand, you must replace it with the other?"

Again the baffled Pharisee acknowledged, "That also is the law."

Bartimaeus continued, "Is it against your law that no one should be healed on the Sabbath and that no doctor or midwife can perform any function on this day?"

With arrogant confidence the Pharisee sarcastically said, "That is correct. For one who has not studied the law, you are well versed in the statutes."

Bartimaeus knew his next question would inflame the conflict, but it had to be posed. "Is it better to let a person die on the Sabbath because of the law, or to save him that he may continue living?"

This time the Pharisee paused before replying. His skeptical expression indicated he was pondering the intent of the question and did not want to get caught by reason or logic. "The law is quite clear there is to be no healing on the Sabbath. That should be sufficient to answer to your question. What is your point in making such a trivial inquiry?" He was beginning to feel nervous.

"Because your law does not focus or care about the soul, that which is inside the person. How many laws do you break during the course of a day or a week? In such instances, do you lament breaking the law or disobeying God's Word and not the man-made law your superiors have devised?"

Bartimaeus added, "With your man-made law and rituals there is guilt and no possibility of true repentance. This is not what Christ Jesus taught or what God's Word says. Your focus is on the law made by your superiors instead of on God's holy teaching. Should you commit true sin, it is only God who can forgive and restore, not your man-made laws and rituals."

The young Pharisee was taken aback by Bartimaeus' rebuke. He could not refute Bartimaeus. He sullenly admitted to himself that he had not won the round, and skulked off to avoid further arguments.

The onlookers turned their heads back to Bartimaeus and several said, "Never have we heard anyone speak to a Pharisee in the manner that you just did. You speak with boldness and authority that must come from God! You have revealed to us that Christ's words and teachings are true." As a result, the majority accepted Christ as Savior.

During this time God's Holy Spirit was moving powerfully within and around Bartimaeus, Hadassah, Mattan, Devorah, Barabbas, and Zacchaeus in such a way that many Jews and Gentiles sought them out for teaching about the freedom available through Christ Jesus. As the small group of evangelists continued seeking and following the guidance and direction of God, Judea and Samaria's numbers of followers of Christ began to grow.

The Sanhedrin became more nervous and infuriated with the growing number of converts to The Way; they were particularly incensed by how effective these particular individuals were in rebuking the dictates of the Oral Torah and the Talmud.

High priest Ananias ben Nebedeus commented to the full Sanhedrin on one occasion in AD 50, "The passion and persistence of these people are causing the rabbis difficulty. There are more converts to this blasphemous craze with each passing day. Members of the Sanhedrin, I fear we will have to take stronger measures to curtail the growth of this sect."

It was getting out of hand. In AD 52, shortly after Marcus Antonius Felix was appointed procurator over Judea and Samaria, the high priest Nebedeus approached the regional governor, pleading for his intervention in order to curtail the efforts of the evangelists. He was met with Felix's firm refusal, declaring, "High priest, I do not care about this sect of your religion. This is your responsibility. Are you not the leader of your religion?"

Felix did not wait for an answer from Nebedeus, before he added, "These people do not cause me or Rome any problems in this region. In fact they are easier to work with than the rest of you Jews. Beware, high priest, do not make any effort to cause harm to these people called followers of The Way lest I bring harm to you."

Nebedeus left Felix's palace in Caesarea and brooded discontentedly throughout the long journey back to Jerusalem. When he told the Sanhedrin of Felix's proclamation of non-involvement and even his dire threat, the religious leaders muttered and murmured their displeasure with the Roman Procurator's decision.

Chapter 22

One of the issues that stood out in the mind of Procurator Felix was the ability of the insurgent Jewish group called the Zealots to harass both the Romans and the Greeks who were scattered throughout Judea and Samaria. He analyzed their tactics and grew to admire their audacity, but he was also concerned about their growing power.

"These bandits steal from Roman citizens and the Greeks, often in broad daylight. They have no fear of our soldiers. I must watch them closely," Felix confided to his secretary. "We must find ways to use this group to our benefit. They could be useful for my purposes."

Late in his tenure as procurator, Felix unwittingly started the wheels turning that would end in his humiliating recall back to Rome.

He tired of the incessant whining of Ananias ben Nebedeus. So, Felix utilized his power and authority to appoint a new high priest named Jonathan. This was done as a courtesy and reward to Jonathan for his successful influence on his Roman contacts to get Felix appointed as Procurator. Within a short time after his appointment, Jonathan began advising Felix on matters relating to the Jewish religious leaders.

During one of his visits with Felix at Caesarea, Jonathan informed the Procurator, "I can benefit you, Felix, in dealing with both the Sanhedrin and the rebel group the Zealots. My influence is sufficient to sway the opinion of the Sanhedrin positively towards the Zealots. They are revered by the Jewish people and causing harm to them would not be advisable."

Felix listened to the high priest. "These Zealots rob and pillage Roman citizens. I don't care so much about the Greeks, but I am accountable to Caesar for the Romans who decide to live in this land and those who do business here. How do I appease both Rome and your Jewish people?"

Jonathan smiled inwardly about his position of advantage with this Roman official whom he barely tolerated. Felix was both easily manipulated and gullible, and was the reason why Jonathan had sought his appointment to Judea. He answered the procurator, "So long as the Zealots do not kill any Romans, you do not have to take drastic action. Regarding the economic loss by the Romans, you can replace what they lose by taking from the Greeks or from the trade caravans that regularly pass through this region. In addition, I will meet with the Zealot leader and give him, shall we say, private information about Rome's limit to their interference. I will state basically what I've told you today—that the Zealots will not be actively pursued so long as they ensure no Roman is killed in their raids."

Felix sat in his chair and placed his fist under his chin as he pondered the high priest's proposal. He thought of another way to sweeten the pot. "Also, do this. Inform this Zealot leader that so long as he and his wild bunch do not physically harm any Roman who lives or travels through Samaria or Judea, I will not raise the taxes on the Jews."

This proposal was exactly what Jonathan wanted to hear. He fought hard to hide the smug feeling he was enjoying over Felix's words. "Very good. I truly believe the Zealot leader will have no problem with this arrangement. I will inform him of such immediately upon my return to Jerusalem."

The Zealot leader John of Gischala met with Jonathan at the smaller meeting room in the Temple. After hearing the arrangement devised by Jonathan and Felix, Gischala curled his upper lip and replied, "I know you have some hidden aspect of this treaty that will benefit you personally, high priest. I do not trust either you or the Roman dog in Caesarea. Be that for what it is, I will instruct my warriors as you say." John of Gischala snarled, "But high priest, the first Roman soldier who kills one of my warriors or a member of his family will be dealt with in kind. This treaty will then cease and we shall come after both you and the Roman dogs who rule us."

High priest Jonathan inwardly shuddered. He knew John of Gischala did not make idle threats. The high priest momentarily visualized his own death which he quickly shook off. Even in hypothetical terms, Jonathan did not like thinking about what would come from Gischala's wrath.

From his throne-like chair, Jonathan watched the Zealot leader march out of the smaller meeting room in the Temple. He wanted to devise a plan that would not require the services of the Zealots. These thoughts were brief; however, as he knew his purposes actually could not be achieved without them.

In AD 58, fate and the Roman gods seemingly gave favor to Felix. In mid-summer, the commander of the Roman garrison in Jerusalem, a man named Claudius Lysias, arrived in Caesarea from Jerusalem with a prisoner named Paul. Lysias and a contingent of soldiers immediately met with Felix and explained how Paul had incited the Jewish leaders. Lysias told Felix, "The Jews made a plot to kill this man, so I brought him to you. He is a Roman citizen and as such must be heard by you."

Felix knew of Paul and his evangelistic work among the Gentiles about the so-called Jewish Messiah who had been put to death years earlier. Felix thought it odd for someone to speak highly of a man who never accomplished what the Jews sought. The procurator was well aware of the power Paul had among the converts to The Way.

He immediately thought there was potential to extract money from either Paul or his followers. The procurator told Lysias, "You have acted correctly and it is my duty to ascertain if this man has committed a crime against Rome. Depart now; for I shall have this citizen watched from his cell in the palace here."

After Lysias and his solders left for their return trip to Jerusalem, Felix conferred with his third wife, Drusilla, who was a Jew. He hoped her heritage would give him insight that as a Roman he wouldn't imagine. "Do you think I can secure money from either Paul or his followers once they learn he is in my custody?"

Drusilla shrugged her shoulders and replied, "He has many followers. Some years ago, he and another man brought money to the members of The Way during the famine. The Jews attempted to starve these Way members because they considered them blasphemous to the Jewish traditions. I believe he is capable of obtaining large sums of money. Hold him and find out what happens."

Following her advice, Felix detained Paul under arrest in a cell above his living quarters. Paul's detention elongated into two years. During that period of time, the corrupt procurator was not able to obtain a single shekel, despite letting Paul have frequent visitors including Bartimaeus, Mattan, their wives, and Zacchaeus.

Paul's brethren from Jericho made several trips from Jericho to Caesarea to visit and to bring their mentor items of clothing and food, but no money. Felix monitored these visits closely and was always disappointed to determine there was no money to confiscate.

In AD 59, Felix erupted emotionally against Jonathan. Informants had kept Felix apprised of how the high priest repeatedly ridiculed the procurator. The arrogant Jonathan made one disparaging remark once too often. For Felix, it was time to take action against the high priest, and in so doing the rest of the Sanhedrin as well.

An infuriated Felix met with the leader of a sub-group of the Zealots, a man named Menachem ben Jair. Felix traveled to Galilee to meet with Menachem. The meeting would ultimately have dire consequences throughout the land.

Menachem sat on his fainting couch surrounded by bodyguards as Felix was pushed into the meeting room by members of the rebel clan. He was directed to a chair and Menachem immediately fired the first question. "Procurator, you have come a distance here to Bethsaida just to meet with me. What is the purpose of your visit?"

Felix was keenly aware of Menachem's probing eyes as well as those of the bodyguards all staring at him. He was extremely uncomfortable and began to perspire. Summoning his courage, Felix stammered, "I, I have a proposal that might interest you." Felix paused to gauge the interest of Menachem, but saw only a scowl.

Fire was shooting from his eyes. "Don't play such foolish games with me, Procurator! I do not like such naïve and vague statements. Be advised that, here, you really have no control. You have come unattended by soldiers, obviously for secrecy. It would be easy for me to cut your throat, throw your carcass on the side of the road, and blame it on bandits."

Menachem waited for his words to penetrate Felix's corrupt mind. Beads of sweat were giving away the procurator's great discomfort. "Now Roman, state your purpose! Otherwise I shall feed you to the buzzards."

Felix cleared his throat and said, "I can arrange a way that will be easy for you to do away with the high priest Jonathan and not be charged with his demise." Surprised at seeing no reaction at all from Menachem, Felix quickly added, "Within a few days Jonathan will be my guest at an event in Jerusalem. It will be very crowded and your men can dispose of Jonathan without fear of reprisal by me. I can arrange that only a few soldiers will be present and will not interfere."

Menachem's facial expression remained stoic, causing Felix's nerves to rattle. The cult leader merely stared at the procurator, but his mind was relishing the possibility of doing away with his hated enemy. Jonathan had betrayed Menachem, and it had nearly cost the rebel his life.

The rebel leader pretended disinterest. He waved off Felix's statement saying, "Why don't you approach the Zealots with this plot? You have dealings with John of Gischala. Get him to do your killing."

Felix quickly answered, "John of Gischala refuses to get involved with the Sanhedrin. Jonathan has convinced the members of the Sanhedrin not to show favor to the Zealots as they have in the past. Anyway, the Zealots are more focused in efforts against Romans, the Greeks, and Jewish collaborators."

"You are telling me, then, that John of Gischala has turned you down in your plot to assassinate Jonathan?" coaxed Menachem. Reluctantly Felix nodded. Menachem threw back his head and laughed heartily. Then he leaned forward with fiery eyes aimed at his guest and said, "I will think your proposal over. Return to Caesarea. I will contact you there with my answer."

Five days elapsed and Felix heard nothing from Menachem. The procurator became anxious and wondered if his plot had been made known to Jonathan. The worry that these Jews could not be trusted turned in his mind constantly. It was heightened by the fact that the event Felix originally chose for the assassination was occurring that very day and, as such, was no longer viable. Anger joined his simmering anxiety. Felix vowed to teach this Jewish rebel a lesson not to trifle with a Roman official.

However, any action from Felix was pre-empted. Late that night, as Felix lay asleep in his bed, a dark figure crept into his bedchamber and swiftly placed his hand over the sleeping procurator's mouth. Felix awoke in alarm, but could not move to release the hand over his mouth. With wide eyes he stared into the night shadows, but could not distinguish his assailant's identity.

The powerful figure spoke softly to Felix, "Menachem sends his greetings to you. He says he is agreeable to your proposal. You are to go to the docks tomorrow to the far corner of the harbor where the small boats are kept. There you will be met and taken to Menachem to finalize your agreement. Should you fail to show, you will be killed."

The powerful figure then placed a damp cloth over Felix's nose and mouth. Fumes in the cloth caused the procurator to shake his head but he could not dislodge the cloth. Almost immediately he passed out and the night visitor slipped out the same window of the bedchamber that he had just entered.

Felix awoke early the next morning with a slight headache from the powerful herbs used to render him unconscious. He remembered the chilling words spoken to him and knew he had to do as he was told.

After his usual morning meal, the procurator went about his normal routine, but with his emotions and stomach churning over the scheduled meeting. When most of the official business had been conducted, Felix told his secretary he needed to do some work for Rome. As casually as possible, he left his headquarters and made his way to the harbor per the instructors of the nighttime intruder.

When he reached the harbor where the small boats were docked, a hunched over man approached him and quietly said, "Get in this boat. I will take you to meet with Menachem." Felix did as instructed and the hunched body cast away from the dock and began to row the small fishing vessel out from the harbor.

The rowing shadow made sure no one was watching or following them before he changed the boat's direction and headed around the harbor's edge to a rocky point. The shrouded boatswain stopped rowing and instructed his passenger, "Get out of the boat and make your way ashore. There you will be taken to Menachem."

Awkwardly, Felix removed his outer cloak and eased himself over the side of the boat. The water was waist level, and part of his outer cloak soaked up the sea water. His intent on preventing his new garment from getting stained from the salt water was of no avail. This irritated him greatly, but he managed to control himself. He was able to reach shore without any difficulty and, just as he had been told, another dark form met him saying, "I will take you to Menachem."

The pair made their way to a cave hidden by several rocks and trees. Once inside, he saw dim candles illuminated the interior enough that Felix could identify Menachem sitting on a tree stump, surrounded by several of his followers.

Menachem pointed to a second tree stump where Felix was to sit. Felix's irritation escaped his lips, "Why such clandestine efforts to meet, Menachem? I don't believe this is really necessary."

The Zealot leader frowned and said, "You are a fool, Felix. Should anyone see us together, it will not go well for either of us. You, of all people, should realize spies watch prominent people such as us. Now, tell me how you propose to make it possible for me to do away with Jonathan."

Felix felt he must not annoy this bandit leader any further, and got right to the point. "My original plan cannot be possible, now, as the optimal time has elapsed. However, in three days, I will be in Jerusalem. At that time I will invite Jonathan and several of the Sanhedrin members as well as other Jews to join me at the hippodrome for the horse and chariot races. It will be very crowded and once the races have concluded, you can kill Jonathan when he and his entourage leave the amphitheater. I can assure you, no Roman soldiers will be at that location to interfere or capture you."

Menachem studied the face of the procurator through the dancing light of the candles. He picked up a stick and stirred embers at the edge of the warming fire. The only sound heard was the slight popping of the flames as air swooshed into the cave from its seaward entrance. Finally the rebel bandit leader said, "I am aware of the hippodrome. Its configuration makes for crowdedness. But what of the Zealots? Will they be there to protect Jonathan?"

Felix indicated no Zealots would be in the vicinity, and that Menachem and his men would have free access to their despised foe.

Menachem pondered Felix's words and their mutual distrust. He stated, "I shall contemplate this plan." The rebel narrowed his eyes and pointed the stick he was holding directly at Felix's face. He ordered, "Do not make any further attempts to contact me. Go about your normal routine and meet with Jonathan. Should I decide to act on this plan, it shall be done. Depending on your honesty with me, you will either live—or die should I detect this is a setup."

The schemers ended their meeting and one of the bodyguards grabbed hold of Felix's arm, jerking him to his feet. Pain shot through his shoulder. He was pushed through the cave to a different access point. There the bodyguard turned the procurator over to another small group of bandits who put Felix on a horse and led him through the trees to a road that took him back to Caesarea.

The next day, Felix and Drusilla got into their carriage for a dusty journey south to Jerusalem. At Jamnia the carriage and the mounted archers turned east and headed for Jerusalem. Once there, Felix appeared enthusiastic about attending the races scheduled for the hippodrome.

It was difficult for Felix to act and think normally during the races, but he forced himself to converse with Jonathan as well as the other dignitaries he invited to the festivities. The races were excellent and the crowd was loud and exuberant.

At the finish, the majority of the crowd had made their way ahead of the dignitaries. Felix grabbed hold of Drusilla's arm and said, "Let our guests go ahead of us. They can pave the way for us." Drusilla did not think anything was amiss by this suggestion, and she lingered with her husband while the rest of the group went ahead.

Felix grew more nervous with each step. He wondered if Menachem would indeed act on his proposed plan. His eyes darted from side to side, attempting to see anyone who resembled those who were with Menachem at the cave. His hesitating steps caused Drusilla to question why her husband was delaying their exit from the hippodrome.

Outside the seven-columned entrance to the arena, the crowd was backed up due to an overturned cart carrying caged chickens. The driver and a couple of onlookers were gathering up the cages while several other onlookers had uprighted the two-wheeled cart.

Jonathan and his entourage could not see the ruckus but could hear some commotion. Without warning, Jonathan let out a groan and slumped to the ground. As those close to the high priest saw him go down, several other members of his group also keeled over and fell on the hard terrain. Shouts behind the Jewish leaders hollered for the crowd to move quicker. The din was ear-splitting. The unrelenting force of the pressing crowd caused some of the hippodrome attendees to step on the fallen religious leaders.

Suddenly, someone exclaimed, "These men are dead!" By that time, Felix and Drusilla had reached the scene of the assassination. Immediately, three Roman soldiers appeared and cleared a small area around the fallen bodies. Felix recognized one of the soldiers and asked gruffly, "What goes here?" The soldier bowed to the procurator and informed him four men had been killed. Felix moved to where the dead men lay. He pointed to one corpse and looked at the soldier with feigned shock. "That is the high priest Jonathan, and the others are his fellow Sanhedrin members! We must remove them immediately away from here."

Five more soldiers quickly arrived at the scene of the crime, and Felix ordered all the soldiers to carry the dead religious leaders away from the crowd to the edge of the hippodrome entrance. He directed the soldiers to a stone silo attached to the entrance. This provided sufficient time for the assassins to make their escape undetected. Once inside the silo that stood nearly three stories tall, Felix and the sergeant inspected the corpses. "Procurator, these men have been stabbed through the heart. There is only one wound."

Felix looked at the blood-soaked wounds and eyed the sergeant, "What do you make of this, sergeant?"

The soldier cocked his head sideways and said, "It is the work of true assassins. I have heard of similar killings. It is the handiwork of a group from Galilee called Sicarii, or dagger men. There have been only a few such killings, but now it appears these assassins have made their presence known here in Jerusalem."

Felix feigned surprise. "Sergeant, make sure these bodies get to the proper Jewish religious leaders. Afterward, come to my quarters at the garrison and report to me all that you know of these Sicarii." The sergeant agreed, and Felix and Drusilla made their way back to the garrison under armed guard. Drusilla looked quizzically at Felix, wondering if he was involved with these killings, but she kept her secret suspicions to herself.

Both the sergeant and the garrison commander agreed the killings were religious in nature due to the feud that existed between the Jewish Sanhedrin and the Sicarii. The dagger men hated those in the Sanhedrin who collaborated with the Romans. The Sanhedrin collaborators were primarily the Sadducees. "Procurator, we do not believe these Sicarii will make any assassination attempt on Roman citizens, yourself, or businessmen here in Jerusalem. Nonetheless, for your safety, we shall increase the mounted archers who will accompany you back to Caesarea."

It was difficult for Felix to contain his elation along the journey back to his headquarters in Caesarea. Drusilla did inquire if Felix was involved in the murders, but Felix calmly and nonchalantly told her about the Sicarii. This was enough to placate his wife's curiosity and she dropped the subject.

At Caesarea, he met with his secretary and ordered wine for the meeting. The procurator held up his goblet in a toast and his secretary did the same. "To success. I have rid myself of that despicable Jew who sought to control me. Menachem did an excellent job in arranging the timing and performance. He will receive a bonus for having several of the key Sanhedrin members there as well. Maybe I should have charged him for making that opportunity possible." Felix snickered at his own tongue-in-cheek commentary, but his secretary did not share his glee. Felix noticed this and prodded him, "Why are you silent, my friend? This is a time for celebration! Now I can appoint a new high priest that is to my liking. In addition, I have eliminated those who could cause me problems in dealing with these Jews."

The secretary contritely answered his employer, "I feel I must point out that this Menachem ben Jair and his Sicarii have now been emboldened to do away with those they deem supportive to Rome. I fear, Felix, this will not bode well for you in the future."

Felix looked at his secretary and retorted, "Nonsense! These Sicarii will do nothing without my approval."

Jonathan and the other Sanhedrin members' deaths spurred Felix into greater acts of corruption, forcing the new high priest Ishmael ben Fabus to acquiesce to the procurator's every demand. The elderly Ishmael willingly went along because Felix overlooked his debauchery with young Jewish virgins and his thefts from the Temple.

For the next fourteen months, Felix proceeded at breakneck speed exercising his combination of greed and cruelty. During this time many insurgencies took place throughout both Samaria and Judea. Many of the more moderate Jews became irate with the procurator.

It all came to a head when the Jews and some Syrians had a dispute that escalated to the point of potential war. Felix ordered the slaughter of both antagonist groups, causing significant bloodshed. Word of this horror reached the ear of the new Emperor Nero who angrily had Felix recalled to Rome. Nero was intent on executing Felix, but an influential intervention by Felix's brother Pallos saved his life. Instead, Felix was sentenced to exile for life.

Much to his dismay, Felix was most saddened that he never could secure extortion money from his house prisoner,

Paul. Nevertheless, Paul was left in prison for his fate to be decided by the newly appointed procurator Porcius Festus. Of the seventeen procurators assigned to the province, Festus was the most honest of the group.

Within a short period of time, Festus held court over Paul to determine why Felix had him incarcerated two years. Festus learned of the plot by the Sanhedrin to assassinate Paul. When the evangelist invoked his Roman citizenship and requested to be heard by Nero concerning his alleged crime, Festus was happy to comply.

When Bartimaeus, Mattan, their wives, and Zacchaeus went to visit Paul, they were shocked to learn Paul had been rushed aboard a ship the night before and sent to Rome. The distraught mentees of Christ's faithful servant would never have contact with their beloved mentor again.

Chapter 23

In the wake of Felix's treacherous dealings, the Sicarii became more prominent, escalating hostilities between the Zealots, the Sicarii, and the Sanhedrin. It was a very difficult situation for Festus and the three procurators who followed Felix's brief reign.

In AD 64, Procurator Gessius Florus commented to the garrison commander in Jerusalem, "I do not foresee any way to contain these rebels. The Zealots commit acts of violence against the Romans who live here, as well as the Greeks and the Jews who they believe collaborate with us. The Sicarii assassinate Jews whom they feel stray from their original religious doctrine. It is very difficult to suppress these two wild religious factions."

The garrison commander added, "For some time I have suspected many Zealots to also be part of the Sicarii. Our interrogations of those fringe elements indicate such is the case." With a heavy sigh the garrison commander finished, "I do not see a way we can eliminate these warring factions from Samaria or Judea. I believe this will only continue to grow."

In 66 AD, the shifting magma of religious discontent boiled alongside Roman paganism. Pressure resulting from their philosophical/religious collision erupted like a long-simmering volcano. The top blew apart midsummer when the Zealots combined with the Sicarii and took a stand against the Sadducees who collaborated with the Romans.

Much to the ire of the Jews, the Sadducees for years had conducted an offering in the Temple to honor the Roman Emperor. The Pharisees and the Jewish populace were furious with this perceived desecration of the Temple. The Zealots/Sicarii union took control of the Temple and stopped the sacrifices made by the Sadducees, who normally performed all sacrifices in the Temple.

Several of the Sadducees were killed by the Sicarii and word was relayed to the Jews throughout Judea that this heinous practice was to be no more. Procurator Florus met with the Jerusalem garrison commander in Caesarea concerning the situation. "Commander, give me details about the takeover of the Temple by these rebels."

The commander gave his version of the takeover. As he spoke, Florus shifted in his chair and his face blazed crimson. When the commander finished his depiction, Florus thundered, "These insolent Jews have gone too far! Enough of this religious tolerance!" he snorted. "It is time we take back control of Jerusalem as well as all of Judea and Samaria from these insidious rebels before others adopt their methods of rebellion."

Florus rose from his chair and placed both hands on top of his desk. In a rage, the procurator commanded, "I will order the garrison commander here in Caesarea to provide you with two-thirds his troops. In addition, you will also receive two-thirds of the troops stationed in Jericho. Take these men and secure control of the Temple."

The Jerusalem garrison commander meekly bowed to the procurator and calmly stated, "It will be as you say, Florus." The procurator's gaze remained locked on the Roman commander.

In a sinister tone Florus ended, "Maintain control of the Temple and bring me the Temple treasury."

The commander's eyes grew wide at this added command. "Are you completely sure you want to confiscate the Jews entire treasury?"

Florus pounded his fist on the desktop and hoarsely demanded, "That is what I said and that is what you will do, Commander!"

Two days later the raid was made on the Temple, but the Zealot/Sicarii forces escaped capture, having received advance warning of the impending Roman raid. The shaken Sadducees were thankful the Roman soldiers remained in the Temple. They were sadly mistaken in their perception and were horrified at the Romans' demand for the Temple's treasury. They futilely argued and begged the Roman military to change their orders. Soon the Sadducees protested to Florus, but to no avail.

Their ineffective pleas led to more grim action. The Pharisees, Zealots, and Sicarii incited the Jews to riot and hurl stones at the Roman soldiers. When Florus heard of this action he sent back troops who assisted in taking over the Temple. After giving his order, Florus smiled ferociously at his secretary and pronounced, "NOW we shall see how much these despicable Jews like Roman justice."

When the additional troops descended on Jerusalem there was no mistake about their purpose. Like a giant scythe the Roman soldiers moved throughout Jerusalem indiscriminately murdering, raping, and plundering whoever and whatever was in their path of destruction.

The clash lasted two days. When the soldiers withdrew, they left nearly four thousand men, women, and children dead in the streets. The ruthless troops returned to their original posts. Jerusalem was stunned and immobilized.

Gessius Florus was quite content with the results, and boasted to the commander of Caesarea, "Rome's soldiers performed admirably and were a testament to its power. I believe these Jewish pigs will now submit to Rome the way all others have submitted."

The garrison commander cautioned the exuberant procurator, "Florus, I'm not so sure that these Jews will cease their protests. The rebels that operate throughout the entire province are strong, determined, and very angry with Romans."

His statement agitated Florus. His face contorted, and he scoffed, "Commander, are you telling me these boorish bands of ruffians are stronger and greater than the armies of Rome?"

The commander looked down and made an appeasing statement to the procurator. "Not at all, Florus. I am telling you in my humble opinion as a military leader with experience in many battles, these rebels will probably initiate future action. What kind, I do not know. I tell you this so that preparations can be made when such an event takes place."

Florus thrust out his chest and grabbed the colored stripe on his toga. It was a deliberate act to remind the commander who was in charge. "That is exactly why, Commander, you have spies and scouts to infiltrate these rebels and learn beforehand of their plans!" he bellowed. In the next breath, he lowered his voice to a quiet tone that only added a more sinister flavor to his threat, "I trust you are capable of carrying out this tactic for Rome. If you have difficulties in this area, I can replace you with someone more capable."

The commander bit his tongue and refrained from castigating the ignorant and prideful procurator. Instead, he softly answered, "I will do as you order, Procurator." He knew this was another grave mistake of Florus' dealing with the Jews, the Zealots and the Sicarii. And it would not be his last.

When word of the atrocity reached Jericho, Zacchaeus called together his fellow disciples for Christ at his mansion. "Brethren, I have news from Jerusalem that Christ's disciples there escaped the Roman swords due to our Lord's protection over them. However, I have also learned the Zealots and the Sicarii are forming a counterattack."

Alarmed, Mattan quickly asked, "Do these informants know exactly when this counterattack will take place?"

Zacchaeus shook his head. "I am not told, but I believe it will be soon. The mourning period for the dead is almost completed. The rebel factions will honor and obey the observances for the dead. But once this is satisfied, they will retaliate with deadly vengeance."

A shocked silence filled the room until Bartimaeus voiced what everyone was contemplating, "This does not bode well for either the Jews or the followers of Christ Jesus in Jerusalem or Judea. There will be much bloodshed."

In late summer, the volcano of discontent erupted one more time with great force. John of Gischala secretly met with his Sicarii counterpart Menachem in a cave located near Herodium. The two leaders sat on wooden logs facing each other in the candlelit cave. Their colleagues surrounded them, leaning against the cold damp earthen walls.

"My sorrow is great for all who died at the hands of the Roman dogs," said John of Gischala. "I'm sure you agree with me, Menachem, the time has come for us to lead our people into liberation from these curs."

Menachem nodded his head in full agreement. Overpowering their sorrow over the conflict and casualties, emotions of fiery hatred ignited. The Sicarii leader stated, "Together we have sufficient manpower to take on these Romans. In addition to our forces, Simon bar Giora has agreed to join his forces in Galilee in our rebellion."

John of Gischala at once raised his head toward heaven and proclaimed, "Praise you, Almighty God, for this extra provision." Then he questioned Menachem, "How do you believe we should start our revenge against the Romans?"

Over the course of the next two hours, the two warrior leaders discussed various options available to them. Every detail was hashed out until finally Menachem said, "John, we have a good, workable plan. Let us notify Simon of the start of this glorious campaign that he can be prepared."

Carrier pigeons flew the simple message to the Zealot leader in Hippos, Galilee. The wheels of destruction had begun to turn.

Shortly after the carnage inflicted by the Romans, the elders of Christ's followers in Jerusalem held a conference in Bethlehem. There, one of the elders recited a warning issued by Christ before His crucifixion. "Our Lord and Savior prophesied, 'When you see Jerusalem surrounded by armies, then recognize that her desolation is at hand. Then let those who are in Judea flee to the mountains, and let those who are in the midst of the city depart, and let not those who are in the country enter the city because these are days of vengeance, in order that all things which are written may be fulfilled."

When the elder finished, there was a stream of murmuring and groaning from the others in the group. One elder stood and looked at his counterparts, saying, "Let us not tarry, for word has come the rebel forces will soon act out their revenge. They attack at the end of the mourning period, which is soon. We must do as our Savior instructed. We must send word to all who live outside Jerusalem to act on Christ's prophecy."

The elders were in complete agreement for this course of action and the gathering concluded.

Almost immediately, the followers of Christ began a mass exodus from Judea. Those living along the two trade routes began their trek out of harm's way. From Gaza the refugees went north up the Via Maris trade route, gathering more of Christ's disciples. They stayed on the trade route for fear of retaliation from the Samaritans as they passed through their land.

When the group was safely outside Caesarea, some members sailed north on the Mediterranean Sea. Others proceeded north to Ptolemais. Followers of Christ living on the southern part of the Dead Sea traveled north on the King's Highway route. Many stayed in the region of Galilee while others continued their trek to Damascus, then west to the Phoenician cities of Tyre and Sidon.

Oddly, when this influx of humanity arrived in Caesarea, Gessius Florus paid little attention to them or the reason they were in exodus. The garrison commander attempted to bring their movement to the procurator's attention. "Florus, large numbers of people who are called members of the Way are inundating Caesarea. These people are fleeing all of Judea. I believe it's because the rebels will soon attack Jerusalem. We must give fortification to the garrison in Jerusalem; otherwise they risk being overrun by these aggressors."

Gessius Florus waved off the warning of the Roman military commander. "These people who call themselves members of the Way are simply avoiding persecution by the Jews who call them blasphemers of their religion. This is of little matter to us so long as no Romans are harmed, which I do not foresee. I tell you, Commander, we have nothing to fear."

An exasperated military commander stiffly turned and left Florus' office with clenched fists. He decided to take matters into his own hands and placed his entire garrison on standby notification to leave on a moment's notice for Jerusalem.

The businessmen and the farmers/shepherds throughout Judea who had converted to being followers of Christ had little difficulty disposing of their businesses or animals. The Jews were quite happy to rid themselves of these Christ-follower pests and to acquire value in the process. They interpreted their exodus as a sign God was blessing them. The majority of refugees took only their personal items and money from the sale of their businesses and animals.

It was decided by John of Gischala and Menachem ben Jair to make their attack right after the Feast of Tabernacles. They reasoned that the Sanhedrin leaders would be focused on the festival and the massive influx of pilgrims who would attend. The religious leaders would also be focused on the added influx of money issuing from the sale of sacrificial animals and other items. The windfall profits would greatly add to the depleted treasury confiscated earlier by Florus. The Roman soldiers would be on high alert with many additional troops on hand to quell any difficulties that might arise.

After the festival observance, both the Jewish leaders and the Roman military would relax, thereby making themselves more vulnerable.

Twelve days after the Feast of Tabernacles, the attack was initiated. The spark of revolt set by Florus fanned into an open flame that quickly spread destruction throughout Jerusalem.

With precision and deft accuracy, the Zealot/Sicarii forces slaughtered Roman citizens living in the city. By employing guerilla tactics, even the less trained rebels were able to wreak havoc on the Roman military stationed in Jerusalem.

The garrison commander was unable to counter the assaults from the rebels. In the process he lost over half of his men. Faced with total annihilation, the commander abandoned the garrison and successfully escaped to Caesarea. Abandoning a post in a crisis was sufficient for execution. However, he felt the circumstances demanded a retreat to reform and plan a reprisal.

Zacchaeus quickly learned of the rebellion in Jerusalem and once again called his friends and adopted family to his mansion. He looked tenderly at Bartimaeus, Mattan, and their wives, and informed them of the earthshaking news. "There is much bloodshed taking place and the rebels will not be satisfied until they drive the Romans out of Judea. Rome will not allow this to happen," said the saddened business administrator.

Mattan was the first to speak. "Followers of Christ daily come through Jericho. More will follow now that the floodgates of rebellion have been opened. We must minister to all who make their way here." All acknowledged the need and were ready in their desire to help.

Zacchaeus and the rest were aware also of Mattan's concern over his sister, Channah and her family, who probably were in harm's way. The former shepherd wasn't worried about his brothers and their families because they were on the grassy plains, far removed from the slaughter in Jerusalem.

The business administrator attempted to console his adopted nephew. "Mattan, rest assured I have my informants in Emmaus and others near the wintering grounds of the Jordan Valley. They have been instructed to keep me informed as to the plight of your sister and your brothers."

Bartimaeus suddenly asked, "And what about Barabbas? Beersheba is not beyond the possibility of impact from this rebellion."

Zacchaeus assured him, "There are informants located there, as well. Should hostilities make their way to our loved ones, I have plans to get to a safe place either here in Jericho or north in Galilee." There were murmurs of relief from the group and they turned their focus on ways to minister to the invasion of refugees.

In Jerusalem the Sicarii made it their assignment to do away with the Sanhedrin priests who aided the Romans. High priest Mattathias ben Theophilus was stabbed to death, as were the majority of the Sadducees. The former high priest Ananus ben Annaus who really controlled the Sanhedrin's decision-making had his throat cut. In the ugly conflict, the Zealots burned the homes of the Sanhedrin members, destroying all archived Jewish public records. Parts of Jerusalem were ablaze. Shock and terror spread throughout the population.

After the siege of Jerusalem, Menachem split from the Zealots and took his forces to the Roman fortress of Masada where he took control over the strategic military outpost. John of Gischala set himself up as dictator over Jerusalem. The moderate Jews and the wealthy elites met with the Zealot leader to negotiate and gain his favor.

The garrison commander in Caesarea sent all available troops to Jerusalem to aid the Romans there and to end the rebellion. An exasperated, stunned, and defeated Florus turned control of the situation over to the commander.

Emperor Nero recalled Florus when word of the rebellion and the resulting carnage reached his ears. The unstable monarch was livid with Florus and forced him to commit suicide after reaching Rome. Nero would have been satisfied with deposing Florus, but knew the issue in Jerusalem remained in need of a permanent solution.

While the troops based in Caesarea were on their way to Jerusalem, another Zealot leader, Simon bar Giora, heard of the Roman plans and led his own army south to Jerusalem. He caught up with the advancing Romans and caught them completely by surprise.

The startled Romans were under weak leadership; they scattered and returned to Caesarea. Bar Giora took the booty, consisting mainly of the beasts that carried weapons of war, and turned them over to John of Gischala.

Within only a few weeks, the Zealots and the Sicarii had accomplished what the majority of the Jews had longed for—liberation from the hated Romans. The wave of success in Jerusalem made its way to Gaza, and on up north. Many of the remaining Roman citizens living in the coastal port cities fled to Rome by ship.

In Beersheba, Jesus Barabbas was noncommittal to the success of the Zealots and the Sicarii. But his previous reputation for leadership and resistance was still circulating. One day, soon after the liberation of Jerusalem, Barabbas was approached by a small band of Zealots who were cleansing the south central part of the Jordan Valley of Romans and collaborators.

"Jesus Barabbas, we are part of John of Gischala's army. He has sent us here to talk with you about rejoining the Zealots." Jesus Barabbas surveyed his flock that surrounded him on the vast grassland before he answered the Zealots. "Let us sit down at the base of his knoll. You must be tired from your journey here." The nomad shepherd dismounted his horse and led his visitors to the base of the knoll where several small rocks provided seats for their discussion.

Jesus Barabbas took his time before inquiring of the Zealot leader, "Now, tell me why John of Gischala desires my return to the Zealots? He knows I have disassociated myself from all activities with all Zealots."

The leader of the men said, "John knows of your fighting spirit and how well you fought the Romans. He wants you to utilize your abilities here and throughout all of the southern Jordan Valley to Gaza, to keep this land free from the Roman dogs and their filthy allies. Your battle prowess is valuable to our cause." Their admiration was sincere, but they hoped their flattery would help persuade Barabbas to consider their request.

Jesus Barabbas saw their hope that he would answer yes to their request. He lowered his head and rubbed his eyes with one hand. Then he directed his comments to the leader.

"I ceased being a member of the Zealots cause when I accepted Christ Jesus as my Lord and Savior. The Jewish traditions and beliefs mean absolutely nothing to me anymore."

These words completely took the small Zealot group by surprise. Incredulity was on each face. Jesus Barabbas evaluated their response to his proclamation. Gesturing with his hands, he added, "I am too old for such involvement. My bones ache and are stiff from all the years of being a nomad shepherd and the earlier battles while I was part of the Zealots."

The visitors listened in total disbelief. The impact of Barabbas' statement left them mute. They merely stared at the old shepherd. Leaning towards them with firm resolve, he continued, "My purpose is to live every day of life as Christ's servant, not any man's. My war is against those who persecute those who have chosen to follow Christ Jesus first and foremost. In this war I go as Christ directs me."

Jesus Barabbas barely finished his last sentence when an enraged Zealot rushed at him, driving his knife deep into his heart. Barabbas let out one final breath, and in a twinkling of the eye found himself in Heaven. The remainder of the bandit group looked on in shock.

"You fool! What have you done? John of Gischala did not instruct us to kill this man! He has great standing with John. Now you have put us in grave danger. When John finds out what has happened here this day, he will surely kill us."

The evil assassin looked at the leader unemotionally and said, "Should we cut out a space in this knoll and place this traitor's body inside? We can cover it well, and no one will know that he is dead, or that we had any part of his death."

The leader considered his colleague's suggestion while the others stared in morbid horror. After a few minutes, the leader said, "We will do as you suggest. The ground is soft and should not pose a problem for us." The Zealots quickly cut out an opening deep inside the knoll and placed Jesus Barabbas' body inside. They covered up the opening and replaced grass and a few rocks to conceal the grave.

The men mounted their horses and looked closely at their handiwork. "The grass and the weather will hide this grave," said the leader. "Now let us leave and go to Gaza as John has instructed us to do so. Let us hope no one has witnessed what we did here today." The bandit leader sternly warned everyone to inform John of Gischala that Jesus Barabbas had died before they could make contact with him.

The next day several of Jesus Barabbas' hirelings came to the spot where Barabbas was killed. The sheep and the goats were wandering nearby eating the succulent grasses. One of the hirelings noticed a cloak nearby a pile of rocks. He inspected the find and said to his companions, "This is Barabbas' cloak." He held it up for the others to see and continued, "There is blood on it and also blood and parts of a sheep here as well. It appears a predator killed both the sheep and Barabbas. Look! There are signs that something was dragged away."

Thus, the Zealots' savage plot was completed and Barabbas' family was notified that a predator killed him while he protected his flock. Later the family sold the flocks, left Beersheba, and joined the seemingly endless procession of refugees as they headed north, away from the Jewish conflict.

For the next year the Zealots and the Sicarii completely ruled the region. They made no effort to interfere with the continuous procession of Christ's converts. They were as glad as the Jewish religious leaders these blasphemers were leaving. In fact, they were content the disciples of Christ were vacating the region, and thereby eliminating what they thought was a potential threat to their reign. Ironically, the exodus of the converted followers of Christ nearly paralleled that of the Jewish multitude when Moses led them out of bondage from the Egyptians.

In AD 67, under considerable pressure from Rome, the Legate to Syria, Cestius Gallus, was ordered to quell the insurrection.

With the lauded 12th Legion, Gallus set out for Jerusalem. Along the way he encountered sporadic skirmishes with rebel factions, but was able to quickly squash the insurgents. On the outskirts of Jerusalem, Gallus' forces faced heavier resistance, but he was stopped short of the Temple walls.

A week of repeated attacks by the 12th Legion resulted in the rebels considering surrender. John of Gischala met with his commanders. "The Romans have inflicted great damage upon us. They are very strong. They believe we will surrender to them very soon, but they are mistaken. We shall never surrender!" he emphatically declared. The commanders were in agreement and prepared to fight to the death.

The next day to the complete surprise of John of Gischala and the moderate and elite Jews, Gallus pulled his troops back and hastened a retreat from Jerusalem. The Zealots quickly took advantage of this retreat and counterattacked.

The semi-trained Jewish army capitalized on the ineptitude of Gallus and his lack of strategic planning. The Jews inflicted heavy losses on the Roman forces. And the Zealots captured the Romans' entire siege equipment. The most embarrassing and humiliating loss to the Romans was that of their famed eagle masthead that was never to be surrendered to the enemy as long as one Roman soldier remained alive. The debacle lasted only two days. Gallus and less than one third of his forces escaped back to Caesarea.

The astounded Zealots and Jewish elites were ecstatic. Their initial revolt now allowed them full independence. They set up their own government in Jerusalem, created seven military districts that included the surrounding towns, and minted their own silver coins.

They believed that soon the world would recognize their independence and seek to establish diplomatic relations with them. They believed this victory was the precursor to the promised Messiah who would inflict more pain and destruction on the hated Romans.

Close to the time of the Jewish revolt in Judea, Nero was under considerable pressure from the Roman Senate over his declining ability to govern. The Senate and the general populace of Rome were extremely suspicious that Nero had started the great fire of AD 64 that burned vast areas of Rome. To deflect their suspicions, Nero blamed the new sect called Christians.

Attempting to fortify the credibility of his accusations, Nero set about killing known Christians and falsely accusing them of crimes they never committed. Among those executed was the Apostle Paul, even though in AD 62 Nero had acquitted Paul of the crime of high treason earlier espoused by the Sanhedrin. Soon after Paul's release, he and several other disciples had ventured into Spain. Paul had returned to Rome in AD 67, only to be arrested as a scapegoat and imprisoned. Despite Paul's birth advantage of being a Roman citizen, Nero refused to hear his case and ordered Paul to be beheaded. Nero knew that Paul was a Roman citizen and punishment and executions were limited to prescribed ways, which in this case was for a more merciful and immediate means of death. Other disciples of Christ suffered horrible deaths of burning alive or by crucifixion.

Word quickly reached Zacchaeus in Jericho of Paul's execution. There was deep sorrow and lamenting by Paul's mentees. "We indeed mourn the loss of our mentor, yet praise God for Paul's obedience in carrying out God's plan for him. Paul was a faithful servant and great mentor to us all," wept Zacchaeus.

Bartimaeus suggested, "Let us have a celebration feast to honor God and thank him for his grace to us in bringing Paul into our lives."

The group readily agreed and a joyful feast was held that same evening. Bartimaeus called the attention of his fellow revelers and bravely encouraged them all, "Paul taught us the importance of true love. He lived what Christ taught him. Now let us continue to live and manifest Christ's love during this time of crisis. In so doing, we will honor both Paul our mentor, and Christ our Savior."

Throughout Judea the Jews boasted of their triumph over the Romans. The Jewish leaders erroneously contended this victory confirmed to the common man how God protected them and gave them the power to defeat such a powerful enemy. Again they emphasized their expectation of the promised messiah.

The Jewish leaders instructed the rabbis to use the momentum to pressure those followers of Christ Jesus into either forsaking their belief in the convicted blasphemer or forcing them out of Judea.

The vast majority of Christ followers chose to leave, adding their numbers to the continuous line of refugees. Christ's followers were escaping two enemies, the Jews and the Romans. Surprisingly, the greater threat at the time was the Jews.

Chapter 24

In January of AD 68, Nero was summoned back to Rome from Greece, where he was spending the majority of his time. Conditions in the capitol city were in great disarray. On the economic side, a food shortage partially caused by the disruption of trade caravans through Judea brought great hardship. Roman citizens grew more discontent each day. Adding to their discontent and anxiety were stories from Roman citizens who had been assaulted by the Jewish Zealots and had had their businesses destroyed.

On the political front, Nero was successful in killing senators, noblemen, and even generals whom Nero feared were plotting against him. His actions caused the remainder of the Senate to view him as a death-monger out to silence those who disagreed with him. This was the last straw of tolerance the Senate had held out for Nero's narcissistic ways.

By March of AD 68, the Senate had regrouped sufficiently to demand Nero either commit suicide or be put to death. The despot ruler opted for suicide. He attempted to evade the ruling, but eventually gave in to his fate. For the next year and a half chaos ruled the Roman Empire.

It was also early in AD 68 that the Roman general Vespasian was assigned to regain control over Judea and those parts of Samaria that had joined the great revolt. With battle-hardened warriors and the reorganized 12th Legion that was most eager to avenge their earlier humiliating defeat, the juggernaut began their campaign of revenge.

Mattan's sister Channah and her husband realized the Roman tsunami of death was approaching Emmaus. Several unsuspecting or cavalier Jews chose to remain in the targeted city and eagerly bought out Channah's husband's business. With a few clothes and several bags of money, Channah and her family crossed the ridge route trade bridge into Jericho.

The reunion between Channah and Mattan was intensely emotional, with much hugging and laughing, mingled with tears of sadness. "I'm so glad you were able to get here safely. We have prayed you would be able to escape the impending destruction. It is good to have you with us again!" declared Mattan.

Soon after Channah's arrival in Jericho, word came to Mattan that his three brothers were not far behind Channah. They had decided to push their flocks steadily to Jericho rather than at their normal easy pace. By late January, all of Terach's offspring were together in Jericho.

At the beginning of Passover, the three brothers sold a sufficient number of lambs and older ewes, both sheep and goats, which pared down their flocks by one third. Gavriel made a somber announcement to Mattan and to Zacchaeus. "We do not believe it is safe for us here in Judea. As such, after Passover we believe we must proceed north to Damascus. We have learned that between Damascus and the two port cities of Sidon and Tyre, the land is lush and capable of sustaining our flocks."

Zacchaeus concurred with Gavriel's assessment. "My informants tell me that Rome is staunch in their desire to rid themselves of Jews, Zealots, and the Sicarii. All they need is a single word that anyone in their path is associated with any of these elements and death comes swiftly to those deemed guilty."

Mattan did not appear shocked by this news. He spoke with resignation, "I agree with your decision, my brothers. We are growing older and our children must be protected from the certainty of Roman revenge. They will be intent on doing harm to all Jews, even those who have no intentions against Rome, but have only chosen Christ over religion and ritualism."

Zacchaeus looked at the four brothers and Channah and suddenly felt very old. He saw signs of age clearly in the faces of his adopted family members. Their hair, too, heralded advancing age. The business administrator inwardly cringed, admitting he too was old, much older than his adopted family members.

The Passover was extra special for them this year. Mattan held the Tanakh up as he had done every year since Terach's death. Gavriel had presented Mattan with his father's prized possession after their father's death when he reached Jericho for the annual Passover celebration. It was Terach's decree that Mattan should have the Tanakh and none of the other family members disagreed.

The former blind shepherd exchanged the words of prophecy for those of hope as written by King David. Mattan felt under the circumstances this was the proper thing to do. Gavriel and the other siblings were quite proud of their younger brother. After the reading, Channah spoke for the family, "Mattan, you do our father honor, taking his place as the patriarch in the reading of God's holy word. More importantly, you honor our Heavenly Father by leading us as a good shepherd does." Mattan's heart swelled with her loving affirmation.

Paul earlier had taught Mattan and the rest of his mentees that reading and studying the Tanakh was allowed since they surrendered their hearts to Christ. "The Tanakh contains God's word He has given to His children. It is not the same as the Talmud, which is the man-made law written by the Pharisees and the Sadducees. Study God's Word and let it rest forever in your hearts."

Tears began well up in the eyes of Zacchaeus who said a brief silent prayer, thanking God for blessing him with such a godly adopted family. The old adopted uncle gathered his clan around him and gave each a strong, encircling hug, powerfully delivered, even for an old man.

Following the Passover observance, Gavriel and his brothers headed the flocks north. Channah and her family remained in Jericho.

By April of AD 68, Vespasian's blood-thirsty warriors had killed thousands of Jews and totally destroyed many towns in their quest to retake Judea and Jerusalem.

Over dinner one evening, Zacchaeus looked at his family and began a sorrowful litany. "Each of you is very dear to my heart. I love you all as if you were my flesh and blood. I loved your father like a brother. This love I have for you is strong and life-long. For this reason, I have secured your safe passage out of Jericho to Sepphoris in Galilee."

The diminutive elder statesman looked at his family with tear-filled eyes. He took a deep breath and continued, "Within a very short period of time the Romans will march through Jericho. Their past actions indicate they will do great harm to the city. All who remain here put themselves in harm's way. I will not allow the Romans to execute you like they have done to others."

Zacchaeus trembled and had to pause a second time. As he did so, Channah rose up from her chair and went to him placing her arm around the frail old man's shoulders. He looked up at her and faintly smiled. "Tomorrow you all shall leave. There are three wagons that have been loaded with your tools. Mattan, your pottery implements are in one wagon. Your family possessions that you want will also go there as well. There are sufficient horses for you and your sons to ride, thereby making room for the women and the young children in the wagons."

The hushed gathering stared at their beloved uncle who took a sip of wine to steady his emotions. He cleared his throat and continued, "Bartimaeus, there is a wagon for you and your family, as well. Your leather utensils and some premium hides await you. In addition, I have hired some people to escort you safely to Sepphoris. Once there, you will find arrangements have been made for your housing and your business."

Zacchaeus could not continue. He shuddered and sobbed. Channah grabbed hold of his shoulders tightly and placed her cheek on the top of his gray-haired head. Nobody said a word, but tears formed in their eyes as they witnessed their emotional surrogate uncle succumb to the moment.

Finally Devorah spoke for the group. "Uncle, will you be coming with us in your own wagon?" Her tone of voice conveyed hope, but no confidence.

Zacchaeus' answer confirmed the apprehension each member of the extended family felt. "I will not. I must remain here and do my duty as business administrator for the procurator, now in this case the Legate of Syria... besides, I have no desire to start over. God has blessed me more than I deserve. My trust is in Him that His Will will be done."

Early the next morning the group found their respective wagons just as their surrogate uncle had described. Each family member personally embraced Zacchaeus and expressed their love. Zacchaeus sobbed and shook. It was not easy having to say a final goodbye to those so deeply loved.

He watched them slowly make their way to the main trade route. As the precious parade receded further into the distance, Zacchaeus' throat constricted and his stomach tightened and he tearfully turned away to continue his preparations for the imminent arrival of his Roman superiors.

In mid-June, Vespasian and his warrior horde reached Jericho. Within a six-hour time frame the hub of commerce was destroyed for approximately the tenth time since its formation. Vespasian burst into the mansion that once belonged to King Herod and was now Zacchaeus'.

The old business administrator sat peacefully behind his desk as Vespasian entered the office. The Roman general observed Zacchaeus' calm demeanor and queried, "You are Zacchaeus, the business administrator over Judea?"

A soft reply came from behind the desk. "Indeed, I am he."

Vespasian looked around and one of his aides quickly brought forth a chair for him to sit.

The tired general wasted little time in questioning Zacchaeus. "Do you have all the necessary documentation I requested about the economic condition of this land?"

"Everything you requested is here in these documents," he calmly answered.

The general's aide stepped to the desk and retrieved the voluminous assortment of heavy files. As he turned to present them to Vespasian, the general waved him off. "Keep them safe. I will read them later. Right now I have business to conduct with Zacchaeus. Leave us alone."

The aide bowed in submission to his commander and left the office with the documents. Vespasian's eyes did not follow his aide. Instead they remained fixed on Zacchaeus. Once the room was down to the two Roman servants, Vaspasian spoke. "Zacchaeus, Rome has been quite pleased how you have conducted business here despite all the mayhem." Zacchaeus detected a small smile on the general's lips but he did not speak. The general continued, "Because of the great changes being invoked in this despicable land, Rome has decided to retire you from the combined position of business administrator and tax collector. That will be my responsibility until such time as order is restored here."

The general paused and gauged Zacchaeus' reaction. The old administrator softly said, "I completely understand both Rome's and your assessment of what's needed."

The general's eyes slightly twinkled hearing Zacchaeus' keen assessment that the decision to remove him from office was mainly Vespasian's.

Zacchaeus asked, "What are your plans for me?"

Vespasian relaxed and congenially stated, "Take your personal treasury and anything you wish to keep and make way to Antioch. There you will advise the Legate about certain matters from time to time when he needs advice concerning this region. Basically you will be in retirement."

The general looked closely at the frail old man before him. Zacchaeus showed no reaction.

Zacchaeus matched the general's pleasant demeanor as he answered his proposal. "I am deeply honored by your decision, General, concerning my welfare. It will be with great pleasure for me to be of service to the Legate. I can be ready and will leave within the next three days, assuming you will be finished with me."

Vespasian quickly answered, "I will immediately read the documents you have compiled about this region. I'm sure there will be questions. Please remain in your mansion that I may meet with you."

Zacchaeus nodded his understanding. The little man then offered, "General, please be my guest here in this mansion. There is plenty of room for you and your aides. It will be much more comfortable for you." Vespasian smiled in surprise at the invitation. He was glad that Zacchaeus realized Vespasian had the power to commandeer the mansion and anything else. It was always much better when there was no opposition to authority.

True to his word, Vespasian reviewed all the files Zacchaeus had recorded about Judea. The general was pleased that the little administrator did not steal from Rome's treasury. Vespasian expected a certain amount of money to be in any administrator's private treasury. It was part of doing business in these outlying regions. What Rome did not tolerate was undoing theft.

Two days after evaluating both the files and Zacchaeus, the general informed the now former administrator, "Zacchaeus, I find everything in order and it will be easier for me to address the economics of this region. When you leave, I have a personal escort that will travel with you to Antioch."

After pillaging Jericho, the Roman army went south the short distance to Qumran located at the northwest corner of the Dead Sea. There, Vespasian captured a small group of Jews known to be both sympathizers and members of the Zealot sect. The Roman general had them bound and shackled together and proceeded to throw them en masse into the Dead Sea. To his surprise along with the soldiers assigned the duty of the drowning, the Jews bobbed to the surface.

"I had heard of the buoyancy of this water because of the salt, but this is the time I've seen how buoyant the water really is," marveled Vespasian. He and the soldiers retrieved the bouncing Jews and placed them back into the boats reserved for the drowning. Back on land, Vespasian had the Jews crucified making a wry comment, "These Jews will not float off their crosses."

Vespasian halted his army at Qumran because he was recalled to Rome where he became involved in straightening out the chaos in the Senate. After Nero's forced suicide, a succession of short-lived emperors and a year of civil war required Vespasian's presence. Judea got a brief reprieve and the Roman army regrouped and added to their arsenal of weapons.

At the same time, John of Gischala and Menachem also went about preparing Jerusalem for a potential siege. Part of John's action was overthrowing the newly established Judean Free Government led by the moderates and the elites of Jewish society. Soon after establishing himself as the Jewish despot, the moderates and elites made an agreement with Simon bar Giora to return to Jerusalem to drive John Gischala and Menachem away.

Simon and his fifteen thousand men quickly took control of the upper part of the city, but Gischala and Menachem maintained power over the lower part of Jerusalem. There was much infighting between the different factions. During this internal squabble, Menachem was killed leaving John and Simon vying for control. Their internal disputes proved disastrous in the spring of AD 70.

Vespasian had gained sufficient control over Rome that he ordered his son Titus to resume the march to Jerusalem, determining this would be the key to breaking the Jews' spirit.

Titus arrived at the outskirts of Jerusalem just before the Passover observance. All the chaos and the warring between the Jews and the Romans prevented many Jews living in the outer regions of Judea from making their desired pilgrimage to Jerusalem. Fear of death overcame the call of religious duty. Titus' siege caused the inhabitants of Jerusalem great hardship.

John and Simon had all the storerooms emptied, forcing the Jews to follow their plan of insanity. The patient Romans simply waited at the parameters of the Jewish capitol. In August, five months after the siege began, Jerusalem fell to the ecstatically victorious Titus.

Roman hatred towards the Jews was so great that Jerusalem was completely destroyed and many Jews killed. In the process, Titus personally participated in the demolishing of the Temple. Herod the Great had begun the construction of the second Temple and it was completed in AD 61, barely nine years before its total destruction. All the Temple's ornate golden

313

fixtures were confiscated by the Roman soldiers as part of their booty.

When Titus completed his work, there literally was nothing left of the Temple. The entire city was burnt, destroyed, and dismantled.

Prior to the siege, many Jews knew the Romans were about to raid Jerusalem and as such they had hastily gathered all that they could before scurrying out of Jerusalem and beyond. This third exodus by the Jews caused a theological crisis. The Pharisees and the Sadducees lost control over the people.

Some members of the Sanhedrin who were fortunate enough to survive made their way to Joppa and to Lydda where they attempted to re-establish their religious rule, but without success. As the Jews embarked on a similar exodus as Christ's followers had in AD 66 - AD 68, there was much wondering and unsettledness.

Many asked, "How can the God of Israel allow His sanctuary to be completely destroyed and His people vanquished by the Romans?" Many heads shook in disbelief and were prone to say, "Why did God allow good and decent Jews to suffer? Did we not obey His laws?" The surviving rabbis had trouble adequately answering the questions posed by the Jews. Nobody thought to contemplate that the Jews were more intent on obeying their man-made laws and rituals than accepting the Savior their God had sent them, Jesus Christ. Their faith was not in Christ but in their religion to the extent of worshiping the grandeur of the Temple rather than God. Neither the Jewish populace nor their religious leaders wanted to remember the fateful words spoken by the jeering mob at Christ Jesus' trial. "His blood be on us and on our children." And so it came to be.

After the total destruction of the Temple and the majority of Jerusalem, Rome brought in foreigners to inhabit much of Judea. A minority of Jews were allowed to live in the outer towns, but none in Jerusalem. Those Jews who escaped the carnage spread far and wide to Gaul, Germania, Persia, and beyond—never to return to their homeland until nearly 2,000 years later.

The emotional impact of the Roman retaliation hung like a heavy cloud throughout all of Judea as well as Samaria. Although the Samaritans did not incur quite the extent of destruction as did the Judeans, nonetheless the Samaritans were quite fearful of what the Romans would do to them.

This cloud of heaviness drifted north into the region of Galilee. The migrating followers of Christ infiltrated Galilee's communities of Pella, Bethabara, and Scythopolis in the south and Hippos, Nazareth, Sepphoris, and Tiberias in the central part and Bethsaida and Ptolemais in the north. Some of Christ's migrants even settled in the Phoenician towns of Tyre, Caesarea, Philippi, and Sidon. In all, nearly ten thousand converts to Christ resided in this area.

One migrant among this horde of displaced humanity stopped in Sepphoris. Unlike the rest of the refugees, this migrant was happy and pleased. It was Zacchaeus, and he enthusiastically sought out his adopted family whom he earlier had established in the city.

The reunion between Zacchaeus and his adopted family was celebratory. There was a feast and party atmosphere in great contrast to the rest of the refugees. Zacchaeus informed his family about his meeting with Vespasian and the consequent decision. When he announced his new assignment to the Legate in Antioch, the family let out a howl of joy. "We were worried what would happen to you, Uncle!" said Hadassah. "And now, here you are!"

Mattan chimed in, "Uncle, indeed Almighty God has blessed you with favor!"

Zacchaeus stayed with his family an entire week. His Roman military escort did not attempt to interfere and force him to leave early. They were under his command. During his stay in Sepphoris, Zacchaeus insisted his family should stay in the hub of commerce rather than accompany him to Antioch. "It would not be wise for you to be with me at my new home. I have my duty to the Legate, and you have your life and duty to our Lord to be His servants here."

At the end of his respite with family, Zacchaeus left the city with his impressive escort. The diminutive man and his family's hearts were somewhat saddened again at the departure, but full of peace that God's plan for all was taking place.

It did not take either Mattan or Bartimaeus long to get established in their God-gifted trades. Soon they were flourishing economically and were being used extensively by God in spiritual ways.

As the shell-shocked immigrants either passed through or settled in Sepphoris, it wasn't long before Mattan, Bartimaeus, their wives, and their now young adult children engaged many of the refugees, helping them and evangelizing.

Mattan came up with the methodology for the ultimate approach for evangelizing. "These people are suffering physically as well as emotionally from what happened in Judea. First, we must comfort them with food, find them lodging, and listen to their experiences. When the Holy Spirit speaks to us about their readiness, only then shall we give them the gospel of Christ."

Many of the stressed refugees were at the end of their ropes physically, spiritually, and emotionally, experiencing aspects of depression, anxiety, and particularly hopelessness. The numbers of these people were so large that Mattan and Bartimaeus secured a sheep shearing facility where over three hundred refugees could gather at once. The refugees received a warm meal, replacement clothing, and what they needed most of all—hope. Not earthly hope, but the eternal hope offered and available only through Christ Jesus.

Bartimaeus led his family and nearly fifty other followers of Christ in securing food and clothing. Following the meal, Mattan stood and gave the message of hope to the hopeless. As Mattan looked around the crowd, he saw many long, drawn faces of despair. Inwardly, he prayed for words of power and to be the servant Christ wanted him to be for that moment. In a flash, Mattan remembered the words spoken by his mentor the Apostle Paul when he and Barnabas came to deliver money to the people of the Way, back in AD 47. With a rush of excitement Mattan opened his mouth and addressed the throng of refugees.

"You all have experienced both a physical and an emotional milestone that will impact you the rest of your lives. Your homes are destroyed, friends and family killed, and now you must leave your cherished homeland, maybe forever. No doubt many of you are wondering why God allowed such a thing to happen and what will become of you."

Mattan began to walk among the seated refugees. He made a point to meet the eyes of certain individuals and speak directly to that person. As he moved, the servant of Christ felt more confident and relaxed and he continued only as he sensed he should. He spoke sincerely and honestly.

"You have been let down by your government, and especially your religious leaders. In fact, the Sanhedrin is the cause of much of your despair." Mattan felt his voice grow bolder, "Verily, I tell you that your hope and your future does not lie within any religion or ritual. Your hope can only come from Christ Jesus who died on the cross, that you may have relationship with Him and eternal life with Him in heaven."

The evangelist saw some eyes that looked down and heads that shook in doubt or disagreement. Undeterred, Mattan grew louder and bolder. "I tell you forthrightly that no religion can fill the void you now are feeling. If that were the case, why do you feel the way you do, having closely observed and obeyed the laws set forth by the Pharisees and the Sadducees? Your religious leaders do not travel with you. They do not have the answers you seek, nor do they have the power to take back Judea."

Taking a deep breath, Mattan asked the all-important question, "If religion was the answer, why didn't your religion save you from the Roman destroyers?" The evangelist's frank words echoed loudly and went to the hearts of his audience.

Many in the crowd cringed at the blunt truth spoken by the former blind shepherd. Without hesitating, Mattan persisted. "It is the Risen Christ who stands ready and eager to give you His hope and eternal life. Only He can heal your heart, take away your fear, your depression, and your hopelessness. He will do so without asking any monetary price on your part. All He asks is that you follow Him...Surrender your will to His. Be obedient only to Him and not to any religion or idol. He will act within you in the twinkling of an eye. You will feel and experience His compassion, His love, and His grace like you have never felt before in your life."

At that point there was a mix of reactions. Some in the crowd began to sob and placed their hands on top of their heads or clutch them together next to their hearts. Some stood up and glared at Mattan. One man said, "I will never follow this convicted blasphemer! I would rather be a Roman slave first." The man and his family stomped out and a few others followed him.

Mattan remained calm and evenly countered, "Neither I nor Christ Jesus force you to accept His offering of relationship and eternal life. It is your choice, and yours alone. Do not be swayed by others. Follow your heart and let Christ rule in your life. He wants to give you abundant life."

The evangelist looked skyward. In an emphatic voice Mattan gestured and proclaimed, "Who shall separate us from the love of Christ? Shall tribulation, or distress, or persecution, or famine, or nakedness, or peril, or sword?"

Mattan pointed to the heavens. "Yet in all these things we are more than conquerors through Christ who loves us. For I am persuaded that neither death nor life, nor angels nor principalities nor powers, nor things present nor things to come, nor any other created thing shall be able to separate us from the love of God, which is in Christ Jesus."

Devorah stood to the side watching her husband give his divinely inspired message. Her skin tingled as Mattan spoke. She could see the reaction of many in the crowd. Her attention to the people moved to her husband as it always did when Mattan told his personal story to finish.

"Once I was a shepherd taking care of my father's flocks, until a battle with a wolf caused me to go blind. As a shepherd and a blind man, I was deemed an outcast by the Pharisees and their religious laws. I had little hope, became angry with God, and had little desire to even live. Then one day Christ Jesus extended His grace to me and restored my physical sight. He asked no money or favor of me, all He said was to follow Him."

The crowd became very attentive, hushed, and leaned forward to listen. "When Christ asked me that, my heart unhesitatingly said yes! I immediately felt the warmth of his eternal love within my entire body. I felt cleansed like I had never been before. I felt rejuvenated, it was easier to breathe. I felt more alive than at any other moment in my life."

Mattan surveyed his audience and let his words sink into their minds. The evangelist continued, "That is when and how I knew that Christ Jesus was Lord of Lords and King of Kings, the Son of Almighty God. I knew in my heart and my mind Christ is the Promised One, the Messiah to all the world. He is real, and He is alive."

Mattan stopped in the middle of the wide-eyed mass of lost souls. He took a deep breath and exhaled passionately, "I implore each of you, listen to your heart. Listen to your heart and let Christ into your life. Accept His gift of eternal salvation."

A few in the crowd verbally said yes to Christ Jesus. As they did, more came forth and did the same. When it was all said and done, nearly 250 of the lost souls became saved through the power and the presence of the Holy Spirit.

Devorah looked lovingly at her husband through flooding eyes. Her heart leapt with joy. She said to herself, "Mattan is once again the shepherd he used to be."

When Mattan finished and the people dispersed, one lone man in tattered clothes came forward and said to Mattan, "Shepherd, do you remember me?"

Mattan looked closely at the man and saw black and blue bruises and a few cuts to his face and body. "No, I do not. Please tell me how you came to know me?"

The disheveled man easily said, "Some years ago, you and Bartimaeus spoke about Christ. I was one of the young Pharisees instructed to disrupt you and challenge your belief in the man Jesus, the one deemed a blasphemer. You effectively cut through our religious arguments. After that debate I kept thinking about your words; they plagued me both day and night."

Both Mattan and Devorah were transfixed by the man's narrative. "Nearly one year after arguing with you and Bartimaeus, I fell into great emotional turmoil and could not understand why. Finally, I could not contain myself and cried out to Jesus to make Himself known to me."

The man stopped to clear his throat before continuing. "He did, and my life has not been the same since. I tried to remain a Pharisee but to no avail. Each day after I made my decision, Christ opened my eyes to the deception of the philosophy taught by the Pharisees and the Sadducees."

He looked first at Devorah, then back at Mattan, and said, "I ceased my association with the religious leaders and the rabbis. I sought out those who followed Christ for help in my understanding. Some were able to clarify things, but I request your help in better understanding how I should follow my Savior, Christ Jesus."

There was a slight gasp of surprise from both Devorah and Mattan. Devorah looked at her husband who had a glowing peace about him. "I will gladly do my best to teach you what it requires to be a true follower of our Lord Jesus," the shepherd of men commented.

For several weeks every day thereafter, the man met with Mattan, with Bartimaeus sometimes joining them. He ate with them and spent hours during the day peppering them with deep and personal questions. On one such occasion the man asked, "How do I know what Christ wants me to do?"

Mattan answered first, "Listen carefully for His still, small voice. He will speak to your heart through His Holy Spirit who resides within you. You will feel a strong compulsion to either do something or to refrain from such activity or words."

Bartimaeus nodded his head in agreement and added, "It will be the strong guidance and conviction of God through His Holy Spirit. In the process, as you seek Him, you will experience His peace; and afterwards His joy in carrying out His plan and purpose."

On another occasion, the man questioned, "Should I continue to observe the holy feasts established by the Jewish leaders?"

This time Devorah, who was serving them, answered for the group of mentors. "Do not be a double-minded man. Christ Jesus said you cannot follow two masters. You have a choice to either follow Christ or the religious rituals. You also must not follow man's institutions, for these are the ways of the world, and the world is at war with Almighty God."

The former Pharisee looked wide-eyed at this woman, turning over her wise words in his mind.

Devorah continued, "The main thing to remember is that Christ died, was buried, and rose from the grave to give you eternal life. Honor Christ daily by surrendering your will to His. Follow what the Holy Spirit teaches you and guides you, and no one else."

The man looked perplexed, "There have been times I thought I was doing this only to find out afterwards I was wrong. How can this be?"

Mattan replied, "Remember that the deception of the enemy is great. He is the father of all lies and has the ability to make things appear to be good, honorable, and right. When we succumb to this deception, we soon learn it was wrong. This happens as we grow spiritually, just as children learn as they grow physically."

Bartimaeus could not help himself and interjected, "Mattan is right. I will add that after the deception, the enemy entices your senses and heightens your desire to give in to the temptation again. This is because the enemy knows your weaknesses and attacks them fiercely and relentlessly."

There was a moment of silence as the man pondered these words. His eyes narrowed and he peered at Mattan saying, "After these moments of giving in to the temptation, I feel sad and wonder if Christ even loves me or cares about me because I am so weak of spirit. Does He still love me?"

Mattan had no hesitation in answering him with soothing truth, "Christ has said He will never forsake anyone who truly gives his heart to Him. He knows our frailties. He convicts us of our sin but His Holy Spirit also leads us to confess our sin to him and helps us to repent. When we fail, we ask His forgiveness. Your willingness to follow the prompting of the Holy Spirit brings repentance and obedience. Only our defiance stands in the way of our relationship with our Savior. Our eagerness to please

Him and let Him work in or thoughts and desires reveals our heart and our passion for Christ."

The man's eyes widened with an epiphany moment. "Now I understand what you are saying. I have been very confused by what others told me about obeying Christ."

There was gladness and relief in the man's voice. His whole body showed a great burden had been lifted from him. Encouraged, he confessed, "There are those areas deep within me that are very susceptible to answering the temptation thrown at me."

Mattan looked squarely into the man's eyes and emphasized, "That is why you must be very vigilant. Do not let your guard down for one moment. Trust in Almighty God. As you pass through the valley of the shadow of death, God alone will bless you with His discernment, His wisdom, and His discerning of spirits to identify the ploys of the devil. He will be your strength and weaponry to fight off evil deceptions. Ask God's Holy Spirit to guide you through those tempting moments."

The man listened earnestly to his mentors and two months later informed them, "I must leave Sepphoris. I will go to Damascus. I feel in my heart this is where God wants me to go, at least for now." His mentors gave him a farewell dinner and early the next morning the man set off the next phase of his walk as a true follower of Christ.

Chapter 25

Smoke from the dreadful fires in Jerusalem had barely lifted and the dust from the destruction of the Temple and many of Jerusalem's buildings had settled to the ground as the Romans continued their purging of Judea.

Throughout the entire region, the Romans destroyed synagogues, killed many rabbis, and those who were deemed part of the insurrection, as far south as Masada, west to Gaza, and north to Joppa, and all the towns and villages in the central part. When the ethnic cleansing was completed, the world heard the proud boisterous voice of the Roman Empire declaring its dominance.

The grace of God was such that the Roman army did not invade the regions of Decapolis or Galilee. Their focus was on Judea and Samaria because those were the centers of the Jewish revolt.

Soon after the Roman slaughter in Jerusalem, Jews who escaped the Roman sword made their way to the towns and cities of Galilee where they attempted to infiltrate the ranks of Christ's followers. God's blessing of wisdom and discerning spirits exposed these charlatans, but they refused to repent and truly follow Christ. The discovery of their true natures forced them to vacate the region when their intentions were identified and rejected.

By AD 75, the impact of the Jewish revolt and the Roman response had settled down. The trade routes resumed their regular treks through Judea and Samaria. Jerusalem was rebuilt and became a pagan city. The only vestige of Jewish presence was one wall of the city the Romans let stand, mainly as a monument to remind dissenters of the price of opposing Rome.

The Roman Legate at Antioch received much pertinent information and advice from his new consultant, Zacchaeus. That lasted well after the situation in Judea had settled into complacency. During this time the Legate noticed the declining health of the new consultant.

One morning, Zacchaeus did not appear at a scheduled appointment with the Legate. A servant was dispatched to the home of the consultant and the servant found Zacchaeus dead. Limited medical knowledge at the time could only speculate on the cause.

It really didn't matter, because even before his body was found by the Legate's servant, Zacchaeus was already in heaven. His earthly mission completed, God's servant was available for the next phase of his servanthood to Almighty God.

In the spring of AD 77, Bartimaeus' old body became weak; he was barely able to eat or to move. With each passing day, his body deteriorated. Mattan and Devorah visited him and Hadassah every day. One month after contracting his sudden illness, Bartimaeus weakly called for Hadassah who quickly dashed to his side.

"My beautiful wife, you have been so wonderful to me all these years and I love you deeply." Catching his breath, he labored to continue. "Now I feel the time is here for me to go be with our Savior."

Bartimaeus offered a faint smile and closed his eyes. Hadassah gripped his hand between hers, and could feel his life ebb away. She stared at his peaceful face for some time not saying a word, just clinging to his lifeless hand. Finally she placed her cheek against Bartimaeus' face and began to sob.

After the celebration of Bartimaeus' life, Hadassah reminded Mattan, "Bartimaeus loved you like a brother. He valued your friendship and was glad the two of you had experienced so much together." The grief-stricken old woman finished, "I, too, am glad to know you and Devorah. We are brothers and sisters in Christ and I cherish you as I would any brother."

Mattan softly replied, "I, too, am glad to have known Bartimaeus and experienced so much of life with him. He was not just my brother, but fellow bondservant to Christ. I shall miss him greatly."

The elderly shepherd of men held Hadassah as tightly as his old bones could. Hadassah felt his love and compassion for her grief. Mattan drew away and said, "You are every bit my sister as Channah is."

Hadassah left Sepphoris and went to live out the remainder of her days with her daughter and husband in Tiberias until she joined Bartimaeus in heaven in AD 78 where, similar to Bartimaeus, she was welcomed to eternity with rejoicing from the angels. With her beloved husband, they enjoyed their treasures built up while on earth carrying out Almighty's God's plan and purpose for them.

In AD 79, Mattan and Devorah grew too old and frail to continue creating different forms of pottery. They were saddened that time was stealing away their ability to be productive. In the fall of that year just before the beginning of the rainy season, Mattan and Devorah were moved to the port city of Ptolemais by one of their sons and his wife. The offspring were eager and willing to care for those who had cared for them so many years when they were young.

Both Mattan and Devorah enjoyed the sea air, the breezes, and the fresh fish. What they enjoyed the most was spending each new day of life with each other. One of their new routines was to sit on a rock that overlooked the sea. They talked about and smiled about the beginnings of their love for each other and reminisced about how they had been able to witness and evangelize about Christ.

During the mid-winter after a period of chilling rain and cold temperatures, Mattan became ill with pneumonia. With each passing day, Mattan's condition slowly grew worse. At the same time, Devorah also came down with the dreaded illness and began to weaken.

Devorah realized their time on earth was extremely short. With tenderness, she struggled to move and place a cool cloth on Mattan's forehead. Seeing it brought him comfort, she placed her head lovingly on his chest. She could feel and hear his faint heartbeat, which relaxed her and brought a smile to her old weathered face.

With great effort, Mattan reached for Devorah's hand, and tightly held it. The shepherd-turned-potter-turned evangelist did not speak, but with his free hand he touched the back of her head and gently moved it up close to his lips. The dying disciple of Christ whispered in Devorah's ear his never-ending love for her. As she had so many countless times,

Devorah responded, softly pronouncing her undying love for the man she had shared so much of life with.

The sick and feeble Devorah could not hold back tears which trickled down her cheeks—not tears of sorrow, but of joy. She realized that her beloved husband of these nearly sixty years was about to meet with Christ Jesus.

Tightly, she clutched her beloved's hand and kept her head on his chest. Without any other words, the old shepherd breathed his last breath of earthly life. God's grace was rich and sweet. He called Devorah home at the same and she followed Mattan into eternity.

In a twinkling of an eye, both Mattan and Devorah were standing in the presence of Christ Jesus and basking in His full glory. Their Savior opened his arms wide, beamed a welcoming smile at them, and pronounced, "Well done, My good and faithful servants."

OTHER BOOKS BY TOMAS W. SCHAFER

The Prisoner of Rome

Mentoring God's Way – Fulfilling the Great Commission